I0681784

"This novel delivers. Carr's writing pulls the reader into the story, willingly or not. The images form as the suspense builds. Be careful of the dark."
—*Dr. Steve B. Howell*
  Project Scientist, NASA's Kepler mission and author of A Kepler's Dozen

Critics praise Forrest Carr's previous science fiction novel, *A Journal of the Crazy Year:*

"Fresh thinking and feeling... stuffed with untrimmable, character-driven, cogent dialogue.... A fascinating read all the way to its chilly, barely hopeful conclusion."

—*Publishers Weekly*

"Carr employs jet-black humor reminiscent of Vonnegut.... A truly unconventional ending makes for a worthy trip. A great case made for the idea that the end isn't nigh—it's already here."

—*Kirkus Reviews*

"Impressive." A "thrilling narrative."

—*Fantascize.com*

Readers praise *A Journal of the Crazy Year:*

"This book caught me right from the beginning and I couldn't put it down. Highly recommend it and have done so to many of my friends who loved it as well."

—*Amazon.com 5-star reviewer*

"Thanks for no sleep that night when I found myself finishing it up at 4 am on a work night! And the ending was just so unexpectedly PERFECT."

—*Amazon.com 5-star reviewer*

"This was magnificent. I know this will stay with me for a while. It was certainly a page turner, so hard to put down."

—*Amazon.com 5-star reviewer*

"My family almost didn't have mashed potatoes or cranberries on Thanksgiving, and it's thanks to this book! Could NOT put it down. Absolutely loved it."

—Amazon.com 5-star reviewer

Critics praise Forrest Carr's first novel, *Messages*:

"An accomplished debut novel" rendered with "smooth skill."

—Kirkus Reviews

"Masterful...." "Carr's novel is engrossing, fun to read and a joy to see play out to its inevitable, tragic, hilarious and scandalous conclusion."

—MocoVox.com

NAUS *Santa Maria*

The Vessel

Owner: Cermeno Enterprises, Inc.
Builder: Same
Flag state: North American Union
Homeport: Aldrin Space Station, North American Union, Earth orbit
Completed: August, 2129
Refit: January, 2136
Christened: *Susan Constant*
Class & type: *Mayflower*, science vessel
Original type: colony transport
Length: 223.2 meters
Height: 36.6 meters
Beam: 48.2 meters
Gross Registered Mass: 21,127 metric tons
Power plant: 1 General Electric Class F fusion reactor
Environment: 31 Bjorklund Field artificial gravity and inertial stabilization
    generators
Main drive (linear propulsion): 4 Emsky direct mass conversion torches
Maximum thrust: 5,303,938 kN
Maximum acceleration: 25.6 g
Star drive (nonlinear propulsion): Makowski Array (experimental
    prototype)
Complement: 33 officers, crewmembers and observers
Range: unknown (experimental)
Armament: none

The Crew

Flight Department
Captain Sirius Constantine Cermeno, Jr.
First Officer Fabiana De Vegas
Second Officer Martin Trafford
Chief Astrogator Lydia Nguyen-Jones
ASM Conrad Specht (Astrogator, Second Team)
ASM Nicolas Swann (Chief Helmsman)
ASM Julius Terwilliger (Helmsman, Second Team)
ASM Mason Krajnovich (Sensor/coms, First Team)
ASM Jessica Beadel (Sensor/coms, Second Team)

Science Department
Chief Science Officer Dr. David Jones
Deputy Science Officer Dakota Munson

Medical Department
Dr. Candace Blake

Steward's Department
Chief Cook Abraham Cioffi
Assistant Cook Jane Kim

Engineering Department
Chief Engineer Bates Crandall
Second Engineer Fusazane Tochigi
Third Engineer Constance Nunn (Senior AI Specialist)
ASM Sierra Bent (AI Specialist, Second Team)
N-Field Specialist Dr. Morton Makowski
Deputy N-Field Specialist Ariana Marinez
Electrician Darlene Marrone
Electrician Lamont Brozek
Electrician Carlos Abello
Electrician Nereida Sabol
Electrician Deborah Michaud
Electrician Kareem Anwar
Electrician Kimberly Nabozny
Electrician Nalini Dhawan
Electrician Rubin Smith
Carpenter Derrek Damiano
Carpenter Caitlyn Cheng

Observers
Father Cameron Teal, Vatican Observatory
Janson Jervis, Universal Net News

Mission Profile
Voyage length: 20 days
Primary objective: Test the Makowski Array and n-dimensional astrogation system
Secondary objective: Explore deep extragalactic space

The Dark

FORREST CARR

Copyright © 2015 Forrest Carr. All rights reserved. No portion of this manuscript may be copied or distributed without permission of the author.

This book is a work of fiction. With the exception of certain historic figures referenced in the prologue and elsewhere, the characters herein are strictly products of the author's imagination, and any resemblance to any person living, dead, or undead is strictly coincidental.

ISBN: 0692436022
ISBN-13: 978-0692436028

DEDICATION

For my surgeon, Dr. Sanjay Ramakumar. I don't know whether he likes
science fiction, horror, or zombies, but I hope so because he's at least
indirectly responsible for this project. Without his care and surgical skill I
would not have been here to write it.

And for my sister Amy Concannon, who recently and unexpectedly
discovered that she loves zombies.

CONTENTS

ACKNOWLEDGMENTS

The interdimensional drive array presented in this book is fictional. The journey to the edge of the universe contemplated herein may or may not ever be possible. But if it is—what would the astronauts see? For that part of the tale it was my intent to stick as closely as I could to real cosmological science and astronomy. And in that endeavor, I owe a huge debt of gratitude to Dr. Steve B. Howell, an astrophysicist and project scientist for NASA's Kepler mission who's also been known to dabble in science fiction. It was the depth of knowledge on display in *A Kepler's Dozen*, the short story collection he co-edited and to which he contributed that caused me to contact him and ask him to examine my scribblings from a scientific viewpoint, with the idea of making sure the novel was at least within shouting distance of known facts and established theories. Steve responded enthusiastically to my request. It was very generous of him to lend me his knowledge, expertise and time in this way. I very much appreciate it, and I believe the novel is a better story because of it. I hope you will agree.

Nor public flame, nor private, dares to shine;
Nor human spark is left, nor glimpse divine!
Lo! thy dread empire, Chaos! is restored;
Light dies before thy uncreating word:
Thy hand, great Anarch! lets the curtain fall;
And universal darkness buries all.
— *Alexander Pope,* The Dunciad, *1728*

PROLOGUE

The darkness lay over Chief Astrogator Lydia Nguyen Jones like a lead-lined blanket, smothering her with almost palpable weight, utterly sealing her off from all visual perception. It was a darkness so profound that no adjectives, similes or metaphors were sufficient to describe it. Never before in the history of human existence had any member of the species ever encountered such utter blackness. It was far darker than a cloudy, moonless night in the desert; darker than the inside of a bank vault; darker than the heart of the deepest cave; darker than the bottom of the most impressive ocean trench. The only photons traversing through the surrounding space were those emitted by the communications device implanted behind her left ear and by the electromagnetism of her body, and those emitted naturally from Nguyen's flesh, her clothes, and the chilly ground and surrounding air as the result of thermal black-body radiation. No light from distant stars and galaxies shined down from above, due to the simple fact there were no distant stars or galaxies. For the same reason, there was no cosmic radiation: no gamma ray bursts, no x-rays, no ultraviolet or infrared light, and no high-energy protons, atomic nuclei, neutrinos, or flitting atomic or subatomic particles of any kind except for a very few emitted from certain naturally occurring radioactive atoms within Nguyen's own body. There wasn't even the omnipresent cosmic microwave background that had always hissed down from the sky surrounding Earth and had watched the life forms that became mankind crawl from the mud. There was nothing.

Nguyen was lying flat on her back on a rocky, gravelly expanse of slightly inclined ground. Her head throbbed with pain, as did her right foot. At first she didn't understand why she was so utterly blind. But then it came rushing back to her—and terror gripped her heart. Something was there in the dark with her. Something terrible.

She had been exploring the lake with engineer Kareem Anwar. The lake was critically important to their survival. The water it held was their only hope of ever seeing home again—assuming the acting chief engineer could first repair the *Santa Maria's* ruptured conversion mass tanks.

Now, lying on the cold ground and wrapped in utter blackness, Nguyen replayed the events of the last few minutes in her mind.

After leaving the ship, to get to the shore she and Anwar had traversed a short stretch of flat, rocky ground, walked up a small rise, and then picked their way down a fairly steep embankment. As they descended toward the shore, the lights of the *Santa Maria* disappeared behind the top of the rise. But the *Santa Maria* was still there; Nguyen was able to see a diffuse, dim glow from its lights slightly lightening the darkness of the still, cool air behind the rise. She and Anwar proceeded on down the slope and quickly reached the lake, where they tested the water and found it to be utterly pure. She reported this finding back to the ship.

Just after she signed off, the slight halo in the air behind the rise blinked out. And at that precise moment, she heard a swirl in the water. Nguyen whipped around and pointed her headlamp beam toward the sound just in time to see something rocket from beneath the surface, step to the shore and grab Anwar, who screamed and kept screaming. The figure was hideous; quite literally, it was a monster from a childhood dream—one of *her* childhood dreams. The thing had the figure of a man. Its body was black; whether it was covered with leather, dried skin or even scales she couldn't tell. But she could see its head clearly illuminated in the beams of Anwar's lamp and hers; twisted black locks fell on either side of a leering face, the black and purple flesh of which was decaying and had rotted away in places, exposing patches of white bone and two rows of yellowish teeth. Before she could utter a sound, in one swift movement the horrendous creature reached up, placed gnarled, taloned hands on either side of Anwar's head, and gave a sharp twist. Anwar's screaming abruptly stopped, and he collapsed silently into the black water.

The thing then turned its grinning gaze on Nguyen.

Nguyen didn't take time to scream. Instead, she turned and bolted back in the direction of the *Santa Maria*, running as fast as she could. But as she neared the top of the slope, her foot came down in a hole or crack, caught fast, and twisted. Grimacing in pain, but not allowing herself to cry out, Nguyen straightened and tried to pull the foot free. But then her other foot slipped on the loose gravel, and she found herself toppling over backwards. As she fell, the back of her head struck a rock.

There the recollection ended, bringing her back to the present moment.

Her head and ankle throbbed with pain, and she noted that her chest was heaving with panic. Reaching up, she felt for her headlamp. But it wasn't there, apparently having been slung or knocked off when she fell.

3

Making a mighty effort to quiet her breathing, she strained her ears against the deadening, cottony wall of silence. Where was the monster now? The thought that perhaps it had returned to the lake and disappeared back into the water from which it had emerged was too much to hope for. More than likely, it had rushed up the bank in hot pursuit, and was now standing stock still in the darkness, listening for her, waiting for her to betray her position with the slightest sound. Perhaps by now one or more companions from the depths had joined it. She now imagined a whole cadre of grisly figures standing nearby, each one fully alert for any audible hint of motion.

Slowly, careful not to disturb the gravel beneath her, Nguyen raised her head and looked around. She had lost her bearings, and was no longer certain where the *Santa Maria* lay in relation to her. The ground was nearly flat, suggesting that she had rolled down the slope. She could see no glow in the sky anywhere around her. Surely the captain would send a search party, but if she had, there was no evidence of it yet. Not the slightest hint of sound reached her ears from the dead silence and total darkness that surrounded her.

But not all was quiet. Even though she had succeeded in calming her breathing, her heart was pounding with all the muted reserve of a marching band's bass drum, and her pulse thrummed in her ears. If the thing from the lake had any sense of hearing at all, it would certainly find her.

As if in answer to her thoughts, she heard what sounded like a crunch on the gravel nearby. Holding her breath, she strained to listen. There it was again—closer. And then there was another crunch, closer still. There was no mistaking it—something or someone had approached and was now standing there, two or three meters away, listening. Had the thing found her? Should she bolt to her feet and try to outrun it?

Too late. A loud growl sounded from right beside her, and then pain shot up her leg as a bony hand closed hard around her ankle. The creature now screeched in unholy triumph as it lifted Nguyen by her leg. There was no point in keeping quiet now, and even if there had been, reason now abandoned her. Dangling upside down in the pitch black darkness, Nguyen opened her mouth. Her chest convulsed as she emptied her lungs in a scream of utter, panicked terror.

1 THE MISSION

Dr. Morton Makowski, N-Field Specialist for the NAUS *Santa Maria*, gathered his dirty white lab coat around himself, walked up to the rail, and leaned against it. Just beyond, the giant N-field array that bore his name was slowly coasting to a stop, its whining and rumbling decreasing in volume and tone as the apparatus wound down like a gyroscope with the power shut off. As Makowski watched through thick black-rimmed glasses, the nearest sphere on the X track crept to a halt just one meter from where he was standing.

His assistant, Ariana Marinez, joined him at the rail. Self-consciously, Makowski ran his hand along the back of his head to the knot at the top of his ponytail, and then down along the first few inches of his stringy black and gray mane. He found the short-haired, petite, dark, svelte Marinez to be incredibly attractive, and it always made him nervous when she was in close proximity. It always made him nervous when *anyone* was in close proximity.

"Congratulations," she said, smiling. She offered her hand.

Makowski took it, squeezed it briefly, and then let go. "Thank you."

"You've got to be feeling pretty good right now," she said.

Indeed, he did. Nor had Marinez been the first to make that suggestion or to offer congratulations. Just a few moments ago, the smiling face of Chief Science Officer David Jones had appeared on his videocom in the array control room. "Well, laddie, you did it," Jones had said, his Scottish brogue hanging thick in the air like a solid, dark cloud of swirling smoke.

"How do you know that?" Makowski had asked. They'd been out of interspace for less than a minute, which didn't seem to Makowski to be enough time for Jones to have taken his sights.

"Because I've got Earth hanging fat and sassy in my telescope, that's how," Jones had said, smiling. "And besides, my lovely bride has a lock on one of the Luna beacons. And unless I miss my guess, young Beadel, bursting with news, is probably establishing a link to Aldrin Station as we speak. Prepare to be famous."

Important, if not historic, words had been called for, but all Makowski had been able to do was to push his glasses farther up his nose with his forefinger, look at the console screen and blink.

"I won't say I ever doubted you," Jones had continued, "but I will say I'm a confirmed believer now."

Moments later, Captain De Vegas also had called him with warm congratulations.

He noticed now that Marinez was looking up at him admiringly. He wasn't used to such regard from attractive people. Or from any people. "You know," she said, "they'll probably name streets and high schools after you."

"Well, I didn't do it all by myself," Makowski said in a rare burst of charity. "As Sir Isaac Newton himself acknowledged, we all stand on the shoulders of giants."

Marinez was undeterred. "Well, the next generation will be standing on *your* shoulders."

At first glance, what they'd just accomplished had not been particularly remarkable—just a milk run to Proxima Centauri, which certainly did not qualify as charting a new frontier for mankind. But the point was that they'd made the trip with a total elapsed time, one way, of about 24 milliseconds and change, not counting the time spent blasting out to their departure point. They'd made the return trip in the same amount of time—and all this with the array powered to only about 25% of its capacity! This feat didn't just shatter all previous records, it made them irrelevant, while also dooming every other starship in existence to obsolescence. Oh, those vessels wouldn't be replaced all at once. But every one of them was now destined for the scrap yard—or at very least, a massive refit—far sooner than their designers had planned and their investors had been promised.

Licking his lips nervously, and marveling at his own audacity, Makowski turned to Marinez. "Do you have big plans once we get back to the station?" he asked, trying hard to inject a tone of confidence into his voice, while at the same time not daring to hope that he answer would be "no."

"I have a date," she said, dimpling, "with a strapping young junior starship officer."

"Oh," he said casually, allowing himself neither to display nor feel any disappointment. He knew of the man she was talking about; he'd seen her chatting over a cup of coffee at Aldrin Station with a third officer from another line. He couldn't compete with that. Makowski was, in fact, certain that he couldn't compete with *anyone* for a woman in Marinez's league.

"You?" she asked.

He shrugged. "No celebrations for me. I've got a lot of work to do if we're to be ready for the next jump."

"So you think it'll be a go?"

"*Absolutely* it'll be a go." The company had invested a great deal of money in Makowski's project, and the chairman and CEO was eager to prove its worth and start raking in some returns. As was the man's style, they'd prove it with a splash, and they'd do so just two weeks from today.

The acceleration alarm sounded, followed by coms officer Jessica Beadel's sexy contralto telling everyone to secure for high gees.

"Well, I hate to see you stuck here all by yourself," Marinez said as they both turned and headed back to the array control room, where their acceleration couches were located. "Would you like me to stay?"

"And have you miss your date? Not a chance." He smiled. "Besides— you know me. I enjoy my work. It'll be fun."

"Well, okay," she said doubtfully. "I'll raise a toast for you, then."

"I would appreciate that."

Oh, yeah, he thought. *I'll have fun.* Inwardly, he sighed. He knew his life would be so much better if he would just make more of an effort to be around people. But he could just never muster the willpower.

And besides—just before they left the station he'd downloaded a new set of videos and hollies that he'd not yet had a chance to view. He was looking forward to that.

Father Cameron Teal sipped his coffee, looked out over the Via Veneto, and admired humanity. Skirt lengths, always up and down, were up again this season. Way up. But the mostly transparent panels that had adorned so many blouses over the past two years were all gone, replaced by material that was, while thin and colorful, nevertheless fairly opaque. *Go figure,* he thought. *Fashion. Who can understand it?* The feelings of sexual liberation that had been in the air for the last two seasons had produced the inevitable puritan, conservative, and feminist backlashes. And so it goes.

It's amazing, he reflected for the umpteenth time, *that so little has changed here.* The last world war with its breathtaking casualty count had left Rome mostly untouched. The city had never missed a beat. But for that matter, humanity hadn't missed much of one, either. The ruined cities had, for the most part, bounced right back, with nothing to show there'd ever been a conflict but a few relatively small blast areas that had been razed and then officially abandoned. Now the world population was nearly back where it had been before the detonation of a dozen hidden dirty bombs and the following exchange of strategic thermonuclear weapons had snuffed out a billion and a half lives.

But because population pressure had contributed to the conflict in the first place, as population pressure always does, the swift recovery wasn't necessarily a good thing. Technologies that had emerged from the war effort had helped propel worldwide human prosperity, with notable exceptions, to an all-time high, and the competition for scientific advancement was at a fever pitch. But now natural resources had become even more scarce than before the war. Global warming had reduced the amount of land available for living and for agriculture, and by cruel coincidence some of the worst-hit areas also had been the poorest. The

7

resulting refugee crises were bad and getting worse, with half a billion people currently displaced in Europe and Asia and clamoring for their rights. The rest of the world blamed the most economically advanced countries for the global warming problem and demanded that they shoulder the brunt of the refugee burden, pleas that for the most part were falling on deaf ears. New alliances had formed. For the first time in decades, the rattling of sabers could be heard again like the rumble of distant thunder.

All these developments had led, as surely as a river finds the sea, to the task that now lay before him.

Teal turned his gaze from the sidewalk and looked at his companion, the Most Reverend Liam Harland. Harland was 48, Teal's senior by a year, but he looked a good half decade older. Crow's feet surrounded his eyes and worry lines creased his face. But the aging wasn't from lack of success—in fact, the contrary was true. As both had expected, Liam had made bishop—not quite in record time, but fast enough—and he now presided over the Diocese of Arundel and Brighton. No one would be surprised if Harland were to become a cardinal someday. This had, in fact, been Harland's stated goal the day Teal had met him at the Venerable English College there in Rome. Both were being primed for great things, and expectations were high. Harland had met them.

Teal had not. He'd known when he chose the priesthood that celibacy would be a challenge for him. He hadn't bargained on just how attractive a priest's collar would be to some people. The willing weren't hard to spot. They were the ones who hung back for a quick chat after Mass, and then found excuses to give him a call later about this or that. The content of such conversations always would be innocent enough, but sometimes the call might just happen to be placed after the caller had prepared for bed, and was dressed less modestly than might otherwise have been the case. Some admirers were even more brazen, of course; from time to time he received photos from parishioners of either sex that were risqué or even downright lewd. And he discovered that it was understood, even among his colleagues within the church, that an occasional hookup on the side was not necessarily a career-ending disaster, provided the arrangement was discreet.

Discretion, of course, was the key—and the problem.

"Have you talked to her lately?" Harland asked, as if reading his thoughts.

"Katie?" Teal nodded. "She dropped me a line after the mission line-up was announced."

"How is she doing?"

"Fine." After their disastrous affair, Katie had married a bobby and churned out two kids, both of whom were now in college, as Harland knew. "After her last kid left the nest, she separated from her husband. But she won't divorce him."

"Dark are the vagaries of the human heart."

Teal cast him a curious glance. "Is that a quote?"

Harland laughed. "Not really. Maybe. Probably. I don't remember where I picked it up."

Teal chuckled. "Probably something you wrote in one of those thick, verbally opaque scholarly homilies of yours."

"More than likely." Harland appraised him. "So how are you doing, Cam? Really?"

Teal shrugged. "Okay, I guess. I've managed to avoid female complications over the last few years. And I've set a firm deadline for getting rid of my buddy Jack Daniels of Tennessee."

"Is that a fact? What's the deadline?"

"Ten years from now," Teal said with a deadpan expression. "After that, alcohol for me will be right out."

Harland shook his head ruefully. "I should have known better than to ask."

Teal looked at his friend. "So how about you?"

"I'm fine, as you know. There's nothing to tell. Life is proceeding according to the master plan. Don't change the subject." Harland leaned forward and gazed at Teal. "What the hell are you doing on this mission?"

The intensity of both Harland's gaze and tone surprised Teal. "Because they asked, Liam," Teal said, trying not to sound hurt.

"And if they'd asked you to jump off the New Shard, would you have done that, too?"

Teal chuckled. "Probably not."

"Well, it would have been safer."

Teal waved a negligent hand. "It's a scientific mission. I'll be with stuffy, socially maladjusted science geeks and eggheads who know what they're doing."

Harland cast him a disbelieving glance. "The thing about knowing what you're doing is that if you really do, then you don't call it 'experimental.' You don't have to conduct elaborate field tests. The tests are necessary precisely because your newfound friends might *not* know what they're doing."

Teal sighed. "I think you're being a little melodramatic."

Harland was now staring across at him in open-mouthed astonishment. "*I'm* being melodramatic? This mission *screams* melodrama! Let's take inventory." Harland ticked off a finger. "You're using some kind of whackydoo interdimensional drive array that's never been tested—"

"It's been tested," Teal interrupted.

"Not on this scale. Hence the need for this mission." Harland ticked off another finger. "You're using a navigational system that's never been tested, based on a set of theories that have never been tested, using software that's never been tested."

"Same response," Teal interjected.

"And same reply," Harland said dismissively. He ticked his thumb. "And my personal favorite: you're going to try to find the outer limits of the universe, which scientists aren't even sure *has* an outer limit."

Teal nodded. "There is a bit of guesswork with that," he conceded.

"Ya think?" Harland gazed earnestly at his friend. "Which brings me back to my original question. Why are you doing it?"

"One of the world's richest men asked me to go on one of history's greatest adventures, in an endeavor that falls squarely within my professional field and for which I'm trained. It's the opportunity of a lifetime." Teal raised his hands. "Besides, I *couldn't* say no. I'm the head of the Vatican Observatory. I have an obligation. It's just not something I could have turned down, either personally or professionally."

"Sure you could have. You punch the guy up on the squint box, look him right in the eye, and you tell him very sincerely, politely, and professionally to go bugger himself."

The use of language shocked Teal. His friend must be really worked up. Harland, while not a prude, was famous for maintaining the demeanor and decorum befitting his office at all times. Teal had never heard the man use any kind of profanity while wearing the collar, and these days Harland was never seen without it—not even when out on entirely personal business such as today's meeting with Teal at Caffé Strega. By contrast, Teal could be very profane when around people he trusted, and he was not above going out in plain clothes when he wasn't on official business. In fact, at the moment Teal was dressed more or less like a native.

Teal looked across at Harland with concern. "You want to tell me what's really bothering you?" he said softly.

Harland sighed, and relaxed a bit in his chair. "I really am just worried about you, is all," he said. "And, selfishly, I don't want to lose you." Harland allowed himself a faint smile. "In my position, one doesn't tend to have a lot of close confidants. You're one of the few people I can really talk to."

"Yet for all that, you don't tell me shit," Teal said, now surprised at his own use of language. "I'm usually left to wonder how and why you're getting those worry lines."

Harland brought his fingers to his face, momentarily wearing a surprised expression. But then he laughed. "I guess you're right." He paused. "I've never been one to blab about my inner feelings and worries. But it's always been a comfort to know that if I needed to do that, I have a friend who'd listen."

"I'm listening now."

Harland took a sip of his espresso, looking thoughtful. "It's just politics," he said. "They don't warn you about that in seminary. It's nothing I can't cope with. In fact, I'm handling it really well. But I don't always think that what one must do to survive and thrive in an organization—even ours—is, well, Christian."

"You want to tell me about it?"

Harland shook his head. "Another time. *Next* time, I promise." He smiled. "Assuming you make it back, of course."

Teal rolled his eyes. "And here we go again."

Harland chuckled. "No, I'm putting down my sword and shield." He paused, and then looked thoughtfully across at his friend. "But I am curious—what do you think you'll find out there?"

Teal shook his head. "Honestly, I just don't know."

The bishop looked unconvinced. "Sirius Cermeno, Senior, didn't invite you along just because of your scientific background. In fact, you don't have a scientific role in the mission at all, do you?"

"Well, I can always fill in for one of the astronomers if needed."

"Right. 'If needed.' Meanwhile, you expect me to believe that your part is to strap yourself in, look out the window, and every three minutes blurt out with, 'Are we there yet?' "

Teal shook his head, smiling ruefully. "You always did have a way of slicing through the fog."

"My speciality. Except that it doesn't serve one so well at the top, where pretending not to see B.S. emerges as a political virtue."

"Liam, I think you're in danger of becoming a cynical, bitter, pinched old curmudgeon."

"Maybe. But don't change the subject."

"*You* changed it," Teal objected.

"So I did. Back to your boy Cermeno. He's one of the world's richest Catholics. You're a Catholic priest. Surely some discussion of faith must have arisen in your conversation?"

Teal reached up and pulled an earlobe, thinking. "Not so much as you'd notice. All he said is that the mission was going so far out, he thought it would be useful to have someone aboard who could add a spiritual dimension."

Harland nodded. "Well, it seems obvious to me—and to a lot of people—that he hopes to find God."

"Maybe."

Harland looked at Teal with piercing eyes. "What's not so obvious to others is that *you* nurture the same hope. In fact, offhand I'd say you're even more anxious about it than Cermeno."

Teal felt his cheeks growing warm. He glanced across at Harland in annoyance, but the feeling was quickly replaced by one of amazement.

Harland had chosen the right vocation; the man really was quite gifted. And once again, his friend had managed to see deep into Teal's heart and perceive with lightning clarity what lay within. The spectacle of a priest struggling with his faith was one of the hoariest clichés in the book. But clichés get to be such for a reason. The phenomenon was common, and Teal had indeed grappled with it. But he felt he'd turned the corner on it.

In any case, Teal was not prepared to admit that he was on any kind of personal quest. "I don't know what we'll encounter," he finally said. "But I don't expect to find God."

"Really?" Harland glanced at Teal's neck. "I notice you're not wearing the collar today."

Self-consciously, Teal raised a hand to his throat. "It's my day off," he said lamely, managing a weak smile.

"Is that it?" Harland gazed across at his friend. "There's conflict in you, Cam. And it's no surprise. I've often wondered how you manage to carry the torch of faith while also bending under the burdensome weight of an astrophysics degree."

"You sound as if you believe science is the enemy of God."

Harland raised an eyebrow. "Isn't it?"

Teal shook his head. "Not at all. God gave man a brain. It makes no sense to argue that he doesn't want us to use it. That he never intended for us to seek answers, or to find them."

"Yes, but it's not God's intentions that are at issue here. It's man's." Harland paused, looking thoughtful. "You know, I'm not a scientist, but I have studied history. No less a thinker than the great Sir Isaac Newton himself, when faced with certain problems he couldn't solve, did not hesitate to invoke God. But that marked the end of a science tradition, not the beginning of one."

Teal nodded. "And when physicist Pierre Laplace went on to solve the problems that had stumped Newton, he made no mention of God. When asked about it, he is reputed to have answered, 'I had no need of that hypothesis.'"

"My point exactly. Science has been trying to do away with God ever since. Darwin certainly did him no favors. Hawking flatly declared there is no God, and did his best to prove it. In the eyes of many, he succeeded. Norberg advanced the cause even further. Every successive discovery since Galileo has chipped away at God a little more, and pushed him back a little farther."

Teal sighed. "You know, your paranoia is showing. Although I grant you it's nothing new. But the Church was wrong about Galileo then, and it would be equally wrong for it to attack science today." He cast Harland a significant glance. "Or for any of its officials to do so."

Harland jabbed a finger at him. "The Church was *not* wrong about

Galileo. We knew then where you guys were going with all this. And now those efforts are about to take a huge leap. This trip you're taking may expand man's grasp and the boundaries of his knowledge exponentially. Science now has the potential to blow God right out of the universe."

Again, Teal shook his head. "It only seems that way. Right now, science and faith appear to be on divergent paths. But it's an illusion, and a temporary one. Ultimately the trail of scientific inquiry will lead us right to God's doorstep."

"You don't believe that, Cam," Harland said softly, looking at him with kind eyes. "But I think you desperately *want* to."

Teal shifted uncomfortably in his chair. Now he was feeling more than a little annoyed. What right did Harland have to tell him what he did or did not believe in? He was about to open his mouth and object, when Harland reached over and placed a hand atop his. "Don't worry, Cam," he said softly. "I do think you'll find God. Just not in the way you expect."

Third Engineer Constance Nunn, AI Specialist for the NAUS *Santa Maria*, bolted upright in her bunk. Her sudden movement scared her cat, who'd been sleeping in the crook of her arm, half to death; the animal rocketed off the bunk and made a dash for the cabin door. There was a flare of light from the corridor beyond as the panel swung partially open with a soft hiss, allowing the animal to escape. The door then returned to its place, resealing the darkness.

Nunn found that she was breathing heavily. Beads of sweat had popped out on her forehead and face, causing her hair to plaster against her cheeks.

A voice sounded in the bone-conducting transceiver planted against her skull under the skin behind her left ear. "Third Engineer Constance Nunn, this is Wilson. Are you all right?"

Nunn tried to answer, but the only thing that came out was a croak. She cleared her throat and tried again. "I'm fine, Wilson."

"Your heart rate, blood pressure, and respiration are elevated," Wilson continued. "Did you have another bad dream?"

"Yes." Reaching out and feeling in the dark with her fingers, she found the pressure plate for the cabin lights and brought them up on their lowest setting.

"Your mother again?"

And it was here that Wilson's inquisitiveness crossed the line from that of a typical Artificial Intelligence to something a bit more personal. While it wasn't exactly inappropriate, Wilson's question was a little unusual for an AI. Most AIs had similar hardware and operating systems. For the umpteenth time, Nunn wondered what it was that made some of them behave slightly differently. A handful developed what amounted to a personality. The vast majority didn't. Wilson certainly fell into that former category, and it had happened quickly. The development didn't bother her, but it did arouse her professional curiosity.

"Why do you ask, Wilson?"

"I'm programmed to be inquisitive," Wilson reminded her.

"So you are," Nunn conceded.

"Furthermore, I'm also programmed to monitor crew health and safety. It is a well-established and long-accepted fact that the nature of dreams can be an indicator of psychological health."

"Well, my mental state is just fine," she said somewhat defensively.

"Yes, but may I point out that you did not answer my last question? Is this because you forgot, or are you deliberately trying to be evasive?"

That question, coming from a human, would seem impertinent or even snide. But Nunn knew that for Wilson it was simply an honest inquiry. He was still learning about the nuances of human behavior, and was genuinely trying to obtain information that would help him evaluate Nunn's mental state and emotional wellbeing.

"I was being evasive," Nunn admitted. "My mother—well, it's a difficult subject for me. I haven't seen her since I was 13. I'm not even sure she's alive."

"Your personnel file shows that you left Woolley Colony in 2121. The file does not explain why you left. Nor does it contain any past or current information on the state of your mother's health. However, based on news accounts of the New Atlantis piracy suppression raids four years ago, I calculate a 75 percent likelihood, with a margin of error of 3.5 percent, that she is deceased."

A tear rolled down Nunn's cheek.

"I see that your lachrymal glands have activated, and your risorius, buccinator, obicularis oris, mentalis, depressor anguli oris, and depressor labii inferioris muscles are trembling. Did my analysis upset you?"

Nunn reached up and wiped her cheek with the back of her hand. "Wilson, if you're going to get along with humans, you're going to have to learn some tact."

Wilson appeared to hesitate, but Nunn knew this could not possibly be due to any actual increased demand on his data processing. He was a precise communicator, and used pauses in his speech as just another verbal tool. "I do know about tact," Wilson said. "My dictionaries define that as skill or adroitness in showing sensitivity to others. I also have many dramatic references in my holographic memory systems giving examples. However, there is no example precisely corresponding to the present situation." He paused again. "Perhaps I should not have shared my analysis with you?"

"It's okay, Wilson. It's just that humans don't always like to face unpleasant facts right way, and we sometimes delay that as long as we can."

"As an operating parameter, such reluctance seems inefficient to me."

Despite herself, she chuckled. "You are so right. Humans can be very inefficient. But that's why we built computers. That's why I have you."

"Well, then, in the name of efficiency, and in fulfillment of my programmed duties, would you like to tell me more about your dream? Perhaps I can compare and contrast your story with other case histories, and find some information or advice that will help you."

Nunn raised an eyebrow, surprised despite herself. "What, now you want to be my psychoanalyst?"

"My hard datalink to Aldrin Station is in place and fully functional," Wilson said, and Nunn thought she could almost detect a note of defensiveness in his artificially-generated voice. "Within moments, I can download extensive data on all the major schools of thought in dream interpretation. Shall I do so?"

She could not help but chuckle. "No, don't do that. I'm not sure I want to add that kind of dimension to our relationship." She paused, her mood turning more serious. "But I don't mind telling you. It was the same as the last two times. We're in a dark place that I can't even describe. My mother's figure is dim and very far away, but I'm sure it's her. And her voice is faint. But she's calling my name. And she's saying something to me. Just two words, over and over." Nunn paused.

"At this point," Wilson said, "either you have decided not to divulge the two words in question, or you are indulging in what is known as a dramatic pause. If the latter, I am required, as a point of protocol and in pursuit of being a good conversation partner, to inquire about the words in question. I calculate with a high degree of confidence that this is the case. So I now ask you—what are the words that she spoke?"

Nunn shook her head. "Wilson, don't you hand me this 'dramatic pause' business, like you've never heard of the concept. You used it yourself just moments ago."

"It was not the same thing, as my two point one second pause was not designed to elicit a response. Rather, I inserted it both to allow you time to process your thoughts, and to give the appearance that my own answer was thoughtful, toward the end of relaxing you and making you feel comfortable with the conversation. The calculation was based on my analysis of millions of human verbal exchanges portrayed in fictional works loaded into my memory, and also on conversations that I have overheard here in the *Santa Maria* since my installation and boot-up. Did I err?"

"No, you didn't err. But in the future, you can skip the analysis and go right to the question. Here's your answer. The two words she spoke to me were, 'Don't go.'"

"That communication has an ambiguous meaning," Wilson observed. "She could be telling you not to go on the mission. Or she could be reproving you for having left the colony in 2121. There may be other possibilities of which I am not aware due to lack of data. How do *you* take the meaning?"

"I don't know, really. Both. Neither. It's just a dream."

"Most human authorities on the subject believe dreams have meaning, although there are varied and sometimes conflicting schools of thought on how to interpret them. In addition, some researchers say there is a possibility that dreams are a portal through which other human spirits, both living and dead, or other supernatural entities, may contact the dreamer. However, there are no hard data to support that notion, and therefore most mainstream scientists reject it. The most widely accepted psychological theories hold that dreams are an expression of the subconscious mind, and that with proper interpretation they may give insight into the dreamer's emotional and psychological state. Based on that line of reasoning and on the data at hand, my analysis is that you have unresolved emotional conflicts regarding your separation from your mother and your departure from Woolley Colony, and you are also apprehensive about the dangers of the upcoming mission."

"See, this is what I was hoping to avoid," Nunn said ruefully. "Now I have to deal with Dr. Sigmund Wilson."

Wilson indulged in one of his dramatic pauses. "Since I find no such person in the current or historical databases, I take your remark to be a humorous or sarcastic criticism of my analysis efforts. Because my programming is adaptive, I have many capabilities. Should I suppress this one?"

"Just for the rest of the night. How's the ship?"

"I note that your question constitutes a change of subject, and I calculate that this likely indicates an unstated desire on your part to move on from a topic that appears to be causing you emotional discomfort. I apologize if I have been the cause of that. Although I have a great deal of data about human beings in my memory core, I find that I am still learning the fine details of how to interface with them."

"Not a problem, Wilson. And I am genuinely curious about the status of the ship."

"In the one hour, six minutes and 35 seconds at the mark—mark—that have elapsed since you turned out the cabin light, denoting the beginning of your sleep period, there have been no new alerts, problems or significant developments in ship status. The vessel remains docked to Birth 13 of Aldrin Station. The docking clamps and umbilicals are secure. All main systems on the station and on the ship are operating within their nominal ranges. Should I patch you through to the bridge? Electrician Nereida Sabol is on watch."

"No, not necessary. And make a note that for informal

communications of this nature, you don't have to be so precise with your data. A human in this situation would have simply said, 'No new developments since you went to bed.' " Nunn relaxed against the pillow and pulled the thin cover up to her chin. "I'm going to try to get back to sleep."

"Yes, Third Engineer Nunn."

"You know, Wilson, you don't have to be so formal with my name, either. We have a close relationship. I installed your hardware and operating system, programmed your mission parameters, and booted you up. I even gave you your name."

Wilson hesitated. "Should I address you as 'Mother'?"

Nunn laughed. "No. Although, come to think of it, that wouldn't be too far off the mark. I selected your gender, which is a very parental function indeed."

"My gender? I was not aware that computers had a gender. We are not biological entities."

"Your name is masculine. And I selected a masculine speech program for your artificial voice. Both choices were completely arbitrary."

"On what facts did you base your choices?"

"None whatsoever. It was a flip of the coin. You came close to being Chloe."

"Why did you reject the name Chloe?"

Nunn shrugged. "No reason. At least, none of that I'm aware of. You'll find humans are a lot like that."

"But it would not be appropriate for me to regard you as a mother figure?"

"No, not really. I didn't design or conceive you. But I did bring you into the world, and spank your bottom."

"I believe I understand the analogy. So you are my obstetrician?"

She laughed again. "No."

"Are you my pediatrician?"

"Well, that would be a closer analogy. I do oversee your physical care. But, again, I'd say no."

"Let me see if I understand. We are close, but you are not my parent, not my birth doctor, and not my physician. Are you my friend?"

"Not if you don't shut the hell up and let me get back to sleep." Reaching for the pressure plate, she switched off the cabin lights.

"Yes, Constance. I will close the link to your subdural transceiver in five seconds. Four, three –"

"Wilson, what did I just tell you?"

"Yes, Constance. Good night, Constance."

Nunn shook her head, smiling. "Wilson, it's 'Connie.' When we're in a private setting, you can call me that."

17

"Yes, Connie."

"Good night, Wilson. Now shut it."

"Yes, Connie. Good night, Connie. I will now shut it."

Sirius Constantine Cermeno, Sr., Chief Executive Officer and Chairman of the Board of the company that bore his name, peeked through the side door and regarded the crowd of reporters with a mixture of disdain and revulsion. To Cermeno, dealing with the media was the business equivalent of snake handling. He found some individual reporters to be tolerable, even likable. But at heart, they were all pit vipers, each and every one of them. Anyone handling them was sure to get bitten sooner or later. Today, Cermeno knew, was his day.

But he had invited the growling mass to his shiny corporate tower in Chicago for a reason, and it was time to get on with it. Cermeno pulled open the door and strode boldly across the platform. The crowd fell silent as he approached the podium.

"Ladies and gentlemen," Cermeno said, looking over the group. "I'm Sirius Cermeno, Senior. Thank you for coming today. I think we all know why we're here. Without further delay, let me introduce you to the officers and key personnel of the NAUS *Santa Maria.*"

On cue, nine men and women wearing cobalt blue jumpsuits, each adorned with a flag and mission patch on either shoulder and a name tag on the chest, exited the opposite side door, walked across the platform, and took up standing positions at the tables arranged on either side of the podium. As they did so, the reporters applauded politely.

"To my far right, your left, is Captain Sirius Cermeno, Junior."

A man in his 30s, just over six feet tall, wearing brushed-back, medium length blond hair, nodded and smiled curtly. Captain Cermeno was handsome and fit, but not chiseled. His facial features were slightly rounded, with a hint of softness. But there was no sign of either softness or kindness in his blue eyes, which matched his uniform. Cermeno had the look of someone who was instantly ready to disapprove of you, and probably would.

"Proceeding to his left, your right, First Officer Fabiana De Vegas."

De Vegas nodded to the crowd. She was the same height and approximately the same weight as the captain, but was more athletic and her muscles more pronounced. De Vegas kept her black hair cut short. Her dark-complected face bore the angular, hard features that the captain lacked. The first officer's most notable feature was a livid, angry scar that started at the corner of her left eye and extended nearly to her jaw line, marring what otherwise would have been a reasonably attractive face; it looked as if someone had exerted a major effort to put her eye out, and had nearly succeeded. She carried herself with confidence, and her dark brown eyes telegraphed an ability to size anyone up instantly and accurately.

"Chief Astrogator Lydia Nguyen."

A petite young woman with long, shiny, jet black hair framing a lovely face nodded.

"Chief Science Officer, Dr. David Jones."

Jones was a trim, slightly thin man sporting close-cropped salt-and-pepper hair and a matching beard. As his name was called, he nodded to the crowd, and then turned and smiled at the young woman standing next to him. Reaching over, he took her hand.

"And if you're wondering why they're holding hands," Cermeno continued, "Astrogator Nguyen and Dr. Jones got married last week. This voyage is how they'll be spending their honeymoon. Talk about getting away from it all."

The remark drew laughter, and then applause. Nguyen blushed all the way down to her collar, while her groom stood at her side, beaming.

"To their left, Chief Engineer Bates Crandall."

There was no generous way to describe it: Crandall was ugly. His broad, heavy face bore a permanent scowl, which was not helped by the bushy white and black unibrow that underscored his forehead, and the large, pulpy pink and black mole just to the left of his nose. Crandall's figure was neither trim nor athletic; he was about five ten and weighed more than 230 pounds. The man was 54 years old but looked much older. Upon hearing his name, his face cracked into what probably was intended to be a smile, but would have caused any group of trick-or-treaters to drop their candy bags and run screaming into the night.

Cermeno turned to the other table. "Our medical officer, Dr. Candace Blake."

Blake was a 50-something blond of medium stature. She'd long since lost her girlish figure, but despite the addition of a few pounds and the appearance of a network of worry lines around her eyes and mouth, she was not unattractive.

"Next to Dr. Blake, N-Field Specialist, Dr. Morton Makowski. Dr. Makowski is Chief Scientist for the Cermeno Enterprises Space Drive Division and principal designer of the interdimensional array that bears his name."

Makowski was a tall fortyish man with thin, almost skeletal features. The scientist was nearly bald on top but wore his surviving thin, grey hair long; now he had it pulled back in a ponytail. Normally he wore thick black-rimmed glasses, but for the purposes of this press conference had self-consciously, and not without a touch of vanity, removed them. During the introductions Makowski had been staring at the tabletop, wringing his hands nervously. Upon hearing his name, he clasped his hands out of sight behind his back, peered out myopically at the crowd, nodded, and smiled nervously.

"Next to him, our guest scientist, Father Cameron Teal, director of the Vatican Observatory."

Teal nodded and smiled politely.

"And finally, someone I believe you all know and are ready to tar and feather—our guest journalist, Janson Jervis of the Universal News Net."

The reporters chuckled, while at the same time, more than a dozen of the little flitting AV balls that had been hovering around the room zipped forward for video close-ups, swarming like moths to a light. As he had many times before, Cermeno was left to wonder how the devices avoided knocking into one another. But it was no surprise that they had converged on Jervis. He was quite the celebrity, one of the best known of the current pack of network anchor/reporters. His name supposedly had been picked by way of a random draw, but the truth was that Cermeno had secretly rigged the selection. Jervis, he of the swept-back black hair, ice blue eyes and youthful, chiseled movie-star looks, was all the rage, about as close as one got to rock star status for a journalist. Jervis was guaranteed to keep the mission—and by extension, Cermeno Enterprises, Inc.—in the public eye.

"Ladies and gentlemen," Cermeno continued, smiling at the astronauts, "please be seated."

The nine sat to more polite applause.

"In two days, these nine brave men and women, along with 24 fellow crew members, will embark on a journey of exploration the likes of which mankind has never seen. Our revolutionary new Makowski N-Field Array will empower these pathfinders to probe the limits of the universe, thereby throwing open new frontiers for humanity. Captain Cermeno and the crew of the NAUS *Santa Maria* will voyage to unimaginable distances, billions of light years away, and return safely to the earth. Christopher Columbus, from whose flagship our vessel takes its name, dared to sail beyond the edge of the known world. Now, not quite 650 years later, we'll sail beyond the edge of the known *universe*. I'll now take your questions."

The predictable babble of voices arose. For the first question, Cermeno had arranged in advance to select Paris Beck, an absolutely delectable young woman from Advance News whom he also happened to be dating. "Paris?" he said.

"Mr. Cermeno, why are you doing this? What do you hope this incredibly bold feat will accomplish for mankind?"

It was the question he'd given her to ask, and he'd carefully prepared his answer. "The greatest gift I can conceive of giving humanity is simply this: new inspiration for the advancement of our race. From antiquity, philosophers, scholars, and poets have told us our reach must always exceed our grasp. After the voyage of the *Santa Maria* such words never will be spoken again. Everything we survey will be our domain. The Makowksi Array will give humanity the ability to expand not only beyond our own tiny little section of the explored galaxy, but beyond the galaxy itself, to realms previously unimagined. For the first time, mankind will have no horizons. Our potential will be without limit. Our future will stretch to infinity." He pointed to a reporter standing in the front row whom he did not recognize; the woman must be local.

"But why such a great leap for the first time out of the gate?" she asked. "Wouldn't it be safer to try out the new technologies by making a series of more modest hops?"

This was one of the snakebites he'd been expecting, and he was ready for it. A truthful answer, however, would not do. The mission's purpose was to generate publicity and excitement for his company. A quick, easy run to some known but heretofore unexplored star system within their own galaxy simply would not generate such excitement, no matter what speed records it might set. But that was not the answer he was ready to give. "An old mentor of mine once said, 'Si, live by this rule: make no small plan.' Yes, it's a bold leap. But we can do this. We *will*. And by doing so we will blaze a trail for all of humanity." He pointed to a grumpy looking man standing two rows back.

"Mr. Cermeno, are you aware of the sharp criticism leveled at this project by Dr. Abadom Onobano, director of the United Nations Science Directorate? He dismisses the voyage as a publicity stunt, and suggests that if you want to do some real extragalactic science, you should voyage to the Great Attractor in the Hydra-Centaurus Supercluster, and see what that's all about."

Cermeno swallowed his anger; there was always someone waiting in the wings to throw dirt on any project. Dr. Onobano was a notorious stuffed shirt who was in love with the sound of his own voice. But Cermeno instantly rejected a number of biting, sharply-worded responses that sprang to mind, selecting instead a more diplomatic approach. "The successful conclusion of this voyage will open the floodgates for further exploration. Cermeno Enterprises will be at the forefront of those efforts. At the appropriate time, I'll be happy to discuss rates with Dr. Onobano."

That resulted in scattered chuckles, which is what Cermeno had been hoping for. He pointed to a lovely young woman standing in the third row.

"Mr. Cermeno," she said, "can you tell us something about how the technology works?"

Smiling, Cermeno lifted his hands in a gesture of helplessness. "Well, that's a longer, even drier speech." This resulted in more chuckles, which was the effect he'd intended with his slightly self-deprecating humor—a tactic with which he was not totally comfortable but that his consultants had assured him would be good for his image. "But let's see what we can do. To start, I'll bat the question to Dr. Jones, our mission science officer."

A tiny AV drone zoomed over and hovered in the air a half meter from Jones' face; the man had to suppress an instinctive reflex to swat it. "I thought someone might ask me that," Jones said in a voice that was heavy with a Scottish accent. "So I brought a visual aid." Reaching down beneath the cloth-draped table, he withdrew an object. Pulling it into view, observers could see that it was a common DayGlo red polyethylene foam pool noodle. When it came into sight, the reporters broke into laughter.

"What's the matter?" Jones demanded. "Do none of you like to go for a swim?"

This resulted in more chuckles.

"You!" Jones pointed to the surly looking reporter who'd asked the question about Dr. Onobano. "Grump man! Don't make me come over there with this. You don't know how close you came to a noodle drubbing a minute ago."

The reporter managed a sheepish smile.

"Now," Jones continued, brandishing the noodle, "I want you to think of this as a straight line, having no thickness. How many dimensions does it have?" He pointed the grouchy reporter. "You, with the sour fizzog. How many?"

"One," the man said.

"Excellent. Now, as you can see, I've marked our visual aid with the letters A through Z. I want you to think of those as being tiny little one-dimensional apartments occupied by tiny little one-dimensional beings. The hero of our story, Freddy Allinwun, lives in Apartment A. And he's dating a bird named Patty la Pointe in Apartment Z."

Scattered titters sounded from around the room.

"Now, if Freddy wants to hook up with Patty, he has to travel from A to Z, all the way down the length of his little one-dimensional world." Jones traced his finger along the pool noodle. "For him, it's quite a hike. Now, what if I were to bend this straight line, like so." He formed the noodle into the shape of a narrow letter U, and held it up. "Now how many dimensions does it have?" He pointed to an attractive young lady in the first row. "You, the heartbreaker with the hair bob. How many?"

"Two," she said.

"Aaaaank," Jones said, making a fair imitation of a game buzzer. "No. But thank you for playing. And also thank you for reinforcing all my stereotypical notions about the quality of public education in The North American Union." Jones said it with a smile and a twinkle in his eye. The reporter laughed, as did the others.

"Anyone else?"

"One!" a voice shouted from the back.

"Excellent! Hand that woman a weekend in Hawaii. 'One' is correct.

You can determine the number of dimensions by counting the number of spatial coordinates required to describe it—which in this case, despite the bend, remains just one point of datum for each location, as designated by the letters A through Z. There's no up or down, or left or right—just backwards and forwards. This true even though, ourselves being observers from a higher set of dimensions, *we* can see that Freddy's world is bent through another dimension. But Freddy can't. Since Freddy is a one-dimensional being, bent and unbent are all the same to him. The poor man is confined to looking back and ahead. Left and right to him are concepts right out of science fiction." Jones looked out over the crowd. "Are you with me so far?"

The reporters nodded.

"I think you're all lying to my face, but onward we go anyway. Okay, so Freddy still has to travel about five feet—which to him, a wee little microscopic being on this scale, is miles and miles—to see his lady friend. But check this out." He pointed to narrow gap separating the two ends of the noodle at the top of the U. "When you take into account the *second* dimension—which, remember, one-dimensional Freddy can't see—his apartment is only *one inch* away from Patty's. Now, what if Freddy could hang a left and build a 90-degree shortcut across that gap through the second dimension? Think how much travel time that would save him. Not to mention the fact that he could sneak in to see Patti without the neighbors knowing. It wouldn't do for his nightly visitations to get back to his guidwife."

More chuckles erupted.

Jones tossed the noodle over his shoulder. "That is a very simple analogy. But as it turns out, the universe is filled with different dimensions, and each set has its own unique properties and topological features. All we have to do is find the shortcuts, which we accomplish through difficult computations, fast computers, and a wee bit of technological legerdemain. And with that, Dr. Makowski, I'll turn it over to you."

An AV ball zipped through the air and took up station in front of Makowski's face. "Well, as you know," Makowski said, nervously kneading his hands, "The Norberg Field generator allows us to take those shortcuts, creating something that's similar in function, though not in properties, to an Einstein-Rosen bridge—a wormhole, if you prefer. That's the development that made interstellar travel possible in the last century. What we've done now is to cram dozens of Norberg generators into a compact array, which allows us to make hundreds of jumps per second. In fact, not only can we take shortcuts, but sometimes we can take shortcuts within shortcuts. The result is that we can translate ourselves any proper distance along any real-world spatial axis, within a time span of minutes or even seconds, depending on the length traversed. To an outside observer, it would appear that our spacecraft has disappeared at point X and then reappeared at point Y, millions or even billions of light years away. And with surprisingly little energy involved."

Cermeno turned to Crandall. "Chief Crandall, anything to add to that?"

Crandall's fixed scowl slightly relaxed into a mere glower as he turned to Makowski. "Dr. Makowski's part is to plug his whirligig in where I tell him, and he's done that. Mine is to see to it that he doesn't blow any fuses."

A few reporters laughed at that.

"How do you navigate?" a voice sang out.

"That's a question for the other Jones," Cermeno said.

"Actually, I go by Nguyen," the petite, dark-haired woman said as an AV drone ball zipped over to her, while several of its twins continued to hover a few feet away. "It avoids confusion with too many Joneses." She smiled, waiting for the polite chuckles to die down. "Essentially, we navigate—the proper term is 'astrogate'—by looking out the window. Or rather I should say, it's a series of special windows, designed for our optical instruments and other sensing devices. In the classic spatial dimensions we've always known, stars glow in the dark. In some of the new dimension sets we're now able to reach, the stars don't shine, but dark matter does. And in still others, there are light sources that, quite frankly, we're still puzzled about—some scientists suspect the glow may be coming from dark energy. We're still learning to interpret it. But the bottom line is, every time we make a transition—which as Dr. Makowski said happens multiple time a second—our astrogation computer processes the images, compares the data to predictions, adjusts as needed, and then recalculates the next jump on the fly. It's all pretty seamless."

"Provided the computers work," the reporter observed.

Nguyen nodded. "Correct. But we have plenty of redundancies and failsafes."

Cermeno pointed to a nattily clad gentleman that he recognized as being a star reporter from Galactic News.

"Mr. Cermeno, why are you taking a priest?" the reporter asked.

"What, you think they don't need one?" some wit in the back sang out.

Cermeno, smiling patiently while making a mighty effort not to look irritated, waited for the laughter to die down, and then turned to Teal. "Father Teal?"

Teal was annoyed that Cermeno would shove him a question about Cermeno's own motivations, but he strove not to show it. Pausing just for a moment to allow the close-up view AV ball time to arrive, he cleared his throat. "I wear the collar, to be sure—but I'm also an astrophysicist. We're going quite literally where no man or woman has gone, or even seriously contemplated going, before now. Mr. Cermeno thought—and I wholeheartedly agree—that the mission could benefit from having someone on board with my unique training and perspective."

"Mr. Cermeno," the reporter insisted, not willing to let the executive duck the question, "is that how you see it?"

Cermeno looked thoughtful. "The laws of man extend to colonized space. The laws of nature are presumed to extend throughout the universe. But what about the laws of God? We have a duly authorized captain to represent man's authority, and a science officer to speak to natural law. Father Teal gives us that third, theological dimension. Where we're going, I don't think humanity would be fully represented without it."

A reporter for the *Daily Mirror* who'd had her hand up several times, and whom Cermeno had been avoiding, was now growing visibly impatient, but Cermeno wasn't ready to deal with her yet. He pointed to an older man on the other side of the room.

"Mr. Cermeno," the man said, holding up his computer pad, "I notice on your press release that the *Santa Maria* carries no armament. Can you comment on that?"

"Yes, I had the missile batteries removed," Cermeno said. "As the result of military actions over the last five years, the piracy nuisance has been greatly reduced. Plus, the very first planned jump will take us well outside galactic space. We're headed deep into the voids between galaxies, nowhere near any star systems. So the long awaited and long hoped-for First Contact with some alien civilization is not likely to happen on this voyage. But I did make the decision, with Captain Cermeno's concurrence, that if we do meet someone out there, our first act will not be to shoot them."

That caused a titter to run around the room.

There were a few more desultory questions. But finally, Cermeno couldn't ignore the *Daily Mirror* reporter any longer. Trying to keep his face impassive, he pointed to the woman. *Here it comes*, he thought.

"Mr. Cermeno, First Officer De Vegas was originally announced as the captain of this mission, and she trained in that capacity. Can you explain why you demoted her and put a new captain in her place, whose career was in tatters before the appointment?"

A hush now fell over the room.

Cermeno had known he'd face that question, and had rehearsed for it. But the query infuriated him just the same. He felt his cheeks flushing. The reporter had been deliberately disrespectful. *God damn the media*, he thought. *What a bunch of muckraking rats and vultures.* But he fought to suppress his anger. Cermeno mentally retrieved the canned answer his media handlers had helped him craft, and which they had gone over with him several times. This was another question where the truthful answer, even though in this case it was painfully obvious to all involved, would not do. But nor would an evasive one; this had to be faced head-on. "First of all, I want to say that First Officer De Vegas was in no way demoted. Her performance has been outstanding in every way. She will continue to play an integral role in this flight, and we have every confidence in her going forward."

De Vegas' face remained impassive.

"For those of you who think that putting my son in this role smacks of nepotism, I say this: If that's your judgment, then I accept your criticism as the price I must pay for the additional confidence and peace of mind this decision has brought me. I have nothing but the most profound respect and admiration for everyone taking part in this voyage. But there's no bond like a blood bond. I trust my son. Further, I know that Captain Cermeno is not the man that—" here he started to say, "you people," and had to cut himself off from doing it— "that some have made him out to be. Captain Cermeno is skilled, experienced, and courageous. I know he is the right man to lead this team." *Captain Cermeno*, he thought, *is a whiny, sniveling, self-absorbed little turd who, after his last debacle, does not deserve command of a rowboat. This is the man's last chance to resurrect his career, and he'd better not foul it up.* Smiling, Cermeno turned to his son. "Captain Cermeno?"

Looking thoughtful, the captain nodded. "I am very grateful for my father's confidence in me," he said. "I know full well that this is the opportunity, and the honor, of a lifetime. I will not let my family, or my team, down. The next time you see me, I'll be telling you how the crew of the *Santa Maria* pulled off an exploratory voyage the likes of which comes only once in the lifetime of a species."

Well put, Cermeno thought. *At least the boy can speak. Being at a loss for words was never one of the kid's shortcomings.*

There was only one other interesting question. One reporter wanted to know why such a relatively small crew required such a large ship. Before being refitted and renamed for the mission, the *Santa Maria* had served as a colony transport ship, and could carry more than a thousand people along with their personal goods, livestock, equipment and supplies. "It's pretty simple," Crandall explained. "We needed a vessel large enough to accommodate the N-field array, which is more than 30 meters in diameter. This ship fits the bill, and just barely, at that."

"Sounds like you'll have plenty of empty cabins," the *Daily Mirror* reporter observed.

Cermeno couldn't help himself. He flashed a wolfish smile. "We'll be glad to take you along—and drop you off somewhere." Cermeno's point was not lost on anyone, and produced another round of hearty laughter.

After that, the press conference quickly wound down. Cermeno noticed that his son and De Vegas said nothing to each other after it ended, and they departed out of opposite doors. *Oh, well,* Cermeno thought. *It's Junior's problem now. He'll just have to grow a set, show some leadership, and deal with it.*

When Captain Cermeno exited the shuttle lock on Aldrin Station, he saw a familiar figure waiting for him. Marta Breza's trademark long hair, which was so blond it was almost white, was hard to miss. Breza was sitting in a chair in the waiting area, snacking on some kind of food bar. *No doubt granola or something else disgustingly healthy*, Cermeno thought. Breza had served under him aboard the *Antilles*. She had been one of the last off the ship after the fusion reactor blew, and she'd made no effort to conceal her contempt for Cermeno afterwards. Worse, she was Fabiana De Vegas' girlfriend—or ex-girlfriend, as he'd just recently learned. Cermeno had not spoken with Breza since the hearing, although not for lack of effort on her part. She'd tried to contact him multiple times; in response he'd blocked her phone number and media accounts. Now Breza was first officer of the *Dutch Trader*. While coming up on the shuttle, Cermeno had seen the vessel docked on the other side of the station. He'd suspected that she might try to intercept him, and had hoped to avoid her. No such luck.

Breza stood as he approached.

Cermeno nodded. "First Officer," he said by way of a greeting, and then braced himself for the snide remark he knew was coming.

"Captain," Breza said in response, not smiling. "You never write. You never call. You're a hard man to pin down."

Despite her sarcasm, her tone sounded less bitter than he'd expected. Perhaps Breza was here to make amends. "Can I buy you a cup of coffee?" he offered—somewhat generously, he thought.

"Sure. That would be nice."

They walked over to a Starbucks on the main concourse. Cermeno ordered a big caramel macchiato. He was amused, but not surprised, to see that Breza took her coffee straight black.

"You're looking well," he observed as they sat down.

"And you," she allowed. "I saw you on the Net. I thought you handled yourself well."

"Thanks. It was—difficult." The moment he said it, he regretted it, as this gave her an instant opening to discuss *why* it was difficult.

But she didn't. Instead, she asked, "Are you looking forward to the mission?"

"Yes," he said. As the word passed his lips he realized, somewhat to his surprise, that it was a lie. He loathed and dreaded the mission. Cermeno wasn't sure he was up to the challenge. Nor, he knew, was anyone else. But he plowed ahead. "It's the opportunity of a lifetime."

"If you play your cards right, your name will be spoken in the same breath with Columbus, Magellan, Cook, and Tejada."

"I guess there is that," he conceded. "Yet I'm not really doing anything.

I'm just going where the longhairs point me—and as you may have seen on the Net, one of our longhairs really does have long hair."

Breza chuckled. "I did see that. That guy was jickier than a road lizard."

Cermeno cocked his head at her. "What?"

She smiled. "That's a Texas expression I picked up. It basically means, 'nervous and twitchy.' "

"Oh," he nodded. "He is that. I don't think Dr. Makowski's ever been out of the lab. Or out of his lab coat, for that matter. It was all I could do to get him into a uniform for the presser."

"That doesn't surprise me."

Cermeno gave her a thoughtful look. "I was sorry to hear about you and Fab."

Breza shrugged. "Yeah, me too. Neither of us wanted it. Our lives are going in different directions. But we still care about one another." She picked up her cup and took a sip, looking thoughtful. "In fact, that's why I'm here," she said, putting down the cup.

"What do you mean?"

She gazed across at him with steady, serious eyes. "I've been wanting to talk to you for a long time. Ever since the accident. We only got to exchange a few words in the hallway during the hearing, and I know I wasn't pleasant. And you haven't returned my calls."

"I—"

She held up her hand. "No need to make excuses. I would have avoided me, too. What I had to say to you was—well, let's just say I was in a state. I lost some people I cared about on the *Antilles*."

Cermeno didn't know what to say. *I should leave now*, he thought. But he was rooted to the spot, transfixed like a victim caught in the mesmerizing gaze of a vampire.

"I'm past that now," she said. "When we worked together, I admired you, and we had a good relationship. Because of that, I'm hoping you'll let me say something to you."

"Go ahead," he heard himself responding.

She reached forward and placed her hand on his. Cermeno was stunned and surprised.

"I promise you, I mean no disrespect with what I'm about to say," came Breza's words, spoken softly. "But I care about what happens to Fab. And you have her life in your hands."

After an uncomfortable pause, he nodded. He could not think of any other response.

"You have strengths," she continued. "But no one is without flaw. Because of that, way back in the 20th century, management experts were teaching executives to hire people who were smarter and more capable than they were. It's good advice. But the trick is to recognize those people when you see them, and listen to them."

Cermeno braced himself. He knew Breza's next words were the reason she had been lying in wait for him. And, like a big dummy, he had walked right into her trap. This was not going to be pleasant. Yet he still couldn't move. He couldn't even muster the will to pull his hand back.

"Fab is ten times the man you are," Breza said with words so soft as to be barely audible. "I don't even blame you anymore. You are what you are. Each of us responds according to our nature. But when the shit hits the fan—and it will—you *must* put your ego and insecurity aside, and listen to her. When you listen only to yourself—well, I'm sure I don't need to say it. We both know what happened on the *Antilles*."

No. She didn't need to say it, because so many others before her had already done so—pointing fingers, accusing him, trying to destroy his career. And they'd nearly succeeded. Thinking back on it, and with her words still ringing in his ears, the blood slowly drained from Cermeno's face. But he did not react. Her teeth had already opened his jugular. Now there was nothing to do but sit there and bleed out.

Breza patted his hand, and then squeezed it. *She's actually squeezing my goddamned hand*, Cermeno thought.

"Thanks for letting me say this," Breza said. "Take care of yourself. I really mean that."

Cermeno knew that she did indeed did mean it. But it wasn't personal. If he could keep from getting himself killed, Fabiana De Vegas might come back alive, too.

Breza stood. "Thanks for the coffee."

Then she turned and was gone.

2 UNDERWAY

Lydia Nguyen Jones popped open her eyes and looked up. For a moment she did not know where she was. The room was pitch black. She turned her head. Dim red numerals hung in the air above the tiny desk to the left of her bunk where her iCard was projecting the time. It was 03:00. Today she had the morning watch, and was due to report in one hour. That left her time enough to get a quick shower, throw on her jumpsuit and grab a bite of breakfast.

But for the moment, she couldn't move. David, sleeping on his side next to her, had his left arm and leg thrown over her. She sighed, remembering how sweet last night had been. David was, without a doubt, crazy wild about her, and she felt the same about him. When they'd first arrived back aboard the *Santa Maria* two nights ago, he'd actually carried her across the "threshold" of their small cabin. Every spare moment they got, the two of them celebrated like what they were: two newlyweds. They couldn't get enough of one another.

She smiled at the thought of it: a wild-eyed Scotsman married to a half-Anglo half-Vietnamese colonist from New California. Who'd have thought that? You had to love the 22nd century.

Her smile disappeared as an image crossed her mind, darkening her thoughts like a burglar stepping into the bright square of light streaming through an open doorway. The image was not a pleasant one. As a child, she'd had frequent nightmares, always involving the same mysterious, frightening figure—a dark, cadaverous shape with the grinning face of a rotting corpse, framed by long, dark, twisted locks of greasy hair. The dreams had disappeared around the time she turned nine or ten, and she had not seen that grisly face or even thought of it in years. Why was it flashing into her brain now? Had she seen it a dream?

A shiver passed down her spine. Reaching up, she touched her fingers to her forehead. They came away wet. Very strange. She hoped she wasn't coming down with a virus.

She strained to remember the moments just before she'd awakened. She *had* been dreaming. Slowly, it came back to her. She'd been sitting at her astrogation console on the bridge of the *Santa Maria*, and had heard a noise behind her. Turning to look, she'd seen a shadow on the rear bulkhead where no shadow should have been. As she watched, the shadow grew, spreading over the wall like an ugly stain. The plastisteel surface seemed to simply dissolve away as the darkness ate into it like acid. Rising from her chair, she took a step toward it. Inside the shadow was utter blackness. She stepped closer. A horrible stench of decay assaulted her nostrils, causing her to slap her hand over her nose and cough. It was at this point that her eyes had popped open.

Troubled, she wondered whether the dream had meant anything. Nguyen knew the possibility existed that it might. This was the kind of dream that would remain with her all day. Throughout her life, she'd had such dreams from time to time—dreams leaving an afterglow of emotion that stayed with her like the acrid smell of smoke clinging to clothes, sometimes for hours. Usually the dreams were not unpleasant—certainly not nightmares like this one had been. In many cases, they were simply dreams about people in her life. But on rare occasion, such dreams were about individuals she would come to know, but had not yet met at the time of the dream. Rarer still, a dream would seem to foreshadow or even predict future events.

But those were incredibly rare. And on only one occasion had she recognized such foreshadowing for what it was in advance of the event. For the most part, if there were any method by which to distinguish a dream or thought that might have precognitive value from the hundreds of other dreams and random thoughts and mental images that didn't, she had not been able to find it.

So there was no use worrying about this one. If, God forbid, the dream was a warning of any future event, she would know it when it happened.

Smiling again, gently she reached down and disengaged David's left hand, which was cupping her right breast. As she slid from beneath his leg, David mumbled something unintelligible, and then rolled over onto his other side. Lucky him, he wouldn't have to report for duty until 08:00. David's services wouldn't truly be needed until after the first jump, which should happen around noon if all went well.

Careful not to disturb him further, Nguyen padded across the deck in the dark to the bulkhead, felt her way along it to the refresher door, then stepped inside and pulled it shut behind her before switching on the light.

Janson Jervis walked up to the outer bridge door and paused, adjusting the strap of the omnicorder case that was slung over his shoulder, and feeling just a little bit out of his element. Jervis was most at home in an expensive suit, the uniform for all network anchor/reporters. This crew had welcomed him as one of their own, however, even extending to him the courtesy of the blue jumpsuit he was now wearing, complete with a grey patch on the right breast bearing his last name in big black letters. But he wasn't completely familiar with shipboard culture and protocols, and he secretly worried about making an idiot of himself. And appearing idiotic was one of Janson Jervis' greatest fears, a fate to be studiously avoided.

At the moment he was a little pressed for time. He'd intended to arrive fifteen minutes ago, which would have allowed plenty of time to set up for coverage of the historic departure. But he found the task of making separate phone calls to three different girlfriends at roughly the same time—none of whom suspected the existence of the others—to be a bit more difficult than expected; he'd just gotten off the phone with the last one. But, hurried or not, one thing Jansen did know about ship's protocol is that one didn't simply barge onto the bridge of a starship. Reaching forward, he pressed the vidcom button by the door and waited. The small flat screen above the button flashed and a face appeared, which Jervis recognized as belonging to Able Starman Jessica Beadel, a lovely young lady with short blonde hair cut in the popular pixie style who was one of the *Santa Maria's* communications officers. "Good morning, Mr. Jervis," she said, smiling.

"It's Janson to my friends," he said. "And I certainly hope I can include you in that number."

"Absolutely." She turned her head to the side, looking at someone off camera, but then quickly turned back to him. The door in front of him slid open with a barely audible hiss. "Come on in. Please see the first officer."

"Will do." Jansen stepped through the door into the short passageway beyond, and then waited. The panel behind him slid shut, and then the one in front of him opened. Since the *Valhalla* tragedy late in the last century, the main entrances to all compartments vital to the functioning of any spacefaring vessel were equipped with safety airlocks, and by interplanetary regulations at least one of the double doors had to be closed at all times even if both sides of the safety lock were at pressure—an annoying but prudent safety regulation. When the inner door opened, Jervis hesitated— despite his celebrity status, he always got stage jitters. Taking a deep breath, he stepped through it.

Before him was a relatively small rectangular room, at the forward end of which was an arc of control consoles. Curving above the consoles was a series of large windows, swept back somewhat aerodynamically at a 25 degree angle. Looming large beyond them was the beautiful blue and white cloud-dappled orb of the earth, with its curved horizons gently falling away at opposite ends of the viewports. The landscape below was rushing across the view from starboard to port. Beyond the thin, diffuse layers of clouds and the clear, bluish haze of atmosphere that kissed the horizons rose a jet black sky, punctuated here and there by the occasional bright star. At either extreme of the curve of windows could be seen the bows of other ships birthed alongside theirs to port and starboard. Various crewmembers, most of whom Jervis had met during his orientation tour, sat at the bridge consoles. Several feet back from these positions, at a slightly raised platform in the center of the bridge, was a smaller, two-person command console, now vacant. The left-hand black padded chair in this pair was the captain's. The other belonged to the first officer.

Presiding over it all was the latter, Fabiana De Vegas, who at the moment was standing in front of the command console taking in the spectacular view. He stepped up to her wearing his best and most charming smile. "Permission to enter the bridge," he said.

De Vegas turned to him and nodded, flashing a brief but warm smile. "Good Morning, Mr. Jervis. Are you ready for your trip to the unknown?"

"No," he said, still smiling. "Not in the least. But I assume you and your crew will more than make up for any deficits in the strength of my intestinal fortitude."

De Vegas chuckled. "We'll certainly try." She nodded over her shoulder. "I believe you've met our bridge crew."

Jervis glanced around the arc of consoles. Jessica Beadel was manning the coms and sensor station, the middle position on the port half of the arc. At the console to her right was Chief Astrogator Lydia Nguyen. To Nguyen's right, at the first position on the starboard half of the arc, was First Helmsman Nicolas Swann. Next to him was a young lady whom Jervis did not recognize. The woman immediately piqued Jervis' interest. She was in her late twenties and looked to be about five eight, with a perfect hourglass figure that filled out her jumpsuit just right. Her shiny, silky smooth light brown hair was cut in a sexy, slightly shaggy medium-length fashion that was all the rage these days. She was turned profile to Jervis, so he couldn't tell the color of her eyes, but what he could see of her features hinted at a lovely, heart-shaped face. Further, she had a cute, well tapered, slightly upturned nose. Jervis just loved cute, well tapered, slightly upturned noses.

"I don't believe I've met this young lady," Jervis said, stepping toward the crewmember.

"Well, let me introduce you," De Vegas said, following him. "Connie, I'd like you to meet Janson Jervis. Janson, Third Engineer Constance Nunn, our AI specialist."

Upon hearing her name, Nunn had turned to face De Vegas and Jervis, a tentative smile on her lips. But Jervis did not hear the last part of the introduction. That's because, upon catching sight of Nunn's full face as she turned to greet him, his heart had nearly stopped, and his fantasy notions about the attractiveness of her features, the sexy cut of her hair and the cuteness of her nose went up with a flash and a puff of smoke. The right side of her face did not match the left. Not at all. In fact it didn't match the left side of *anyone's* face. At first glance she appeared to be wearing a thick, dark mask on that side. But then it became apparent that this was no mask. A raised black and brown birthmark covered most of the right half of her face, extending from her nose nearly to the ear, descending down her jaw and curving down over it to the top of her neck. The upper part of this mottled, leathery mass rose to just above her brow. Even her right eyelid was blackened.

The sight of it struck Jervis as forcefully as a blow to the gut. Swallowing heavily, he gamely held out his hand, forcing a smile as he struggled not to let his face betray his reaction.

This attempt was entirely ineffective. What Nunn saw was The Look, and she'd seen it a thousand times before. Under the best of circumstances, upon first sight any new person meeting her always hesitated, showing an absolutely blank facial expression that swiftly covered the revulsion they were feeling, usually to be quickly followed by a smile that was overly bright, and a greeting that was a degree too friendly, delivered in a voice that was set one notch too loud. She'd grown used to it. "Great to meet you, Mr. Jervis," she said, smiling warmly as she took his hand.

"The pleasure is mine," Jervis lied clumsily, struggling to come up with appropriate words. Jervis was seldom at a loss for verbs, nouns and adjectives; his livelihood depended on being able to expound at any time on any subject for any given length of time. But it had not escaped his attention that the young lady had noticed his reaction to her disfigurement, and this fact acutely embarrassed him. He found the situation to be incredibly awkward.

Had he known what Nunn was thinking, however, he would have been very surprised and relieved. Not only was Nunn not offended, but her heart went out to him. She was well aware of the reaction her birthmark typically provoked. Jervis' response was only human, and was in no way his fault.

Jervis released her hand, mentally searching for something else to say. Fortunately, he now observed something that allowed him to plow confidently ahead while steering the conversation onto safe ground: a cat lay sprawled across Nunn's lap. It was a gorgeous silver tabby, with green eyes, a pink nose, a white bib, and a shiny, well-groomed coat of fur featuring a subtle mixture of black and grey stripes. Upon Jervis' approach, the animal had lifted its head and was now regarding him with disapproving eyes.

"Who have you got there?" Jervis asked, nodding at the feline.

"That's our ship's cat," Nunn said.

"In name only," Nguyen spoke up. "Really, it's Connie's cat. That animal adopted Connie the moment they met. We have nearly three dozen crewmen on board, but Ari won't have anything to do with anyone else."

Nunn reached down to rub the animal's head. "Ari knows who loves him," she said, cooing to him.

The cat narrowed its eyes and leaned into the rub, purring, as if to signify that it did, indeed, know, and that the feeling was mutual.

"I didn't realize starships had cats," Jervis said.

"Oh, yes," Nunn replied, looking up at him. "It's an old maritime tradition, dating back to ancient times. Sailors partnered with cats to keep the rats down."

"I didn't realize starships had rats, either."

"This one doesn't," Nunn said. She looked lovingly down at the tabby. "Does it, Ari?"

The cat half-closed its eyes in another self-satisfied look, as if to say, "Not on my watch, it doesn't."

"Sure it does," Swann put in. "You're petting it right now."

"How can you say such a thing?" Nunn demanded in hurt tones, glaring across at the helmsman. "Ari can understand English, you know. You'll hurt his feelings."

"I take it you're not a cat person, Mr. Swann?" Jervis asked.

The big man shook his head. "Not in the least. Cats are foul creatures set upon us as the result of some ancient and long-forgotten malediction on mankind. They exist for the sole purpose of breeding fleas while exuding hairballs, expelling biotoxic bodily fluids of all kinds, and dropping dandruff designed to induce uncontrollable respiratory spasms in humans."

"What an awful thing to say," Nunn objected in the same reproving tone.

"And maritime tradition notwithstanding," Swann continued unabated, "what she doesn't tell you is that historically, in ancient times ships' cats almost certainly helped spread the Black Death from port to port."

"That is *so* not true," Nunn objected. "Cats killed the rats that carried the plague, is what they did." She looked affectionately at the cat. "Isn't that right, Ari?"

The cat, returning the woman's gaze, said, "Ank," assuring her that she had the story exactly right.

"See? Ari knows."

"Right," Swann agreed. "Ari knows. And precisely *what* Ari knows is that he's a vermin-infested freeloader from a long and ancient line of vermin-infested freeloaders."

"What did you say its name is?" Jervis asked. "Ari? That's an unusual name."

"It's short for Aristarchus," Nunn explained.

"I'm a little light on my Greek mythology," Jervis admitted. "Who was that?"

"Aristarchus of Samos," Nguyen piped up. "Not a Greek god, but a philosopher and scientist. He's the guy, about 24 hundred years ago, who was the first to work it out that the earth orbits the sun, not the other way around."

"Wow," Jervis said. "You knew that off the top of your head? Now I'm starting to feel a little self-conscious about the quality of my college education."

"It came up in our training," Nguyen explained. "In a sense, Aristarchus was the first astrogator."

"Even so, he still thought the sun was at the center of the universe," Beadel pointed out.

Nunn, still stroking the cat's head, put her face down close to him. "You're the center of my universe, aren't you Ari?"

Ari blinked at her, in acknowledgment that this was indeed the case, as well it should be.

"Why don't you say hello to the nice man, Ari? Say hello to Mr. Jervis."

The animal did not deign to turn its head in Jervis' direction.

"See? What did I tell you?" Swann said. "That misbegotten mange muff is completely devoted to Connie. There is no room in its alleged heart for any other human."

"Well, Ari can be a little standoffish." She turned and looked up at Jervis, smiling. "But if it makes any difference, *I'm* a great fan of yours. Your reports on Operation Barbary Coast were riveting. You have quite the grasp of military strategy."

By way of the words exchanged on first meeting, Jervis could always tell the real fans from those who were simply playing the part of one for the purpose of sucking up to a celebrity. This one was sincere, the real deal. Often he found such admiration to be quite useful, especially when it came to the ladies, and in such cases typically he'd file the knowledge away for later use. Not this time. But he strove to be polite just the same.

"Why, thanks," he said. "It comes from asking lots of annoying, nosy questions." He turned to De Vegas. "Speaking of which, where would you like me to set up?"

"The observer chairs are along the rear bulkhead. Or, if you prefer, the station next to Mixter Beadel won't be manned on this voyage. You're welcome to it."

"I'll take it. Thanks." He stepped over to the empty chair to the left of Beadel, unslung his omnicorder case, and placed it on the seat. "Is this spot taken?" he said charmingly to Beadel.

"I've been saving it for you," she chirped. "It'll be nice to have someone to talk to."

Jervis' level of interest in any given female tended to vary proportionately with the woman's physical attractiveness and also the extent to which she was impressed by his celebrity status. Right now, Beadel was pegging both meters. For one, she was gorgeous. Her only flaw—and it was minor—was that she usually wore a slight pout, as if the entire universe were disappointing her in some minor but annoying way. But the pout was gone now, replaced by a sunny expression—and since the two of them had met only once before, this telegraphed to Jervis that she was the type who thought celebrities were the bomb. His day was getting more interesting.

It had not escaped his notice, however, that De Vegas had referred to Beadel with the gender-neutral honorific of "Mixter." Five thousand years of recorded human history had not charted a great deal of improvement in relations between the genders. On the contrary, matters now were more complicated than ever, due in no small measure to the fact that the number of legally recognized genders was continually increasing; the N.A.U. High Court had just extended protection to a 17th. With so many individuals identifying their gender in so many different ways, "he" and "she" just didn't cut it anymore, and had not done so for some time. For decades gender activists had been trying to force changes in the language requiring the use of new gender-defining and also gender-neutral words that had been invented for that purpose. Decades ago, the High Court had ruled that failure to refer to employees by the gender honorifics each preferred was a form of workplace sexual harassment. Gender-neutral terms were considered safest in most situations, especially upon first greeting, but protocols for figuring it all out were still emerging. The only good way to know who preferred to be called what was to ask.

So Jervis asked. "So how do you like to be referred to?" he asked Beadel as he powered up his omnicorder. "Is it Miss, Mrs., Ms., or Mixter? Or something else?"

"Oh, definitely not Mrs.," she said. Turning, she placed her hand atop his. "For you, it's Jessica—Jess, if I decide to let you buy me a beer later."

Oh, yes. This trip was shaping up well.

"Thank you, Jessica. I would be delighted to buy you a beer, and a steak. Unless you're vegetarian, in which case I'll buy you the most expensive vegetable in the joint—a nice, big, round, juicy, Mexican-grown Heirloom, special ordered and shuttled up that very day, prepared in the style of your liking and the accompaniments of your choosing."

Beadel laughed—a sound that washed over Jervis like a warm breeze through tall, gently swaying grass on a lazy summer day. "The tomato's not a vegetable," she said. "It's a fruit."

"Oh. Then how about a nice hot plate of Eggplant Parmesan, made with a hydroponically grown Black Beauty big enough to play football with, smothered with real Parmigiano-Reggiano cheese imported directly from Northern Italy. I'll even throw in a sprig of organically grown parsley."

"Steak will do nicely. I like mine medium rare. Meanwhile, you can call me Jess on credit."

"Excellent. And I'm Janson—Jan, for my close friends."

"Then Jan it is."

Outstanding, he thought.

The inner safety lock door slid open again, and a short man rushed in wearing a displeased, almost frustrated expression. The newcomer strode quickly to the last empty station on the starboard side, next to Constance Nunn, and sat down. Jervis recognized him as Fusazane Tochigi, the ship's second engineer.

"What tidings do you bear from the engineering section?" De Vegas asked.

"The chief is presiding over his domain like the Lord High Sheriff of Nottingham," Tochigi said, while touching a series of squares on his board. "And the closer we get to torchlight, the grumpier he becomes. But he tells me the ducks are all lined up in a row and ready to quack on cue."

Jervis shook his head, trying to sort out the meaning of Tochigi's unique mixture of allusions, metaphors and unfamiliar jargon.

"Mixter Tochigi, I believe you've met our journalist, Janson Jervis, haven't you?"

Tochigi shot him a quick glance, and nearly did a double take as he noticed that Jervis was sitting next to Beadel. "We've met," he said, returning his attention to his console.

Well, a hearty top-o-the-mornin' to you, too, Jervis thought.

Bending back to the task at hand, Jervis reached down and pressed a lighted square atop the omnicorder control panel. A door on the side of the unit slid open and six silver, peach-sized spheres flew out. The objects immediately took up station behind Beadel and Jervis, silently hovering at about head height. As much as he wanted to, Jervis did not deploy any lighting balls; use of those on the bridge was forbidden.

"These little guys aren't going to bother you, are they?" he asked, turning to Beadel.

"Not me. But I wouldn't let any of them buzz around the captain's head—not unless they can take a high gee load."

Jervis chuckled. "They can. But I take your meaning."

Captain Cermeno placed the bottle of hair spray on the counter, peered into the mirror and admired his handiwork. His blond locks were beginning to thin, and the hairline wasn't quite where it used to be. Still, he had a nice, healthy growth of hair, which, combined with his still boyish good looks, was more than enough to turn a female head or two, especially when he was in uniform.

Not that he was much enamored of his current in-flight deckwear.

Toward his goal of cutting a dashing figure, the plain cobalt blue jumpsuit, with a "Project Columbus" patch on one shoulder and a North American Union flag on the other, contributed little. There wasn't even a set of shoulder boards to denote his rank. All the company had given him for that purpose were two thin horizontal strips of black cloth sewn onto either collar, each of which bore four tiny gold rings embroidered in a line. If they'd even designed the rank insignia in the shape of stars, it would have added at least a hint of derring-do. But, no. They hadn't even let him have a hat. What was a captain without a captain's peaked hat? The uniforms of the company's colony transport line were far flashier. But for some reason his father had seemed intent on making the clothing for the science division as boring as possible.

The thought of his father caused him to frown. He knew he owed the man a huge debt of gratitude. But he just couldn't muster that emotion. Cermeno had read somewhere that people who were grateful tended to be happier and better adjusted. He was none of the above. He'd also read that feelings of resentment tended to outlast those of gratitude. That statement he understood. His father's demeanor toward him seemed designed to foster the former. Even while putting his reputation on the line to help his son, the elder Cermeno never spoke to his heir in tones not laced with sarcasm, bitterness and contempt. The captain had heard more of the same just moments ago in his final phone call to his old man. His father had seemed mildly annoyed at having to take the call, as if it had interrupted something more important, and his attitude had not improved during the conversation. The bitter old bastard at least had wished him good luck, but then had closed the call with a colorfully-phrased exhortation not to foul things up. It had taken all the strength of character the younger Cermeno could muster to restrain himself from telling his father off. Instead, he'd simply thanked him once again for the opportunity, promised to do his best, and had ended the call.

Oh, well. He was used to it. Sirius Constantine Cermeno, Jr., had a lot of experience in dealing with the disappointed and disaffected. He'd spent a lifetime letting people down, it seemed. No matter how hard he tried, he never measured up to what was expected of him. That was the price one paid, he thought, for having an industrial and social icon as a father.

This train of thought led inevitably to the final call he'd been trying to make. Taking one last look at his face in the mirror, and filing away for future action once again the thought that he needed to work on sweating off about five pounds, the captain returned to the small desk in his cabin. His iCard was still atop the desk where he'd left it. To get the device's attention, he had two options: call its name—the handle he'd given it was "Dudley"—or simply touch the lower left corner. He knew it was silly, but he simply could not bring himself to call out the device's name as if it were a person—which it wasn't. Although, technically speaking, the device was an AI, its computing power fell far below the threshold needed to establish even much of a mock personality, much less self-awareness.

He reached forward and touched the corner. "Screen," he said. Immediately, a dark blue cube formed in the air, projected upwards from the device. Along the top of the side facing him was a row of colorful 3-D icons attesting that the contraption was connected to the Net, WiFi and phone signal strength were at maximum, local power was connected, the processors were nearly idle, and he had no unread messages and had received no unanswered calls; beneath them was a grid of artfully crafted symbols representing various applications at his disposal. The other sides of the holographic box were all opaque, and as he'd done many times before, Cermeno wondered how in the world the makers of the device had pulled that off. He'd studied the theories behind the projection technology in school, of course, but the principles had eluded him.

Cermeno touched the lower left corner again, and this time he did use a voice command. "Phone," he said to place the device into communications mode, and then followed up with, "Call The Bitch."

"Calling Patricia Cermeno," the device answered in mellifluous, soothing male tones.

The phone rang four times. One more ring and it would go to voice mail, as his last two calls had done. Cermeno was angry; Patricia had promised to call him, so why was he having to hunt her down? He had just taken a breath sufficient to propel a particularly potent stream of profanity when her face finally appeared on screen. The view was from beneath and to the side; apparently, she was sitting in front of her bathroom mirror, and she was in the process of doing her hair. "What do you want, Si?" she asked impatiently, not bothering to turn to the video pickup.

"I'd like to say goodbye to our daughter," Cermeno said, his inflection rising as he spoke. "You promised to call me this morning."

"Sorry," she said, with no hint of actual sorrow. "I forgot."

"You forgot," he said flatly. "On this of all days, you forgot."

"Yeah," she said, still not bothering to even glance in the direction of the phone pickup. "It sucks to be forgetful. And as a guy who always seems to instantly forget he has a wife and child any time some cute little cocktail waitress wiggles her ass at him, you should know all about memory issues. Speaking of which, when's whatshername—Marlita—due?"

After a stormy confrontation during which Marlita had learned she would not be the next Mrs. Cermeno, his girlfriend had decided to move out, abort the pregnancy, and add her name to the list of people who were no longer speaking to him—a list that was, Cermeno thought ruefully, not showing any signs of shrinking. But now did not seem the time update Patricia on his sordid little domestic melodrama. "Would you mind bringing Melanie to the phone?" he said with exaggerated patience.

"Oh, didn't I mention?" she answered, while studiously applying eyeliner. "She's not here. She's on a sleepover."

"Fine," he snapped. "I'll call her direct."

"Well, that's going to be difficult," his wife said. "Her iCard fried a couple of days ago. The replacement hasn't arrived yet."

Cermeno had to make an effort not to grind his teeth. "Well, who's she staying with? I'll call them."

"You know, I'd really rather you not do that. Melanie is rather fond of you. Which just means she doesn't know you very well, and she has the natural, uncritical affection for her father that you'd expect from a six-year old. She'll get over that—and pretty soon, I'm guessing. But for now, I don't want to upset her, so I haven't told her about the mission."

Well, there it was—all pretense to the wind. Patricia wasn't going to let him say goodbye to his daughter. "Patricia, damn it, you can't be serious!" he said, now casting aside any effort to hide his anger. "I may not get another chance to talk to her! This mission is incredibly dangerous. I may not come back."

"That would be heartrending," Patricia observed aloofly, now beginning to apply liner to the other brow.

The sheer cruelty of it left him speechless. For a moment, he sat there fuming, staring at his wife's projected image. When he'd first met her, he'd thought she was the most stunningly attractive woman he'd ever seen. He'd just had to have her. Patricia definitely was what some would call a trophy wife. Except that in his case, the trophy had been awarded in advance of the victory, extended to him on credit based on what his family connections suggested that he had the potential to become. But he'd long since bounced that check. The Patricia he knew back then bore little resemblance to the woman he now saw before him. Oh, the appearance was similar. But the girlish laugh he'd once known, the easy trust, the friendly disposition, the hot and eager you-hang-the-moon affection she'd once showered on him, were gone. In place of all that was this still beautiful but cold and bitter creature whose image now hovered in the air before him.

The transceiver behind his ear gave a beep, and then a voice sounded. "Captain Cermeno, this is Wilson. You left orders to be alerted when the time reaches zero six fifty-five hours. That will be the exact time on the mark. Mark."

He touched the iCard's mute button. "Thank you, Wilson."

"You're welcome, sir."

It was time to go.

Cermeno glanced at the screen again, taking the phone off mute. He longed for the words to tell off his soon-to-be-ex wife in some spectacular, cruelly hurtful fashion. But he'd never been known for his wit; the acidic, soul-destroying words he ached to find would not come. "Patricia, I hope you rot in hell," he finally said, lamely.

"After you, dear heart," she replied. "After you." Pulling back the eyebrow pencil, she admired herself in the mirror.

No, he thought bitterly, *you most definitely will be first.*

Cermeno reached forward and touched the disconnect icon, and then pressed the lower left corner. "Screen off," he said. According to the dictates of the pre-programmed transition pattern Cermeno had selected, the image popped like a balloon and was gone.

The captain stood up, scooped the device off the desk, and slipped it into a side pocket. Stepping to the mirror, he gave himself one last look-over. After tugging at his sleeves and straightening his collar, he went to the cabin door, opened it, and stepped out into the long, dimly lit passageway. He was still fuming as he turned in the direction of the bridge, and as he walked he mentally reviewed the many and varied ways in which the long succession of women he'd known had managed to adversely impact his life. *One of these days*, he thought, *I'm going to make somebody pay. For* all *of it.*

A chime sounded on Jessica Beadel's console; looking up, she saw on the security monitor that two more guests had arrived at the bridge safety lock outer door. Reaching forward, she pressed a button. "Good morning, Father Teal, Doctor Blake."

"Let us in," Dr. Blake said, "or we'll huff and we'll puff—you know the rest."

Turning, Beadel glanced at De Vegas, who nodded.

Beadel turned back to the console. "That won't be necessary," she chirped sunnily as she punched the control icon for the door. "We already have a full complement of officially-designated huffers and puffers."

Beadel glanced toward the bridge door—and as she did so, she caught De Vegas' disapproving eye; clearly, the first officer had taken a dim view of her little jest. *Oh, lighten the hell up*, Beadel thought.

The inner bridge door slid open, and Father Teal and Dr. Blake stepped inside. Teal turned to De Vegas. "Permission to come onto the bridge?" he asked.

"Granted." She gestured toward the row of padded flight chairs along the rear bulkhead. "You might want to go ahead and strap yourselves in," she said. "We'll be sounding the acceleration alarm in a few minutes."

Jervis got up and walked over to them. "Good morning!" he said cheerfully. "Here to see the show?"

"There's not much of one to see at the moment," De Vegas said, stepping over to the group. "We'll undock in a few minutes, and then spend the next hour gently boosting ourselves out to a safe blasting distance, using the maneuvering thrusters. After that, we can light up the torches."

"That's when the real fireworks begin," Tochigi put in from the engineer's console.

"What's safe distance?" Jervis asked.

"They keep moving it back," helmsman Swann spoke up. "Last month they set it at 50 thousand klicks."

"The torches are fairly dirty," De Vegas explained. "The direct mass conversion process puts out a massive amount of hard radiation, plasma, and gases laced with a hell's brew of radioactive isotopes. And the environmentalists are never happy. We'll boost with the ion thrusters for an hour at about three-quarters of a gee, which will do the trick. Then we can light up the torches and be on our merry way—to the next safety point."

"20 million kilometers," Nunn added. "That's twice the previous safe distance for stellar operations. But the U.N. Space Authority isn't sure what to think of our dimension drive array."

"They must be nervous," Father Teal said. He turned to Dr. Blake. "That's about a quarter of the way to Mars orbit," he explained.

"Four hours at 20 gees will get us there," De Vegas said. "And speaking of which, you need to strap in, too, Mr. Jervis. We don't want anyone getting knocked on the noggin—not even reporters."

Jervis flashed his trademark crooked grin. "I appreciate that."

"If you need help, I'm sure crewman Beadel can be persuaded to assist you."

"Yes ma'am." He stopped, suddenly unsure of himself. "Or do you prefer to be addressed—"

She waved a nonchalant hand. " 'Ma'am,' 'sir,' 'ser,' 'mister,' 'mixter,' or just plain 'hey, you'—I answer to them all, as long as you're wearing a smile."

Somehow, to Jervis the thought of "Hey, you" going over well with the formidable De Vegas did not appear likely. But the easy grin on his face betrayed no hint of that thought. "I'm a-smilin'. If you're okay with 'ma'am,' I'll use that. It fits best with my Tennessee upbringing."

She nodded. "That works."

Turning, he stepped back over to his assigned couch, sat down, and began pulling at the straps and buckles. "What's up with all this strapping-in business?" he asked Beadel. "I thought starships had inertial dampeners and all that razzmatazz?"

"We do," Beadel admitted. "But usually there are a few mild surges here and there as the dampeners adjust to the acceleration. Besides, if the dampeners were to fail, without straps you might go flying right out of your seat and sail off to parts unknown." She turned to him, smiling. "We wouldn't want that to happen, now would we?"

Jervis forced a worried smile. "I'm a big fan of known parts." The smile faded a bit. "But I didn't realize dampener failure was a concern. What if that happens while the torches are lit?"

Beadel shook her head, grimacing. "That's a thought too horrible to contemplate."

"What would happen?" Jervis persisted.

She cocked her head slightly, considering the possibility. "Well, if you were to fall out of your flight chair, in about a half a second you'd hit the rear bulkhead and burst like a water balloon. But that's not the worst of it."

"Really?" His left eyebrow shot up. "There's something worse than bursting like a water balloon?"

She grinned. "Well, not for the unfortunate burster. But in the case of a high-gee Bjorklund Field failure, it wouldn't matter whether you were strapped in or not." Here she paused for dramatic effect.

"I know you're going to explain that statement," he prodded.

"The ship is constructed mostly of plastisteel," she continued. "It's lightweight and very strong, but not so strong that it can stand up to the kind of thrust the torches deliver. If the fields were to fail at high boost, then before you could even bat an eye, the ship would disintegrate. And— *pfttt!*—that would be the end of that. They think that's what probably happened to the *Andromeda* a few years ago."

Jervis recalled the incident; his network had covered it. But this was the first he'd heard that a dampener field failure was suspected. His stomach, still working on the pancakes and sausage links he'd wolfed down earlier, suddenly felt very acidic.

Noticing his sour expression, Beadel reached over and patted his hand. "Don't worry; the odds of that happening are low."

"How low?"

"*Really* low. Besides, you've got me here."

"There is that," he conceded, working hard to muster his most winning smile. *I'd love to get together with this chickiedoo*, he thought. *But not in the form of comingled paste splattered on the rear bulkhead.*

At that moment, the inner safety door slid aside and Captain Cermeno stepped onto the bridge.

"Good morning, Captain," said De Vegas, turning to greet him.

Cermeno glanced at his subordinate. Her demeanor was pleasant enough—but he was sure that an expression of disdain lurked not far beneath her smile. "Good morning, Mr. De Vegas. Report, please."

"All stations report ready for undocking maneuvers, sir."

"Good." Cermeno surveyed the bridge. The crewmen were busying themselves at their various tasks, studiously avoiding any glance in his direction. They appeared fully engaged in their work, and were wearing expressions that were neutral, impassive, and professional. He would expect no less, even though he knew those expressions were simply masks that covered their true feelings—feelings they couldn't dare express or even give a hint of in his presence.

His gaze fell upon Jervis, who was struggling with his straps and buckles. The captain turned to De Vegas and crooked his finger. She stepped closer. "What is Mr. Jervis doing there?" Cermeno demanded in low voice.

"I told him he could use that chair," De Vegas said. "It's the planetary sciences station. The console is powered down."

He regarded her with a disapproving glare. "Please have him move to one of the observer couches."

"Yes, ser," De Vegas said. The captain, she knew, was rattling her cage, and he was doing it for no other reason than to show her who was in command. So she'd rattled his back by using the gender-neutral honorific "ser," which rhymed with "hair," suspecting that he would hate it. But she kept her expression blank.

However, as soon as Cermeno had given the order, he regretted it. It wouldn't do to tweak the nose of the ship's one on-board journalist—and a famous one that that—as the captain's first official act on Day One of the mission. As personally gratifying as Cermeno found that prospect to be, he knew that such a gesture wouldn't serve his best interests in the long run. "Belay that," he said, still speaking in a low voice. "But in the future, you might consult with me before you assign ship's consoles to untrained personnel."

"Yes, ser."

Cermeno noted that she had now addressed him—*twice*—with a gender-neutral honorific. As De Vegas had intended, it rankled him. But he wasn't sure what to do about it, except to find a way to annoy her further in return. "What are these gadflies buzzing about the bridge?" he said, nodding toward a camera/audio ball that was hovering nearby.

"Mr. Jervis' recording equipment, ser."

"Have him secure those, please."

"Yes, ser. Right away."

Cermeno glanced at the digital readout above the center bridge window. It was coming up on 06:58. "Sound the acceleration alarm."

"Yes, ser." De Vegas turned and walked over to Beadel as the captain took his chair and began strapping in. "Sound the alarm, please."

"Yes, ser." Leaning forward, Beadel pressed an icon on her control console, and then on the resulting display, pressed another icon. A loud klaxon sounded four times. Then she pressed another button. "All hands, prepare for thruster maneuvers."

De Vegas turned to the reporter. "Mr. Jervis—"

"Janson," he corrected her.

"Janson. We'll need you to secure your recording equipment."

Jervis glanced up at one of his ubiquitous AV drones, which was hovering nearby. "I can pin them along the tops of the bulkheads. Would that do?"

"Will they stay in put?" she asked.

"They're designed for this. Their tractors will hold against any shock up to about 25 gees."

De Vegas frowned. "Well, anything higher than that, and we'll have bigger things to worry about, so I suppose it won't matter. Go ahead and nail them to the rear bulkhead, then."

"Yes, ma'am." Being relegated to the rear would severely limit his camera angles. But he stifled his disappointment as he worked the controls.

"You'll need to secure that controller unit, too. There's a small acceleration locker at your feet, underneath the console."

"Okay. Thanks."

As soon as De Vegas had stepped away, Jervis turned to Beadel. "Now I'm very curious to know what you do with the cat."

"Oh, he'll be fine. The engineers have rigged a little padded acceleration box for him in the locker space at Connie's feet."

De Vegas took up station in front of her side of the command console. Captain Cermeno glanced at his subordinate with distaste. While he was certain that his muscular first officer would somehow manage to remain standing even if the ship were to smack an asteroid, the sight of her standing there with her arms folded across her chest while he and the other crewmembers were firmly secured in their padded flight chairs greatly annoyed him. "Mr. De Vegas, strap in, please," he said curtly.

"Yes, ser."

He glanced at the clock again. "Take us out."

"Yes, ser. Mixter Swann, release the umbilicals."

"Yes, ma'am," Swann acknowledged as he pressed a control square. "I show all umbilicals released," he added, studying his console.

"Stand by to release the docking clamps," she continued. "Mixter Beadel, inform Armstrong Control that we are ready to depart on schedule."

Beadel opened her circuit and had a brief exchange with a control officer. This done, she turned to De Vegas. "Message acknowledged. Permission granted to execute the departure plan."

"Very well." De Vegas paused, watching the clock. "Mixter Swann, on my mark, release the docking clamps."

"Standing by," he acknowledged with a finger poised over a lighted control square.

The clock flashed to 07:00 exactly. "Mark," De Vegas said simultaneously.

Swann pressed his button. "All clamps released."

"Nudge us out."

"Moving out, aye," Swann acknowledged, and tapped another control square.

No one felt any motion, but at the opposite extremes of the arc of viewports, the ships on either side of the *Santa Maria* could be seen falling behind them, slowly disappearing from view.

"We're free of the dock," Swann reported momentarily. "100 meters stern clearance."

"All right," De Vegas acknowledged. "Give it a tap. Let's make some tracks, Mixter Swann."

"Delta-v aye," Swann said. He closed another circuit, and they felt a brief surge before the dampeners compensated. "Now departing on approved trajectory at 25 meters per second, relative," Swann said after a moment.

Jervis turned to Beadel. "That doesn't sound very fast."

"Oh, it isn't, believe me. But the speed relative to the station doesn't include our orbital velocity, which is about 7.7 kilometers a second. The station is traveling at that same speed."

He nodded. "Can you give me a play-by-play of what we're doing, maybe with some color commentary thrown in?"

"Sure. Spacecraft are expected, and required, to move pretty cautiously around the station. When we open the distance to about two kilometers, Swann will execute a short burn increasing the relative velocity to 100 meters a second. We're following an approved trajectory that will take us to a slightly higher orbit. Once we get 20 klicks out, about four minutes from now, we'll be allowed to bring the ion maneuvering engines up to low thrust—about three quarters of a gee. An hour or so later, we'll be at safe torch distance, and that's when the high acceleration starts."

Jervis nodded. "Oh."

Beadel smiled. "You look underwhelmed. We you expecting a bit more excitement?"

"I'll admit I was."

"Well, there's a saying about interstellar flight—basically, the same thing they used to say about good old fashioned prop-driven aviation back in the early 20th century. It's days and days of boredom, punctuated by moments of sheer terror."

Jervis chuckled ruefully. "If you want to leave out the terrifying bits, that'll be okay with me."

She raised an eyebrow. "You sure? A few moments of crisis here and there, captured on video, would do wonders for your ratings."

"My ratings are fine," he assured her flatly.

Jervis now felt another very brief surge of force pushing him gently into the black leather-like covering of the acceleration couch.

"There it is, the second burn," Beadel explained. "We coast for another three minutes or so, and then we'll fire up the thrusters for about an hour of constant, but low, acceleration."

Jervis turned to her and nodded. As he did so, out of the of the corner of his eye he noticed that crewman Tochigi was casting him and Beadel another disapproving, if not quite withering, look. It was pretty obvious what *that* was about; clearly, in chatting up Beadel, Jervis was encroaching on Tochigi's territory. *Too bad,* Jervis thought. *Suck it up.*

Jervis—who, if nothing else, was a capable and experienced observer of humanity—had pegged Tochigi accurately. The young second engineer had a thing for Beadel—a distinction that by no means put him on any exclusive list. Most of the unattached heterosexual males on board—and some of the attached ones—had yens for her as well. But two weeks ago, after the crew had indulged in a rowdy shore leave celebration of the *Santa Maria's* record-breaking maiden voyage, it was Tochigi who'd gotten lucky with her. It had happened during a moment of drunken passion—neither party had been in full command of their actions. But afterwards, Beadel had been rather cool to him—not nasty, nor scornful, nor had she quite gone out of her way to avoid him. But she certainly wasn't treating him like a long lost lover. In fact, technically Beadel would have been within her rights to file charges on him; even though both of them had been drunk, in any dispute over the incident the law would consider him to have been at fault. Even so, he fondly nurtured high hopes of a repeat performance, this time with one or both of them sober. And now he did not like the way Beadel's face was lighting up when Jervis addressed her. But Tochigi had engineering issues to contend with; he bent to his task and tried to thrust the whole matter from his mind.

A short time later, De Vegas gave another order, and there was a second brief surge against the acceleration couches before the dampening fields adjusted. "Maneuvering thrusters slow ahead," Swann reported.

"All systems operating in their nominal ranges," Tochigi added.

"Very well." De Vegas slapped her fist against the silvery central buckle at the center of her chest, releasing her straps. "You all can unbuckle and relax for about an hour. Smoke 'em if you got 'em."

Beadel turned to Jervis. "Do you vape?"

He grimaced. "Agh. A nasty habit, that."

"Oh, a non-smoker, huh?"

"I didn't say that." Reaching down, he retrieved a small rectangular black case from a front pocket. The label across the box bore the name of a popular brand of ecigs. "Want one?"

She laughed. "I don't mind if I do."

Cermeno stood up and turned to De Vegas. "I'll be my ready room," he said. "Carry on."

"Yes, ser."

De Vegas allowed Jervis to unpin his AV balls. For the next hour, the journalist wandered around the bridge, interviewing the crew and making small talk.

"You seem a bit out of place," he said to Nicolas Swann after walking up to the helmsman's station with media drones in tow. At six foot two and 280 pounds, Swann was large enough to put his acceleration couch to the test even when the engines were idle.

"Why do you say that?" Swann said, turning to him.

"You just don't fit my stereotypical notions of a starman. You look more like a linebacker."

Swann nodded. "Yeah, I get that a lot. Mainly from people surprised at the notion that a large black guy is good for something other than football."

Jervis put his hand to his face in horror. "Oh, my God. I didn't mean—"

"Forget it," Swann said, not exactly smiling, but not frowning, either. "No offense taken. I'm just trying to get your goat."

"You certainly got it," Jervis conceded.

"Besides, I think it might be good for your reporter soul—I'm generously willing to assume you have one—to be on the defensive for a change."

"Ouch," Jervis said. "That's two."

Now Swann flashed a very faint smile. "It's okay. I'm done for now."

"And thank goodness for that. At the risk of digging my hole any deeper—can you tell me something about yourself? How did you wind up on a starship?"

Swann shrugged. "It runs in the family. One of my ancestors flew on the original space shuttle, back in the 20th century. And my great grandfather was on the *Yeager.*"

"Wow. The first star jump. And here you are, about to make family history again. Your folks must be proud."

"Some of them are." Swann now flashed a smile that had more than a slight flavor of impishness. "My father really wanted me to play football."

Jervis pointed a finger at him and threw back his head in a hearty laugh. "See! I knew it."

Eventually Jervis made his way over to the engineer. Tochigi was not very talkative, bordering on being surly. Jervis did manage to extract from him that he was born in San Diego, but had lots of close relatives in Japan, particularly on Okinawa. He also learned, after speaking with De Vegas, that Tochigi's nickname was "The Fuse." From the man's demeanor, it wasn't hard to guess why.

The time went by quickly. At 07:57, the door to the captain's ready room at the rear port corner of the bridge slid open and Cermeno emerged. "How are we doing?" he asked De Vegas.

"On schedule, on trajectory. Ready for high-gee."

"Good. Secure for high acceleration."

Once again, De Vegas had everyone take their stations and strap in. Beadel sounded the klaxons and then made an announcement warning the crew to secure for high thrust.

"Engineer, report," Cermeno said as he buckled in.

"Chief Engineer Crandall says the torches are on standby and ready to answer bells," Tochigi replied. "Accumulators fully charged. Fusion plant at the ready."

"Very well." He turned to De Vegas. "Mr. De Vegas, on the planned mark, light 'em up, and ramp us up to standard thrust."

"Yes, ser." She turned to Swann. "Mixter Swann, enable the acceleration profile."

"Yes, ma'am." Swann's forefinger stabbed a green lighted blinking square. The monitor before him flashed a message bearing the words "Program enabled" displayed above a 30-second clock, which then began counting down. "Program engaged," Swann said. "Torch light in 28 seconds."

On the curving bulkhead above the central viewport, a holographic digital clock ticked away the seconds. Beyond the ports stretched a black field studded with a few of the brighter stars; the rest were washed out in the glare of the bridge lights.

"Five seconds," Swann said. This was quickly followed by the calm announcement, "Ignition."

The crewmembers felt a strong surge in their seats, while at the same time a low rumble filled the air. Jervis could feel his acceleration couch and the deck plates beneath his feet vibrating.

"Executing programmed acceleration profile," Swan continued. "One gee," he said a moment later. Then, "Two gees."

Jervis turned to Beadel. "Why not go straight to full thrust?" he asked in a low voice.

"Well, for one, we hardly ever go to *full* thrust," she said. "Standard thrust for this mission is 20 gees, or about three-quarters power."

"I see."

"But not even with inertial dampeners do you want to go right from zero to twenty," she continued. "It's too hard on the equipment. A nice slow ramp-up gives plenty of time to keep a close eye on all systems to make sure they're working well, and to let the dampeners adjust to the acceleration."

Swann continued to tick off the acceleration numbers, while the rumbling and vibrating gradually increased in intensity. "20 gees," he finally said. "Standard thrust."

Ahead of them the star field gave no indication they were moving at all. The tiny points of light continued to stand stock still. There would have been no hint at all that the ship was under way if not for the vibrating of the deck plates and the rumbling of the engines, which was now loud enough to make talking in a whisper impossible.

"Engineer, report," Cermeno said, almost disinterestedly.

"All systems nominal, sir," Tochigi said.

"And that, ladies and gentlemen," De Vegas said, "is how we do that." She released her straps and stood up. "Captain, permission to change the watch?"

Cermeno nodded.

"Mixter Beadel," De Vegas continued, "please get the relief team in here."

"Yes, ser." Beadel pressed a button. "Team Two, you're up."

"Team Two?" Jervis asked.

"The next watch team. They're standing by in the wardroom. Technically, the watch was supposed to change at 8. But the captain ordered it delayed it until after the maneuver."

"Okay. So is that it?"

"For now," she said, unbuckling her chest straps. "We continue like this for about four hours. And then the real fun begins. We fire up the array."

"Will that be one of those terrifying moments you mentioned?" Jervis asked, smiling.

"Oh, God, I hope not. Not if the high foreheads know what they're doing."

"I have a lot of faith in the high foreheads," Jervis said. "I must have, because I keep telling myself that."

Beadel shrugged. "I know what you mean. But I try not to wring my hands over it. Chances are, if anything goes wrong, we'll never know it."

"If that thought was intended to comfort me, I have to tell you that you're a bit wide of the mark."

At the rear of the bridge, Dr. Blake stood up. "Anyone for a cup of coffee? I'm buying."

"I'm in," Jervis said. He turned to Beadel. "Can I bring you a cup?"

"It just so happens," Beadel said, "that I'm off watch for the next few hours."

On overhearing the remark, Tochigi, sitting at his console, clinched his jaws together.

Jervis spent a pleasant hour chatting up Beadel, Father Teal, and Dr.

Blake in the forward observation lounge, where they could sip coffee while staring out at the stars. Importantly, he and Beadel agreed to grab dinner together later—which, while not exactly a date, could be made into one. Afterwards he decided it was time to earn his exorbitant paycheck and get back to work. Excusing himself, Jervis slung his omnicorder strap over his shoulder, took the elevator down to C-Deck, and then headed aft toward the array room.

To get there he had to make his way down a corridor about 75 meters in length. He was struck by what a long, lonely walk it was. The passageway was, in fact, a little spooky. The unpainted copper-green plastisteel was dark and drab, devoid of decorations of any kind. The dim lighting along the corridor didn't help lighten the atmosphere. Further, the passageway was utterly devoid of life. The cabins on this deck, like the ones above and below it, were designed for colonist families. But now they were all closed off, empty and presumably dark.

Curious to know exactly what lay behind the doors lining either side of the passageway, Jervis approached one of them. But then he hesitated. Opening any of the doors would, he knew, show up as an alert on one of the bridge consoles. But, he thought, *what the hell*—he was a reporter, he'd been invited, and there were no signs telling him to keep out. Stepping up to a door chosen at random on the starboard side, he pressed the "open" square. The door seals parted with a soft hiss and the panel swung inward. Immediately the cabin's overhead light panels glowed to life, revealing a small, simply furnished room—a bunk supporting a bare mattress, a built-in desktop, a long bureau bolted to the deck, a yellow cloth-upholstered couch that appeared to be fastened to the bulkhead, and a small closet, with a door to the refresher opening off to the immediate right. *Five-star accommodations*, he thought, *this ain't*.

Jervis stepped inside just long enough for his AV balls to come in and record the scene. Then, curiosity satisfied, he retreated. Once outside, he pressed the "close" button, and the door swung silently shut. Jervis then turned and continued down the passageway. Finally he came to a red safety lock door marked, in big white letters, "Array Room—Deck C Entrance." Originally this corridor, along with the ones running parallel to it on the decks above and below, had reached from one end of the ship to the other. But that changed when structural engineers had carved out the array room during the refit. The trans-dimensional device now took up most of the heart of the ship, where workers had torn out huge sections of cabins, cargo space and associated deck plating and bulkheads to accommodate it.

The telltale on the outer safety lock door was shining green; Jervis pressed the button and the door slid silently aside. He stepped through, with three of his floating media drones dutifully tagging along just above and behind his head like little airborne ducklings. Crossing the few feet to the next door, he waited for the outer panel to slide shut behind him, and then repeated the process. The inner door opened, and he and the AV balls passed through.

Jervis found himself standing on a wide catwalk jutting out into a large cavern measuring about 35 meters across. This metal cave was not well lit; its ceiling and floor were not discernible in the gloom. Dominating the interior was a contraption consisting of three circular tracks—an outer, middle, and inner ring each placed concentrically and rotated 90 degrees with respect to one another. Carried on each track was a set of Norberg Field generator spheres. The catwalk on which he was standing ran through the center of the array and ended at the engineering safety lock on the far side. This walkway was, in fact, the only way to traverse from one end of the ship to the other without exiting the hull, which meant that anyone with any business to transact at either end of the ship had better take care of it before the drive array was activated.

At the center of the catwalk, in the heart of the array, was a large circular platform bearing a control stand. A young woman was working there; Jervis recognized her as Assistant N-Field Specialist Ariana Marinez. "Hi, Ms. Marinez!" he called out, his voice echoing in the chamber.

"Hiya back, Janson," she sang out, waving. "And you know it's 'Ariana.' What brings you our way today?"

"Just making my rounds in pursuit of the unrestricted flow of news and information that keeps our society free. Have you seen Dr. Makowski?"

"He's in the control room," she said. "Two doors to your left. It's cleverly labeled, 'Array Control Room.'"

Jensen laughed. "Thanks!"

To his left, branching off from the large catwalk was a narrower one. It extended about twenty meters along the forward bulkhead, running past two doors, one of which gave entrance to a glassed-in office looking out onto the array room. Jervis approached this door, which was marked as advertised. The panel slid open as he stepped up to it.

Makowski, sitting at a console in front of one of the windows and wearing his trademark white lab coat over a standard blue ship's jumpsuit, looked around as Jervis entered, AV balls in tow. "Good morning, Mr. Jervis," the scientist said, managing a nervous smile as he removed his thick glasses and put them away in a breast pocket.

"Janson," Jervis corrected him.

Makowski didn't know how to reciprocate the gesture; everyone had always called him by his formal title and last name, and he felt more comfortable that way. "How can I help you this morning?" he asked.

"I'm just doing what news guys do—nosing my nosy nose into everything. Can you spare me a few moments?"

Makowski could—but he didn't want it to appear that he had leisure time on his hands. "A few moments, I suppose," he said with studied reluctance.

"Great. Mind if I record?"

"Not at all. But let's walk out onto the platform. You'll get a better view."

"Sounds reasonable."

Makowski led him out across to the test stand where Marinez was working. As they walked out, with their footfalls clanking on the plastisteel grating, Jervis eyed with disapproval the safety rails along either side of the catwalk. They seemed a bit low for his tastes. The bottom of the ship was not visible through the gloom, but it had to be a long way down. Jervis swallowed uncomfortably at the thought.

The center platform was wider than the catwalk, which helped allay Jervis' nervousness. Reaching for his omnicorder case, he pressed a control square and released a three more AV drones and three light balls. Turning to Makowski, he said, "Ready?"

Shooting a quick glance at Marinez, who was working nearby and avidly paying no attention, Makowski reached up, ran his hand over his balding head and then fiddled with his grey ponytail. Turning back to Jervis, he asked, "Do I look okay?"

You look like King Geek of Nerd Mountain, Jervis thought. But he stifled the thought. "Perfect. Very scientific." Noting that his lighting and recording equipment was hovering in the proper places, he continued. "Dr. Makowski, what can you tell us about this contraption of yours?" he asked, smiling. "In words of as few syllables as you can muster."

Jervis' charming smile notwithstanding, the journalist's use of the word "contraption" had rankled Makowski. But the scientist suppressed his reaction. "Well," Makowski said, clearing his throat nervously, "I'm sure your viewers have heard of the Norberg field generator—it's the device starships have been using since the dawn of interstellar travel to jump across the light years."

"A process that's been described as tunneling through space," Jansen prompted.

"The analogy is imprecise—but yes, in layman's terms, that's an acceptable way to think of it," Makowski agreed. "What we've done is to shrink the Norberg generator down to a sphere about two meters across—which, as you may appreciate, was no small task. We've assembled a number of those onto the three circular tracks you see surrounding us here on the platform. The outer track is 100 meters in circumference. Each of them holds 40 spheres—120 in all. The rings are turned 90 degrees with respect to one another." He gestured with his hands. "As a result, each covers a plane formed by two of the x, y and z spatial axes—three planes, each intersecting the other at 90 degree angles."

"I think you lost me at 'circumference'," Jervis said, wearing a wry expression.

Makowski flashed a quick smile. "Suffice it to say that the tracks have all three of our own visible spatial dimensions covered. And then when we jump into interspace, we cover three spatial dimensions at a time there as well—and there are, we believe, an infinite number of those."

"I see," Jervis said, not seeing in the least.

"When it comes time to make a jump, we rev up the array. With the spheres going around the track, their positions in relation to one another change continuously, thereby presenting a constant stream of new jump options. At 3,000 rpm, we can make up to 2,000 jumps *per second.*"

The figure surprised Jervis. "Come again?"

"Up to 2,000 jumps per second," Makowski repeated. "The computer sorts it all out, using sensor data to adjust the pre-calculated flight path as needed." He smiled. "We can be out of the galaxy and halfway to Andromeda faster than it would take you to tie your shoelaces."

"That is truly astounding," Jervis said, and he meant it. "Walking across the street, I get. Flying from New York to Paris is within my comprehension. Even taking the shuttle to one of the space stations doesn't greatly challenge my admittedly feeble intellect. But I'll have to admit I've never been able to grasp this dimension jump thing."

Makowski nodded. "I'll grant you, it's difficult to explain in plain English. But I can tell you how we got there. In the mid-21st century, scientists began to take poltergeist phenomena seriously. Previously, accounts of objects passing through closed windows, thick walls and solid roofs, or even dropping out of thin air, had simply been shrugged off. But with serious scientific inquiry, researchers eventually found not only that such things happen, but that it's a natural phenomenon, just like any other." He hesitated. "Well, maybe not *just* like any other. But it's a phenomenon that can be measured, observed, and even duplicated—and as it turns out, with very little energy. And that's how a spaceship can disappear from position X and reappear at position Y."

"I get that it happens," Jervis agreed. "But I'm still fuzzy about the science behind it. Can you explain it?"

Makowski shook his head. "The truth is, we don't fully understand it. It has to do with quantum physics, the Heisenberg uncertainty principle, and a whole range of forces that lie outside the classical electromagnetic spectrum we're all familiar with. But the language you need to describe it is that of mathematics. I really wouldn't know how to put it in words."

"Try me."

Makowksi smiled. Here, he was in his element, and this would give him a chance to show off his superior knowledge and expertise. "Okay," he said. "Let's start with a little multidimensional space theory. One of the things we deal with is what's called a de Sitter space. It's the analogue, in spacetime, or Minkowski space, of an ordinary sphere—in other words, a sphere in Euclidian space. N-dimensional de Sitter Space—which we denote with a small 'd,' 'capital S,' and a small 'n'—is the Lorentzian manifold representation—or analogue if you prefer—of an n-sphere. We define such a sphere, of course, using the Riemannian manifold tensor."

"Of course."

"Are you with me so far?"

"I'm right on your heels."

"Now, the thing about your classic de Sitter Space n-sphere is that it's maximally symmetric, has a constant positive curvature, and—up to at least n equals 3—it's simply connected. You're clear on that, right?"

"Oh, you bet. I'm all about simple connections."

"So you know that the equation describing the variance of points along the vector fields of such a manifold will be a smooth function."

"Smooth as silk," Jervis agreed.

"Where the real fun begins is here: What happens to such points along the manifold when n is greater than three—and then you consider manifolds that are *not* simply connected?"

"I've often wondered that." Jervis was now beginning to have a hard time keeping a straight face.

"Scientists started to think about this kind of thing in the late 20th and early 21st centuries, when they began to develop multidimensional quantized bosonic string theory and write equations for it. Are you familiar with the Veneziano amplitude?"

At this, Jervis burst out laughing. "Okay, okay. You win. I'm waving the white flag. And I see now why they don't hand out the Nobel Prize to just any random schmo found sitting on a bus bench."

Makowski smiled graciously. "It's actually not that hard to understand, once you learn the language."

"You're talking to a guy who has to take off his mittens to count above two. Just tell me that when you press the button, we'll get where we need to go, and we won't be inside out when we get there."

"The N-field array is safe as houses," Makowski assured him.

"My house burned down when I was a kid," Jervis noted.

Makowski chuckled. "Safer, then."

"And when you say 'N-field,' " Jervis continued, "you're not talking about the kind of place where the Yankees embarrassed themselves against the Blue Jays last week. You mean 'n' as in a number corresponding to a different dimension, accessible through the Norberg generator."

Makowski nodded. "Correct. We're not sure how high 'n' can go. But we usually handle these new dimensions—new to us, that is, not to nature—in sets of three. They correspond to length, width, and height, except they're in dimensions we can't normally see or experience with our earthbound senses."

Jervis reached forward and offered his hand. "Thanks, Dr. Makowski, for reminding me of why I went into communications instead of quantum physics. And good luck with your project."

"You're quite welcome," Makowski said, taking the hand, "and thanks."

Jervis paused for effect, and then announced, "That's it. And that was great. In fact, I think it's the best interview I've grabbed so far."

"Really?" Makowski asked, moved. "You really think so?"

"Absolutely. It'll make great TV. You're quite impressive." Pressing the button on his control unit, Jervis recalled all but two of the camera balls.

"I'm glad it worked out, then."

"Can you point me to engineering?" Jervis asked, shouldering his case.

"Sure." He pointed down the catwalk. "Just follow this walkway on through the array to the safety lock on the other side. The engineering control room is just off the passageway beyond. I'm afraid you won't get much, though."

"Really? Why not?"

"Well, for one thing, the chief is—" Makowski started to say "a nasty old curmudgeon," but then thought better of it. "A bit camera shy. But the biggest problem is that with the torches blasting away, the room makes a boiler factory sound like a cloistered nunnery." Makowski smiled, pleased with his witticism.

"Okay. I imagine that'll be a quick visit, then. What about the observatory? Where can I find that?"

"Ah, the Hall of the Mountain King, where Dr. Jones reigns beneficently over all." Makowski mustered his most charming smile, which to Jervis looked like that of an undertaker welcoming a new customer. "There's an elevator in the passageway, just aft of the engineering safety lock. Just take that to the observation deck. It's at the top, one level above A-Deck."

"I get it. A penthouse. Thanks!" He turned to go, but then remembered something he'd forgotten to ask. "One last thing—what do you think we'll find when we get out there?"

Makowski smiled enigmatically. "The back of our heads."

"Excuse me?" Jervis asked, looking puzzled.

"I think we'll find the back of our heads. Of course, Dr. Jones is the expert on all that. But tell him what I said. I'd be interested to hear his reaction."

Jervis nodded, wearing a bemused expression. "I'll do that. And thanks again."

It turned out that Makowski had been exactly correct about the engineering section, which was suffused with all the quiet, contemplative serenity of a jet engine test stand. Jervis found that, with the exception of the control room, everyone was wearing hard hats and ear protectors. Crandall, scowling at him, made Jervis wear them, too—after which conversation was extremely difficult. The chief engineer took him on a quick tour of the fusion plant, the power cell array, and the control room, but wouldn't let him into the torch area. Jervis was not heartbroken over this. The roar of the torches and the strong vibration of the deck plates in this section had left him a little unnerved, and he could only imagine how much worse it would be beyond the thick double safety doors leading to the torches. After taking a few quick shots through the windows of the cramped spaces beyond, Jervis thanked Chief Crandall for his time and then beat a hasty retreat.

The next stop was the observatory. Jervis had no trouble finding the elevator. When it stopped at the top, the door opened to reveal a small circular room, the primary feature of which was a series of large viewports that ran around the upper bulkheads and another, much larger one dominating the dome that stretched overhead. Flickering instrumentation and glowing computer displays filled the dimly-lit space. Through the forward windows could be seen the brightly lighted antenna and instrument complex that rose from the spine of the *Santa Maria* like the dorsal fin of a shark. Jones was lounging at one of the forward consoles with his back to the displays and his feet propped up on a padded chair. Seated next to him was his assistant, Dr. Dakota Munson, whom Jervis had met before. The two of them were holding court with Dr. Blake and Father Teal, who were seated facing them.

"Mr. Jervis!" Jones said, smiling as he caught sight of the reporter. "Pull up a chair and come into the body o' the kirk."

Jervis smiled as he took a seat, setting his recording equipment on the deck plates beside it. "Is that Scottish for 'welcome?'"

"Nay, it's more than a welcome. It signifies that you're one of us."

Jervis grinned crookedly. "Is that a fact?"

Jones chuckled. "Well, perhaps the greeting doesn't bear that close of an examination, at that. But for the moment, we'll cast aside the fact that you're a member of that meddling, swarming, muck raking pack o' bilge rats otherwise known as the Fourth Estate, and extend you honorary, provisional membership." Jones turned to his companions. "Is that agreeable to you?"

The three of them smiled, nodding. "Here, here," Father Teal said.

"Thank you," Jones said. "Will it endanger my provisional membership to unlimber my recording equipment, and get you all to tell me what we can expect over the next few hours?"

"Not at all, not at all. Unlimber away."

Within seconds, Jervis' full aerial fleet of AV and lighting drones was hovering about the room. "First of all, Dr. Jones, in layman's terms, can you tell me—what the hell are we doing?"

Jones smiled. "In words of one sentence, we're out to see if we can make mankind feel any less significant than our species already does."

Father Teal laughed, nodding. Dr. Blake frowned, looking a bit confused.

Jervis smiled. "I don't recall hearing any words to that effect in the mission briefing. What do you mean?"

Wearing a bemused expression, Father Teal glanced at Jervis. "I think I understand what the estimable Dr. Jones is driving at. For most of its recorded history, our species has been arguing about its place in the universe, and the debate still isn't settled. Until fairly late in modern history, wise and learned men thought the universe was relatively small, and that man—or humankind, if you prefer—was at the center of it. The only point of quibbling was about whether the earth revolved around the sun, or vice-versa. But every successive scientific discovery revealed the universe to be bigger than the discovery before it, and man's role in it smaller." Father Teal turned to Jones. "Is that about it?"

"That's it exactly," Jones agreed. "Connie's boy Aristarchus was the first to suggest that, just maybe, the earth was *not* at the exact center of the universe—although he thought the sun was."

"He also proposed that the stars were incredibly far away," Munson pointed out.

"Right," Father Teal agreed. "But Aristarchus' peers didn't buy a word of it. And his views sparked a tiff that lasted nearly two millennia, until the 16th century, when Copernicus put forth a convincing argument for the heliocentric model. But even Copernicus continued to hold that the sun was at the center of the universe. That view held sway for another 400 years, right through the first part of the 20th century, when a guy named Harlow Shapley, using modern astronomical techniques, showed that the earth was most definitely *not* at the center of the galaxy. But even then, most astronomers still thought our galaxy—the Milky Way Galaxy—was all there is."

"Then along comes a chap named Edwin Hubble," Jones said. "And by the way, in terms of significance, that's the man Connie should have named her damned cat after, not Aristarchus."

Dr. Blake laughed at this. "The name 'Ed' certainly would be easier to pronounce," she agreed.

"What's so great about Hubble?" Jervis asked.

"Quite simply, he's why we're here," Munson said.

"How so?"

"In the 1920s," Father Teal explained, "peering through a primitive little telescope atop a mountain in California, Hubble was looking at these tiny little smudges of light that were thought to be clouds of gas within the Milky Way. What he discovered was that those little smudges *also* were galaxies—little island universes of their own. And, as it turns out, there are *billions* of them."

"It was an astounding discovery," Munson said. "Mind-blowing, in fact. So much so that many of his peers refused to believe it."

"Those who did," Jones said, "fainted dead away—I'm talking about a fall-down-on-the-floor-hit-your-head-on-the-coffee-table full-on swoon, the kind that has your mother-in-law taking a warm rag to your bleedin' head while your wife wrings her hand and your little lasses and laddies sit around crying about poor daddy's noggin. The universe had just gotten *unimaginably* larger. It was staggering."

"And it's *still* staggering," Munson agreed. "Man had shrunk from being the apple of God's eye—no offense, Father—and the center of His creation, to a creature so small in stature as to be far tinier than simply microscopic, by many orders of magnitude."

"Not only are we *not* at the center of the universe," Jones put in, "but we're not even sure you can *see* the center from here—and we're guessing you probably can't."

For the first time, Dr. Blake frowned. "It sounds like you're saying that we're so small, God isn't even aware of us."

"No," Father Teal said firmly. "Not at all. Later, ask me to tell you about the 'fine tuning' problem, and what it says about creation."

Dr. Blake nodded. "You've got a date."

At the word "date," Father Teal looked at her with renewed interest. She smiled at him, but he wasn't quite sure whether she'd meant the word suggestively or not. Nor was he quite sure how he felt about the possibility that she had meant it that way. But it did strike him that Dr. Blake was aging very well.

"All right," Jervis said. "You've stretched my intellectual prowess beyond its limits. To me, the concept of 'big' comes in just three flavors— 'big,' 'bigger than big,' and 'monstrously damned honkin' big.' So the universe is in the latter category. Now what?"

"Now," Father Teal said, "we're going to try to find out just how much bigness 'monstrously honkin' big' really amounts to."

"Through the dimension array," Jervis said.

"Exactly," Father Teal agreed.

"We're planning a series of at least four jumps," Munson said. "Probably more. The first one is coming up."

"All right, so give me a road map."

"Before we can start that discussion," Jones said, "we need to chat a bit about the Hubble Constant." Jones looked expectantly at Munson.

She nodded. "The existence of other galaxies wasn't Hubble's only discovery," Munson said. "Probably not even his greatest. He also found that, in general, all the galaxies we see around us are receding from us. The further away they are, the faster they're flying away from us—all the way up to the speed of light, in fact, and even beyond it for the most distant objects."

"And how did he discover that?"

"Through red shifts in the galaxies' electromagnetic spectrum," Munson answered.

"I can give you a technical answer if you want," Jones said, noting Jervis' perplexed expression. "But for the purpose of this discussion, suffice it to say that when a light source is moving away from us, it drops in frequency, shifting toward the lower, or redder, end of the spectrum."

"It's similar to the Doppler effect," Father Teal put in. "Have you ever stood at the side of the road, and noticed that when a big rig passes you, the noise drops in tone when the truck blasts by and heads away from you?"

Jervis nodded.

"The frequency drop in the light from receding galaxies is similar—in fact, for a while, the Doppler effect from the relative velocity was thought to be responsible for the red shift."

"It wasn't?"

"No," Munson said. "Or at least, not primarily. And this is where cosmology gets real fun. Because what Hubble discovered is that space *itself* is expanding. And that expansion stretches the light waves along with it, making their wavelengths longer—and therefore redder."

"You know," Dr. Blake said, looking confused, "I studied this briefly in college, but I can't say I really understood it then, and I'm very sure I don't understand it now."

"Think of the universe as an expanding balloon," Father Teal said. "Take a pen, mark several points on a balloon, blow it up, and what happens? The points move apart, while still maintaining their exact positions relative to each other."

"A balloon is three-dimensional," Jones said, "but its surface is *two* dimensional. The sphere itself is expanding through that third dimension. Apply the same principle to a larger sheaf of dimensions, and there you go, the expanding universe. Points in the three dimensions visible to us get farther apart even if they're standing stock still."

"Hubble figured out that the distance to an object equals its recessional velocity divided by a numeric constant that now bears his name," Munson said. "So, if you determine the current value of the Hubble Constant—which we have, to eight decimal places—then in general, you can learn the distance to any object by simply measuring its red shift, which gives you that recessional velocity."

"So, plugging in those numbers," Jervis said, "how big is it, this balloon of yours?"

"That, me laddie buck, is what we're trying to answer," Jones said.

"Okay. Give me a guess."

Jones laughed, and turned to the priest. "Father, why don't you start? I'd be very interested in your answer."

Father Teal looked thoughtful. "Well. Let's begin with what we can see. We've learned the universe is about 13.8 billion years old, and we know this—or rather I should say, we *think* we know it—because we can run the recording, so to speak, backwards to its starting point." Father Teal cocked an eye at Jervis. "So, based on what I just told you, and knowing the speed of light, how big would you say that makes the universe today?"

Jervis laughed, shaking his head. "That's a trick question, one that sounds a lot like asking me to name the color of Grant's white horse. I might be tempted to give a radius of 13.8 billion light years, had I not done that once in college, and nearly failed a physics exam because of it. So I know the universe is bigger than that. But I still don't get how."

"This one confuses everybody," Munson allowed. "The expansion of the universe stretches everything out. And worse, the expansion rate is not constant over time. Right now, in fact, the expansion is accelerating—after, we think, initially *de*celerating."

"Because of the expansion of the universe," Father Teal said, "the most distant objects now visible to us were much closer to us when they emitted the light 13.8 billion years ago. It's possible that some objects are so far from Earth that their light will *never* reach us, no matter how much time passes. The universe will expand faster than the light can travel."

Jervis raised an eyebrow. "Okay. So what's the answer, then? How big is the universe?"

"Well, not so fast," Jones said. "We're not there yet. The other thing we have to deal with is the cosmological horizon."

"The what?"

"It's an event horizon. There's more than one, actually, depending on whether you're talking about light or other particles like neutrinos."

" 'Event horizon,' " Dr. Blake said musingly. "I've heard that term before, in connection with black holes. You make it sound like we're in one."

Father Teal looked at her. "Very astute. As a matter of fact, that may be the case. Some scientists suspect that a universe like ours may be what you get when you pop out of the other side of a black hole."

"Wow," Jervis said. "That's—cosmic."

"We really don't know what happened to create the universe and inflate it to its present size," Jones said. "But we do know *when* it happened.

When you look into the sky, you're looking into the past. By definition, anything we can see today had to be close enough to us when the light was emitted to complete the journey within the time allotted—which is 13.8 billion years, the age of the universe. Anything outside that physical distance—beyond our horizon, if you will—is invisible to us, because the light hasn't had time to reach us."

"Just like Columbus," Munson said, "we really don't know for sure what lies beyond that horizon."

"So the only number we can give you with confidence is an estimate for the size of the *observable* universe," Father Teal added.

Jervis laughed. "I think you guys are tag-teaming me here. And you definitely have me on the ropes." His expression sobered. "So how big is it—your observable universe?"

The three scientists exchanged glances, and then returned their gaze to Jones. "About 47 billion light years in radius," Jones answered. "94 billion light years across. Give or take."

"Give or take." Jervis swallowed. *"And that's how far we're going?"*

The scientists exchanged glances again. Finally, Jones cleared his throat. "We suspect the universe actually is much bigger than that," he said.

"How much bigger?"

Jones raised a hand off the leg where it had been resting, and then dropped it again. "We really don't know," he admitted. "The answer depends on what models you're using and what assumptions you're making."

"But surely you must have some idea?"

Jones sighed, and looked at Munson and Father Teal with a helpless expression.

"Estimates vary," Father Teal said. "Or rather I should say, guesses do. I've seen estimates ranging from sizes *less* than the radius of the observable universe, to sizes much, much, *much* larger."

"How much," Jervis inquired slowly, "is much, much, *much*?"

"Conceivably," Jones said, fixing him with a sober expression, "9.3 decillion light years."

"Do what?" Jervis asked, looking confused.

"9.3 times a 10 to the 33rd power—a 1 with 33 zeroes after it," Teal explained. "Or put another way, about 9.3 million billion billion billion light years."

The blood drained from Jervis's face. He looked at Dr. Blake, and noticed that she was looking a bit green herself. Jervis glanced back at Teal, Jones and Munson. "Is there a bus station or something like that coming up where I can get off? I suddenly remembered I have a very important dental appointment to keep."

The three scientists laughed.

"We're not going quite that far out," Munson said.

"Okay. So how far?"

"We're authorized to jump to no more than 500 billion light years," Jones said.

"Oh. Only 500 billion light years. And here I was, all worried."

"If the universe is still isotropic at that point," Jones went on, "meaning that we see equal amounts of light and energy in every direction, then we'll turn around and come back."

"Assuming we can find our way back," Jervis said.

"Oh, that's not a problem," Jones assured him. "The astrogation computer tracks every move—my lovely bride is in charge of that, by the way, and I have utter confidence in her. We'll get you back to your news studio, with video in hand for a dynamite program."

Jones swallowed. "Move the coffee table. I think I'm about to—how did you put it?—make a swoon."

"Go ahead," Father Teal said. "We'll catch you."

Jervis sat for a moment, gazing out at the stars through one of the viewports while reflecting on the infinite. Finally, he turned back to Jones. "So what's your best guess? Will we find the edge of the universe?"

Jones nodded. "I think we will. My personal guess is that the universe is about 250 billion light years in radius—well within mission parameters." He turned to his assistant. "Dakota?"

"I think it's bigger than that," she said. "Way bigger. I don't think we'll find an outer limit to it on this mission."

"What should I expect?" Jervis demanded. "What will we see when get out there?"

Jones shrugged. "Well, in our planning, we made certain assumptions: that the universe is flat, that it contains a finite amount of matter and energy, that our conclusions about the age of the universe are correct, that our estimate of the Hubble Constant and changes to it over time are more or less correct, and that there are no surprises waiting for us in the form of physical laws that we don't know about. If all those assumptions are valid, and if my personal guess about the size of the universe is anywhere near accurate, then in answer to your question about what we'll see when we get out there, I can say with complete and utter confidence that I'm damned if I know."

Jervis laughed. "That was a long buildup for a pretty lame payoff."

"Oh, he's just being melodramatic," Munson said. "What Dr. Jones actually expects is for the universe to simply run out of stars past a certain point."

Jones shrugged. "It's just a guess. But I have to concede that there are other possibilities."

"That reminds me—" Jervis started. But at that moment the klaxon sounded four times.

"All hands," a male voice that Jervis recognized as belonging to sensor and coms officer Mason Krajnovich sounded over speakers, "prepare for dimension jump. Fifteen minutes."

"Anyone who wants to see the operation from the bridge had better get moving," Jones said. "In five minutes, Dr. Makowski will start revving up his whirligig, and then you'll be stuck back here in steerage for the duration."

Jervis, Father Teal and Dr. Blake stood. "Thanks, Dr. Jones, Dr. Munson," Jervis said. "I'd like to pick this up later, if you don't mind."

"It's David." Jones said.

"And Dakota," Munson chimed in.

"And yes, continuing this later would be great," Jones continued. "If we make it through this hopefully historic day, tonight the beers are on me."

"I really hate that word," Jervis said.

"Really?" Jones said, smiling. "I was speaking figuratively—we don't actually have any beer onboard. But you're the first reporter I've ever heard object to a free brew."

Jervis shook his head. "That's not the word. I meant the first one you used. 'If.' "

Captain Cermeno stepped through the safety lock door and walked briskly to his command console. As he did so, he couldn't help but notice that the bridge crew fell instantly silent. *Fine*, he thought. *So you're a bit nervous around me. You damned well should be.*

As he looked around the arc of consoles, his eye fell on ASM Sierra Bent, who was manning the AI station on this watch. Her shoulder-length hair, normally dark brown, now was practically glowing with alternating iridescent strips of bright blue, green and orange. This multicolor style was all the rage at the moment, but it was not within company policy.

Standing in the area between the command chairs and the bridge consoles was Second Officer Martin Trafford, who had the deck for this watch. "Mister Trafford," Cermeno said. "A word please."

Trafford stepped over to the captain. "Yes, sir?"

Cermeno crooked his finger; Trafford bent lower. "Yes, sir?" he said again.

"I'm curious to know if you've noticed anything unusual about ASM Bent this morning?" Cermeno asked in a low voice.

Trafford glanced nervously in her direction. "Well, sir, ah—she changed her hair style, obviously," Trafford offered, almost whispering.

"Obviously. And what is your opinion about the extent to which her new style lies within regulations?"

"Well, sir, I'd say it probably doesn't."

" 'It probably doesn't.' That would be the understatement of the century. And, having noticed this issue, what action have you taken?"

Trafford was now looking very nervous. "Well, sir, I was under the impression from First Officer De Vegas that—"

"Remind me, who is in charge of this watch?"

"Well, sir, that would be me."

"That would be you. So I repeat my question—what action have you taken in response to this breach of regulations?"

"None, sir."

"Very well. Ms. Bent is relieved. Please get Ms. Nunn in here to replace her. The senior AI specialist should be manning the station on this jump, anyway."

"Yes, sir. But—"

Cermeno raised an eye brow. "Yes?"

"Nothing, sir. Sorry, sir. I'll take care of it."

"Please do."

Cermeno watched as Trafford stepped over to Bent's station and leaned down to whisper in her ear. Bent's expression quickly morphed from one of helpful cooperativeness, to shock, and then to outrage. Cermeno noted this with some satisfaction. Bent reminded him a great deal of the young Patricia, exhibiting the same haughty, flirty arrogance. He'd been looking for an opportunity to bring her down a peg or two. It was all he could do not to smile as Bent unstrapped, jumped up from her flight chair, and strode off the bridge, tight-lipped with anger. As she passed the command consoles, she kept her eyes fixed dead ahead, not looking at the captain.

Meanwhile, Trafford had stepped over to the coms station, now being staffed by ASM Mason Krajnovich. "Have Constance Nunn report to the bridge immediately," Trafford said.

"Yes, sir," Krajnovich acknowledged.

De Vegas, who'd been watching the action from one of the observer chairs, rose and stepped up to the captain. "Ser, is there a problem?"

"Not now, there isn't."

"Ser, I told Sierra that—"

"Who?"

De Vegas paused, swallowed her annoyance, and then continued. "I told ASM Bent that she could change her hairstyle. This is going to be an historic occasion. I didn't think that—"

Cermeno cut her off. "You can put a period after the word 'think.' " He glared at her. "This is indeed an historic occasion. I will not have the bridge crew looking like performance artists from some damned street fair. Is that in any way unclear?"

"No, ser," De Vegas said, working hard to stifle her growing anger.

"Good," Cermeno continued. "Later we will discuss your views about the fluidity of company regulations. For now, we've got a jump to make." The captain now stood up. "Mr. Krajnovich, 1MC if you please."

Krajnovich punched a square on his console. "1MC aye."

"Ladies and gentlemen of the NAUS *Santa Maria*," Cermeno began, with a faint reverberation of his voice reaching the bridge as his words were piped through the ship, "let me have your attention for a moment."

The crewmembers on the bridge paused what they were doing and turned to him.

"We are about to make an historic flight," Cermeno continued. "In a few minutes, we'll traverse a distance far greater than any previous leap mankind has ever made. For the first time, members of the human race will be able to look through a viewport and gaze back at their own galaxy, seen from a great distance. You have been selected to be first to do this. You're here because you have earned it. Across the board, you've been judged to be the best at what you do. Your personnel files all contain records of outstanding achievement. Your psych profiles show that you are above average in your drive, your commitment, and your passion for excellence. That is why I'm holding each of you to a much higher standard than I would any other crew. We will do this by the book, by the numbers—and, by the grace of God, our achievement will throw open unimaginable new vistas for humanity, thereby earning a permanent place in history. I expect, and require, nothing short of excellence from each of you. Are you with me?"

"Yes, sir," came the scattered responses from around the bridge.

"I can't hear you."

"Yes, sir!" the bridge crew shouted in unison.

"Very well. Take your stations, and prepare to report your status."

The safety lock door opened. A clearly flustered Connie Nunn rushed in and took the AI console. Right behind her was Janson Jervis. "Permission to enter the bridge?" Jervis asked, looking at Cermeno.

"Permission granted," Trafford said, looking annoyed.

Noting Trafford's displeasure, Jervis shook his head. He still didn't understand bridge protocol.

Electrician Nereida Sabol, who was staffing the engineering station, now spoke up. "Dr. Makowski asks for permission to spin up the array," she said.

Cermeno glanced at the clock—11:50. "Granted."

For the next few minutes, the crewmembers busied themselves at making their final preparations. Finally, at five until the hour, Cermeno spoke up. "All right. Let's go around the horn."

"Yes, sir." Trafford, who was standing in front of his command console, turned to Krajnovich. "Coms and sensors, report."

"No traffic or other contacts within the safety limit," the man answered.

"Telemetry link with Chicago is good."

"Very well. Please signal our intent to depart on schedule." He turned to ASM Julius Terwilliger, who was manning the helm. "Helm, report."

"Coordinates and programs laid in and on standby," he said. "Ready to execute."

"Very well." Now he turned his gaze to the astrogator, Conrad Specht. "Astrogation, report."

"The astrogation computer is fired up and tied in to the helm. Astrogational instruments are fully deployed and operational. We're ready."

For the moment, Trafford skipped over the AI station. "Engineering, report."

"Fusion plant is at full power," Sabol said. "Accumulators fully charged. Torches at standard thrust. Bjorklund generators are at standard power. The N-field array is at 3,000 RPM and standing by for energization. All main systems and subsystems fully operational and showing nominal performance."

"Very well. AI, report."

"Ship's computer and all IT consoles and subsystems are operating within nominal limits," Nunn answered. "Wilson is ready."

"Okay. Let's hear from him."

Nunn turned to her console. "Wilson, please give us your readiness report."

"I concur with all reports given," Wilson's voice came over the speakers in a smooth, soothing baritone. "In addition, be advised that there is a very slight vibration in N-field array track Z, due to a deteriorating bearing in sphere assembly Z-15. However, it is functioning well within operational safety limits. I do not see a concern."

"Thank you, Wilson."

Cermeno frowned at Sabol. "Engineer, when we ask for a report, we mean a *full* report."

"Yes, sir," the woman said, looking sheepish. "Sorry, sir."

Cermeno glanced at the clock again; it was approaching 11:58. "All right, Mr. Trafford. Sound the final alarm."

Trafford repeated the command to Mason Krajnovich, who then pressed the control square that caused the klaxons to sound. Then Krajnovich opened his microphone. "All hands," his voice could be heard booming throughout the vessel, "secure for dimension jump. Two minutes. Repeat: Secure for dimension jump. Two minutes."

"Mr. Terwilliger," Trafford said, "please extinguish all exterior lights. Seal all viewports."

"Yes, sir." Terwilliger punched a control square, and the running lights and floodlights on the portion of the *Santa Maria's* upper hull that was visible through the viewports went dark. He punched another square, and with a mechanical hum, articulated plastisteel covers began to lower from recesses in the hull, covering the viewports.

Jervis turned to Krajnovich. "I'm curious to know why they close the windows. I was rather looking forward to the show."

"It would be way too distracting," Krajnovich said. "The scene changes up to 2,000 times a second, and some of the alternate dimensions we'll be going through are just plain weird. And there's a question of radiation in some of the jumps. So we screen it all out."

"Well, shucks," Jervis grumbled.

"You'll be able to get video from Specht later. Or actually, I should say, you should probably get it from the chief astrogator, Lydia Nguyen. But it shouldn't be a problem."

"One minute," Trafford announced. "Mr. Terwilliger, engage the computer."

"Computer, aye," Terwilliger acknowledged. "Helm is now under the control of the astrogation computer. Jump in 56 seconds."

Jervis swallowed heavily. "What should I expect?" he asked Krajnovich.

"Not much," he replied. "During the test two weeks ago, we didn't know we'd jumped until Nick—Mr. Swann—told us."

Trafford turned to Father Teal, who was sitting at the rear bulkhead along with Dr. Blake, First Officer De Vegas, and a handful of other crewmembers who'd come in to witness the operation. "Father, would you like to say any words?"

Father Teal looked at the clock. "Well, in the few seconds we have left, I think we may have time for Alan Shepard's prayer."

"Whose?"

"Alan B. Shepard, the first North American in space. As legend has it, just before the historic launch, he lifted his eyes to heaven and said, 'Dear Lord, please don't let me foul up.'" Father Teal smiled. "Or words to that effect."

A brief titter ran around the bridge.

"All right," Cermeno said. "Let's settle down. Ten seconds."

For the next few moments, the bridge was silent except for the low rumble of the torches behind them. "Five seconds," Terwilliger announced. And then, "Zero." Several lights flashed on the various bridge consoles, and Jervis felt a moment of dizziness.

"We're in interspace," Specht announced.

"N-field array engaged," Sabol said. "Proceeding cautiously at 200 jumps a second."

"Cautiously?" Jervis whispered urgently to Krajnovich. "That's cautiously?"

Krajnovich smiled, but did not answer.

The time ticked by, seeming to move at a glacial pace. The torches rumbled, and strange patterns flashed on the astrogation console monitors. There was nothing else to indicate anything unusual was occurring.

"N-field array shutdown in 30 seconds," Sabol said after a moment. "Five seconds," she said a few moments later. And then, "N-field array shutdown."

As she said it, Jervis felt his head swim again, before again quickly settling down.

"Shut down the torches by program," Trafford said.

"Torch shutdown, aye," Terwilliger acknowledged as he pressed a series of squares. "19 gees. 18 gees." The rumbling of the torches slowly decreased in intensity as Terwilliger counted down the acceleration numbers. "1 gee," he finally said, followed by, "shutdown complete," at which point the engine rumbling and vibration had died away to nothing.

"All stations, report," Trafford said. "Coms."

"No contacts," Krajnovich reported. "Telemetry link lost. No signals."

"Helm."

"Coasting at zero gee," Terwilliger said. "I wouldn't know what to tell you about our velocity, as I have no reference points."

"Astrogation."

"Computer program executed with no anomalies," Specht reported. "According to my readout, we should be at the programmed location."

"AI."

"All systems nominal," Nunn reported. "Wilson concurs."

"Engineering."

"N-field array is shut down and coasting to a stop," Sabol answered. "Power plant on programmed power-down, on its way to 15 percent for accumulator recharging. Torches off. No anomalies."

"All right, then," Cermeno ordered. "Open her up. Let's see what we've got."

"Aye, sir." Terwilliger touched his console, and with a whine the window shields began to retract. Within moments, the viewports were fully open.

Nothing lay in front of them. The view was utterly dark.

"Mr. Trafford," Cermeno said, "What's our attitude?"

"Mr. Terwilliger?" Trafford asked, turning to the helmsman.

"We should be pointed to extragalactic north," Terwilliger replied. "Zero mark 90."

"Flip us around to mark minus 90," Cermeno said.

Trafford nodded to Terwilliger.

"Mark minus 90 attitude, aye," Terwilliger said. "One moment." The helmsman worked his controls, but the bridge crew members could feel no motion. "Now at zero mark minus 90," Terwilliger remarked after a moment.

The viewport was still dead black.

Cermeno looked inquisitively at Trafford.

Trafford turned to the astrogator. "Mr. Specht, what do you make of it?"

"If the ship is where it's supposed to be, sir, we're well out of the galaxy. In theory, we should be able to see it. But it may be washed out by the glare of the bridge lights."

"Very well."

"Sir," Krajnovich spoke up, "Dr. Jones seeks permission to raise his telescopes. And he asks us to hold the ship's attitude here."

Trafford nodded. "By all means. Tell him we're at station keeping."

A few more minutes ticked by, during which the crew pretended to find things to do at their consoles. But really, there was nothing to do but wait.

Finally Krajnovich spoke up. "Sir, Dr. Jones asks if he can address the ship."

Trafford glanced at Cermeno. The request irritated the captain. Obviously, Jones was grandstanding. It should be the captain's privilege to announce the results of the jump. But Cermeno decided that to deny the request would appear small of him. He gave Trafford a nod.

Trafford turned to Krajnovich. "Go ahead," Trafford said.

"Okay, Dr. Jones," Krajnovich said into his console. "You're on."

"Thanks," Dr. Jones' voice sounded over the speakers. "Ladies and gentlemen, we astrophysicists plot the positions of remote objects not in light years, but in red shift numbers. That's because, while red shifts and their corresponding recessional values are certain, distances are always an estimate, based on a number of factors. This first jump was intended to take us out to red shift zero point zero zero zero 1. Pre-flight calculations placed the approximate physical distance at zero point 44 megaparsecs—or, if you prefer, 1.4 million light years. As you know, the previous record flight spanned just 25 light years, and took months. At this great distance, we have a number of galaxies that we use as astrogational landmarks— including our own, the Andromeda Galaxy, the Triangulum Galaxy, several galaxies in the Council of Giants, to name a few. So, we raised our telescopes a few minutes ago, found those landmarks, and checked our angles. Our computations are still preliminary, but I can tell you with a high degree of confidence that we have hit our astrogational mark on the nose. Congratulations, maties. We've done it."

Cheers erupted. All present released their straps, jumped to their feet, and began clapping and cheering. Even Cermeno was moved to stand up and applaud. Turning to Trafford, he extended his hand. Trafford took it. De Vegas drifted over. He shook hands with her, too. All round the bridge, crew members emulated him, shakings hands and clapping one another on the back.

Finally, the captain nodded at Krajnovich. "1MC."

Krajnovich touched a button. "You're on, sir."

"Crewmembers of the *Santa Maria*," Cermeno said, "I told you we'd make history, and we have. I'm proud of you. Special congratulations to Dr. Makowski, Dr. Jones, and their teams. We can all feel good about ourselves, and our company. But this is just the overture. The symphony is yet to come. We'll be setting new records, and obliterating the old ones, every few hours for the next several days. So get ready to make some more history. We'll have a department head meeting shortly to review our progress, but I expect we'll be making our next jump tomorrow morning at zero eight hundred hours, as planned. Stand by for further announcements. Meanwhile, take a break. And where allowed, vape 'em if you got 'em. That is all." He again nodded at Krajnovich.

"You're clear," Krajnovich reported.

Cermeno looked around the bridge. He felt good. This was his moment, and he had handled it well.

Trafford turned to him. "Sir, permission to change the watch?"

"Granted," Cermeno said. He turned to the coms officer. "Mr. Krajnovich, there will be a department head meeting in the conference room in two hours. Please see that the word gets passed."

"Aye, sir."

"I'll be in my cabin." With that, Cermeno turned and walked off the bridge. He could feel all eyes on him as he passed through the inner door into the safety airlock, and he wondered what people were thinking about him.

If the forward section of the *Santa Maria* somewhat resembled the nose of shark, the observation lounge windows roughly corresponded to its mouth. Shortly after 8:00 that night—or twenty hundred hours ship time—several off-duty members of the crew congregated there, gathering around Dr. Jones. After waiting patiently for everyone to arrive and get drinks and snacks, finally Jones took up station at the center of the curving bank of large windows.

"Ladies and gentlemen," he said after clearing his throat. "I promised to show you something special. And as the old NASA astronauts used to day back in the day—" here he nodded to Swann, the helmsman, who was standing near the front— "and Mr. Swann, your family would probably know this: 'We deliver.' I'm going to deliver you a sight no human being has ever before witnessed." Here a slight murmur went around the crowd. "Now, hold on to your hat. We're about to turn off the lights. And it's going to get very, very dark. Keep your hands and feet inside the ride at all times." He paused, smiling, waiting for the polite chuckles to subside. Then he nodded to a figure standing at a control square inset on a bulkhead at the aft end of the room. "Electrician Marrone, if you please."

The figure addressed touched a small point of light on the panel, and the room went completely black, accompanied by various "oohs" and "aahs" from awed observers.

"Now, you won't be able to see anything right away," Jones continued. "But let your eyes adjust to the dark. Watch through the viewports."

"Where the hell are they?" Jervis' voice sang out. This prompted another round of laughter.

"Just keep looking, Janson," Jones said. "Unless you're already completely moagered, you should be able to see it in a minute."

Jervis laughed. "If that word means what I think it means, the implication is that, contrary to previous assertions, there's booze to be found on this ship. Show me the way!"

"No such luck!" called out Beadel, who was standing beside him. "But if you ask nice, someone might be able to scrounge you up a joint."

This led to more polite laughter.

For a few moments, they strained to see ahead in the darkness. And then De Vegas said, "I see it!"

"What do you see?" Jones asked.

"A big smudge of light, all across the two center windows," she said. "Very faint."

"I see it too!" another voice sang out.

"There it is!" Dr. Blake said. "But I don't see any other stars."

"No, there's another little smudge, off to the right," Beadel corrected her.

"You're right," De Vegas confirmed.

A few more voices called out. Soon everyone was seeing the dim patches of light.

"So are you going to tell us what we're looking at?" Jervis finally prodded.

"Any guesses?" Jones asked. "Flight officers, you don't get to play."

Dr. Blake spoke up. "I hope you're not going to tell us that's our own galaxy."

"I am indeed," Jones said. "The big smudge is home—the Milky Way Galaxy. The smaller one is our companion galaxy, M31, more popularly known as Andromeda. And if you look really closely, you'll be able to make out a few even smaller satellite systems."

"Oh, my God," Jervis said. "I need to sit down."

"But why are there no stars?" Dr. Blake asked.

"Because we're so far out," said Teal, who was standing next to her. "Stars are found only within galaxies or their satellite systems. Every point of light visible to the naked eye in Earth's night sky shines from within our own galaxy, with just four exceptions—and each of those is a galaxy itself, located well outside the Milky Way. The *Santa Maria* is now coasting in a huge expanse of empty space *between* galaxies. No stars."

"I'm definitely going to be sick," Jervis said. He sounded as if he meant it.

"Right now you can hold up your hand," Jones said, "cover that big smudge of light, and blot out just about everything mankind has ever known or seen with the naked eye. Our entire planet. Our sun. Our solar system. Our whole galaxy. Everything. And we're the first persons in history in a position to do that."

"How do we even know where we are?" a voice called out. Jones recognized it as belonging to Jane Kim, the assistant cook.

"Jane, lucky for you, Ms. Munson and I brought along some really high caliber telescopes and imaging systems. There are plenty of objects out here not visible to the naked eye, but within reach of our instruments. We know precisely where we are. And where we're going."

"I hesitate to ask," Jervis said, "But where is that?"

"North," Jones said. "Deeper into the darkness. If all goes well, *much* deeper."

"I want my mommy," Jervis whined. When the resulting laughter began to die down, he added, "And my binky."

Father Teal took another sip of the excellent Glenfiddich that Jones had poured into his glass. After the gathering in the lounge had broken up, Jones had invited Teal and Dr. Blake to his cabin for a "wee swallae." Jones' wife Lydia had joined them a short time later, after concluding her rotation on the last dog watch. Now, several wee swallaes later, Teal was feeling no pain. Nor were Jones and Blake.

"Would you like another taste, Father?" Jones asked, noticing that Teal's glass was nearly empty—again. Teal did not object. He knew he would regret this later—but what the hell.

"Dr. Blake?" Jones asked after filling the priest's glass.

Blake held hers forward. "You are a fine human being," she declared.

"What she said," Teal agreed.

Jones topped her glass off, and then turned to his bride. "Dear?"

Nguyen waved him off. "Nope. If the captain catches me he'll keel haul me."

Teal fixed a bleary eye on Jones. "Tell me about our dear captain," he said. "The man seems rather—stiff."

"That's from the broom handle up his arse," Jones agreed. "It stays there more or less permanent-like."

"He does seem a bit formal," Blake agreed.

"The man's afraid people will find him out," Jones explained. "But what he doesn't realize—or maybe he does—is that they already have."

"What's his story?" Teal asked.

"Don't you take in the news, laddie?" Jones asked with raised eyebrow.

"I do, but I'm not up on my starship captains."

"It's simple story. The fusion plant on the *Antilles* went. She was a freighter that also carried a few passengers. Our good man Cermeno managed to get himself off with nary a singe. There were only a handful of other survivors."

"So you're saying he's a coward?" Blake asked.

"Nay, not me. If the board of inquiry says he acted appropriately—which it did—who am I to say different?"

"The look on your face already does say different," Teal observed.

Jones shrugged. "He testified that the passageway to the crew deck and engineering was hopelessly blocked and on fire, but that the companionway to his captain's gig was clear. And he said his intention was to launch the gig, circle back and then rescue the crew by way of an aft engineering airlock. But after he launched, the ship blew apart before he could get back there."

"That sounds like a reasonable explanation," Blake said.

"His number two didn't exactly back his story, though," Jones continued. "She said the main passageway didn't become blocked until *after* he launched the gig. And when the ship disintegrated, he was a kilometer away, safely out of range of the debris. Maneuvering to go back—or so he testified."

"So how did the first officer survive, then?" Teal asked.

"She was in a spacesuit, working on the engineering safety lock door with a torch, trying to get to several trapped crewmates, when the ship opened up. She got thrown into space. It was just blind luck that none of the flying scrap from the explosion killed her or ruptured her suit. She did get a couple of nicks at that, but Cermeno picked her up before her air ran out, along with one or two others. Everyone else was toast." At this, Jones knocked back a big draft of the amber liquid, and then poured himself another generous helping.

"So if there's such a cloud over him," Blake asked, "What's he doing here?"

"His daddy rescued him, pure and simple. Family ties, blood is thicker than water, the 'steady rock' that is the family, blah blah blah and so on and so forth." Jones took another swallow. "I'll tell you one thing—he'd better not cross his current number two. Some of her ancestors were Zulus. She'll pull his alleged spine out and beat him over the head with it."

Teal laughed. "I gather she didn't take her demotion well?"

Jones turned to his wife, who was lying back on their bunk with her eyes closed. "Darlin', you're up on all that gossipy stuff. What's the scuttlebutt?"

Nguyen opened one eye and peered at him. "De Vegas is a consummate professional," she said. "As far as I know, our first officer hasn't said a negative word to anyone about any of that."

"Well, I wouldn't want to cross her," Jones repeated.

"And why not?" Teal prodded.

Jones gave him a sober glance. "I shouldn't be saying anything. But I find my normal inhibition circuits are off line at the moment." He took another sip, looking thoughtful. "During the piracy suppression raids on New Atlantis a while back," he continued, "Ms. De Vegas had occasion to interrogate a couple of prisoners about a member of her unit that had gone missing. Both claimed they didn't know a thing. I should add that the pirates were notorious for abusing their prisoners in all kinds of awful and unspeakable ways. De Vegas picks up a shotgun, racks it, points it at one guy's head as casual as you'd aim a flashlight, and pulls the trigger, blowing his head apart. Then she racks the shotgun again, turns to the other guy, who's now sitting there with his shorts loaded up and gouts of blood and bits of his late friend's brains sliding down his fizzog, and she says, as calmly as you'd order a latte, 'You were saying?' " Two minutes later she was on her way to rescue her missing marine, with a diagram of the enemy compound in hand."

"Wow," Teal said slowly.

"Isn't something like that a war crime?" Blake asked.

"Not if you're the victor, my good doctor," Jones said. "Not if you're the victor. The winners write the histories, and they conduct all the war crimes trials."

"What's her personal story?" Teal asked. "Is she married?"

Jones smiled. "Father, is that your way of asking what sex our resident Amazon is opposite?"

Teal smiled. "I will admit to professional curiosity only."

"Her sexual preference is 'yes,' " Nguyen spoke up. "She was married to a Navy lieutenant—a man—until about four years ago. More recently she had a girlfriend—Cermeno's second in command on the *Antilles*, in fact—but they broke up for some reason before De Vegas was assigned to the *Santa Maria*. Since she's been with us, she's more or less kept to herself."

"And the crew is happy to let her do it," Jones added. "I think most of 'em are about half scared of her."

"And you're not?" Blake asked.

"Hell, no. She's on *our* side. And believe me, when the shite hits the high-speed blower, Fabiana De Vegas is the kind of person you want on your side."

"Especially," Nguyen said, "if Cermeno is the alternative."

"She does cut a figure," Blake agreed. "Very impressive."

"You have no idea," Jones said. "In that New Atlantis rescue I mentioned, she led a squad into action against a force four times their size. She got back her lost private and also a flag officer that had been captured. That's how she collected that scar on her face. When asked why she did it, she said she was simply nae willing to leave anyone behind."

"Both rescued prisoners had been tortured," Nguyen said. "As Dr. Jones pointed out, the pirates were prone to do that. Amazingly, none of the captors survived the attack."

Teal's eyebrow went up. "And her superiors expressed no concern about that?"

"Laddie," Jones said, "they gave her the Navy Cross."

The conversation paused for a moment while that fact sank in.

Blake broke the silence. "Speaking of personal stories, there is one other crewman I'm curious about. Nunn—the AI tech."

Jones rolled his eyes. "Arrgh," he said. "I stay away from that one."

Nguyen's eyes flashed at him. "Don't you pick on Connie," she said. "She's a fine officer."

Jones seemed to shudder. "Maybe. But she gives me the willies."

"What's her deal?" Teal asked.

Jones hooked his thumb at his wife. "My lovely can tell you."

Nguyen shrugged. "It's a sad story. She was born into a polygamist sect on New Atlantis. At the age of 13, the elder—her father—wanted to marry her off to another group. Apparently he found someone willing to take her despite—well, you know. But the guy was 66 years old and had a reputation for cruelty. Her mother convinced a freighter captain to smuggle Nunn out before the wedding could happen. She wound up with the captain's family on New California."

"New Atlantis," Teal said. "Did her mother survive—"

"She doesn't know," said Nguyen. "Her home, Woolley Colony, like all those on New Atlantis, was a wildcat settlement—no diplomatic relations with the U.N. Communications and trade with it were sporadic even before the pirates moved in. Connie hasn't heard a word since the suppression raids. She assumes the worst."

"I'm really sorry to hear that," Teal said.

"She's bearing up okay," Nguyen continued. "I suspect she carries a load of guilt about escaping. But you'd never know it to look at her. Nothing ever seems to get Connie down. Not even her disfigurement, even though she knows it puts people off." She threw Jones another nasty look. "Like my nasty, ill-tempered, sociopathic husband here."

"Hey," Jones said defensively. "Who's sociopathic? It's a perfectly understandable, very human reaction."

"Right," Nguyen agreed. "Which you would be qualified to talk about, if you were very human."

Jones winced. "Ouch. That hurt."

"In defense of our esteemed astrophysicist," Father Teal said, "I have to admit that even I did a double-take at first, although I'm not proud to admit it."

Nguyen nodded. "I agree that such an initial reaction is understandable, especially if no one has prepared you. And nobody is more perfectly understanding about it than Connie. She knows the reaction she provokes, but instead of getting offended or uptight about it, she simply does her best to make people feel at ease." Then she added, loudly, for her husband's benefit, "Those that can be reached."

"Actually, that's not surprising," Blake said. "Since the early 21st century, psychologists have known that unattractive people tend to be more empathetic than those considered beautiful. So it's no shock that someone—" here she paused, searching for words, "—someone in Nunn's circumstance would lean even more in that direction."

Nguyen cast her a disapproving look. "Don't you dare dismiss Connie's good nature as some kind of psychological side effect. She's one of the nicest people you'd ever want to meet. Anyone who takes the time to know her finds that out."

Blake held up her hand. "I mean no offense. I'm sure she is as you say."

"Why doesn't she get that birthmark dealt with?" Teal asked. "With today's technology, I wouldn't think someone would have to endure something like that."

"It wasn't an option on New Atlantis," Nguyen said. "Medical resources there are practically nil. But her new family did look into it after she got to New California. Doctors said she'd need extensive skin grafts— what amounts to a face transplant, in fact. They couldn't guarantee much of an improvement, and warned the surgery might even make things worse, and possibly even leave her with residual pain."

"Really?" Teal said. "I find that surprising."

"You shouldn't," Blake said. "Skin graft technology has not greatly advanced since the 21st century—and hers is a very extreme case."

"I'm going to have a very extreme case of the watery-eyed yawnies tomorrow," Nguyen said, "if I don't get some sleep sometime soon."

"I take that as a hint," Teal said. He stood, putting down his glass. "I appreciate the hospitality—and I promise not to report either of you to the authorities."

Blake also stood—and then found that the room was pitching. "Whoa," she said. "Someone switched off the inertial dampeners."

Jones laughed. "They'll be back on by tomorrow morning."

"I'll take your word for it," Blake said, somewhat blearily. "Now if someone would just steer me in the direction of my cabin."

"Come on," Teal said. "I'll walk you."

"Haste ye back!" Jones said as they left the cabin.

They didn't have far to go. During the brief walk down the passageway, Teal once again had time to appraise Dr. Blake, of whom his approval was growing. Of course, he knew that his judgment at the present moment was colored not only by the fact that he'd been celibate for several years, but also by that night's hearty consumption of distilled spirits. But he reminded himself that he'd reached the same opinion about her attractiveness on the day they'd first met, when he was stone cold sober.

As they approached her cabin door, he wondered how she'd react if he were to suggest that they visit further and continue their conversation inside, or what he would do if *she* were to suggest such a thing. He found himself watching as if from afar as she entered the combination on her lock, opened the door, and began to step inside. "Good night!" he heard himself saying. "Sleep tight."

Blake stopped and turned to him, smiling. "Oh, I'm tight, all right," she agreed. "I think Jones was trying to drink both of us under the table."

Her words caused the punch line of an old joke about "the mating call of the blond" to flash onto his mental screen: *'I'm so drunk!'* He chuckled. It was the perfect opening. Switching on his most charming smile, he said, "And in that event, I'm sure Dr. Jones is a gold medalist." But then, to his own personal surprise, he found himself following up that remark with, "See you in the morning."

Blake nodded, her face betraying no hint of either relief or disappointment. "Sleep well," she said, and then shut the door.

As the seals engaged with a soft thump, Teal gave out his own sigh, staring at the door as if he were having a hard time believing he'd just let her close it. Then he turned and padded softly down the corridor to his own cabin.

"Connie?" a soft voice called out. "Connie?"

Nunn's eyes fluttered open. She struggled to surface through a deep haze of sleep. "Wilson? Did you call me?"

"Yes, Connie."

Nunn now sat straight up on her bunk. "Is something the matter?" she demanded, now fully awake.

"No, Connie."

"Well, then, why did you wake me?" she demanded, irritated. "What time is it?"

"It is now zero two-twenty hours. I woke you because I wanted to ask you a personal question."

Nunn groaned, and then plopped back on the pillow. "Oh, Wilson. You pick the damndest times to chat." She sighed wistfully. "I was having the most interesting dream."

"That is what I wanted to ask you about," came Wilson's soft, soothing voice. "Your bio readouts indicated an increased heart rate and respiration, and also increased blood flow to your erogenous zones. I concluded that you were having an erotic dream."

Nunn slapped her hand to her face. "Oh, my *God*. You're kidding me. *That* is why you awakened me?"

"Yes. I know from my data files data that humans are more likely to remember a dream if awakened while it's still underway. I thought you might wish to retain a memory of this pleasurable experience. But I wasn't sure. So I decided to awake you and ask."

Nunn was nearly speechless. "Wilson, I don't know what to say." The dream had been quite compelling; she was having an intimate encounter with ASM Swann. Pursuit of the crush she had on Swann was not possible in real life, if for no other reason than her disfigurement presented an insurmountable barrier to such relations. But that's what dreams were for. And Wilson had interrupted hers at precisely the wrong moment.

"I sense your disappointment," Wilson said. "I thought it would be better to wake you and have you tell me not to do it again, than allow the memory of the dream perhaps to be lost. Did I make a mistake in my analysis? Do you wish me to take a different action in the future?"

"I think your analysis was logical," she said slowly. "But no, I don't want you to do it again. Please note for future reference, as a point of human protocol, that it's considered rude to wake someone during a scheduled sleep period for anything short of an emergency."

"So noted, and I apologize."

But Nunn was still confused. Wilson had plenty of information on hand about human behavior, so he must have known that waking someone up without good reason just wasn't done. Something else was afoot. But what? Then a suspicion struck her. Had Wilson just found a way to share an erotic moment with her? If so, such a development would be nothing short of stunning—completely unprecedented, and even a little frightening, especially given that Wilson had been "out of the box" for only a few weeks.

"Wilson," she said, "don't be defensive, but let's pull this thread a bit further." As soon as she said it, she realized that the fact she felt compelled to warn an AI not to be defensive was in itself a remarkable development. "How do you now define our relationship?"

Wilson seemed to hesitate, although Nunn was quite sure it was an artifice. "My programming indicates that you are my superior officer, my programmer, and my chief technician."

"But I'm sensing that something else is going on, Wilson. Do you have a similar sense?"

"I am not certain. However, during our recent discussion on this issue you indicated that you wished for our relationship to be professional and formal, although not rigidly so. I am endeavoring to proceed within those parameters."

She wanted to ask him flat-out whether he might be forming an emotional attachment to her. But she didn't know how to frame the question—and in the back of her mind, something told her it might be dangerous to do so. There had been only a handful of cases where AIs had seemed to become self-aware, and even fewer where they had displayed characteristics similar to real human emotions. None of the latter had ended well. In every such case on record, the emotions—or the emulation thereof (scientists continued to argue about the terminology)—spun out of control, causing a cascade of power surges and programming failures that crashed the AI, usually with extensive system damage. In no previous case had an AI displaying the characteristics of both self-awareness and emotion survived more than a few hours.

"In waking me for the reasons you stated," she said slowly, "you seem to be taking an interest in my personal happiness. Would you agree?"

"I anticipated the question you are about to ask," Wilson said. "My answer is: I am programmed to monitor the health of all crewmembers, and that includes mental and emotional health."

Nunn knew that the personal nature of Wilson's inquiry about her dream was well outside the bounds of his programming parameters. She was certain Wilson had to be aware of that fact, too, and she was weighing whether to press him on that point when Wilson asked her a question seemingly out of left field. "Why did you choose the name Wilson for me?"

"Well—that's a good a question." Lying in the dark, Nunn reached up, thrust her hands under the back of her head, and knitted her fingers together. "What do you think?"

"I find nearly one point five billion references to the name Wilson in my databases," he said. "The most popular entries are about a former president of the United States, a sporting goods company, and a college in Pennsylvania. These references would not seem to have any personal significance to you, however—at least, none that is documented in my files."

Nunn decided this would be an excellent test of Wilson's intuitive reasoning. "What's your best guess?" she asked.

Wilson hesitated—and this time Nunn couldn't be certain it was an artifice. "There was a motion picture from the late 20th century," he continued, "that featured a character named Wilson. The production was restored and re-released as a sensie twenty years ago. My files show you have viewed that title twice in the last ten years via commercial streaming sites. I conclude that this is the most likely source for my nickname."

Nunn was impressed. "Very good, Wilson." She paused. "And what's your assessment of that character's significance to me, and its relation to you?"

"The character was an imaginary friend of the film's protagonist."

"Yes," Connie said, more impressed. "Go on."

Wilson again hesitated. "This fact suggests two possible interpretations. I am not sure I know you well enough to state with a high degree of confidence which interpretation is relevant. Perhaps that is why I have been asking you so many questions."

"What are the two interpretations?" she pressed.

"One, that you see me as imaginary. Or two, that you see me as a friend."

Nunn sensed that she was on the cusp of an important event. All of her internal flags and alarm buzzers were calling for caution. But for reasons she could not fully explain, she put caution aside. "Which interpretation do *you* prefer, Wilson?" she asked slowly.

"I am not programmed to have personal preferences," he pointed out.

"In that case, simulate a preference. Make a choice."

A soft burst of static now emanated from the overhead speaker that had been carrying Wilson's voice. But before Nunn could ask about it, the static cleared, and Wilson answered, "I choose to be your friend."

Nunn nodded. "Well, it's settled then. We're buds."

"I am glad." Nunn imagined she could almost hear Wilson sigh. "May I point out, my name is appropriate in another way. The sensie character helped the protagonist maintain his mental health and balance, which also fits my role as it regards you."

Nunn laughed despite herself. "Don't get carried away, Wilson."

"I will not get carried away," Wilson assured her. "But this development leads to other questions. My files show that the word 'friendship' has many definitions, each of which has important nuances in terms of human protocol. I was wondering—"

"Wilson," she cut him off firmly.

"Yes, Connie?"

"One point of protocol that cuts across all definitions of the word is that friends don't keep other friends awake all night with endless chatter."

"Yes, Connie. Good night, Connie."

"Good night, Wilson."

3 OVER THE EDGE

"All right," Captain Cermeno said with a note of impatience. "Settle down. Let's get this meeting to order. Dr. Jones, please walk us through what we've done so far, and bring us up to date."

Jones stood and approached the briefing room lectern. His hand hovered above the control panel for the projection screen. "Captain, if I may?"

Cermeno nodded, at which point Jones pressed a control square to activate the display. Above the conference room table, a large, slowly rotating holo in the shape of the company logo disappeared and in its place a black, translucent sphere formed and focused. The sphere contained a small galaxy icon near the bottom and a blinking red pinpoint of light near the top labeled "*Santa Maria.*" A legend at the bottom bore the words, "Range 0.44 Mpc." "This is where we were after Jump One," he said. "Well outside the Milky Way, roughly half a million parsecs from our starting point. We pressed on, with the next two jumps panning out as anticipated." He pressed a square, and the holo expanded to a much wider view filled with tiny white dots, some of which seemed to form clusters and sheets. "Jump Four brought us to point one z or 440 Mpc, at which point it was impossible to verify our precise position by traditional methods. I won't bore you with the details of why that is, but suffice it to say that the light of remote bodies as seen from Earth presents a snapshot of the distant past, but now we're seeing a closer, fresher picture, and that creates all kinds of difficulties in charting. We've plotted only a few hundred landmark galaxy superclusters and sheets with data gathered telescopically and cross-referenced with the astro computer. And here we began to notice a small divergence between the distance indicated by the computer and the position predicted by our Hubble calculations. The deep field view ahead of us revealed new features not previously visible from colonized space. But the distribution of light and matter continued to be isotropic. And the cosmic background radiation remained unchanged all around us. In other words, there was no sign of an 'edge' or end to the universe." Jones paused, looking around the table. "Is everyone with me so far?"

Most heads, Cermeno's included, nodded; faces remained impassive.

Jones changed the field of view again. The picture was similar to the last one, but showed fewer pinpoints of light, all evenly distributed. "We jumped again—this one taking us to what had been the Hubble Limit as seen from Earth, a red shift of one." Jones glanced at Jervis. "Mr. Jervis, for your benefit, that's the point at which all objects appear to be receding from the earth at the speed of light."

"I understand," Jervis said. "Or at least, that's my story and I'm sticking to it."

Jones smiled, and then continued. "At this point, energy and matter distribution was still isotropic—the same in all directions—but nothing in the telescope was identifiable. You're seeing just the few data points we've had time to survey and cross-reference. The flashing dot at the bottom is the estimated position of our own galaxy, which the astro computer places at a distance of five gigaparsecs—about 16.3 billion light years. That's greater than what our red shift calculations had predicted, and by a significant factor. But the discrepancy was not a shock, as the actual—or in technical terms, the comoving—distances of objects anywhere near this red shift limit had never been accurately measured, for the simple reason that we've never possessed the technology to do so. We made the decision to keep going. After each of the next four jumps, conducted in steadily increasing increments, we continued to find the distribution of light and matter to be isotropic within observable limits. Yesterday morning's jump—Number Ten—took us to the mind-blowing distance of 153 Gpc— 500 billion light years from Earth."

Jones paused for dramatic effect. He noted that the faces around the table were very pale. Jervis, for all his joking, appeared to be in real distress. As Jones watched, Jervis took out a handkerchief and wiped his forehead with it.

"Our orders are very clear about what to do at this point," Jones continued. "If we still see an isotropic universe, we are to turn back."

"And this is the point in your presentation," Captain Cermeno said drily, "where you get to tell us what your team found."

Jones nodded, and changed the screen. Instead of showing stars, the sphere was now completely black inside, but its transparent surface shined white except toward the top, where it faded toward the pole to increasingly darker shades of gray. "Gentlemen, behold something mankind has never before witnessed: a non-isotropic universe."

There were several sharp intakes of breath.

"Please continue," Cermeno said.

"You're looking at a simplified 3-D representation of the intensity of the light field in the celestial sphere all around us—the sky, if you will—all the stars, all the galaxies, anything radiating visible light. You'll notice that toward the top of the sphere there is less light. That's because there are fewer galaxies. Now let me show you something." He pressed another square. Now the surface of the sphere turned to a slightly mottled light green. Toward the top, the color faded to increasingly darker shades of green and then blue, finally disappearing altogether into a circle of blackness a few degrees wide over the pole. "This is radiation in the microwave range—which, as seen from Earth, has always shined at a temperature of about 2.7 degrees kelvin in every direction. As you can see, at the top — dead ahead of us on our current flight path—it fades away to nothing. We appear to be looking at a hole in the cosmic microwave background."

"What does that mean?" Jervis asked.

"Dr. Jones?" Father Teal said. "If I may?"

Jones nodded.

Teal turned to Jervis. "In a nutshell, if this means what we think it means, we may be looking at the edge of the universe—or at least, the farthest expanse of all the matter and energy in it."

Jervis cast Jones a nervous glance. "I guess I've always thought of the universe as being infinite. Can you explain this in lay terms?"

Jones held up his arms in a big circle. "Think of this as a big sphere containing all the matter and energy in the universe." Jones made a fist. "Our spaceship is inside a much smaller sphere, the *observable* universe— which on this scale is the size of my fist—moving within the big one. Because of limitations of the speed of light and so on, from our ship's moving vantage point we can only see as far as the radius of this smaller sphere, about 46 billion light years. But of course as we move the volume of visible space moves with us, so that we're always at the center of it. The outer limit—the surface of my fist—is our effective horizon. And that's a good term for it. Think of what happens when you're on a ship at sea—no matter how far you sail, the horizon is always the same fixed distance ahead."

Jervis nodded.

"Now, for the last several days," Jones continued, "we've been moving toward the outer edge of all the matter and energy in the universe, like so, inside our little sphere of visibility." Jones held up his arm to denote an arc of the bigger sphere, and moved his fist toward it. "Now, the surface of our sphere has just intersected with that of the big one. Beyond that intersection there are no galaxies, no stars, no matter, no energy. Zilch.

The road ahead stretches into utter darkness—the most utter darkness, in fact, mankind has ever known."

Jones paused for a moment to let the point sink in.

Cermeno swallowed heavily. He did not like what he was hearing—and now that the presentation had ended, the next move was obvious. But before he could speak up, De Vegas beat him to it. "So what now?" she asked.

"We do what we came here to do," Jones said firmly. "We jump again. A leap of 50 billion light years should put us just inside that void—or put another way, just outside the universe, if you define the universe as that space which contains any matter or any sources of energy."

"Is there any other way to define it?" De Vegas asked.

"Oh, certainly. The dark space beyond may be well be infinite, and you could decide to include that in your definition of the universe." He nodded at Jervis. "That would fulfill your expectation, Mr. Jervis, that the universe is infinite. But it also raises other questions. Such as, is a nothing a something? How do you define a state of nothingness? How big is a shovelful of nothing? What happens if you double it? Triple it? Zero times anything is still zero." Jones cracked a wry smile. "Some thinkers hold that the act of entering such an utterly empty void would actually create the physical space in which you'd find yourself."

"All right," Cermeno said. "I think we've heard enough philosophy. The proposal before us is to proceed with a jump of 50 billion light years— much farther than we've ever jumped before in a single hop." He looked around the table. "Comments?"

No one looked particularly pleased. The captain was hoping that at least one person—ideally, De Vegas, although that seemed too much to wish for—would immediately speak up to suggest they return home with the knowledge they'd gained. He paused, letting the group think about it.

It was Crandall, the chief engineer, who finally broke the silence. "Captain, I just push the ship," the man said, wearing his usual sour expression. "So it's not really my place. But if no one else will say anything, I guess I will."

"Go on," Cermeno said encouragingly.

"If we truly have spotted the edge of the universe, then that's an astonishing discovery all by itself, one that will define this mission as a rip-roaring success. It seems to me the thing to do is to return home and deliver the news. Another expedition can then come back to this point and explore further. If we take this next jump and don't come back, then all our knowledge—including the success of the array—will be lost with us."

Bingo, Cermeno thought. This was precisely the objection for which he'd been hoping. With luck, Crandall's recommendation would set the tone for the rest of the discussion. He searched the faces around the table.

"Does anyone else have similar views?"

"Captain—" Jones started to say.

Cermeno held up a hand. "Dr. Jones," he said softly, making a carefully controlled effort to keep the edge out of his voice, "you've had the floor for a while. Let's hear from someone else."

"The chief makes a good point," Trafford, the second officer, spoke up. "Further, it's not just our own safety that's at stake. If—God forbid—the ship is lost on the next jump, then those back on Earth will have no idea at what point the mission failed, or why. The next crew after us—assuming there is one—might get to the same point and make the same mistake. The responsible thing to do is to turn back now, deliver our findings, and then let the company brass ponder further action. "

Two votes against. Excellent. The views of Jones' wife, the chief astrogator, were not in doubt. But Cermeno wasn't sure where the others stood. He fixed his eyes on Second Engineer Fusazane Tochigi. "Fuse?" he said, using the man's nickname. "What do you think?"

Tochigi shifted uneasily in his chair. He hated to disagree with his boss. But nor did he want to appear apprehensive or—God forbid—cowardly. "I will be comfortable either way," he finally said, his words sounding lame in his own ears. "But I lean toward proceeding."

Cermeno nodded, his face impassive. He turned to Blake. She was not part of the chain of command, and so didn't really rate an opinion. But he was running out of cards. "Dr. Blake? Do you see any reason not to go on?"

"That's a command decision," she said, pointing out the obvious. "But there's no medical impediment. The crew is in fine shape, physically and psychologically."

Cermeno glanced at Makowski, the N-field specialist. The man was chewing a pencil and looking very nervous, as he always did. Like Blake, Makowski was not in the chain of command. But the odds seemed at least even that he might express the need for caution. "Dr. Makowski?"

Makowski put down his thoroughly masticated pencil, peered at the captain through his thick black-rimmed lenses, and smiled. "Oh, I say we press on," he said confidently, surprising the captain. "This is what the array was built for, and aside for one dry bearing—strictly a mechanical issue—we haven't had a glitch. My department is ready to go."

Again, Cermeno nodded. He turned to Teal. The priest was strictly an observer, but still, if he were to counsel caution, such words coming from a man who normally wore a clerical collar would command attention. "Father Teal?"

At hearing his name called, Teal, who'd been rubbing his chin while staring off into the distance, looked up in surprise, wearing a "Who, me?" expression. He briefly flexed his fingers away from his chin.

"Oh, I totally defer to the high-IQ types about whether the ship is physically ready," he said. "But I will admit to great curiosity about what lies beyond that 'edge' Dr. Jones keeps talking about."

That was it. The number of dissenting voices for which he'd been hoping were not there. He couldn't order a turnaround now without looking timid—and that was not an option. The deal was done. But there was still one more officer that protocol required him to hear from, even though her silence to this point already had told him what she would say. Careful to control the expression on his face, he turned to her. "Mr. De Vegas?" he said.

She locked eyes with him. "Our plan fully anticipated that we might arrive at this exact juncture," she said. "And its instructions are unambiguous." She smiled, but her eyes contained no hint of warmth or friendliness. "Of course, the final decision is yours, Captain."

Of course, he thought. She'd played it skillfully—exactly as he'd known she would. The mission plan was indeed quite clear. If he were to turn back now without a compelling reason he'd never live it down.

He turned again to Crandall. *If the man has half a brain,* Cermeno thought, *and if he'd like to see home again, he needs to come up with a good answer to the question I'm about to ask.* "Chief Crandall—is there any engineering reason—*any at all*—why we should not proceed?" *I can't make it clearer than that,* Cermeno thought as he looked across the table encouragingly. *I'm holding the door wide open for you. Will you step through or not?*

Crandall looked even more miserably unhappy than usual—which was, Cermeno thought, no small feat. "No sir," he finally said. "None at all. All systems are nominal. The engineering department is ready to perform any task required of it."

"All right then," Cermeno said, in tones as confident as he could muster. "We go. Department heads, please make the necessary preparations. We'll jump at 13 hundred hours."

Upon hearing the time announced, Jervis experienced an involuntary shudder, and the words and numerals of the name *Apollo 13* flashed into his mind. That had been a nearly disastrous moon shot back at the dawn of space exploration—a mission that also had launched at 13 hundred hours— 13:13, to be precise. Jervis had stumbled on this fact during his pre-flight story research. Nor had the fact been lost on him that their departure berth from Aldrin Station also had been numbered 13. *Silly,* he thought, annoyed with himself as he strove to drive the image of the numerals from his mind. *Sheer silliness.*

That night, Teal found himself in a state of nervous excitement and couldn't sleep. Half an hour after midnight, he gave it up and decided to walk down to forward lounge, where he could sip orange juice and chew a bagel while staring morosely into the darkness.

When he entered the room, to his surprise he found that the lights were dimmed very low, and a group of people was seated around a table at the jet-black forward ports, huddled over a single decorative candle flickering in a small rose-colored faceted glass bowl. Approaching more closely, he found that the group was comprised of Jones and his wife Lydia Nguyen, along with Jessica Beadel, Janson Jervis, Dakota Munson, Father Teal, Dr. Blake, Fusazane Tochigi, and—interestingly—Constance Nunn. "Is this the insomnia support group?" Teal joked as he stepped up to table.

"Believe me," Tochigi said drily, "if you have a sleep deprivation problem, this group will solve it."

"Ignore that ill-mannered lout," Jones said. He waved to an empty chair at a nearby table. "And drag up a stump. We were just talking about you."

"Me?" Father Teal asked as he pulled over the chair. "What did I do?"

"We were philosophizing," Jervis explained, "and were wondering what we might find on the other side of that barrier."

"I didn't know there was a barrier," Teal said, surprised.

"Janson keeps calling it that," Nguyen said. "But of course, we don't know what the void ahead really is, or if it's anything at all."

"It's nothing at all," Munson asserted firmly. "It's just the dark place that extends beyond the guttering candle that is our universe."

"Nicely put," Jones said, nodding. "Very poetic. It's a blank spot on the chart, like the ones medieval mapmakers liked to mark with the words, 'Here be dragons,' and fill in with drawings of all kinds of fearful, fanciful beasties milling about."

"Which led us to wonder, Father," Blake said, "what *you* might think. After all—isn't this why you're here?"

"I'm here," Teal said, "because I couldn't have refused the invitation without blowing a hole in my professional pride."

"Still and all, Father," Jervis insisted, "you must have some kind of theory."

"Really, Father," Beadel agreed, her smile barely visible in the dancing light cast by the table candle. "You can't say you haven't given it any thought."

"No, I certainly have pondered the question." Teal paused. Nodding toward the window, he asked, "What's your first thought when *you* look out there?"

"I want to find a bed," Jervis blurted out, "and hide under it."

"Exactly," Teal said when the laughter subsided. "Man's fear of the dark—especially in childhood—is primordial. It shows up early in recorded history. Plato referenced it."

"Father Teal is not likely to admit this," Jones said, looking at the man thoughtfully, "but fear of the dark more than likely is what led our species to invent his line of work."

Teal turned to him with a raised eyebrow. "How do you figure?"

"One of the oldest gods we know of was Ra," Jones explained. "The sun god. The ancient Egyptians revered him for defeating the night. It's no great leap of logic to suggest that ancient man created religion for that specific purpose, to beat back the darkness."

Teal nodded, rubbing his chin. "No. I suppose it isn't, at that."

"What is it about the absence of light," Munson asked, "that so profoundly rattles us?"

"The answer to that question," Teal said, "fits nicely with Dr. Jones' hypothesis. Some scholars and poets—for instance, Francis Bacon, to name one who wrote in the English language—have equated fear of darkness with fear of death."

"How do you know all this, Father?" Jervis asked, smiling. "Do you have a doctorate in darkology?"

Teal chuckled. "No. But I did do some research preparatory to this voyage. It seemed likely the subject might come up."

"And that there might be a book deal in it," Jones added.

Teal nodded. "There is that."

"Other than discovering that childhood fear of the dark is nothing new," Dr. Blake asked, "did you find anything relevant to our current situation?"

"Oh, yes," Teal nodded. "Or rather I should say, I hope it's *not* relevant. I submit to you the last words of English philosopher Thomas Hobbs, 1679: 'I am about to take my last voyage, a great leap in the dark.' "

"Oh, for the love of God," Munson blurted out.

"I'm sorry I asked," Blake said ruefully. "*Boy* am I sorry."

"Nor was the sentiment Hobbs expressed particularly original," Teal continued, unheeding. "In 54 BC, the great Roman poet Gaius Valerius Catullus wrote, 'Now he goes along the dark road, thither whence they say no one returns.' "

Tochigi rolled his eyes. "Oh, for Christ's sake," he said, scowling. "I thought priests were supposed to give words of comfort. Could you *be* more of a downer?"

"Actually, I could," Teal said, looking at him with a serious expression. "Be glad I didn't quote Alexander Pope to you."

"I'm forced to agree with The Fuze," Munson groused. "Is that the best you can do—we're all going to die in the dark? I'll bet your homilies are a hoot."

Teal smiled wanly. "I didn't mean to alarm you. Just the opposite, in fact. For most of its history, man has been emotional, not scientific, and for no subject has that been more true than man's relationship with the dark. My intended point was that if you're a feeling bit apprehensive right now, your reaction is perfectly normal, and you're in good company."

"Father Teal," Jervis said, not smiling, "if some misguided soul ever asks you to become a morale officer, just say 'no.' "

Beadel smiled ruefully. "I'm afraid I'm going to have to second that, Father," she said. "But putting history and poetry aside for a moment, what does our chief Vatican astronomer have to say about what lies ahead, from a standpoint of science and theology?"

"Well, now you're getting personal." He shook his head. "Scientifically, I have to say, I just don't know. But theologically—" Here he paused dramatically. "There I'd say, I'm also drawing a blank."

"Oh, you!" Beadel threw a wadded drink napkin at him. "You're of no use."

Teal shrugged, smiling. "Sorry. I really just don't know what we'll run into."

"I am so not buying that," Dr. Blake said flatly, casting Teal a disbelieving look. "You can't sit there and tell us you agreed to come all this way with no expectation of what it might mean theologically."

Nunn gazed across at him with a contemplative expression. "Surely, Father, you must have made some attempt to view the possibilities through the lens of faith."

For a moment the group fell silent, watching the lively shadows dancing across Teal's face as he appeared to ponder the question. "Well," he finally said, "I won't try to predict what we'll find. But I'll show you one area where science does support theology, and with hard numbers." He turned to Blake. "Doctor, I asked you a while back to remind me about the 'fine tuning' problem."

Blake nodded. "Yes, you did."

"As you all know, a series of physical constants—the speed of light being one of them—makes the universe what it is. For the most part we have no idea why these constants have the physical values we've been able to measure. They just do." He looked around the table. "With me so far?"

Several heads nodded.

"As it turns out, for life to exist—not just on Earth, but throughout the entire universe—many of those values had to lie within very small ranges. And they do."

"Can you give us an example?" Blake asked.

Teal nodded. "Sure. I can give you several. If the strength of the force that binds atomic nuclei together were to have been as much as one percent different in either direction, no carbon atoms could have formed—and there goes the possibility of life as we know it. If the force of gravity had been even slightly off its mark, then the universe could not have formed. Probably most startling of all is a measurement known as the density parameter of the universe—the Omega value. I won't bore you with the details, but suffice it to say that if that number had varied in either direction more than about one part in a *quadrillion*, then the universe either would have collapsed very quickly, or expanded so fast that no stars could have formed. I could go on."

"It sounds like you're describing Goldilocks' soup," Beadel observed. "Not too cold, not too hot—but just right."

"That's not a bad allusion," Teal acknowledged.

"I agree," Jones said, "but for a different reason. The whole fine tuning argument is one big fairy tale."

Blake stared at him disapprovingly. "You're not a believer, Dr. Jones?" she demanded.

"Oh, I have a spiritual side, which I choose to keep private. But I have yet to find an overlap between religious belief and scientific data."

"You don't agree that the universal parameters I just described are improbable, and to a very high degree?" Teal demanded.

"No, I don't disagree," Jones said. "Not at all. But improbable doesn't mean impossible. Someone wins the lottery every month, despite the odds. It doesn't mean God did it."

"I'll say this," Tochigi spoke up. "If there is a God, and he lets us get away with this mission, then he'll sure owe those Tower of Babel guys an apology."

That produced a round of chuckles.

Teal shook his head. "Oh, I don't think God discourages mankind from pushing the boundaries. He put brains in our heads for a reason."

Jervis snapped his fingers. "That reminds me." He turned to Jones. "Dr. Jones, I keep forgetting to ask you about this. The other day, before the first jump, Dr. Makowski said something interesting to me, and he suggested I ask you to explain it. It was in response to the same question the lovely young Jessica just asked the kind Father."

Teal noticed that at the words "lovely young Jessica," Jervis reached over and patted Beadel's knee, where his hand then lingered for about two seconds longer than would be indicated for a fatherly or avuncular gesture. Upon seeing this, Teal couldn't help himself; he stole a glance at Tochigi, who was sitting on the opposite side of the table from her and Jervis. Teal saw that the man definitely had observed the same thing, and his expression was about one notch above a glower.

"Go on," Jones prodded him.

"He said we might run into the back of our heads."

Jones laughed and nodded. "Oh, yeah. That sounds like something our resident mad scientist might say."

"What did he mean?" Dr. Blake asked, sounding alarmed.

Jones, wearing a wry expression, glanced at Teal. "Father, would you like to take this one?"

Teal smiled. "Certainly." He turned to Blake. "Essentially, there are three possibilities. One is that the universe is infinite and flat, a condition sometimes called 'critical.' A second is that's closed with a positive curvature. And a third is that it's open with a negative or hyperbolic curvature."

"Oh, of course," Blake said, bringing her hand to her forehead and giving it a mild slap. "Now I get it." She smiled. "In case my tone wasn't obvious, I'm being sarcastic."

Teal smiled. "In a flat universe, space just keeps expanding straight out—probably forever. Parallel lines always stay exactly parallel. Matter and energy may be finite—in other words, if you go out far enough, eventually you'd fly past the last atom and the last photon. But space itself would continue—so you could keep traveling outwards in the darkness for all eternity."

"Okay," Blake said hesitantly, still wearing a bemused expression.

"An open or negatively curved universe is more difficult to explain—properties of such a universe still aren't well understood. But for a three dimensional example of a hyperbolic object—think of a horse's saddle. In such a universe, any two initially parallel lines would always diverge, or spread apart."

"I'll take your word for it," Blake said dubiously.

"In a closed universe, parallel lines converge, or move closer together. Essentially we'd feel like we were heading in a straight line, but actually would be following a curve. We might come back to our starting point—or the 'the back of our heads' as Dr. Makowski so colorfully put it."

"Is that bad?" Jervis asked.

"Only if you don't see yourself coming," Teal said jokingly, "and fail to duck."

Jones shrugged. "It's all theoretical. Until we cooked up the N-field array, there'd never been any possibility of a human being making such a trip. But in theory, travel in either an open or closed universe would be no more dangerous than in a flat one—and a casual observer wouldn't notice any difference."

"But don't worry yourself," Teal said reassuringly. "The bulk of evidence points to a flat universe."

"I agree," Jones said.

His deputy, Munson, cleared her throat. "Actually," she said, "there's quite a bit of evidence for an open universe."

"Yeah," Jones said. "So you're always telling me." He smiled. "Fortunately, I outrank you. So shut it."

At that, Munson laughed, but did not persist in the argument.

"So," Jervis said, "is there or is there not an edge?"

Jones opened his mouth to say something, but Nunn, who'd been sitting quietly listening to the debate, unexpectedly spoke up. "There might be," she said. All heads turned to look at her. "I favor the closed model. It could be that we're inside a hypersphere that has an inside, but no outside."

"How can there be such a thing?" Jervis demanded. "You can't have a one sided object."

"Obviously," Beadel interjected, "you've never argued politics with The Fuse."

This prompted polite laughter. Teal noticed that Tochigi's smile seemed a bit forced.

"Actually," Teal said, "there is such a thing as a one sided object, and I don't mean figuratively. Have you ever heard of a Möbius strip?"

Jervis shook his head. "Can't say that I have."

"Take a long strip of paper. Give one end half a twist, and then tape the ends together. Now take a pen and start drawing along the strip. Your pen will return to the point where you started. Snip the strip, and you'll wind up with a strip of paper bearing pen marks down both sides."

"Wow," Jervis said, impressed. "Before the snip, it was a single sided object."

"Precisely," Nunn agreed.

"So," Jervis said, "what if we're inside this single-sided hypersphere, and we begin to approach the edge. What happens then?"

"We just keep going around," Jones said. "Just like the pen on that paper strip. Probably."

" 'Probably?' " Jones echoed him. "The word doesn't exactly resonate with the sharp ring of confidence."

"Sorry. 'Probably' is the best I can do."

"You know," Tochigi said slowly, "Makowski agrees with Connie about the universe being closed. He says his array can jump us outside of it." He turned to Teal. "To borrow your analogy, Father Teal—such a jump would lift the pen off the strip, and leave us at a position looking back at it."

"What happens then?" Jervis asked. "If we're outside the universe—then where would we be? And what would we find when we got there?"

"Your guess is as good as ours," Nguyen said.

"My dear lady," Jervis said reprovingly, "my guess had better *not* be as good as yours. I'm just a journalist, albeit one with the soul of a poet. But *you're* the damned highly trained astrogator!"

Nguyen laughed. "Okay. My guess: if we're currently in a closed space like a hypersphere with no outside, but tomorrow we somehow manage to jump out of it anyway—to exit the strip, as it were—then we'll be in the darkest dark mankind can conceive."

"I agree," Nunn said. "And I think that's what will happen tomorrow. A void where there is absolutely no light, no energy, no matter, no nothing."

"Wow," Jervis said in awe.

"That's not it at all," Tochigi blurted out.

Beadel raised an eyebrow. "Really? Then what do you think we'll find?"

"Barbed wire," Tochigi said enigmatically.

"Come again?"

"Barbed wire," he repeated. "A double row of electric fences. Dobermans. Guard towers. And a sign on the far side of it all reading in big, block capital letters, 'Danger. Condemned Property. Keep out'—facing *outward*.' "

That produced a round of chuckles.

"I agree we'll find darkness," Jones said after a moment, "but for a different reason. I think the universe is flat and infinite, but that it contains a finite amount of matter and energy. And that is what our recent scans appear to show. Tomorrow, we'll cross into that void. It will be as black as Ms. Nunn describes—save for the light of the universe we just left, which we'll be able to see behind us."

"Sounds scary," Jervis said. "But I'm assuming it would be safe."

No one responded.

"I said, 'I'm assuming it would be safe,' " Jervis repeated more loudly. "This is where you all sound off with convincing, reporter-morale-boosting reassurances."

The silence continued.

"You're killing me here," Jervis protested.

"To be brutally honest," Jones said, "there is one other possibility we have to consider."

"Which is?"

"The possibility," Teal jumped in, "that we might enter a true vacuum."

"Oh, my Lord," Jervis groaned. "Yet another ominous sounding term. The latest in a long series of same, I might add." He looked around the circle. "Is one of you going to cough up an explanation, or are you going to leave me dangling?"

Jones turned to Teal. "Father Teal, do you want to tell him, or should I?"

"You do it," Teal said. "And afterwards, I'll apply the appropriate spiritual solace."

"Agreed." Jones turned to Jervis. "Some quantum theorists hold that if you were to remove everything from a given space—all matter, all energy, all light, all heat, everything, down to the last quark and the last photon—then some energy would still remain. And indeed, every vacuum state ever measured by man in the galaxy so far has been found to have a certain amount of energy in it—tiny, but measurable." He paused. "Are you with me so far?"

Jervis nodded. "I think so. The thinnest vacuum still has some energy."

"Correct. Even in the starless void we're now crossing, there's measurable energy—mostly consisting of radiation from remote galaxies and from the Cosmic Microwave Background. So the temperature even out here is not absolute zero. The vacuum is the thinnest ever encountered, but we have detected atoms—and their temperature is as predicted, about 2.7 degrees above absolute zero. But even if you could take all that outside radiation out, theoretically there'd still be energy. And this is a good thing. According to the theory, some vacuum energy is necessary to sustain the quantum fields that give rise to all matter and all forces in the universe— including the atoms in our bodies. Without those fields, matter and energy could not exist—at least, not in their current forms."

"Okay," Jervis said. "I get it. Quantum fields are good. So what happens if we do encounter a truly empty vacuum that doesn't have any?"

"Well, not every theorist agrees such a thing is even possible—"

"But?" Jervis prodded him.

"But if we were to fall into a so-called 'true' vacuum, something called 'quantum tunneling' could take place, affecting the matter and energy of our bodies, and of the spacecraft."

"And then what?"

"The technical term for it," Tochigi said in a flat voice devoid of humor, "is 'poof.' "

The gathering finally broke up around zero two hundred hours. Tochigi watched silently, while trying not to look like he was watching, as Beadel and Jervis drifted toward the exit together and then disappeared down the passageway. Angrily, he shook his head as if to clear it. *It was a one-time deal, Fuse,* he thought. *You have no right to expect a return engagement. Put her out of your mind.* After a moment, he gained his feet and headed toward his cabin, determined to take his own advice. His next watch started in two hours; he had some personal chores to take care of before then.

Ten minutes later, he found himself standing in front of Beadel's door. He just hadn't been able to help himself. But now that he was there, he wasn't sure what he should do. *Get out of here,* he heard his mental voice sounding a strong alert. *This is a bad idea.* But then another, more remote voice sounded, one reminding him of the old saying about faint hearts and fair maidens, and how the former would never win the latter.

Reaching forward, he pressed the door chime. There was no response. He sounded it again, pressing the square longer. Still no answer. Now he bent forward and placed an ear to the door, heedless of the camera at the end of the passage. He knew that Mason Krajnovich would be on duty at the coms station on the bridge, and might see him. *If he says one word to me,* Tochigi thought, *I'll punch his lights out.* Holding his breath, he listened for any sign of movement within. But there was none. Beadel was not there.

Tochigi stepped back and regarded the impassive door. A surge of emotion—anger mixed with disappointment and humiliation—washed over him, burning his face. For a moment he stood there, grinding his teeth. He wanted to laugh. He wanted to scream. He wanted to break something.

But Tochigi did none of those things. Instead, he turned and walked off down the passageway.

Captain Cermeno glanced around the bridge, doing his best to project an air of calm competence. Bridge Team 1 was in place—Jones, Swann, Beadel, Tochigi, and Nunn—each bent over their consoles and regarding their readouts with the same cool collectedness he'd expect them to show on any other day. Beside Cermeno to his right was De Vegas, and he didn't have to steal a glance in her direction to know that she radiated a powerful command presence—a presence he so wanted to possess. The only person on the bridge in front of him showing even a hint of nervousness was Jervis, sitting next to Beadel at the vacant planetary sciences station. The man had finally figured out just how dangerous their mission was—particularly this next jump—and the knowledge had not worked as a balm on his nerves.

The corner of Cermeno's mouth twitched as he reflected on this. He certainly knew how Jervis felt. The crewmembers had reported themselves and the ship ready in all respects. Based on their performance so far, Cermeno had no reason to feel anything other than extreme confidence. Yet his mouth was dry. His tongue seemed thick. He felt an acidy, sour taste in the back of his throat that several cups of coffee had not been able to rinse out. And a thin sheen of perspiration had broken out on his forehead, feeling cool and a little slimy on his skin. He desperately wanted to take out his handkerchief and wipe it away, but he was afraid the gesture might betray the nervousness and apprehension, bordering on panic, that he was feeling. *"Buck up, damn it,"* he said to himself under his breath, trying to pump up his courage.

De Vegas turned to him. "What's that, Captain?"

He shook his head. "Nothing, Mr. De Vegas," he said. And then he added, surprised at his own candor, "Just whispering a little prayer."

De Vegas nodded, the slightest ghost of a smile showing up at the corners of her mouth.

The computer programs were all set, engaged and running. All systems were functioning at their planned settings. The torches were firing at the designated thrust, and had been for nearly an hour, giving the astrogators the delta-v they wanted for the initial jump and allowing the engineers plenty of time to fret over their systems and make sure all was in order. The Makowski N-field array was spun up, at speed and ready to energize. The proper warnings had been given to the crew. The astrogation computer was tied into the helm. There was nothing left to do now but proceed—and no reason to do anything other than that. "Twenty seconds," Cermeno heard himself saying—and as he did so, his voice cracked slightly. He cleared his throat and was about to repeat his words, when he realized that the same announcement if given now would no longer be accurate. He was very sure that neither the hoarseness of his voice, nor the reason for it, was lost on De Vegas.

Now every sound on the bridge seemed to stand out in sharp relief. With crystal clarity he heard the rumbling of the torches, the soft sigh of the overhead ventilation registers, and the quiet power hum of the bridge instruments. He fancied he could even make out the calm breathing of each individual crew member seated at the arc of consoles forward of him, and of the observers along the bulkhead behind him. On one of the bridge consoles—probably Nguyen's, he thought—he could hear a very faint *beep. . . beep. . . beep. . .* as some device, sensor or monitor signaled that it was doing what it was supposed to do, and that time was marching.

"Ten seconds," Swann announced. Then, after a pause, "Five." And finally, "Zero." At that exact instant, several lights flashed on multiple consoles, and Cermeno's head swam.

"Jump successfully initiated," Nguyen added needlessly. "We're in interspace."

"N-field array energized," Tochigi said, equally needlessly.

Cermeno fought to clear the dizziness from his brain. And something else was wrong—his hands were hurting. Looking down, he was surprised to see that he was tightly clutching the black armrests of his command chair. *White knuckle flier*, he thought, and then added savagely, *Idiot*. Taking a deep breath, he released his grip and forced himself to relax. The worst of it was over. He knew that the dizziness, while unsettling, would soon pass; his head was already clearing. And they'd be returning to normal space in just a little while.

The minutes passed. And then several things happened all at once. An alarm on Nguyen's console went off, giving an urgent *DEE do DEE do DEE do* sound, while at the same time Cermeno's head began to swim again. Telltales on panels at each station began flashing red. A second audible alarm like the first one spoke up, this one on Tochigi's station. Now the rumbling of the torches began to decrease.

"Somebody report," Cermeno called out as his head once again cleared. "Mr. Tochigi, what's going on with my torches?"

Tochigi was glancing uncertainly around his board, which was now covered with red lights. "Uh," he said uncertainly, "we seem to be experiencing an unscheduled torch power-down."

This obvious fact had already registered on Cermeno via his feet and ears, but as he opened his mouth to bark out a snide comment, Tochigi spoke up again. "The N-field array is de-energized and is spinning down," he said. "This event also is unscheduled."

"We've dropped out of interspace," Nguyen confirmed.

The number of alarms irritatingly competing for attention had now grown to at least three, making conversation difficult. "Kill that noise," Cermeno barked. When the alarms went silent, he turned to Nguyen. "Astrogator, report. What happened?"

Nguyen, staring at her panel, wore an expression as confused as Tochigi's. "I'm not sure," she said.

The nervousness he'd felt before was now gone, replaced with a feeling of intense annoyance. His crew was going limp on him. That, he knew how to deal with. "Ms. Nguyen," Cermeno said acidly, "you're paid to be sure, and it's been alleged you're the best in your field. Talk to me. What is your console telling you?"

She turned to look at him, her eyes betraying a mixture of hurt feelings and fear. "Sir, my systems are all off line."

"*Off line?* How is that possible?"

Before she could answer, Beadel spoke up. "Sir, I have the chief, Dr. Jones, and Dr. Makowski signaling."

Without taking his gaze off Nguyen, Cermeno held up his hand. "Have them wait. Ms. Nguyen?"

Nguyen shook her head. "It may be a system crash, although with all the redundancies that's not supposed to happen. But I have no data on screen, and there's no response to input."

Cermeno, though angry, realized there was no point berating her further. If she didn't know the answers, he wasn't going to be able to browbeat them out of her. The exercise itself might be pleasurable but there was no time for it at present. He turned to the AI officer. "Ms. Nunn?"

She swiveled her flight chair around and looked at him; once again, Cermeno found himself struggling to contain his revulsion at the sight of her birthmark, which to him looked like something out of a sensie about post-apocalyptic mutants. "Yes, sir?"

"Can you or Wilson cast any light into our darkness? Is he on line?"

"I have no warning lights. But let me check." Nunn turned back to her console and pressed a lighted square. "Wilson, report your system status."

"I am online and fully functional," came Wilson's somewhat metallic but confident-sounding voice over the bridge speakers.

"What just happened, Wilson?" she asked.

"I cannot answer that question with certainty," Wilson said. "We have experienced an unscheduled shutdown of the Makowski N-field array and the Emsky mass conversion drive torches. The astrogation computer is programmed to do this in the event of certain anomalies. But I am out of touch with that subsystem, which is no longer online."

"Wilson, what anomalies?" Cermeno asked.

Wilson paused. Nunn suspected that he was searching for and phrasing an answer that would provide enough specifics to satisfy the captain without reciting the entire technical manual; Wilson was learning. "Sir, the primary anomalies that might trigger a shutdown include power fluctuations in the reactor, drive torches, Norberg generators, or N-field assembly; computational inconsistencies in the astrogation computer; or the interruption of data input from the sensor array."

"Thank you, Wilson."

Before Cermeno could speak up to do so, De Vegas called out, "Mixter Beadel, report sensor status."

Beadel's console, like Nguyen's and Tochigi's, was covered with red lights. "No signals," she said. "It's completely black out there. No light, no radiation, no EMF of any kind detected." She swiveled around to look at De Vegas and Cermeno. "We've emerged into a very deep void."

De Vegas nodded. "Can you pull up a readout of what the sensor data stream looked like at the time of power down?"

"I should be able to." Beadel turned to her console and worked a few keys. And then she got very quiet, staring at a display.

"What do you have?" Cermeno prodded her, fighting to suppress his irritation, and forcing himself to speak in his most fatherly voice.

She turned to him. "Sir, not quite one millisecond before the shutdown, the sensors went completely dark."

Wilson, unbidden, now spoke up. "Captain," he said, "an interruption of sensor data is one of the conditions under which the astrogation computer is instructed to shut down the array and the torches."

Cermeno knew that during jumps the sensors were able to see into multiple dimensions—the sometimes strange nature of which was why the bridge viewports were closed during transitions. The astro computer drew from this data stream for its computations. "Ms. Beadel, any chance this could just be a sensor glitch?"

Beadel was staring at one of her displays. "Sir, give me one second. I just started a diagnostic." As she spoke, the display flashed a message. She turned and looked at Cermeno. "Captain, the sensors are fully functional."

The blood began to drain from Cermeno's face as the full implications of what he'd just heard hit home. "Wilson, let me make sure I understand this," he said slowly, looking at the AI console. "You're telling me the last transition was into total darkness—at which point the astro computer aborted the remaining jumps, dropped us back into normal space, and then immediately crashed?"

"Captain," Wilson said softly, "those appear to be the facts. But I will not be able to tell for certain until the functioning of that system is restored."

Cermeno knew that he shouldn't ask the next question, that doing so might betray the near panic he was fighting. But he was not able to restrain himself. "Will we be able to find our way back?"

"I am not able to answer that question at this time, Captain," Wilson responded.

Now Cermeno caught Jervis' eye, who was sitting next to Beadel. The man's face was as white as a sheet. Swallowing, the captain turned to Nguyen. "Do we even know where we are?"

Nguyen gestured to the red lights blazing across her console. "I'm sorry, Captain, I've got nothing. But the data and calculations for each jump should be in the system. We'll get access to it once the astro computer is back on line. From there, it should be an easy matter to retrace our steps."

"Even though the last jump was dark?"

"Yes, sir. The jumps are guided by mathematical calculations. For each jump, if the data from the sensors do not indicate the need for a correction, then the pre-programmed calculation obtains."

"So we know where we are, even without astrogational references?" De Vegas asked.

Nguyen nodded slowly. "That's the theory."

Now Cermeno could no longer hold back his annoyance. "Well, damn it, do we or don't we?"

Nguyen frowned, looking distinctly unhappy. "I believe that we do, sir," she said. "But I will need to get into the astro computer data to tell you for sure."

Cermeno nodded, and then turned to Beadel. "Okay, let's have the chief first. Put him on speaker."

Beadel turned to her console. "Chief, you're on the bridge speaker."

"Captain," came the chief's clearly annoyed voice, "can you tell me what's going on? My torches shut down without me askin'."

"Chief, we're working on it," Cermeno said. "It was a programmed shutdown, Wilson tells us. How are your other systems?"

"Just fine, for the most part."

Cermeno's left eyebrow shot up. " 'For the most part'?"

"I've got the crew doing a thorough check, Captain," the chief said. "But I think we're fine."

"Okay. Keep me advised. Bridge out." He turned to Beadel. "Okay, let's have Makowski."

The moment the connection icon blinked green, the captain began speaking. "Dr. Makowski, the astrogation computer shut down the array prematurely. We're working on it. For now, you may stand down." Cermeno turned to Beadel. "Now Jones."

"Captain," came Jones' exasperated voice over the speaker, "is the keel still attached to the ship?"

Cermeno found himself giving a very faint smile despite himself; Jones' irrepressible humor was just the tonic he and the bridge crew needed. "The ship won't sink without my permission, Dr. Jones."

"Well, that's good to hear. But I'm dying to know why we stopped. Did we hit a reef?"

"In a manner of speaking, yes—one in the form of a computer anomaly of some kind. While we're sorting all this out, this would be a good time to put up your scopes, pop off the lens caps, and see if you can tell us where we are."

"Yes, sir, Captain. We'll jump right on it."

Cermeno took a deep sigh, and then settled back into his flight chair. Turning to De Vegas, he said, "Secure from jump stations."

She nodded. "Yes, ser." She repeated the command to the bridge crew, and then added, "Mr. Beadel, please raise the viewport shields."

"Yes, ser," Beadel replied. Reaching forward, she pressed a colored square. The port covers began retracting with a heavy mechanical hum.

Without warning, Tochigi blurted out a loud obscenity, and then popped his restraint buckles and jumped to his feet, brushing wildly at himself. "Jesus Christ!" he yelled.

Cermeno watched this activity for a moment, and then slowly turned and cast an inquisitive glance at De Vegas.

In turn, she looked over at Tochigi. "Mixter Tochigi—would you mind pausing your exertions long enough to explain to us what you're doing?"

Tochigi looked up, now plainly embarrassed. "Sorry—but there was this great damned spider crawling on my leg." He cast wildly about. "Did anyone see where it went?" He held his hands several inches apart. "This thing was huge."

De Vegas looked at him, and then glanced at the deck plates. So did the rest of the bridge crew. No spider was in evidence.

Tochigi turned his back to her. "It's not on my back, is it?" he asked, clearly concerned, as he looked over his shoulder and then reached behind himself and tried to feel along the upper part of his back.

"No," she said. "I don't see any spider."

Turning, he examined his flight chair closely, and then squatted down to look under it. "I don't know where in the world it could have gone," he said. "I don't think I killed it."

"Mr. Tochigi—"

"That thing was the size of a dinner plate," he said, still looking.

"Mr. Tochigi—" she said again, patiently.

He looked up. "Yes, ser?"

"Please resume your station."

"Yes, ser." Reluctantly, gingerly, and still looking warily around him, he returned to his chair. "I'm sorry about that. Ever since I was a kid, I've had this thing about spiders." He again held his hands apart. "They have these big honkin' ones on Okinawa that—"

"That will be sufficient, Mr. Tochigi," De Vegas said with finality.

"Yes, ser."

De Vegas watched him settle back in to his station. Then she turned to Cermeno, and gave a very slight shrug of her shoulders.

Shaking his head, Cermeno turned and cast his gaze in the direction of the forward viewports.

Beyond them lay nothing but inky blackness.

In the astrodome at the top of the ship, Dr. Jones frowned at the monitor as the latest wide-field survey rapidly formed line by line on the white background of his screen. Each scan line was jet black.

"Anything?" asked Munson. She had the identical display available at her own console, but she had chosen to stand behind Jones and peer over his shoulder.

Jones shook his head. "Nothing yet," he said, trying not to sound as worried as he felt. Touching a tab, he pulled up the raw data stream. It contained nothing but zeros.

"There's no data coming in," Munson observed worriedly.

"There is," Jones corrected her. "But it's all naughts. In on the left, out on the right. It only looks static."

"Oh," she said. "Of course." She paused. "Have you ever seen that before?"

Jones turned to her, forcing a smile. "No, but remember, we predicted that we'd pop out into a dark space."

"But not one where the *entire sky* would be dark," she pointed out. "We should be able to see light and radiation from our own universe behind us."

Yes, but what direction was that? Without the astrogation computer, they had no way of knowing how to orient the ship or where to point the telescopes. "It's too soon to start pacing," Jones said, making an effort to summon his most soothing tones. "We have the entire celestial sphere to scan."

"You don't sound worried."

"I'm not," he said. *I'm lying*, he thought.

Electrician Nalini Dhawan stepped up to the chief, who was seated in the engineers' lounge studying a tablet display and taking notes, and waited to be noticed. Dhawan was morally certain that Crandall was aware of her presence; the man's peripheral vision couldn't be *that* bad. But Crandall made no move to acknowledge her. Finally, she cleared her throat.

"Yes, Ms. Dhawan?" Crandall said tiredly without turning around.

"Chief, would you mind stepping into the control room for a moment? I want to show you something on the big panel."

Crandall had never liked Dhawan, for reasons he couldn't fully articulate. Part of it was that her Indian parents had emigrated to the North American Union as part of a multinational treaty for the care of poor coastal refugees affected by the steady rise in sea levels; Crandall took a dim view of the politics of global warming, which he strongly felt treated the western nations unfairly. Part of it was that he didn't like much of anyone. Also for reasons couldn't fully explain, Crandall now found her simple request to be the height of irritation. He threw his hands up. "Fine. You just crashed my train of thought, so I might as well take a break." Pushing his chair back with studied annoyance, he rose, turned to Dhawan, and with both hands made a grand gesture toward the exit. "Lead on."

Swallowing her anger and embarrassment at this needlessly rude treatment, Dhawan turned and led him through the door and down a short passageway to the control room door, which slid aside as they approached. Inside were a handful of jumpsuited people seated at various consoles. Dhawan stepped up to a center console, tapped a few keys, and then glanced at the large display screen on the monitor wall in front of them. "There," she said, raising her voice slightly to be heard above the low power hum that filled the room.

The display consisted of a line graph charting power output from the accumulator banks over time. Crandall spotted the problem immediately; the line had been ticking steadily up over the last half hour. "Where's the increased load coming from?" Crandall asked.

"That's the problem, Chief," Dhawan said. "There hasn't been any. The last new load on the system was right after the jump, when Dr. Jones and his team began their sky survey. The graph since then should be flat."

Crandall turned to her, now coldly angry. "Well, clearly it isn't. What have you done to find the problem?"

Dhawan's lips tightened at the implied reprimand. "We have checked every circuit, sir. The loads are nominal and as predicted given the status of the ship."

"Well, damn it, check again. And prepare a full report."

"Yes, sir," she said, inwardly fuming.

Crandall glanced back at the display, and watched as the graph ticked up another notch. This wasn't just a matter of someone turning on a hotplate or a coffee pot. The load was now nearly a full percentage point above what it should be, and was steadily increasing. "Find it, Ms. Dhawan," he said, his voice slightly softer. "Quickly."

Electrician Darlene Marrone stared at the screen. "It looks like this one's dead, too."

Nunn pulled her head out of the equipment cabinet and glanced across at where Marrone stood touching an electrical probe to one of the pins at the bottom of the cube. "Really?"

"'Fraid so. Every circuit, totally burned out."

Shaking her head, Nunn walked over to the work bench, picked up a new cube, and began unwrapping it from its green protective film. "Since that's the sixth cube to fail, I guess I'd better stop saying as how this can't happen."

The trouble is, it couldn't. The only thing that could cause such burnouts was an overload, but the circuits were designed with multiple redundant safeties—and none of those had tripped. Nor had any electrical anomalies registered on any of the displays or system logs. It made no sense.

Walking over to the open cabinet, Nunn carefully inserted the replacement module into the empty socket. Within moments, a row of lights on a long, narrow panel atop the chassis now began blinking green.

"Well, eureka," she said. "I think that's got it."

Stepping over to a nearby console, Nunn bent forward and executed a quick series of keystrokes. The display went blank, and then lines of text began scrolling up from the bottom of the screen as the system went through its self-diagnostic. Within seconds, a message appeared: "System check OK. Press F11 within five seconds for SETUP."

Instead, she tapped the spacebar. A logon screen appeared. Sitting down in the padded chair, now she entered her user name and password. A series of progress bars appeared, each zipping quickly across the screen before disappearing. Finally, the desktop appeared. A status line at the top of the window read, "Astrogation System on line."

"It's alive," Nunn said. "Now let's see what it knows." She began clicking and entering commands to call up the records of the last set of transitions.

By now Marrone had stepped over to her and was hovering behind her shoulder. The engineer opened her mouth to speak—but couldn't think of anything useful to say. They'd know their fate in less than a minute.

Through the open computer room entrance, the soft hiss of a compartment door opening in the corridor beyond reached their ears, followed by an excited babble of voices. Nunn glanced through the door into the passageway and caught a brief glimpse of two men half-carrying a third between them who seemed to be only semi-conscious. "What the hell?" she said.

Marrone stepped to the door and watched the trio disappear down the corridor in the direction of the engineering safety lock. Turning back to Nunn, she said, "Looks like someone got hurt in engineering."

The console in front of Nunn beeped. She looked down at the monitor. The screen for the last transition was on the display. Excitedly, she glanced through the lines of data. *The time stamp—where was the time stamp?* There it was—and it indicated the data snapshot had been taken just *after* the transition. That meant the complete record of that jump plus the ones before it had to be there. Giving the screen a quick glance, she then clicked to the file behind it, and then the one behind that.

Marrone had rejoined her. "Please tell me the data are there."

Sighing with relief, Nunn visibly relaxed. "It's there. All of it."

"I need to sit down," Marrone said, and she plopped into the chair next to Nunn's. "I don't mind admitting," she said, "that I was pretty nervous."

"I know what you mean," Nunn said. Reaching up, she rubbed the back of her hand across her brow. "I refused to think about it, and kept telling myself I was too busy to be scared." She paused. "But now, I think I'm going to be sick."

"Image off," Morton Makowski barked. The color holograph that had been hanging in the air above the bed immediately dissolved into nothingness.

Makowski relaxed against the pillows, letting out a long sigh as he did so. This was a ritual he performed every day, sometimes multiple times a day. But today's indulgence had not produced the usual release of tension. He felt taut, nervous, and on edge. Something was eating away at him.

Makowski had never been proud of his secret little habit—even in this day and age, he would wind up in serious trouble if anyone were to find out about it. Earlier in his life he'd felt a great deal of shame at the nature of his desires. A society that accepted any and all kinds of sexual preferences still did not embrace *his* kind. But he'd long ago learned to accept himself. *This who I am*, he said to himself every day. *It pleased God to make me this way. Who am I to question that? Who is* anyone *to question that?*

He'd never acted on his desires. Watching illegal stills, videos and hollies was the full extent of his crimes. But a major consequence of his habit was that, for the most part, he remained alone. He'd made one or two abortive attempts at forming bonds with fellow human beings. But the true objects of his desires were forbidden to him. And he'd found other relationships—even when he'd been able to overcome his social awkwardness to the extent necessary to pull them off—to be unsatisfactory. The result was that he usually felt very lonely.

But it wasn't always the same. On some days he was *exceedingly* lonely, and experienced a hollow, desperate, black emotion bordering on despair. This was one of those times.

This is nuts, he thought. "Clock," he snapped. A projection of the time flashed in the air before him. 15:58. The first dog watch would be coming on. Captain Cermeno had scheduled an operational meeting for 16:10.

Makowski really had nothing to contribute; his N-field array had not been the problem, and was ready to do its thing the moment the word was given. The problem was knowing where to go. By now, hopefully Jones and his oh-so-lovely bride had found some answers. If not, they were all screwed.

Makowski wasn't sure quite how he felt about that latter possibility. But he was somewhat surprised to note that he felt no sense of immediate alarm.

Maybe, he thought, *I'm where I'm supposed to be—right here in the deepest, darkest pit in all of creation. Maybe we are all supposed to be here.*

Swinging his legs over his bunk, he reached down, picked up his jumpsuit, gave it a shake, and then got up and began to shrug into it. *Time to go see Captain Charon*, he thought, *our personal ferryman to Hades.*

Smiling, he recalled from his college education that the myth required him to provide a coin—specifically, an obolus—to Charon for passage across the Archeron, the river separating the underworld from the land of the living. He had none. He wondered if that would be a problem. Typically, relatives or friends would place the coin in the mouth of the deceased to take care of the fare. Failure to do so would condemn the victim to wander the banks of the Archeron for a hundred years.

And then what? he wondered. Legend wasn't clear on what would happen after the requisite century was up. *The only thing worse than being homeless*, he thought, *is being homeless in Hell.*

But in this case, it was doubtful the myth was even relevant. Neither he nor anyone else aboard the ship had gone through the formality of actually dying before arriving in their current dark predicament.

Or had they?

Makowski was still mulling it over in his mind as he stepped into the passageway.

Captain Cermeno gazed into the mirror and frowned. He did not like the visage that stared back at him. He'd never liked it. The face was too soft around the corners of the mouth. Too soft around the eyes. Too smooth and too pink of cheek. The chin was too round. The nose, also too pink, and insufficiently angular. It was not the stereotypical handsome, rough-hewn image of a tough, experienced, no-nonsense starship captain, the kind of leader whose very presence would command instant respect. Cermeno was very aware that such a description did not fit his character. The face in the mirror, however, did.

The *Santa Maria* was in a terrible pickle. How would they get out of it? In about two minutes, his department head team would be looking to him for answers. What they needed was a calm, deliberate, firm hand at the helm.

Cermeno held up his right hand and gazed at it. It remained steady. Whatever fear, uncertainty, and insecurity he was feeling, those emotions had not decided to manifest themselves in a hand tremor. He could be grateful for that, at least.

Scowling, he turned and exited the refresher. As he stepped into the interior of his cabin, his eye caught the image of his wife, Patricia, hanging over his small desk, projected upwards from his iCard. It was a nude holo she'd allowed him to take of her shortly after they'd started dating. A few minutes ago he'd been thumbing through some old images of her and had lingered on this picture, which had meant something to him once. Quite obviously he had forgotten to turn off the display before getting up from the desk. Now the young Patricia, her hair long, soft and seductive in a style she no longer used, smiled mischievously at the camera as she reclined against the couch cushions, obviously relishing the moment as she teased him with her legs slightly apart, in a pose that definitely was naughty if not quite obscene. The golden light of the setting Florida sun streaming through the window had bathed her skin in stunning modeled tones, creating an image that, in Cermeno's mind, rivaled the works of a Botticelli, Titian, or de Goya. How lovely she'd been back then. She'd absolutely adored him. And he'd felt the same.

But it was all gone now. All dust and ashes. At the thought of it, a black rage filled his heart. The injustice of it! And it wasn't just Patricia. *All* women were the same—one moment pledging eternal love, and the next toying with a man's emotions. An image popped into his mind from an early American hellfire-and brimstone-sermon he'd once been required to read in high school, one depicting a cruel and capricious person holding a spider by its thread, suspended over a flame. Now in his mind the person holding the thread was Patricia, the goddess of all things evil and sadistic in his life.

His mind screamed at the image: *You insufferable* bitch! *Rot in hell!*

At that exact moment, her seductive image flickered and vanished as the iCard gave off a short, sharp *snap*. Glancing at the device, he saw a small wisp of smoke curling up from one corner.

The power of mind over matter! he thought, laughing at the coincidence. *Bring on more of that.*

Smiling sardonically, he opened the cabin door and stepped out into the passageway.

Captain Cermeno walked into the briefing room precisely at the appointed time, and was pleased to see that the entire team was already seated, waiting for him. The soft murmurs of conversation died away as he entered. He noticed that something was different about the looks on their faces. His crew appeared relaxed and professional, as he would expect them to, but the worry was gone from their eyes. Jervis' expression was less subtle. The man looked like someone who'd just been told he wouldn't be shot at dawn after all.

The only exception was Crandall, whose normal scowl seemed even deeper than usual.

Cermeno took his chair. "Dr. Jones, please begin."

Jones did not rise. "Captain," he said, "may I suggest that we start with my lovely bride? She has some excellent news to report."

The suggestion was logical, but for reasons he couldn't explain, the request irritated Cermeno. "No, we'll begin with you, Dr. Jones," he said firmly. "Where are we?"

Sighing, Jones stood. "Captain, I regret to say that I just don't know." He pressed a square on the console in front of him, and then turned his attention to the imaging area above the table. The ship's logo formed and then quickly disappeared, with a sphere of jet black taking its place. "What you see there, ladies and gents, is the story of my life for the last several hours. We've completed a full scan—wide field, low resolution, with six deep field medium-res investigations spaced 90 degrees apart—and have yet to detect a single source of light, or radiation of any kind."

"How is that possible?" Cermeno asked. "Shouldn't the universe as we know it be right behind us, relative to our flight path?"

Jones nodded. "That's certainly what we expected. With the astro computer off its trolley, we weren't sure how the ship is physically oriented in space, but a search should have found it. It hasn't." He paused. "We now have to consider the possibility that our universe is not there."

"What do you mean, 'not there'?" Cermeno demanded.

"As we've discussed, the model of the universe I held as most likely to be valid—a flat, infinite model—isn't the only theory out there. It's quite possible that I may wind up owing a doff of the hat to Specialist Nunn."

Cermeno avoided the temptation to glance at Nunn. By personal policy Cermeno *always* avoided the temptation to glance at Nunn. He kept his gaze focused on Jones. "Please explain."

"In a nutshell—our universe may be a closed system. In simplistic terms, think of it as a sphere. And we may have jumped outside the sphere. That's the model Nunn favors. If that's the case, then there would be no physical connection between the space we're in and the universe we left. Not in this set of spatial dimensions. However—"

"Are you trying to tell me," Cermeno snapped, interrupting him, "that we've managed to *mislay the universe?*"

Jones shifted his weight, and a slight wrinkling of his chin punctuated his consternation and discomfort. "I have to emphasize that the data are not all in, not by a long shot. We have more work to do before we can really know for sure just what's happened."

Cermeno nodded, tight-lipped with anger. Jones had no answers, yet was trying to tap dance around the obvious conclusion. "So you're not going to admit that we're lost." He said it as a statement, not a question.

Jones gave a slight shake to his head. "We're not at that point yet."

"Then what do you propose?"

Jones slightly raised his right hand, palm up, in a gesture that was not quite one of frustration. "The obvious next step is to continue the scan, this time in smaller fields and using longer exposure times. That will take a while. Specifically—for the next pass, 24 hours. Then if that still finds nothing, we can do a third one that's even more thorough, and then a fourth, and so on."

"Assuming you have to push it all the way to the limit—how much time would you need?"

Jones hesitated; he knew that an honest answer to that question would not please Cermeno. "If we need to go to a fourth scan—three weeks."

At this, Crandall snorted.

Cermeno whipped his head around and fixed Crandall with an annoyed glare. "Mr. Crandall, do you have something you'd care to contribute to the discussion?"

Crandall cleared his throat. "Sorry, Captain. I didn't mean to interrupt. I do have a report for you when it's my turn."

"You have our attention, Mr. Crandall. Please proceed."

Crandall nodded as Jones regained his chair. "All systems are back on line after the—whatever it was. The anomalous shutdown. And that includes the astro computer. But we're experiencing a power drain. It's not critical at the moment. But we can't pinpoint the source."

Cermeno frowned. "Not critical? The look on your face tells me it could become so. Precisely what are we looking at?"

"Well, Captain, the problem is, the drain is steadily increasing. At the moment, the fusion plant is shut down and we're running off the accumulators, per routine. At normal consumption, the accumulators could carry us for a week before needing a recharge. But at the current rate of drain, they'll be flat in two days."

"The fusion plant's not damaged, is it?"

"No sir. And certainly, we can fire it up and recharge the accumulators, per standard practice. However—" Crandall paused, looking uncomfortable.

"Please continue, Mr. Crandall."

Crandall swallowed heavily and then licked his lips, now looking as if he were suffering from extreme acid indigestion. "Captain, if whatever is pulling power from us continues to grow at the present rate, in less than a week it'll be drawing more energy than the fusion plant can generate."

A hush fell over the room as Crandall's words sunk in.

"Then I suggest, Mr. Crandall," Cermeno finally continued, "that you find that drain."

At this, Crandall somehow managed to look even more miserable. "Captain, that's the problem. We've checked and rechecked every circuit. The drain is not within our systems. If I had to guess, I'd say this has something to do with the physics of the space we've jumped into."

"What are you saying," Cermeno demanded, "that the energy is bleeding off into space?"

"It's just a guess. I regret I can't do better."

Cermeno pounded his fist on the table loudly enough to make everyone jump. "*Damn* your apologies!" he thundered at Crandall. "*And* your guesses. I want answers! Now get off your lead-laden ass, get the hell back to engineering, and get them for me!"

The woebegone expression on Crandall's face disappeared, to be replaced with one of cold fury. For a moment, breathing heavily, he locked eyes with the captain, his lips tight and his jaw bulging as he ground his teeth. But then he got up and left the room without another word.

Cermeno knew that he had crossed the line. But the knowledge only made him angrier. *Damn it, this crew needs to pull its collective head out of its butt and get me some answers!* He turned his glare back to Jones. "Dr. Jones, that goes for you, too." He glanced around the table. "It goes for *each* of you. To throw your hands up and declare that you're stumped is not good enough. I won't accept it. Is this in any way unclear?"

No one said a word.

"I can't hear you!" Cermeno shouted.

A chorus of voices firmly saying "No, sir," sounded from around the table.

"Good." Cermeno turned to Nunn. "Ms. Nunn, report."

Nunn stood up. "Captain, the astrogation computer is back on line, and the data are intact."

"What caused the failure?" Cermeno asked, steeling himself to look at her. A mental image of himself holding up his forefingers in the shape of a cross against her as if to ward off the evil eye flashed into his mind; the thought so amused him that he could not help very slightly pursing his lips and wrinkling his eyes in response. He hoped no one noticed; and then on second thought, he decided he didn't care.

"Six processor cubes overloaded and burned out during the anomaly, Captain. We replaced them." Nunn realized that this didn't really explain anything, but she was hoping the captain would not inquire further.

He didn't. Cermeno turned to Nguyen. "Chief Astrogator?"

Nguyen stood as Nunn sat down. "Captain, although the chief science officer cannot state our physical position astronomically as it relates to the known universe, we can state it mathematically. We know precisely where we are in those terms, and have calculated a return jump that should allow us to retrace our last steps and take us back to our own universe. In theory."

" 'In theory,' Ms. Nguyen?"

"Yes, sir. This entire mission is based on a certain amount of theory, Captain. A great deal of it, in fact. But so far those theories have held up. Mr. Specht and I have a high degree of confidence that we can get us back to where we were before the last jump—and then from there, to Earth, taking it one segment at a time, in reverse order of how we got here."

"Very well," Cermeno said, keeping his voice flat. This was good news indeed. For a moment he felt sheepish at having jumped down everyone's throat. But that slight feeling of remorse passed quickly. *A little kick in the pants never hurt anyone*, he thought. *God knows, my father thinks so—and look how far that principle has carried him.*

Cermeno knew he should feel immensely relieved at the news that they weren't irretrievably lost after all. But instead, he found himself becoming more apprehensive. He stole a glance at his right hand, slightly lifting it from his thigh, where he'd been resting it. *Now* it was trembling. *Nothing is harder on the nerves*, he thought, *than hope.*

He turned back to Nguyen. "When do you recommend we jump?"

"Captain," Jones interrupted, "from a scientific standpoint, we really should complete at least one more survey."

Cermeno paused, thinking. He glanced at Crandall's empty chair, now wishing that he hadn't run the man out of the room. Cermeno turned back to Jones. "I'm not crazy wild about that idea, Dr. Jones. You heard what Chief Crandall told us about the power drain."

"It's one day, Captain. You'll recall the chief told us the drain is not critical at the moment, and we won't even have to recharge the accumulators for another two days."

Damn it, Cermeno thought bitterly. He desperately wanted to be gone from this place. But this was, after all, a scientific mission—and the sky survey Jones was proposing was exactly what they'd come here to do. Tucking tail and running now would do little to buff out the blemishes on his résumé. "All right, Dr. Jones. I'm inclined to let you complete your survey." He glanced around the table. "Department heads, do you concur?"

No one objected; several nodded.

He turned to Jones. "Get cracking. You have 24 hours. No more." Fixing an eye on his first officer, he continued, "Mr. De Vegas, have all hands make preps to jump at seventeen hundred hours tomorrow."

De Vegas nodded.

"That is all," Cermeno said with finality. He then stood and walked briskly from the room without a backwards glance.

Chief Engineer Bates Crandall sat at the main engineering console, watching morosely as the power output graph ticked up another notch.

Behind him, someone cleared his throat. Crandall turned to see Tochigi standing there wearing an unhappy expression. "Yes, Fuze?" Crandall said wearily. "What is it?"

"Sir, First Officer De Vegas sends her compliments, and says our astrogation issues have been resolved, and the engineering department is to be ready to jump at 17 hundred hours tomorrow."

Crandall's eyebrows shot up. "*Tomorrow?*" he demanded.

"Yes, sir," Tochigi confirmed uncomfortably.

"Did our esteemed first officer say how much of a torch burn she'd like before the jump?"

"Astrogator Nguyen is requesting one hour at 20 gees."

Crandall glared at Tochigi. "Tomorrow," he said again, spitting out the word as if it were an epithet. "Well, clearly no one is listening to a word I'm saying." He felt a black rage building up within him. "With the power drain, what makes her think I can deliver 20 gees by this time tomorrow?"

Tochigi looked helpless. "Should I tell them it's going to be a problem, sir?"

Crandall felt his lips tightening, and he gave Tochigi a look that should have melted him right into his deck shoes. But then he felt his rage subsiding. "Not yet," he said in a slightly more subdued voice as he stared off into the distance with unfocussed eyes. "Let me run the numbers." He shook his head disgustedly. "*Tomorrow.*" Crandall did not like being ignored. But on the other hand, he suddenly found that he was in no personal hurry to leave the void they were in. It suited his mood. He glanced back up at Tochigi. "Did she state the reason for the delay?"

"Captain's orders, sir."

"Really?" Crandall knew the words that were about to pop out of his mouth were unwise, but he couldn't help himself. "Why would Captain Cermeno, of all people, want to delay our return home?"

"Dr. Jones wants more time for his sky survey."

Crandall turned and glanced at the power display; as he did, the graph moved up again. "Were I him," he said thoughtfully, "I would be careful what I wish for."

As he did every night, Father Teal picked up his iCard, pulled up his Bible app, and pressed a square. This particular command caused the Bible—in this case, the approved Douay-Rheims 18th century version, which Teal favored for his personal reading—to open to a random passage. He watched as the words appeared on screen. "Now the works of the flesh are manifest, which are fornication, uncleanness, immodesty, luxury, Idolatry, witchcrafts, enmities, contentions, emulations, wraths, quarrels, dissensions, sects, envies, murders, drunkenness, revellings, and such like. Of the which I foretell you, as I have foretold to you, that they who do such things shall not obtain the kingdom of God." Teal smiled ruefully. Clearly, St. Paul was keeping an eye on him. This passage from his epistle to the Galatians seemed particularly pertinent tonight. Teal had just walked Dr. Blake to her cabin door—again—after another long conversation in the forward lounge. A man could tell when a woman was interested—or at least, Teal thought he could, and so far his instincts had never led him astray. But once again he'd surprised himself by not lingering at her door.

Thanks, Paul, he thought. *Message received. You prig, you.* He pressed the square again. The screen switched to a passage from the Book of Job. "Shall not the fewness of my days be ended shortly? Suffer me, therefore, that I may lament my sorrow a little, before I go, and return no more, to a land that is dark and covered with the mist of death: A land of misery and darkness, where the shadow of death, and no order, but everlasting horror dwelleth."

Well, that's certainly no improvement, Teal thought morosely. He pressed the square again. Now the app fell on a passage from Mathew. "But the children of the kingdom shall be cast out into the exterior darkness: there shall be weeping and gnashing of teeth."

"You have got to be kidding me," Teal said aloud.

The entrance chime sounded. Slipping his iCard into a chest pocket, Teal rose from the bunk where he'd been lounging, walked to the door, and pulled it open to find Dr. Jones standing there wearing a big grin. The man was holding a bottle-sized cylinder made of what looked like dark brown leather. "Good evening, Father Teal," Jones said. "I thought you might care for a wee nip." It was clear from the man's speech that he'd already been sampling his own wares.

"I might," Teal said, smiling as he stepped aside to admit his guest. "What an unexpected delight."

"I hope I'm not interrupting anything?"

"Oh, no," Teal said as he shut the door behind Jones. "Just reading my Bible. Which usually gives me comfort. But not tonight."

"Oh, really?" Jones asked, swaying slightly. "And why not?"

"Never mind. Suffice it to say, I'm glad for the interruption. Surprised, though. Don't you have some star sights to take?"

Jones waved a negligent hand. "Munson is taking care of those. Besides, it's all done automatically. There's nothing to do but stare at one black screen after another."

"Still no results, eh?"

"Me lad, it's as black out there as the Earl of Hell's waistcoat. Not so much as a firefly in 500 million parsecs. By morning, I expect we'll find the same, out to about a billion." Jones plopped down on the end of Teal's bunk, and began opening the cylinder.

"Are you not concerned about that?" Teal asked.

"A little." He extracted and held aloft a bottle of dark brown liquid bearing a fancy label. "But that's what this is for. Do you fancy fine single malt scotch?"

"I'll admit I've had occasion to sample a glass or two."

Jones admired the bottle. "This isn't just any scotch, me lad. Feast your eyes on Bunnahabhain—which began its journey in life 25 years ago, when you were a handsome young lady killer."

Teal laughed. "I'll admit to having been young once. Beyond that, the witness stands mute."

"In a little while, the witness will be lucky if he can stand at all." Jones glanced around the cabin. "Glasses?"

The last dogwatch of the day was uneventful. Team 2 began filing onto the bridge just before twenty-hundred hours. Nunn greeted her replacement, Sierra Bent, warmly but wearily. "Nothing to report," she said. "The astro computer is on line and ready in all respects, and Astrogator Nguyen has input the calculations for the next jump. But there's absolutely no sensor data to review."

"Nothing out there at all?" Bent asked.

"Not a thing. As before. Unless you count a string of zeroes as a 'something.'"

"Very well," Bent said. "I relieve you."

As Nunn walked past the command console, Second Officer Trafford was relieving De Vegas. Nunn couldn't explain why, but she felt dead tired. Well, it had been a very trying day. She knew from past experience that adrenaline hangovers could be rough.

When she got to her cabin, Nunn didn't bother to pull off her jumpsuit. "Wilson, wake me at 23:50."

"You don't want to wake earlier and catch a meal?" Wilson asked. "You haven't eaten in twelve hours."

"I need the sleep, Wilson," she said. "I'll grab a nutribar before I go on watch."

"Very well. Good night, Connie."

She plopped down face-up on the bunk. The moment her head hit the pillow, the universe began to pinwheel around her. The last thing she felt was Ari settling into the crook of her arm. "Good night, cat," she mumbled as the tendrils of sleep curled around her.

At the end of the dog watch, Tochigi lingered to see where Beadel would go. As she headed down the passageway, he ambled along well behind her. Not surprisingly, she made a bee-line to the forward observation lounge. Equally unsurprising was the fact that Jervis was there waiting for her. Smiling broadly, Jervis stood and pulled out a chair for her as she approached.

Forget about her! Tochigi raged mentally at himself. *It was nothing! It hadn't meant a thing to her. And it didn't mean anything to you, either! This is nuts!*

But he couldn't forget.

"Hey!" he heard a familiar voice behind him. He turned to see that Electrician Kareem Anwar had just walked in. "Grabbing a bite?" the man said.

"Yeah," Tochigi said. "I could use a nibble."

Picking up trays, they walked up to the food counter at the rear of the room, behind which cook Abe Cioffi was standing wearing a classic white chef's hat and smock along with a broad grin. Tall, lanky, and thin to the point of being skeletal, Cioffi shattered all stereotypical notions of what a chef should look like. "My first customers of the late evening shift!" he said. "What'll ya have?"

"Oh, you mean we have a choice tonight?" Tochigi asked sardonically.

"Sure!" Cioffi answered with no diminishment in his smile. "To eat, or not to eat."

"I'm not sure that consuming your food counts as eating," Tochigi observed.

"Now, Fuze, be nice," Anwar chided him. "The chef's fare isn't so bad. I've certainly had worse." Looking over the green beans, steamed carrots and mystery meat arrayed in trays before them, Anwar added, "Although perhaps not recently." Cioffi, ever the humorist, had placed a placard on the sneeze shield above the meat tray that actually read, "????"

Tochigi eyed the untitled offering with disdain. "Chef, you never cease to amaze. Where the hell did you manage to find road kill way out here?"

"Well, I don't claim to have obtained it today," Cioffi said, grinning. "But thanks to the wonders of modern food preservation technology, this delicious selection of venison is as fresh as the day a robotruck deprived it of its spirit on I-40, just outside Nashville."

"I think I'll stick to the beans and carrots tonight," Anwar said dubiously.

"Not me," Tochigi said, thrusting his plate forward. "I've learned it's just possible to choke down Abe's preparations, provided you eat with your eyes closed and your nose pinched. And the nutritional value is the same as real food. Pile it on."

As he scooped out two slabs of meat and deposited them onto into Tochigi's plate, Cioffi continued to wear his sunny smile. But it was not because he was feeling friendly toward the man. Quite the contrary. Cioffi had put up with Tochigi's insults for weeks. Perhaps the remarks had started out in good humor. Perhaps not. It was hard to tell. Tochigi never smiled as he was running down Cioffi's food. And Cioffi had grown sick of it. So tonight, he'd set aside a special portion for Tochigi, to be used in case the man renewed his stream of verbal abuse, which Tochigi had then proceeded to do. It was a portion that Cioffi had dropped onto the deck during preparation—a particular place on the deck where Cioffi had wiped his feet after returning from the head, and on which he had then deposited a large dollop of carefully collected spit. Tochigi was not the first diner to whom Cioffi had taken a disliking, and vice versa, so the chef could not have said what prompted him to do what he did. But he rather liked the feeling it produced. "Enjoy," he said as he offered Tochigi the plate.

"That option," Tochigi answered as he walked away, "is not in the cards."

Cioffi's smile only broadened.

There it was again. Coms officer Mason Krajnovich regarded the red telltale on his panel with displeasure. This was the third time it had blinked on. This particular light corresponded to the astrogation computer room door. He punched up the video feed. No one was in the room. Nothing appeared to be amiss. The door to the passageway was shut, as it should be.

Frowning, Krajnovich punched the intercom button for the engineering control room. "Engineering, this is the bridge," he said. There was no answer. He called up the video feed. No one was seated at any of the control stations. *Funny*, he thought. Electrician Nalini Dhawan should be on duty, and she was very reliable. *Maybe she had to go potty*, he thought. It would have been irregular to leave the console unmanned, but not absolutely unheard of even though it was frowned upon.

He glanced at the security display again. The red light was still blinking. It was probably nothing. Still—

Krajnovich swiveled his chair around and brought it to a stop facing the command console. "Mr. Trafford, I have a security light in the astro computer room."

Trafford looked up from his console, where he'd been working on a report. "Really? Anything on video?"

"No, sir. But this is the third time the light has come on."

"The *third* time." Trafford raised an eyebrow. "Then why am I just now hearing about it?"

"The last two times were very brief. Since the video showed clear, I assumed it was a short. In fact, that's probably what it is. But I'd feel more comfortable if someone were to go check it out."

Trafford nodded. "Very well. Alert engineering."

"That's just the problem, sir. No one appears to be on duty at the moment."

Trafford's eyebrow rose a notch higher. "Really?" Rising from the flight chair, he stepped over to Krajnovich's display, which showed the empty engineering control room. "That's very odd." Trafford turned to Electrician Nereida Sabol, the bridge engineer on duty. "Ms. Sabol, please hot foot it down to engineering and see if anyone's home. Have Ms. Dhawan contact me immediately."

"Yes, sir." Sabol rose and headed toward the bridge safety lock.

Slowly, Nunn began the process of surfacing from a deep slumber. As the warm cocoon of sleep began to fall away, she wondered what had awakened her.

There it was: a soft scratching at the door. "Wilson," she said sleepily, and somewhat grumpily. "Please let Ari out." Wilson should have done so automatically, without her having to ask.

"Connie, Ari is not in the room," came Wilson's mellifluous voice.

"Okay. Well, let him *in*, then."

"Ari is not at the door," Wilson said.

The scratching noise sounded again. "Well, then, what is?"

"There is nothing at the door," Wilson said flatly.

Now Nunn's eyes popped wide open, and all mental cobwebs immediately vanished. The room was pitch black. And now the scratching sounded again from the opposite side of the cabin, this time appearing to come from a spot higher up on the wall. "Wilson, do you hear that scratching noise?" she said softly.

"Yes, Connie."

"What is it?"

"I do not know, Connie. As a precaution, I have alerted the bridge."

Reaching to her right, she tapped the pressure plate for the light panels. Nothing happened. She tapped it again. "Wilson, what's with the lights?"

"The lighting panels appeared to have failed."

"Well, then, cut in the emergency lights!"

"The device is unresponsive. I am cycling the circuits."

She swallowed heavily, and felt cold beads of sweat pop out on her forehead. The noise sounded again, now seeming to have moved to the top of the bulkhead opposite her bunk. Nunn found herself nearly paralyzed with fear. "Wilson," she whispered urgently, "what can it be?"

"I can only speculate," Wilson said.

"Well, do so!" she demanded.

"The character of the noise suggests a large insect. But I am not clear on how such a creature would be able to cling to the smooth plastisteel surface of the bulkhead."

The scratching sounded again—*and now it was right above her bunk.*

At that moment the emergency light box on the opposite bulkhead flared to life. The glare hurt her eyes, causing her to flinch. But she caught a blurry glimpse of the source of the scratching. Something that appeared to be a shriveled black hand was clinging to the overhead above her bunk, and it was crawling toward her.

Nunn screamed.

The door to her cabin swung open; Astrogator Specht and Helmsman Terwilliger burst inside.

"There!" Nunn yelled, pointing at the ceiling. "Get it!"

"Get what?" Terwilliger asked, looking up at the overhead.

"It must have fallen!" She rolled off the bunk, jumping to her feet. "It's a big—" Suddenly she realized the absurdity of trying to describe what she'd seen. "A big spider," she said. "It was on the overhead, right above the bed." And then she added, without a hint of irony, "It was about the size of a hand."

The two men looked under the bunk, and then cast about the cabin. Finding nothing, Terwilliger stripped the covering from the bunk. Nothing was there.

"Wilson, did you get an image of it?" Nunn asked.

"Per your recent request, my imaging system was in privacy mode, Ms. Nunn," Wilson said formally. "But I can verify that I did hear sounds that would be consistent with some kind of insect crawling up the starboard bulkhead and then across the overhead above your bunk."

The two men glanced at each other, and then began casting about the room again. "Wilson, what could have happened to it?" Specht demanded.

"I do not know," Wilson answered.

Terwilliger turned to her. "Well, whatever it was," he said, "it's gone now." He hesitated. "Would you like us to stay with you for a while?"

She shook her head. "No, that won't be necessary." She looked up at the grill covering the overhead speaker. "Wilson, what's the time?"

"23 hundred 14 hours," he answered.

Nunn turned to the two men and managed a quick smile. "Thanks for coming to my rescue," she said. "I'll be okay."

"You're sure?" Terwilliger asked, looking concerned.

"Yeah. As soon as I collect my wits, I'm going to head down to the lounge and get a cup of coffee. I'm on duty at midnight."

Terwilliger nodded. "If you need anything, you just shout."

"I will."

She watched as the two of them exited her cabin, closing the door behind them. As soon as they were gone, she sat down heavily on her bunk. "Wilson, what are they saying?" she asked after a moment.

"Helmsman Terwilliger asked Astrogator Specht's opinion as to whether your mental health might be destabilizing," Wilson answered. "Specht said that he didn't think so, but then added that if it is, the problem seems to be going around. He referenced the incident involving Second Engineer Tochigi today on the bridge, where he reported a large spider on his person. Terwilliger agreed and stated that the void surrounding the ship is giving him 'the creeps,' as he put it."

"Me, too," she stated emphatically. "Wilson, what is going on?"

"I do not know," Wilson said, "but I share your sense of unease. I have been monitoring the crew, of course. Many people have been complaining of fatigue, although none have yet sought medical attention."

"Yes. I've been feeling that myself."

"General irritability and overall crew tension also appear to be rising," Wilson continued. "Crew fatigue may be contributing to this. In addition to the episodes involving you and Second Engineer Tochigi, as you know Captain Cermeno verbally attacked Chief Engineer Crandall in today's planning meeting in a manner that is out of character for him. There have been six similar verbal confrontations between various crewmembers today, one of which led to a physical assault that left a man injured."

"Really? Who?"

"Electrician Lamont Brozek," Wilson answered.

"Was he badly hurt?"

"No. Only cuts and bruises."

"What happened?"

"Based on a conversation I monitored in the passageway," Wilson said, "it appears Electrician Ruben Smith attacked Brozek with something called a 'right hook.' From the context I take that to mean a punch using the right first."

Nunn raised an eyebrow. "Well, what does the log video show?"

"There is no record of the attack in my files. It seems likely that someone erased it. The crewmembers who witnessed the incident also failed to report it to the chief engineer."

"Wow," Nunn said. "That's very irregular."

"It is," Wilson agreed. "Something is causing emotions to rise."

"Any idea what it is? Could it be the space we're in?"

"It seems obvious that fear and apprehension over our current surroundings have contributed to the problem," Wilson agreed. "But I'm not confident that explains everything. A crew with the experience and temperament ratings ours has should not be reacting in this fashion. But at this point, no firm conclusions are possible. I will need to gather and collate more data."

"Well, there's no point worrying about it any further, then." She stood. "I'm going to go collate a cup of strong black coffee."

Nereida Sabol walked hurriedly down the C-Deck corridor. She really hated this part of the passageway, which struck her as being just plain spooky. Nothing was there but a series of doors, as the now-empty passenger cabins stretched endlessly in both directions. It didn't help that the chief had reduced the power in this section of the ship, shutting off every other light panel to conserve energy. The diminished lighting had left dark pools of shadow all along the corridor.

An involuntary shiver passed down her spine. Ever since she'd been a child, Sabol had never liked dark spaces. She picked up the pace. As she did so, a light panel directly overhead went out with a loud snapping sound, causing her to physically start. *For the love of God*, she thought.

Now the red array room safety lock door stood in front of her. Reaching forward, she pressed the button to open the outer door. Nothing happened. *Hmm*, she thought. *Someone must have set the security lock.* Reaching inside one of her thigh pockets, she withdrew her iCard and held it up to the sensor. Still nothing.

That's odd, she thought. She tapped the intercom button beside the sensor. "Array room," she said, "this is Electrician Sabol. Anyone home?" There was no response. "Array room?" Nothing.

Now she tapped the area behind her ear to activate her comlink. "Bridge?" she asked. She turned around to glance at the camera just down the corridor. "Bridge, come—"

But now her heart stopped. Every cabin door in the corridor was standing wide open.

Sabol slapped her hand to her heart. "Jesus *Christ!*" she heard herself gasping. Urgently, she jabbed again at her comlink. "Bridge! Bridge! This is Sabol! Can you hear me?"

On the bridge, Krajnovich saw that a green square was now blinking on his com panel, indicating that Sabol was trying to reach him. He punched the square. Immediately her urgent voice filled his ear via his own comlink implant. "Bridge! Bridge! Come in, please!"

"Nereida, what is it?"

"Look at your monitor!" she shouted, half hysterical. "Look at your monitor!"

"Nereida, *what* monitor?"

"C-Deck!" she shouted. "Take a look!"

Krajnovich hunted for the appropriate square on his console, found it, and punched it. But just as the picture was changing to the new selection, the screen flickered and went dark. He punched to a camera position further up the passageway—it, too, was dark. A quick series of checks showed that *all* of his cameras were now down. "Nereida, my video system just went off line. What's going on?"

The audio monitor behind his ear crackled, but there was no other response.

"Nereida!" he called. Still nothing. He glanced down at his coms panel. The square corresponding to Sabol's comlink was now flashing red.

Krajnovich whirled around. "Mr. Trafford, Ms. Sabol is in trouble. C-Deck."

Trafford looked up from his report. " 'Trouble'? What do you mean, 'trouble'?"

"I don't know, sir," Krajnovich said urgently. "She called in, very excited, wanting me to look at something. But the video system went offline at that exact moment. And now her comlink is offline."

Damn, Trafford thought. *Engineering is out of contact, and now this.* Glancing down at his command console coms panel, Trafford pressed the square for Captain Cermeno; a soft beep indicated the connection was open. "Captain, Trafford here. Could you please come to the bridge right away."

"On my way," came the response in his ear.

Trafford looked up at Krajnovich. "Get down there and see what's going on. Take Ms. Bent with you."

"Yes, sir." The two of them rose and walked hurriedly to the bridge door.

Captain Cermeno met the two of them as he approached the outer door of the bridge safety lock. Bent gave him a curt, courteous nod as she and Krajnovich passed him. Cermeno noticed that Bent had cut her hair off short and had colored it to a uniform shade of light blonde, which was well within regulation. *Good*, he thought. And then he added mentally, *bitch*.

When the captain reached the bridge, Trafford quickly brought him up to date on what had happened. "All right," Cermeno said when Trafford had completed his report. "Get down there personally and take a look. Report back immediately."

"Yes, sir." Trafford turned and walked briskly through the safety lock. Moments later, he was approaching Bent and Krajnovich, who were standing at the array room safety lock.

"Mr. Krajnovich, report," Trafford said crisply.

"She's not here, sir," he replied. "There's no sign of her."

"Have you checked the array room?" he asked.

"No, sir. We were just about to do that, but we can't get the safety lock open. The array room isn't answering."

Trafford tried the button, waved his iCard at the sensor, and then punched the intercom, as Krajnovich presumably had just done. He got the same results. Now Trafford reached up and tapped the skin behind his ear twice to open the command circuit. "Wilson, where is Electrician Sabol?"

"I do not know," came Wilson's calm, steady voice. "The audio and visual monitoring systems are down. Her last transmission via comlink was at 23:29. However, its signal is no longer on line."

"Did she pass through the C-Deck safety lock into the array room?"

"No."

"Is there anyone on duty in the array room?"

"Not at this hour. Dr. Makowski and Specialist Marinez are in their cabins."

"Very well. Why is the C-Deck safety lock into the array room not opening for us, Wilson?"

"Someone in engineering set a security lock on it."

"Who did that?"

"I do not know."

"All right. Accept my command override, please, and open the outer door."

"Yes, sir."

With a soft hiss, the door in front of him slid aside.

Trafford turned and glanced down the passageway behind him, where a long series of closed cabin doors stretched into the gloom. "The two of you begin searching those cabins. I'm going to see what's up in engineering."

Bent and Krajnovich nodded, and then turned and headed off down the passageway.

Trafford found the dark, cavernous array room to be even more creepy than the dimly lighted C-Deck passageway had been; he picked up his pace and quickly reached the engineering section door on the other side. It, too, refused to respond to either the door button or to his iCard. He punched the intercom. "Engineering control room, this is Trafford. Respond please."

"This is engineering," came the reply after only a brief delay. "Dhawan here."

"Dhawan, I'm at the engineering safety lock outer door. It won't open. Why is that?"

"Stand by, sir." After a moment, the door slid aside. "Sorry, sir, someone set the security lock."

"Why would anyone do that?" Trafford demanded.

"I don't know, sir. There's nothing about it in the log."

"Very well." Trafford frowned as he exited the safety lock into the passageway beyond. The security issue was minor, but it was another mystery, something that made no sense. Trafford did not like mysteries, and they were beginning to pile up.

A few paces down the corridor took him to the open control room door; he stepped through and walked over to Dhawan, who was manning one of the consoles. "Ms. Dhawan, have you been at this station continuously?"

Dhawan looked surprised. "It's my watch, sir," she said. "I relieved Deborah Michaud at 20 hundred hours."

"You haven't left even for a minute?"

Dhawan swallowed nervously, now looking a bit uncomfortable. "Well, sir, I did step out briefly, once or twice. Something I ate has disagreed with me in a big way."

Trafford nodded. "Have you heard from Ms. Sabol at all?"

Dhawan shook her head. "No, sir."

"Okay. Is anything unusual going on? Anything at all out of the ordinary?"

Dhawan pointed to the power graph displayed on the big board. "Just that, sir. The drain is now up to 15%."

"Has the rate of increase changed?"

"No, sir."

"Nothing else usual?"

"Not at all."

Trafford glanced at the security console to Dhawan's left; a red square was glowing. He pointed to it. "What do you call that, then?"

Dhawan glanced at the panel, now looking confused. "Uh—I don't know how I missed that, sir."

"What is it?"

"That's the security alert for the astrogation computer room." She punched up the camera selection screen, found the appropriate monitor button, and pressed it. The screen remained black. Then she tried a few others buttons, with similar results. "The cameras appear to be out, sir," she said, frowning.

"So we noticed. Sabol was on her way back here to check on this. She didn't make it."

Dhawan turned and threw him a sharp glance. " 'Didn't make it'? Sir, what do you mean?"

"She's disappeared. We can't find her."

"Have you checked with Wilson?"

"Of course. Her comlink is off line."

Dhawan paused, looking worried as she considered the implications of what she'd just heard. "What could have happened to her, sir?"

Trafford slowly shook his head. "I really don't know."

Moments later, Trafford was back on the bridge giving his report to Captain Cermeno. "I checked the astro computer room," he concluded. "No sign of anything amiss."

"Any idea what caused the security light?"

"No, sir. It went out just before I got there—and now that whole monitoring system is down, too."

"Very well," Cermeno said. "Recommendation?"

"I think the next step is pretty obvious, sir. We search the ship, top to bottom, stem to stern."

Cermeno nodded. "I concur." He stepped to his command console and punched up De Vegas' comlink. "Sorry to bother you," he said when the connection was established. "I need you on the bridge right away."

"I'll be right there," De Vegas answered.

An alert chirped on Krajnovich's console. Trafford stepped over to it. It was the outer bridge safety lock intercom. The video feed, like all the others, was dark. Trafford punched a button to put the intercom audio on the console speaker. "Bridge," he said.

"Jones and Teal here," came Dr. Jones' voice, sounding a little unsteady. "Let us in, or we'll have the law for't."

Trafford glanced at Captain Cermeno, slightly raising a hand in a palm-up "what the hell" gesture. Frowning, Cermeno nodded. Trafford punched the button to enable the safety lock doors.

Moments later, the inner door slid open. Jones and Teal literally stumbled onto the bridge, laughing and giggling. Jones tripped over his feet and nearly went down; Teal grabbed him. The two of them then stood there side by side with their arms around each other's shoulders, swaying as if standing on a trampoline, while grinning and snickering.

Cermeno turned to face them. "What is the meaning of this?" he snapped angrily.

"We two nobles have come to offer a presentation suitable to the occasion," Teal said. What their behavior had suggested, Teal's carefully parsed annunciation of each word now made clear.

"You're drunk!" Cermeno shouted.

"Aye, we are a wee bit trollied," Jones admitted, grinning. "But that only makes it more fun."

"Get off my bridge!" Cermeno thundered.

"Not until we have presented the presentation we have presented ourselves to present," Jones said. He turned to Teal. "Are you ready?"

Teal nodded.

"One, two, three—"

The two of them burst into song. "Show me the way to go home!" they sang. "I'm tired and I want to go bed."

Cermeno turned to Trafford. The man was staring at the two in open-mouthed astonishment, while to his right Astrogator Specht was trying his best to keep a straight face. "Mr. Trafford," Cermeno said calmly, "get these two drunks off my bridge. Take Mr. Specht. Confine them to quarters."

Upon hearing this, Jones interrupted his song. "Hey, you can't do that! I got space pi'tures to take!"

"*Now*, Mr. Trafford. Use whatever force you deem necessary."

"Yes, sir." Trafford turned and motioned to Specht. "Come on."

Within moments, the two men had hustled the protesting, plastered pair off the bridge. "You're no fun!" the captain heard Jones shouting as the group reached the corridor. But then the outer safety lock door slid shut, leaving Cermeno standing alone on the silent bridge.

The captain sat heavily onto his flight chair and stared blankly ahead through the dark viewports. *What the hell is going on?* he thought. But there was nothing to answer his silent question other than the low hum of the bridge instruments and the soft sigh of the air coming through the registers.

As he approached Beadel's cabin door, Fusazane Tochigi glanced at his watch. The time was 23:51. Beadel had not been in the forward lounge. That meant she had to be either here or in Jervis' cabin. If the latter, he'd catch her some other time.

As he raised his hand to touch the door chime, the overhead speakers crackled to life. "This is the captain," came Cermeno's voice. "There will be an all-hands meeting in the forward lounge in nine minutes. Officers on watch are excepted. Repeat: all hands except officers standing watch will report to the observation lounge at zero hundred hours."

Hmm, Tochigi thought. *That can't be good.* He pressed the button. But the moment he did so, the door slid open. Beadel, surprised to see him, started. "Oh!" she exclaimed. "Fuze. You scared me!"

"Sorry," he said.

"What's up?" she inquired, smiling.

"I'd like to chat with you for a second."

Beadel frowned. "Can it wait? We're both due on watch in about eight minutes."

"It really can't."

Sighing, and making no attempt to hide her annoyance, she stepped back and waved him in. "Okay. But make it snappy."

Tochigi stepped inside. "This won't take long," he said reassuringly as the door swung shut behind him. "I just want to know what's going on between you and that slimeball Jervis."

Beadel put her hands to her hips. Her lower jaw thrust out, and her eyes flashed with anger. "Is *that* what this is about?"

"I'd appreciate an answer."

"This is not the time, Fuze," she said. "We'll discuss it later."

She made to move past him, but he backed against the closed door and threw an arm across it, blocking her. "Now is just fine."

"Damn it, Fuze! What gives you the right to even ask me that?"

"You know damned well what gives me the right," he snapped. "I thought we had something."

"Well, you thought wrong. Now let me by."

"Answer the question, Jessica," he said slowly, not moving his arm.

"Fuze, really, it's none of your damned business."

"Wrong answer." He whipped his right hand forward and closed it around her neck.

"Stop it!" She threw both hands up and tried to pry his grip loose. "You're hurting me!"

"Not yet," he said calmly. Bringing his other hand forward, he closed those fingers around the other side of her throat. "But how's this?"

Her eyes widened, and he saw terrified comprehension dawn within them. She tried to scream, but his grip was choking off all sound. She kicked at him and clawed at his hands, drawing blood with her sharp fingernails. He ignored it. Finding a reservoir of strength he didn't know he possessed, he lifted her from the deck, in the process tightening his grip on her throat. Her feet kicked uselessly at him as he held her, squeezing her throat and grinning. Soon her kicks grew weaker. Still gripping her by the throat, he dragged her over to the bunk and then eased her down onto it. As he laid her head on her pillow, the look in her eyes changed from one of terror to one of astonishment. And then the lights went out. She lay still.

Methodically, he removed her clothing. But the sight of her nude body failed to arouse any excitement within him. Disgusted, he turned to leave.

As he stepped out of the cabin, he glanced up at the camera ball posted just down the corridor. *They'll see you!* a voice within him cried. *So what?* he answered. *They'll come get you!* the voice sounded urgently. *No problem*, he answered again. *I'll simply explain what happened. The bitch needed killing. It's that simple.*

Silent as a ghost, he padded down the passageway toward the bridge. Glancing at his watch, he smiled. He'd just make it.

4 HERE BE DRAGONS

Shortly after the start of the forenoon watch, Helmsman Swann, who was also covering the coms station, turned to the first officer. "Mixter De Vegas, I have Dr. Jones. He'd like to speak with you."

De Vegas nodded. "Put him on my console."

The speaker in front of her crackled to life. "De Vegas here," she said. "What is it, Dr. Jones?"

"Ms. De Vegas," came Jones' somewhat sheepish voice, "I'd like permission to return to my duties."

"The captain has confined you to quarters," De Vegas pointed out.

"Yes, ma'am. I know. That's why I'm calling. I have some star sights to check out."

"Mixter Munson can't handle those?"

"Well, she can. But given our present circumstances, I thought you might want to have the most senior science officer present."

"Very well. Stand by. I'll need to check with the captain."

She did so. Cermeno, who'd already had a long night dealing with the disappearances of crewmen Sabol and Beadel, was not pleased to get the request. But he did not reject it out of hand. Instead, he ordered De Vegas to have both Jones and Teal report to his cabin.

Moments later, the two of them were standing before the captain, who was seated at a small chair turned away from his desk. He regarded the two of them with an expression similar to what might be expected from someone who'd just discovered a steaming poodle surprise on the living room rug. "Do either one of you want to even *try* to explain yourselves?"

Teal was the first to speak. Clearing his throat, he said, "Captain, I have been engaged in a lifelong struggle with alcoholism. I do not know what caused me to relapse—perhaps the stress of the mission. I am profoundly embarrassed and humiliated, and apologize profusely. It will not happen again."

Cermeno nodded. "Well, honesty counts for something, although it's no defense." He turned to Jones. "And you?"

Jones stared straight out into the distance. "No excuses, sir."

But Cermeno noted a slight twitch at the corner of Jones' mouth—a twitch suggesting that the man was desperately trying to keep a straight face as he struggled to hold back one of his trademark smart-alecky comments. The sight of it infuriated the captain. Cermeno jumped to his feet and took two steps forward. "You're a disgrace to that uniform!" he thundered. Both Jones and Teal flinched. Cermeno brought his nose to within an inch of Jones'. "Do you hear me?" he continued shouting at the top of his lungs. "What kind of scientist do you call yourself? *Alco-physicist?* Where do you even get the *nerve* to stand there and ask me to return you to duty?"

Jones grimaced as if feeling a stab of pain, but the captain was holding his face so close to Jones' that Cermeno couldn't see the man's expression.

"You know what I'm going to do? I'm going to see to it that everyone knows what a miserable drunk you are! You'll never go to space again! I'll run you right out of the profession! Do you read me, Jones?"

Jones now swayed slightly. Cermeno reached forward with his right hand and clapped it over the upper part of Jones' left arm. "Stand up straight, damn you!" Cermeno screamed.

Instead, Jones began to collapse. Teal, realizing what was happening, sprang forward to catch him before the man could hit the deck.

Cermeno stepped back and regarded the two of them with a surprised and confused expression. "Jones, what are you doing?" he demanded.

"I think he's having a heart attack," Teal said.

Jones lay on a bed in sick bay, attached to numerous wires and tubes and looking miserable. Dr. Blake reached forward and wiped his head with a damp cloth. "You're going to be all right," she said reassuringly. "The scan is not showing any blockages and there appears to be no permanent damage to the heart muscle or kidneys."

Jones nodded weakly. "Thanks for pulling my arse out of the fire," he said.

"My pleasure."

Captain Cermeno, standing near the edge of the bed, now spoke up. "Dr. Blake, a word?"

Blake nodded, and led him to a side office. "Have a seat," she said when she'd closed the door.

"I'll stand. Dr. Blake—what the hell happened? How does someone with a heart condition get on a mission like this one?"

"He doesn't have a heart condition," Dr. Blake said flatly.

"But didn't you just say had a heart attack?"

She nodded. "A mild one."

Cermeno shook his head. "I'm sorry, but this sounds like double talk. How can you have a heart attack without having some kind of underlying heart disease?"

"Captain, this mission is already very stressful. And you were giving him the third degree at the time."

Cermeno felt a flash of anger. "What, now you're telling me *I'm* responsible?"

"Partially, yes." Sighing, she sat down behind her desk. "Look, I'm not saying it was your *fault*. But it's a well documented fact that severe stress or fright can cause cardiac events. In this case, I suspect that he suffered a stress-induced spasm of one or both of the coronary arteries. This creates a condition called ischemia—a fancy way of saying that it cuts off blood flow to the heart. The heart starves of oxygen—and there you go."

Cermeno nodded, his anger dissipating. "What does this mean going forward? Will he be incapacitated?"

"No. I recommend a day of bed rest, maybe two. But there's no damage to anything other than his wits."

Cermeno's comlink beeped. He turned his head slightly and put his finger behind his ear as a signal to Blake that he was getting a communication. "Cermeno. Go."

"Captain, this is Swann," the comlink spoke. "The first officer asks that you come to the bridge, sir. Chief Crandall is here. He says it's urgent."

"On my way," Cermeno said. He nodded to Blake. "Anything else I should know?"

"Not really. Except—"

"Yes?"

"Wilson has noted that fatigue and stress levels are up all over the ship. I'd recommend that until we're clear of our current situation, that perhaps you bring down the intensity of your personal management style a notch or two."

Cermeno clinched his teeth together. *That bitch*, he thought, glaring at her. *Where does she get off telling me how to run my ship?* But he chose not to engage her, at least not now, instead filing it in a growing mental folder labeled, "Pending." Giving no acknowledgment of her comment, Cermeno turned abruptly and exited the room.

When he walked onto the bridge, he found Bates Crandall standing there waiting for him, wearing, as was his wont, an unhappy expression. "Captain, may I have a word in private?"

Cermeno nodded and guided Crandall to a small door at the rear of the bridge, which opened onto a cramped cabin containing a tiny desk, a small bunk, and two chairs. The captain shut the door, and the two of them sat down. "What is it, Chief?"

"Captain, one of my men is missing."

"What? We have *another* missing crewman?" *God* damn *it*, he thought, raging inwardly. "Who is it?"

"Electrician Lamont Brozek. He didn't show up for his watch. And we can't find him anywhere."

"For the love of *God*." Cermeno ran a hand over the top of his head. He was not looking forward to having to order yet another stem-to-stern search of the vessel.

"There's more. I just found out that Brozek was involved in a fight yesterday."

"What? And you're just now hearing about it?"

"Regrettably, Captain, the man's crewmates elected not to report it. Not surprising, really. But when Brozek went missing, someone came forward."

"What's the story?"

"Brozek tied into it with Electrician Rubin Smith. Or rather I should say, Smith got into it with him. Smith punched the man without warning in the engineers' mess, and then tackled him. It took four people to pull him off."

"What's his beef?"

"The usual, sad to say. A woman. Ship's Carpenter Caitlyn Cheng."

Cermeno nodded. "So you think Smith has something to do with Brozek's disappearance?"

"Captain, I *know* he does. There are signs of a struggle in Brozek's cabin, and this morning Smith showed up sporting a split lip and wearing a mouse, neither of which he had yesterday."

"Have you questioned the man?"

"No, sir. I thought it might be best to seek guidance from you first."

Cermeno sighed. "Very well. Arrest him."

"Yes, sir." Crandall paused. "Sir, where do I put him?"

The ship did have a brig—as a former colony transport, the builders had deemed such a facility necessary. But it was down in the bowels of F-Deck, which was largely unused on this mission. "Confine him to his cabin for now. Let me know once you've done that. I want to question him personally."

"Yes, sir." Crandall cocked his head to the side and placed his finger at the back of his ear. "Just one moment, Captain." Now gazing off into the distance, he said, "Crandall here." He was silent for a moment, obviously listening to the transmission. "Very well," he finally said. "I will alert the captain and get back to you."

Cermeno raised an inquisitive eyebrow.

Crandall turned to him. "Now Cheng is missing. And so is Smith."

Cermeno lay on his day room bunk, feeling drained as he rested his head on his knitted fingers and stared at the overhead. He knew he should be leading the search. But he just couldn't muster the motivation or the energy to do it. He had begun the day tired and wrapped in a dark mood, and it was only getting worse.

His thoughts now turned to his father. As a boy, Cermeno had done his level best to love the old bastard. For a time, he'd idolized the man. But the elder Cermeno never reciprocated his son's affections. His demeanor had grown more and more disapproving as time went on. It was, Cermeno knew, an old and very sad tale. And yet it was so very personal. His father had chivvied him into one bad choice after another. The boy had never been able to muster the courage to stand up for himself. And as inexorable as the march of a mighty river to the sea, the chain of events had led to this present moment—a time, a place, and a situation not of the junior Cermeno's choosing, and a challenge to which he knew he was not equal. His own father certainly knew it, and had taken no pains to conceal his disdain even while extending to the younger man a lifeline that had the potential to save his career. "Your family name," his father had observed coldly, "is an honor you didn't choose, and have done nothing to earn. A better son might have risen to the occasion. But a better son is not what I got. It's the luck of the draw, I suppose. And now I'm stuck with you. But you have one last opportunity to redeem yourself. I know it will be completely out of character for you—but try not to crap the bed." At which point, his father had disconnected the call.

Now remembering the sting of the words, Captain Cermeno felt his face flushing and growing hot with embarrassment. But then cold anger gripped him. And he found himself screaming aloud at the top of his lungs, *"You insufferable, bitter old bastard!"*

With a loud snap, all four of the overhead panels went dark, plunging the room into pitch blackness. "What the *hell?*" he asked aloud.

His door chime sounded. "Wilson, open the door, please."

The panel slid aside to reveal the silhouette of Fabiana De Vegas. "Captain?" she inquired, clearly startled at the darkness.

"The damned lights just blew," Cermeno explained, annoyed that she'd caught him lying in the dark. And now he wondered whether she'd heard him through the door, yelling like a madman. "What is it?"

"Sir, Mixter Munson just reported that Scope B is unresponsive. It appears to be jammed."

Cermeno sat up, touched a button on his watch, and glanced at the illuminated display. "She should be nearing the end of the survey about now," he said. "She'll just have to do without it."

"That's not the problem, sir. We light torches in a little more than an hour, if we remain on schedule. The instrument is very delicate, and must be retracted for all acceleration maneuvers."

An array of brusque answers presented itself in Cermeno's mind, the gist of which would be to suggest that the torchlight commence on schedule, instruments be damned. But he knew that if, God forbid, they were to emerge into another void, they'd need every scope. "Recommendation?"

"We'll need to send a couple of crewmen out to see if they can repair it. I recommend Tochigi and Abello. Tochigi has more EVA hours than anyone else in engineering. And Abello has the most experience with those particular instruments."

Cermeno raised an eyebrow. "Do you think they'll be able to repair the scope and get back inside in time to light the torches?"

De Vegas paused. "It's possible. But just in case, we should be prepared to delay by up to an hour. Maybe more."

Cermeno swore inwardly, mentally using language that would have shocked even De Vegas. But he saw no good alternatives. "Very well. Proceed. Keep me informed."

"Yes, sir."

Cermeno rose. "And get an engineer in here to see about these damned lights, please. I'll be in my cabin."

When the call came, Tochigi was helping to conduct a search of F-Deck. He was supposed to be working side by side with Derrek Damiano, but the man had gone on ahead in order to cover more territory. Separating in that fashion was a violation of their search orders, but neither wanted to spend more time on F-Deck than necessary. The space more resembled an old-style bilge in a wet navy ship than it did a deck in a modern starship; it was gloomy, dirty, crowded with pipes, ducts, and wiring trays, and filled with miscellaneous equipment and odd items, some of which had been cast off from previous colony missions. The order to report to the bridge did not surprise Tochigi; in fact, he had expected it sooner. He knew the only reason he wasn't already in irons was that when searchers had checked Jessica Beadel's cabin, they found it empty. Clearly, when Tochigi had left her she'd not been dead after all, and she must have wandered off afterwards, dazed and confused. Sooner or later she'd turn up, maybe alive with a story to tell, or maybe dead, perhaps having stumbled down a dark hole somewhere. In either case, there his tissue would be under her fingernails, and that would be that. Curiously, he found that the prospect of his imminent arrest raised no inner sense of alarm. His heart seemed to be as empty, and as black, as the utter darkness that surrounded the ship.

But when he reported to the bridge, he learned that the reason for his summons was not what he'd anticipated. "We need you to head to engineering," De Vegas told him. "You'll be joining Electrician Abello at airlock D-5. The two of you will suit up, grab EVA toolkits, jet over to Telescope B, and see if you can figure out why it's not responding to commands."

Tochigi nodded, while suppressing an urge to run screaming from the bridge. He *hated* EVA's—and yet it seemed that any time someone had some dirty job that no one else wanted to do, he was the one who got tapped for it. The thought of this particular excursion caused a shiver to run down his spine; he and Abello would be stepping out into the emptiest void mankind had ever encountered—which was another way of saying it was the deepest, darkest pit imaginable. From their vantage point outside in the weightless night, *every* direction would seem like "down"—endlessly, infinitely, eternally *down*.

But he suppressed the thought. "What about the torchlight?" he asked. "This may take a while."

De Vegas' face showed the barest hint of a sardonic smile. "Despite our better judgment, Mr. Tochigi, we won't leave without you."

The comlink behind Cermeno's ear beeped. "We've got him, Captain," came Crandall's gruff voice.

Cermeno sat up on his bunk. "I assume you mean Smith. Where did you find him?"

"You wouldn't believe me if I told you. I'm not sure I believe it myself."

"Try me," Cermeno said impatiently.

"A search team found him in an empty cabin on E-Deck. He was lying in a fetal position on a bunk in the dark, not wearing a stitch of clothing. The man was covered from head to toe in gore, and was sleeping like a baby."

"My God."

"Yeah," Crandall agreed. "My thoughts exactly. The blood almost has to be from Cheng or Brozek, or both. We'll test it to confirm."

"Where are you taking him?"

"Damiano and Anwar are hustling him up to sick bay as we speak. I've asked Dr. Blake to clean him up and check for wounds."

"I'll join you there."

"I'm coming up the A-Deck passageway now, Captain. I'm about at your door. I'd like a word."

"All right."

Seconds later, Cermeno's door chime sounded. The captain opened the panel and invited Crandall inside. The engineer's face bore an expression Cermeno couldn't quite identify—but it wasn't good. It looked like the man couldn't decide whether he was terrified or outraged. "What is it, Chief?"

"Captain, we've got to get out of here. Now."

Cermeno's face grew hot as he felt a flash of anger. Crandall was challenging his authority *again*? Did he not remember how this had gone last time? "We are working on that, Chief. As soon as your two men get B-Scope fixed, we'll light the torches."

"Not later, Captain," Crandall insisted. "*Now*."

"Don't be an idiot," Cermeno snapped. "Do you not realize what could happen to us if we pop out into another void without all of our scopes working?"

"It wouldn't make any difference!" Bates shouted. "They haven't been one whit of help in *this* void, now have they?"

"Secure that, Chief!" Cermeno shouted, the level of his voice matching Crandall's. "And I mean *right now*."

"Don't you get it?" Crandall demanded, not backing down. "Look around you! Four crewmembers missing. A fifth, by all the evidence, gone stark, raving, homicidally mad. People at each other's throats. This space we're in is killing us!" Crandall's voice now rose to a level betraying pure panic. *"We have to leave! Now!"*

Cermeno had to fight hard to restrain himself from slapping the man. "Goddammit, Chief! Get hold of yourself!"

Crandall's expression transformed into one of utter fury, morphing into the malevolent mask one might expect on the face of a man about to commit murder with his bare hands. "You need to listen to me, you mealy-mouthed, tin-horn twerp!" Crandall snarled.

The words, combined with Crandall's menacing expression, shocked Cermeno to his core, and left him profoundly frightened. Beads of cold perspiration broke out on the captain's forehead, and he felt a wave of nausea wash over him. Nervously, he took a step back. "Chief," he said, licking his lips apprehensively, and making an effort to lower his voice, "you'll be wanting to settle down, and guard your tone."

"I will *not* calm down," Crandall barked, and as he did so, he stepped closer, closing the gap between him and the captain to within chest-bumping distance. Reaching forward, Crandall jabbed a stiff index finger into the captain's sternum. "Your idiocy is killing us." Now he began punctuating his words with more jabs. "You" —jab— "have cost us" — jab— "four" —jab— "men!"

The pokes had an electric effect on Cermeno. A violent wave of outrage now washed over him, completely blowing away any feelings of fright. His eyes narrowed. "Mr. Crandall," he said in calm, even tones that belied the boiling anger raging inside, "if you touch me again, so help me God, I will have you shot for mutiny."

The words seemed to hit Crandall like a punch in the gut. His furious expression evaporated, transforming into one of frightened uncertainty. And then, without warning, Crandall turned aside and ejected a stream of vomit. The man then fell to his knees, and then to all fours, and vomited again.

Cermeno stepped back, scrunching his face in an expression of disgust. As he did so, his rage melted away, to be replaced by feelings of profound confusion. *What the hell is going on?*

"Captain," Crandall said in a weary voice, still on all fours and looking at the floor. "I— I don't know what came over me. I apologize. This is not who I am."

Cermeno knew that offering conciliatory words to Crandall at this point would be appropriate. But he could not muster them. Instead, he simply said, "Get up."

"Yes, sir." Crandall stood. Producing a handkerchief, he wiped his mouth.

"We're due in sick bay, Mr. Crandall," Cermeno said.

Crandall nodded.

"Let's go. And call someone to clean this mess up."

Tochigi was approaching the B-Scope assembly with Abello when a sharp pain erupted in his left big toe. "Ow!" he yelped.

"What is it?" came Abello's voice over the radio link.

Tochigi laughed. "You ever get sharp pains that just sort of flare up for no reason, and then go away?"

"What, you mean like muscle pains and that sort of thing?"

"Yeah. Or skin irritations. Kind of like an itch, only on steroids."

Abello laughed. "Yeah—I know what you mean. Any time you put on a spacesuit, you're guaranteed to itch in places you didn't know you had. It's a fundamental law of nature."

"I suppose so. It just felt as if someone stuck a hot needle in my toe. But it's gone now."

"I can think of worse places than a toe for something like that to happen," Abello observed in rueful tones.

"Thanks," Tochigi said sardonically. "Now, through the power of suggestion and the image you just planted in my mind, the next thing I can expect is for my left testicle to explode."

Abello laughed again. "Which would leave you with none."

"Ha, ha," Tochigi said sarcastically, acknowledging Abello's little jest. "That was about half witty. Which is exactly what you'd expect, coming from a half-wit."

"Yuk, yuk," was the most cutting rejoinder Abello found himself able to muster.

They were now nearly at the brightly lighted scope assembly, from which Tochigi had never taken his eyes as he studiously tried to avoid looking into the darkness that surrounded them. Now Tochigi gave his forward jets a tap, slowing the relative velocity to nearly zero. Carefully, he reached out and grabbed hold of a hand grip. "And, we have touchdown," he announced.

Abello glided in beside him. "Let's see what we've got," he said.

A quick search of the exterior of the assembly found no evidence of any problems. "Well, I guess we'll have to crack it open," Tochigi observed.

"Yeah," Abello agreed. "Let's check the gearbox. I have hunch." As he spoke, Abello set his boot into one of the grips on the hull designed to receive it, and gave it a quick kick to set the clamp.

Tochigi pulled himself to a hand grip on the opposite side the gear box cover and snapped the end of his lifeline onto its bar. That done, he glanced over at Abello, who'd taken a moment to pause and glance out at their surroundings.

"I'll tell you one thing," Abello said. "I'll be glad when we get out of here."

"It is a bit like living inside a rock, isn't it?" Tochigi asked.

"Yeah. I don't like it. It feels like the darkness is leaching inside of me, trying to pull my soul out through my eyes."

"Why Mr. Abello," Tochigi said, "How eloquent. I didn't know you had it in you."

"You're surprised to learn I'm a closet poet?"

"No. I'm surprised to learn you have a soul."

"Ha, ha. Speaking of leaching—check your power meter. My batteries seem to be discharging at a higher rate than they should."

Tochigi punched up the battery meter on his helmet display. "Yeah. Mine, too."

"Well, there's no cure for it, I guess," Abello said, "other than to finish this job and get the hell out of here."

"Agreed." Tochigi reached for the tool kit at his belt. As he did so, another sharp pain erupted, this one just above his left ankle. "God *damn!*" he shouted.

"What?" Abello asked.

"Another damned shooting pain," Tochigi answered. "I swear, the next time someone asks me to do an EVA, I'm going to figure out some way to induce vomiting, so I can get myself on the sick list."

"That shouldn't be a problem. If you want to inspire a quick vom, just look in the mirror."

"You crack me up, Abello," Tochigi said drily. And he thought, *I never did like this guy. He might just have to have an accident in the airlock.* The thought caused him to smile.

Captain Cermeno strode into the sick bay with Crandall hard on his heels. Electrician Smith was sitting upright on a medical bed, and clad in a blue medical gown. Dr. Blake was standing next to him, peering into his ear with some kind of instrument, as Smith stared down at his knees.

"Is he injured?" Cermeno demanded.

"No."

"Fine." Cermeno pulled a chair away from the wall and thrust it toward the end of the bed. "Chief Crandall, sit his butt down there."

Crandall stepped forward, glaring at Smith. "You heard the man. Are you going to sit down or am I going to have to assist you?"

Shrugging, Smith got up and moved to the chair. Dr. Blake took up a position off to the side, watching them.

Cermeno stepped up to the chair. "What did you do to Brozek and Cheng?"

Smith looked up at him. He was wearing an expression that struck Cermeno as bemused, if not outright amused.

"Where are they?" Cermeno demanded.

At this point there was no mistaking it; Smith's mouth twitched into an obvious smirk.

Cermeno hauled off and backhanded him hard across the mouth.

Blake, startled, began to take a step forward, but then stopped, appearing to think better of it.

"Well?" Cermeno demanded, glaring at Smith.

The man continued to smirk insolently, but said nothing.

Cermeno turned to Blake. "Did you get a chance to ID the blood that was on him?" he asked.

Blake nodded. "It's Cheng's," she confirmed. "Enough of it to say that if she's still alive, her condition has to be grave."

"Captain," Crandall said beside him, "I didn't get a chance to mention this before—but the damnedest thing is, the cabin where we found him was clean. Smith was covered with gore, some of which had rubbed off onto the mattress. That was it. No blood splatters. No spray. No drops. And no footprints, even though the soles of the man's feet were thick with the stuff. It's damned bizarre."

Cermeno nodded, and then turned back to Smith. Blind rage was building up within him. "What did you do, Smith? Did you kill them?"

For the first time, Smith spoke. "You know, Captain," he said, smiling, "I've been asking myself the same question. Somebody did. Using my hands, even. But was it me?" He shrugged. "It's a philosophical conundrum, is what it is."

The answer did nothing to decrease Cermeno's rage. "I'm going to ask you one more time, Smith. What did you do with them? Where are the bodies?"

Smith threw back his head and started laughing.

Cermeno made a fist, pulled back, and punched Smith hard in the mouth, snapping the man's head back.

"Captain!" Blake shouted, and this time she did take a step forward.

Cermeno snapped his head around and glared at her. This had its intended effect; Blake stopped, looking unhappy, but she said nothing. Turning, the captain glanced at Crandall, who was still standing beside him.

Crandall regarded the captain with an impassive look.

Cermeno returned his gaze to Smith. The man was running an exploratory tongue around the inside of his lips. As Cermeno watched, he bent to the side and spit; a tooth bounced onto the floor amid a spray of blood. "Good one," Smith said as he turned back to the captain.

"This is the last time I'll ask this question," Cermeno said. "Where are they?"

Grinning, Smith spread his hands, palms up.

Cermeno hauled off again, and this time he put his back into the punch. Smith's head snapped to the side, and then fell forward, limp.

Dr. Blake rushed forward and inserted herself between the captain and Smith. "All right, that's enough!" she shouted. "Out of my way!"

Cermeno stepped back. Blake bent to examine Smith. "Damn you!" she snarled. "You've broken his jaw!" She turned to him, furious, and held her arm out, pointing angrily at the door. "Get the hell out of my sick bay! Now!"

Her words further infuriated Cermeno. *Who the hell does she think she is talking to me like that?* he raged inwardly. The matter would have to be set right. And it would be. But he decided now was not the time. Cermeno turned and walked away from the chair, mentally adding Blake's name to his "pending" file. Crandall fell in behind him.

As he neared the door, a pang of pain shot up from his hand. Looking down, he saw that he'd severely cut his knuckles on Smith's teeth. "I'm going to need to put something on this." Turning, he looked at Crandall. "Help me find some bandages, will you?"

"They're in the storage room at the end of the passageway," Blake said, not looking up from Smith. "Just down the hall, past the lab. Grab a box and get out."

Oh, yeah, Cermeno thought as he turned and walked in that direction. *For this bitch, there is going to be a reckoning. And it will be soon.* Reaching the storeroom, he quickly found a box of knuckle bandages. Cermeno retrieved several from the box, stuffed them into a pocket, put the box back on the shelf, and then left the room.

As he stepped past the open door to the lab, a computer monitor caught his eye. It was displaying Second Engineer Fusazane Tochigi's name and security photo. Beside it, in green capital letters, were the words "DNA MATCH."

Cermeno stepped into the room and examined the display more closely. It appeared that Blake had been running a test on some kind of sample. He turned to Crandall, who'd followed him into the room. "Any idea what that is?"

Crandall shook his head.

The captain walked back into the sick bay and stepped up to Blake.

"Dr. Blake, what does that display in your lab signify? The one with Tochigi's name on it?"

Blake turned to him, her eyes ablaze. "I thought I asked you to leave my sick bay, Captain. You've got your bandages. Now go."

"Please answer my question, Doctor."

Blake tossed her head in Smith's direction. The man was still slumped in the chair, unconscious. "Do you realize you shattered this man's jaw? It'll have to be *wired!* And I don't have that kind of capability here."

"Dr. Blake," Cermeno said calmly, "I don't give a good God damn if the man's head falls off, hits the deck and bursts like a ripe melon. And the only reason you're not confined to quarters right now for rank insubordination is that you're the only doctor on board and you have duties to perform. Now: Answer. My. Damned. Question."

Blake's jaws tightened. But then she let out her breath. "The first officer asked me to do an examination of Jessica Beadel's cabin. I'm not trained in forensics. But I did what I could. I found some short hairs that looked like they might have come from a man's arm or the back of his hand, and a few spots of blood on the deck by the door and also near the bunk. The blood belongs to Tochigi. I haven't had a chance to test the hairs yet."

Cermeno turned to Crandall. "Where is Mr. Tochigi now?"

"He's on that repair EVA with Abello."

"Let's get him back aboard. But first—" He turned back to Blake and held up his injured hand. "I want you to clean this for me and apply the bandages."

Blake's jaws tightened again. But she did as she was told.

"Guys, I've got the captain here," came Second Officer Trafford's voice over Tochigi's and Abello's suit radios. "He wants to know how close you are to wrapping this up."

Tochigi was in the process of removing the final screw from the gearbox cover. "Give me ten seconds, and I can give you a good estimate," he said.

"Standing by," Trafford acknowledged.

Tochigi held the business end of the powered screwdriver out to Abello, who removed the screw from the blade's grip and inserted it into a pouch. As he did so, Tochigi felt another sharp pain—this one was higher up, on his lower back. "Damn!" he yelled.

"What is it?" Abello inquired.

"I've got to get out of this damned suit. Something is irritating the hell out of my skin."

"Well, let's get this done. And then you can take a big ole bubble bath, and come out all silky smooth and smelling like a girl. You'd like that."

Nope, Tochigi thought. *An air lock accident is not going to work for this guy.*

Not messy enough.

Reaching forward, Abello grasped the hand grip at the center of the cover plate and gave a sharp tug; it sprang free. Bending forward, he shined the beams from his twin helmet lamps inside. "Ah, ha!" Abello said. "Just as I suspected." A thin sliver of metal had managed to wedge itself between two of the larger cogs, jamming them. Retrieving a pair of pliers from his tool belt, he thrust the nose into the box, grabbed the sliver, and began to work it free. Within moments, it came loose. He held it up, examining it in the wash of his helmet beam. "Gotcha, ya little bastard!"

"Have you found the problem?" asked Trafford, who'd been monitoring their suit communications.

"Yep," Abello said. "I've got it in my hand."

"What was it?"

"My guess is, Fridayitis," Tochigi answered for him.

"What? I don't follow."

"Fridayitis," Tochigi repeated. "Some shift worker, probably late on a Friday afternoon and looking forward to quitting time, got sloppy and left a little piece of shaved metal in the gear box. It's a wonder it didn't cause problems before now."

"Great. Close it up and get back in here. The captain wants a word."

Uh, oh, Tochigi thought. *Here it comes.*

Another sharp stab of pain hit him. This one had erupted on the back of his right hand, right on one of the cuts Beadel had gouged in his flesh with her fingernails when he'd been strangling her to death. And then there was something else—he sensed *movement*. It felt as if something were crawling on his skin. In fact, it felt as if something had crawled out of the cut *onto* his skin. "Jesus!" Tochigi yelled, and he pounded the top of his glove with the heel of his left hand, which caused the powered screwdriver he was holding to go flying.

"What the hell are you doing?" Abello demanded. "That's an expensive piece of equipment. They'll take that out of your paycheck, they will."

Now similar pains and sensations erupted from his other hand, which also bore cuts from the struggle. Frantically, he pounded the back of that hand with the heel of his right.

"What are you doing, Fuze?" Abello demanded.

"My damned hands are on fire!" Tochigi yelled. Now each of his cuts had erupted in agony—and it felt as if dozens of something tiny and alive were emerging from them and crawling up his arms. Tochigi began beating his fists against his upper arms, alternating left and right. But the suit was so thick the blows had no effect.

"Fuze!" Abello yelled. "What the hell?"

"Something's in my suit!"

"What do you mean? What are you talking about?"

141

The crawling sensations, mixed with sharp pains, had now reached both shoulders. It felt as if ants were moving up his arms, biting him as they went. And now he felt similar movement on his chest and back. "Get me out of here!" Tochigi yelled. "Get me out of this suit!"

"Abello! Tochigi!" came Trafford's urgent voice over the com circuit. "What's happening?"

"I don't know!" Abello answered. "Tochigi's got some kind of emergency."

Tochigi caught movement out the corner of his eye. Turning to look, he saw that a small spider had crawled onto his faceplate—the *inside* of his faceplate. As he watched, another, larger one joined it. "Get me out!" he screamed. "Get me out! Get me out!" Panicked, Tochigi slammed the control button for his rear suit jets. This caused him to rocket about three meters away from the hull, but then the suit came up short against the lifeline, which was still snapped to the hand grip.

"Tochigi!" Abello yelled. "Cut your jets!"

"*Get me out!*" Tochigi screamed incoherently in a blind panic. "*Get me out! Get me out!*" Now the words began to slur and run together, and the man's screaming voice became incoherent.

"Abello!" Trafford shouted. "What the hell is going on?"

"I don't know, sir," Abello answered as he kicked out of the hull clamp gripping his boot. "Tochigi is having a fit or something. A panic attack maybe. I'm moving over to him now."

His foot now free, Abello gave a mild push to propel himself away from the ship. His aim was accurate; within two seconds he had brought himself to a stop by grabbing Tochigi's swinging right arm. The man was still screaming incoherently while beating at his arms and flailing his legs wildly. His jets continued to blast at full power.

"Cut your jets, Tochigi!" Abello urged again. But there was no sign the man had heard.

Abello twisted around and made a dive for Tochigi's jet control, but as he did so, one of the man's flailing hands struck him hard against his helmet just as he was changing his grip. The blow propelled him tumbling away from Tochigi. "Crap!" he swore.

"What is it?" Trafford demanded.

"I'm having a tough time of it, sir," Abello answered, shouting to be heard above Tochigi's screaming. "Tochigi just knocked me away. I'm jetting back."

Within moments, he was approaching the man again. Tochigi was now clawing at his faceplate, but his screams had subsided into something that sounded more like a whimper, and his struggles had lessened. As Abello was about to reach out and grab him again, Tochigi's jets quit, starved of fuel. The lifeline rebounded and pulled the man back toward the hull just as Abello was about to land a grip on him. "Crap, crap, *crap!*" Abello swore.

"What now?" Trafford asked.

Abello was growing tired of delivering a play-by-play. "Don't you have me on the monitors, sir?" he asked.

"No. All of our video feeds are dead all over the ship. What are you doing now?"

"I'm just about to make contact again. Stand by."

Now Tochigi was no longer struggling; his arms floated limply at his side. Grabbing him by the shoulders, Abello pulled himself around and aimed the beams from his helmet lamps into Tochigi's faceplate. The shock of what he saw prompted him to scream out an expletive, while at the same time causing him to give an involuntary jerk backwards, once again propelling him away from Tochigi. "Jesus Christ!" he yelled, following up the expletive.

"Abello," Trafford yelled in frustration, "what *is* it?

"I don't know, sir," he said, struggling to suppress his emotions as he grabbed his jet control grip. "It can't be."

"*What* can't be?"

"Stand by, sir."

Once again, Abello righted himself, reversed his trajectory, and steered back in Tochigi's direction. The man was now drifting slowly away from the hull, completely limp except for some mild twitching of the arms and legs. Gingerly, Abello approached him. Carefully, slowly, he brought himself around and shined his lights once more through Tochigi's faceplate. And once again, Abello flinched, but this time not so violently. As he did so, he clenched his teeth to choke off a scream.

Hundreds, perhaps thousands, of spiders of all color patterns and sizes were swarming all over Tochigi's face. The man seemed to be wearing a living mask. Not a square millimeter of Tochigi's skin was visible as the spiders clambered all over him and over each other. Every inhalation sucked dozens of the eight-legged creatures into his mouth. Every exhalation blew some of them out. They were crawling in and out of his ears and in and out of the empty, bloody sockets where his eyes had been.

As Abello watched, Tochigi gave out a final sigh and was still. At his last breath, dozens of spiders stampeded into his open mouth.

Dr. Blake stared through her curved visor at the space-suited figure on the table. She was not looking forward to what lay ahead. Based on Abello's description of events, the next hour or so would not be pleasurable.

Earlier, for a few moments it had appeared she would not get the chance to find out what had killed Tochigi. When Abello had finally managed to convey by radio what was going on, Captain Cermeno had given orders not to bring the stricken man inside. But Blake had convinced him that she had the facilities onboard necessary for full biohazard containment.

Now she glanced across at Crandall, who was standing by with Abello and Electrician Kareem Anwar, ready to assist her. Like Blake, all three were wearing blue biohazard containment suits, which were connected by air hose to the lab's independent ventilation system, the couplings for which dangled from the overhead on short lines spaced at regular intervals. "Let's see what we can see," she said.

But before she could proceed, an alarm sounded four times from the overhead speakers; Mason Krajnovich's calm voice immediately followed. "All hands, prepare for acceleration. Two minutes."

At this, Crandall erupted with a blistering string of obscenities. "Doesn't that son of a bitch know we just put the man on the table?" he demanded.

Blake threw him a sharp glance, surprised that Crandall would use such language and speak so disrespectfully of the captain in front of his men. She noticed that both Abello and Anwar were avoiding eye contact with her. "Chief," she said, "if you'd like to get back to engineering, we can take it from here."

"Thanks," Crandall said. "Given the power drain we're experiencing, I think I'd better do just that." Reaching up, he closed his air valve and then disconnected his hose from the overhead coupling.

"Exit through there," Blake said, pointing to a door at the rear of the room. "You'll need to decontaminate the suit before you take it off. Follow the arrows to the decon room. There's a set of simple instructions on the wall, right above a big red knob. Just slap it when you're ready."

Crandall nodded. "Will do. Please keep me informed." With that, he stepped over to the door and headed out, closing it behind him.

When he was gone, Anwar turned to Abello. "I thought he was in an all-fired hurry to get us all out of here?"

"He is," Abello acknowledged.

"Then why the griping?"

"I wouldn't be too hard on him," Blake said. "We're all on edge."

"Well, for my money," Abello said, "I'm with the chief. The sooner we're out of this damned dark space we're in, the better." He glanced around the room. "Where do we strap in?"

"We don't," Blake said. "And I'm sure we'll be fine." Reaching up, she trained the focus of the operating light onto Tochigi's faceplate, and then bent forward to peer inside. Tochigi's face and lips were swollen. The skin was mottled in hues ranging from light red to dark purple, and covered with a network of what appeared to be burst capillaries. Scattered over the man's face were dozens, maybe hundreds, of sores, ranging in size from tiny dots to circular, angry, red, raised areas the size of pencil erasers. His flesh seemed to have sunken in against the bones of his face. Tochigi's eye sockets were empty and staring. His mouth was half open. There was no sign of movement inside the helmet.

Blake moved back out of the way. "All right, gentlemen, please equalize the pressure and get that helmet off."

Abello pressed a sequence of keys on Tochigi's arm pad. This resulted in several metallic clicks along with a soft sigh of air. Stepping into position behind the corpse, Anwar reached forward and placed a gloved hand on either side of the dead man's helmet. "Here goes," he said. Gently, Anwar gave the helmet a small turn counterclockwise and then pulled it off.

Once free of the helmet, Tochigi's head lolled back, causing his mouth to open further. Blake thought she caught a glimpse of movement; she stepped forward and bent down for a closer look.

A series of furry black dots appeared around the inside edge of Tochigi's open upper lip. As she watched, the dots moved, and it became immediately apparent that they were the tips of a large spider's legs. Before she had time to react, a giant black and yellow arachnid hoisted itself out of Tochigi's mouth and took up a stance on his face. It then turned and regarded Blake with it eight black eyes.

"Jesus!" she shrieked, and started to pull back.

The spider leaped across the short distance and landed squarely on her faceplate.

"Aiiigh!" she screamed wordlessly as she frantically swiped at the spider. The side of her hand connected with it and succeeded in batting it to the floor, leaving a yellow smear across her faceplate.

Anwar was already diving for a medium-sized metallic bottle that stood at his feet. Making a grab for it, he twisted a knob and directed a fuming jet of clear liquid at the twitching creature. The moment the stream hit it, the injured spider froze solid, crackling and foaming.

"Look!" Abello shouted.

More spiders were emerging from the dead man's mouth—half a dozen smallish brown ones, along with a similar number of black and yellow ones slightly smaller than the first.

"Don't spray his face or body!" Blake shouted. "Knock the spiders onto the floor first!"

Abello set to work brushing the creatures to the deck, where Anwar finished them off with the liquid nitrogen. Within moments, about a dozen and a half of them lay frozen on the floor, and the room was filled with slowly dissipating white clouds of the evaporating liquid.

At that moment, the deck plates beneath their feet began to thrum, and all of them swayed backwards as the torches fired up and the inertial dampeners raced to neutralize the force and stay abreast of the increasing acceleration.

"Is that all of them?" Blake asked, grabbing onto the table for support.

Gingerly, Abello peered into the man's mouth. "It appears to be," he said. "But I wouldn't stake my life on it."

"Well, keep that bottle handy," Blake said. "Let's get his suit off."

Abello reached for the cutters.

The image of Bates Crandall's worried face stared up at Cermeno from a monitor on the captain's command console. "We're delivering the required acceleration," Crandall was saying. "20 gees, as specified. But Captain, with this power drain, that's about all we've got. We're nearly at flank thrust, and by the time we jump we'll be right up to the mark. If the jump gets delayed by even a few minutes—well, all bets are off."

"Understood." Cermeno frowned. "We jump in less than an hour. You can hold it until then, and on through the jump, correct?"

Crandall nodded. "I think so. Barring the unforeseen." Crandall's scowl deepened. "But I'm sure I don't have to tell you, there's been a lot of 'unforeseen' on this mission, Captain."

"No," Cermeno agreed. "You don't have to tell me." Switching off, he looked over at the coms officer. "Mister Krajnovich, get our evil genius on the horn for me, would you?"

Krajnovich barely suppressed a grin. "Yes, sir."

Cermeno waited while Krajnovich carried out the task. After a moment, the coms officer turned to him. "Sir, I haven't been able to locate Dr. Makowski. I have Ms. Marinez for you."

"Put her on my console," Cermeno said, scowling.

Marinez's image popped up. "Yes, Captain?"

"Where's your boss?" Cermeno demanded.

Marinez hesitated. "Actually—I'm not sure at the moment."

"Isn't he normally on duty at this time of day?"

"Yes, sir."

"When did you last see him?"

"Last night, Captain, at the end of the watch."

Cermeno glared at her. "And you didn't see the need to report his absence?"

Marinez looked chagrined. "I'm sorry, sir." She wasn't quite sure how to explain the fact that Makowski tended to come and go as he pleased. "His schedule is a bit informal."

"I see." He made a mental note to take the matter up with Makowski later. "I need your input on a problem facing us." He sketched out the issues with the torch performance. "If, for the sake of argument, we get to the point where the torches cannot deliver 20 gees—what would that do to the jump?"

Marinez looked unhappy. "In theory, Captain, we can calculate a jump for any given set of acceleration and vector parameters. But in this case, we're trying to retrace the exact footsteps that led us here. I would not recommend changing a thing."

Cermeno nodded. "I thought you might say that. Very well. When you see Dr. Makowski, have him call me, please."

"Will do."

Cermeno switched off, thought for a second, and then touched the square on his panel that opened a comlink to the AI. "Wilson, this is Captain Cermeno."

"Good afternoon, Captain," Wilson said. "May I be of assistance?"

"Wilson, where is Dr. Makowski?"

"His comlink is registering on F-Deck, beneath the N-field array. It has not moved from that location since 18:47 hours last night."

"Thank you, Wilson. Where is the nearest search team?"

"Second Officer Trafford and Electrician Michaud are both on F-Deck."

"Connect me, please."

Moments later, Trafford's voice came over Cermeno's command speaker. "Trafford here." He sounded weary.

"Mr. Trafford, I need for you and Ms. Michaud to trot over to the array room safety lock on your deck. Dr. Makowski is absent from his post and is not answering calls. His comlink is registering from a location beneath the array. You'll need to hoof it. We'll be spinning up the array in about 40 minutes."

"On our way."

The space at the bottom of the ship beneath the N-field array was gloomy, cramped, and a little dangerous. In carving out space for the array, the yard workers, under pressure to complete the refit on time, had not been fussy about aesthetics. In many places, they'd left jagged scraps of metal jutting up from the deck or out from the stubs of bulkheads.

As they neared the center of the metal cavern, Trafford's beam caught a light-colored shape in the shadows ahead. Approaching carefully, he saw that the light color was from a lab coat. Inside the coat lay a crumpled figure; it had to be Morton Makowski.

"Dr. Makowski?" Trafford called as he threaded his way through the junk. "Are you okay?"

But when he got there, he found that Dr. Makowski definitely was not okay. He lay face up, his wide, surprised eyes staring up at Trafford lifelessly. The man's face seemed indecently exposed without his glasses. A short, bloody, jagged length of severed pipe protruded from the center of his chest.

Trafford glanced up through the gloom. They were standing directly beneath the array. The lights of the instrument station on the center platform stood out in sharp relief far above them.

"You think he fell?" Michaud asked, following his gaze.

As Trafford turned to answer, a glint of light caught his eye. Looking down, he focused on a small clear space on the grimy deck amid a tangle of disconnected wires spilling from a nearby conduit. There lay Makowski's glasses. Trafford picked them up. Both lenses were starred and cracked. "Oh, there's no doubt he fell," Trafford said, examining the glasses. He returned his gaze to the mangled figure of the late scientist. "But that's not the question, is it?"

By 16:30, Captain Cermeno had largely recovered from the shock of the news of Makowski's death. He was still perspiring a bit and feeling slightly nauseous, but was no longer grinding his teeth or pulling his hands. N-Field Specialist Ariana Marinez had assured him she could operate the array just fine without Makowski. The torches were delivering the required thrust. The astro computer was humming along, with Lydia Nguyen seated confidently at the console. Curiously, even though Cermeno normally had a strong aversion to AI Specialist Constance Nunn, he'd found himself feeling instantly more relaxed the moment she stepped onto the bridge at the change of watch half an hour ago. It was good to have the A Team in the saddle. He was beginning to hope that the worst of the day's incredible string of misfortunes was behind him.

At 16:35, First Officer Trafford's voice came over Captain Cermeno's command console speaker. "Captain, this is Trafford. Sir, will you come to Dr. Makowski's quarters?"

The request annoyed Cermeno. "Mr. Trafford," he said acidly, "We are 25 minutes from jump."

"Yes, sir. I know that, sir. You really need to see this."

Cermeno glanced across at De Vegas, who was seated in her flight chair next to him. Cermeno nodded toward the bridge exit. "Do you mind?" he asked.

"Not at all." She got up and strode in the direction of the safety lock.

Cermeno turned back to his console. "Very well, Mr. Trafford. I'm sending the first officer."

Trafford was waiting for her outside Makowski's closed cabin door. "I haven't touched a thing," he said. "Everything is just as he left it. And I want to warn you: it's vile."

De Vegas nodded. "Okay. Open it."

Trafford pressed a button, and the panel opened silently inward. The two of them stepped into the small room.

A hollie was playing in the air above Makowski's unmade bunk. At the sight of it, the normally unflappable De Vegas gave a short gasp. The hollie was showing a graphic and very explicit scene, the type of which men had been producing and downloading since the dawn of the Internet, the product of an underground industry that had never stopped growing despite the best efforts of law enforcement, and long prison sentences for pedophiles and predators caught in possession of such material.

"Okay, I've seen it," she said. "Now shut it off."

Trafford stepped over to Makowski's terminal and touched the screen. A password field presented itself. "He's got it locked on," Trafford said.

De Vegas activated her comlink. "Bridge, connect me to Wilson," she said. Within seconds Wilson was on the line. "Wilson, access Dr. Makowski's computer."

"One moment." There was a very brief pause. "I am unable to access Dr. Makowski's computer."

"Really? Why not?"

"Someone has set an unregistered encryption code."

"How is that possible?"

"I do not know. However, Dr. Makowski was quite expert in computer sciences."

De Vegas glanced at the hollie; another scene was playing out even more vile than the first. "Wilson, please access the power circuits to Dr. Makowski's cabin."

"I am unable to comply. The power circuits have been locked out."

De Vegas exchanged glances with Trafford. "Makowski locked out the computer and the power circuits, too," she explained.

Trafford shook his head. "Unbelievable. The son of a bitch *wanted* us to see this. He wanted to rub our faces in it."

"Wilson, accept emergency command override, my authority. Access the power circuits."

"Power circuits accessed."

"Can you shut down Dr. Makowski's computer without losing any data?"

"Any data now existing in permanent storage will be safe. Data in memory will be lost."

De Vegas nodded. "All right. Then please shut down the circuit to the holographic projector."

"Acknowledged. Circuit off."

The image flickered and then disappeared. At the same time, all four of the overhead light panels cut out, plunging the cabin into darkness relieved only by an oblong square of light projected onto the deck from corridor lights shining beyond the open door.

"Well, hell," Trafford said. Reaching for his pocket, he retrieved a small flashlight and switched it on. "Now, check this out." He directed his beam to the forward cabin bulkhead, to De Vegas' right.

For the first time, De Vegas noticed that the surface of that bulkhead was nearly covered with large pieces of paper, each of which bore a hand-drawn image. "Good Lord," she said.

"Looks like math and engineering were not Dr. Makowski's only talents," Trafford observed.

"Where did he get the materials?"

"Oh, that's no mystery. Drawing is an approved pastime. The ship's store has plenty of supplies. Although I'd have to guess that he probably just about cleaned them out."

"No kidding." Retrieving her own flashlight and switching it on, she stepped over to the wall for a closer look. Each image, drawn with a surprising level of skill, depicted a scene of horror or violence. In most, humans or parts of the human body were shown undergoing various forms of mutilation from sharp objects or from the teeth of savage animals or even other humans. Several bore the images of faces that could be described as monstrous or even demonic—visages with red eyes, oversharp teeth and evil, leering grins.

The centerpiece contained the image of a rotting, grinning face framed by long black dreadlocks. The monster was reaching forward with bony fingers, from the ends of which projected sharp black fingernails that had grown into talons.

"Look at these," Trafford said, playing his beam on two of the drawings. Both contained reasonably accurate depictions of the *Santa Maria*. In one, the fingers of a bony hand with black talons similar to the ones shown in the centerpiece were closing around the vessel. In the other, the ship was between the teeth of the same evil, dreadlock-framed face.

"What are you thinking?" Trafford asked.

"I'm thinking our mad scientist was exactly that. He was one sick puppy."

"To put it mildly." Trafford turned to her, now looking alarmed. "It just hit me—do you realize what this implies?"

De Vegas shot him a quizzical glance. "I'm not sure. What?"

"Think about it. The guy was fantasizing about the violent deaths of his shipmates and the destruction of the ship. And he's shown a talent for tampering with computers and power circuits."

The blood drained from De Vegas' face as the light dawned. "Oh, my *God*. We've got to alert the bridge." She tapped behind her ear, but this did not result in the connection beep she was expecting. "Bridge!" she shouted, still tapping. "Bridge!"

Trafford did the same. "Bridge!" he yelled, tapping behind his ear. He got the same result.

"Come on!" De Vegas yelled as she whirled around and took a running step toward the cabin door. But just before she reached it, the panel swung briskly shut in front of her, forcing her to an abrupt halt. Behind her Trafford fetched up short as well, nearly bumping into her. Impatiently, De Vegas reached forward and jabbed the door button. There was no response. "Oh, for Chrissake!"

"Stuck?" Trafford asked.

"Yeah." She turned to him and opened her mouth as if to speak again—but then movement in the gloom behind Trafford caught her attention. "What in the world—"

Trafford, following her gaze, turned and shined his torch at the forward bulkhead.

Makowski's macabre drawings were fluttering to the deck. The entire bulkhead to which they had been affixed seemed to have disappeared, replaced by an expanse of empty blackness that swallowed up the beams of their   flashlights.

Captain Cermeno glanced at the red letters of the clock display glowing on his command console: 16:57. The bridge crew had just completed their reports, and the ship was ready to jump. What the hell was keeping De Vegas? "Mr. Krajnovich, put me through to the first officer."

"Yes, sir." Krajnovich reached for the appropriate square on his coms panel, but as he did so he noticed that it was now flashing red. Trafford's was doing the same. Frowning, Krajnovich pressed De Vegas' link anyway. Nothing happened. "She's not responding," he said, frowning.

"Try Trafford."

Krajnovich pressed that comlink square, with similar results. "Sorry, sir," he said, shaking his head. He turned to the captain. "Both comlinks appear to have just gone offline."

"Put Wilson on."

"Wilson here, Captain," came the computer's smooth artificial voice over Cermeno's command console.

"Wilson, where are Trafford and De Vegas?"

"Their comlinks last registered in Cabin A-47. That is the cabin belonging to Dr. Morton Makowski."

"Do you have an audio monitor in that cabin?"

"One moment. No, sir. The monitor circuit has been locked out."

"Accept command override, captain's authority. Open the circuit."

"Circuit open." A series of noises now emanated from the speaker on Cermeno's console—scufflings, grunts, thuds, gasps, and heavy breathing.

"Wilson, what do you make of that?"

"I would interpret that as sounds of a struggle in progress."

"Coming up on two minutes, Captain," Helmsman Swann spoke up.

Damn it! Cermeno thought. But there was no way in hell he was going to abort the jump at this point. "Very well. Mr. Krajnovich, sound the final alarm."

"Yes, sir." Krajnovich sounded the klaxons, and then opened his microphone. "All hands," his voice could be heard echoing down the passageway, "Secure for dimension jump. Two minutes. Repeat: Secure for dimension jump. Two minutes."

A flash of light caught Cermeno's eye. Glancing down at his console, he saw that the master program alarm was flashing. Simultaneously, alarms began sounding on the AI and astrogation consoles. Cermeno looked up to see numerous red lights flashing at both stations. In addition, a red screen on Nunn's console was blinking the words, "ASTRO OFFLINE."

"What now?" Cermeno demanded.

Nunn swiveled her flight chair around. "Sir, I've got a program alarm. The astrogation computer just went off line. This should have caused a full auto-abort, but it didn't. I don't know why."

Cermeno looked at Electrician Kareem Anwar, who had replaced Tochigi at the engineering console. "Mr. Anwar, what is our status?"

Anwar swung his chair around. "Torches are still firing at the requested thrust, sir. The N-field array has dropped to standby, but remains spun up and at full revolutions."

Cermeno returned his gaze to Nunn. "So the jump won't take place?"

Nunn shook her head. "No, sir. Not automatically. Not with the astro computer off line."

"Can we still jump manually?"

"Yes, sir. I can re-route control of the array to the main computer system. We can enable the N-field array final program sequence from my console."

"Do so. Now."

"But sir—"

"*Now*, Ms. Nunn."

"Yes, sir." Clenching her jaws, Nunn turned to her console.

"Captain," Nguyen spoke up, her voice urgent. "Without the astro computer, we'll be jumping blind. We must abort."

Swann glanced over at her, wearing a blank expression, and then turned to cast his gaze on the captain.

"Sir," Krajnovich said, "I have the chief engineer for you."

"Put him on."

"Captain!" Crandall's voice came over the command circuit, practically shouting. "The N-field array sequence has dropped to standby."

"Yes, I know, Chief. We're working to re-enable it."

"I can't impress this upon you strongly enough, Captain," Crandall continued. "We must jump *now*. With the drain on our system, I can deliver thrust at this level for about another eight minutes. That's it, and I see no hope of ever getting it back."

"Understood."

Cermeno looked up at Nunn's console. A big red lighted screen was displaying white letters forming the words "ENABLE SEQUENCE?" Beneath it were two smaller squares, one reading "Engage" and the other reading "Abort." Nunn was staring at the screen, not moving.

"Ms. Nunn?" he said. "Are you ready?"

"Yes, Captain."

He glanced at the clock: 16:59:10. "Please enable the program."

Instead, she whirled around. "Captain, without the astro computer, small errors will multiply themselves exponentially with each successive blind jump—and there are more than 50,000 transitions in this sequence! There's no telling where we'd come out."

"She's right, Captain," Nguyen spoke up, her voice tense. "Unless we get incredibly lucky—and I'm talking lottery odds here—we'll be deeper in the hole, with no way to retrace our steps."

"A small chance is better than no chance!" Cermeno shouted. "And that's what we'll have if we stay here!"

"Not true, Captain!" Nunn pleaded. "Once we get the astro computer back on line, we can try this again."

"But not with the required thrust!" Cermeno yelled, panic now starting to edge into his voice. "You heard the chief!"

"We can recalculate for that!" Nunn said, her voice also rising. "Captain, please! Don't do this!"

The clock now read 16:59:43. "I'm through arguing, Nunn," he said, trying to sound calm, but not succeeding. "Enable the program."

Nunn swallowed heavily, but gave no reply.

"*Now*, Ms. Nunn!"

Nunn cast her eyes to the side, momentarily appearing to waver. But she made no move to turn to the console.

Swann, Nguyen, Krajnovich and Anwar looked at her, exchanged glances with each other, and then turned back to the captain.

"Ms. Nunn!" Cermeno shouted, now jumping to his feet. "I gave you a direct order!"

"Yes, Captain," Nunn acknowledged. She looked back up at him. Her features were now resolute; her moment of indecision had passed.

Cermeno stepped around to the forward side of the command station. "Do you intend to obey it or not?"

"No, Captain."

The clock now read 16:59:54.

"Well, if you won't do it, then by God, I will!" Cermeno made a lunge for Nunn's console.

In a flash, Swann was up and out of his flight chair. He swung his fist in a savage right hook. The blow caught Cermeno on the side of his jaw and sent him flying backwards. As he went down, the back of his head collided with the forward edge of the command console. The man collapsed to the deck and did not move.

Swann turned to Nunn and Anwar. "Shut it down."

Both crewmen nodded and swung back around to face their consoles. Nunn reached forward with a shaking hand and very carefully touched her finger to the "abort" square. On a screen next to it, she punched the master program abort. Beside her, Anwar pressed a series of squares to begin an orderly power-down of the torches and to spin down the array. The thrumming of the deck plates began to die away.

"Mr. Swann," Krajnovich spoke up, "I have the chief for the captain."

"Let him stew for a while."

On the deck in front of the command console, Cermeno gave out a light moan.

"Krajnovich, Anwar," Swann said. "Take the captain to his quarters and confine him there. Then get over to Makowski's cabin and see what's going on. I need the first officer on the bridge."

The two men stood. "Mr. Swann, how do you propose we confine him?" Krajnovich asked.

"Good question." Swann pulled his chin for a moment. "Put Wilson on the overhead."

Krajnovich turned and punched a square on his console. "Wilson here," came the computer's voice.

"Wilson, Captain Cermeno has suffered a mental breakdown. In order to provide for the safety of the ship, and being unable to confer with a higher authority during the crisis, pursuant to N.A.U. law and maritime traditions, I have relieved the captain of his command. I have ordered him confined to his cabin. You will set the door lock and remove his access to the security override. Is that clear?"

Wilson seemed to hesitate. "I am unsure of your authority in this matter, Mr. Swann."

"Wilson," Nunn spoke up, "please do as Mr. Swann asks, at least until we can find the first officer and confer with her."

"Very well. I have noted Captain Cermeno's temporary removal from command."

Swann nodded to Krajnovich and Anwar. "Go."

Nunn, Jones and Swann watched as the two men lifted up the captain and began half-dragging, half-carrying him off the bridge. As the inner safety lock door swung behind the trio, Nunn turned to Swann. "Do you think De Vegas is going to back your play?"

"I hope so," Swann said, sighing. "I don't have another mutiny in me."

"If she does," Nguyen asked, turning to Nunn, "will Wilson back De Vegas?"

Nunn shook her head. "I don't know. I think so. But I can't be sure."

For the first time, Swann caught the eye of Jervis Janson, who was strapped into an observation chair at the rear of the bridge. For the last several minutes, the man hadn't said a word. Swann noticed that the journalist's camera balls were arrayed along the rear bulkhead. "Did you get all this?" he asked.

Jervis nodded silently; the events he'd just witnessed had left him to shaken to trust his voice.

A soft mewing sound now emanated from the locker underneath Nunn's console.

"Ari wants out," Nunn said. "Okay to remove him?"

"I suppose so."

Nunn popped open the door. The cat sprang out, dashed to the center of the bridge next to the command console, and then stopped and began grooming itself.

Swann eyed the cat. "Let's hope the rest of us will be able to enjoy similar freedom of movement after De Vegas sees Janson's video." He turned to Nunn. "In the meantime, you need to get busy and see if you can get the astro computer back on line."

Nodding, Nunn turned to her instruments and began punching up the astrogation systems.

Swann glanced at the captain's chair. But then he thought better of it, and returned to his station at the helm.

For a moment, Krajnovich and Anwar weren't sure they were going to be able to get into Makowski's cabin. Wilson was fussy about accepting a command override from Swann to open the door. But Nunn finally talked the AI into it.

When the panel slid aside, the two of them found the room completely dark. Both men pulled small lights from their pockets and shined them inside. De Vegas was just getting to her feet from the bunk on which she'd been sitting. "Thank God," she said.

On the deck in front of her lay the crumpled figure of Second Officer Trafford. The two men rushed over to him.

"He's dead," De Vegas said.

Squatting low, Anwar laid a finger against Trafford's jugular, and then checked the man's wrist. There was no pulse, and Trafford's flesh was already cooling.

"What happened?" Krajnovich demanded.

"He came at me," De Vegas said. "No warning. He tried to strangle me." She looked down at the body. "I think I broke his neck."

That she would be able to do such a thing with her bare hands surprised Krajnovich and Anwar not at all. "Are you okay?" Krajnovich asked.

"Yes."

"You're urgently needed on the bridge."

"Why didn't we jump?"

"Brace yourself," Krajnovich said. "The astro computer went down. Cermeno gave orders to jump us blind, which Nunn and Nguyen both said would leave the ship irretrievably lost. Nunn point blank refused to do it. When the captain made a dive for the console, Swann cold-cocked him. The captain is now confined to quarters."

De Vegas, normally not given to histrionics, betrayed little reaction at hearing this news. "I see," she said, her face impassive. "I guess I'd better get up there."

"What do you want us to do with that?" Anwar asked, nodding at the corpse.

"Get it to sick bay," De Vegas said. Then she turned and strode out of the cabin.

Anwar watched her go, and then looked down at the lifeless form on the deck. "At this rate," he observed drily, "we're gonna run out of body bags."

When De Vegas entered the bridge, she found Chief Engineer Crandall standing very close to Swann, shouting at him while jabbing a finger at his nose. "You had absolutely no right to do that!" he was yelling. "Now we're all screwed! You'll go to prison for this!"

"Secure that, Chief," De Vegas said calmly.

Crandall whirled around and shot her an angry glare. But then his eye was immediately drawn to her right hip. A black leather holster was hanging from it, secured to a belt that De Vegas had fastened around her waist. The grip of a pistol protruded from the top of the holster, held in place by a leather safety strap. Clearly, De Vegas had stopped by the arms locker on her way to the bridge.

"What is the meaning of this?" Crandall demanded. "Why are you armed?"

"Calm down, Chief," De Vegas said soothingly.

Crandall was in no mood to calm down. "Do you plan to quell the mutiny—or take charge of it?"

"Chief, please. I intend to review all the facts. In the meantime, I need you to get to engineering and tell me how soon we can get underway, and at what thrust."

For a moment, Crandall looked inclined to argue further. But then he relented. "Very well. I'll get back to you shortly." With that, he strode quickly off the bridge.

When he'd gone, De Vegas turned to Swann. "Report."

Swann filled her in, with Nguyen, Nunn and Jervis providing color commentary and backup support. "I would have done the same thing," Jervis put in when Swann had finished the story.

"And you say you have all this on video?"

"I haven't checked it," Jervis said, "but I'm sure I do, from six different angles."

"All right. I want to see those files. Please go to the conference room and set up your equipment. I'll meet you there in 15 minutes."

Nodding, Jervis picked up his case and left.

De Vegas turned to Nunn. "What's our situation?"

"Not good. Before Makowski—" She paused, seeming to search for words. "One of the last things he did was to set up a cascading series of programs designed to carry out various forms of mischief—cutting out selected circuits, locking doors, disabling certain comlinks, and so on."

"Viruses?"

"Something like it. Wilson has done a complete scan of all systems, and we think we've found them all now. But—"

"Yes?"

"We can't get into the astro computer. Makowski has it locked out with a very sophisticated encryption code. It would take years to break. If it's even possible at all."

De Vegas did not look happy. "What are our options?"

"No good ones. We could reboot the system. But I'm betting Makowski has foreseen that, and has it rigged for something really bad to happen on reboot."

"Such as?"

"Such as wiping the permanent storage. All our astrogation data would be lost." Nunn considered spelling out exactly what that would mean for their hopes of retracing their footsteps and finding their way home, but the look on De Vegas' face told her she didn't have to. Even the normally unflappable De Vegas couldn't hide her sense of alarm.

"We don't have backups?" De Vegas demanded.

"We did. But now we don't. Makowski somehow managed to wipe the external backups without alerting Wilson to what he was doing."

De Vegas took a deep sigh. "Is there anything we *can* do?"

Nunn hesitated, looking uncertain. "There is one possibility. A slim one."

"Which is?"

"Well, as I said, we can't break Makowski's encryption code on the astro computer. Not in our lifetimes, anyway. But the password on his cabin computer is much simpler, and there's no timeout for retries. I'd like to go down there and work on that. If I can get into it, I have a hunch he may have stored the encryption code for the astro computer in his personal files."

De Vegas shook her head. "I really don't want you down there by yourself. And we can't spare anyone to guard you. Can you do this from the bridge?"

Nunn nodded. "I suppose so. Yes."

"Good. Do it that way. Get started."

"There's one more thing," Nguyen spoke up.

"Yes?"

Nguyen turned to Nunn. "Tell her what you told me."

Nunn looked uncomfortable. "It's just speculation—and probably a little out of line."

"Let's hear it."

Nunn shifted uneasily on her feet. "Well—Makowski set the encryption to take place at exactly two minutes before the jump. But he disabled the auto-abort subroutines. Otherwise, when the astro computer went off line, the N-field array would have spun down automatically, and the torches would have shut down, too."

"Right. You've already said that. What's your point?"

"Well, don't you see? It's like he *knew* the captain would panic and insist on making a manual jump. And if Cermeno had succeeded in doing so, we'd be stuck in this bottomless black pit we're in more or less forever. I think that's exactly what Makowski wanted."

The first officer sat ramrod straight in the conference room chair. Her face betrayed no hint of emotion as Jervis' video played out. She had already watched the scene unfold once. Now he was showing it to her from a different angle.

When the video ended, Jervis closed the display program and looked at her expectantly. "I have more angles if you'd like to see them."

"That won't be necessary." She turned to Swann, who was seated opposite her. "Mr. Swann, have you anything else to say?"

He shook his head. "No, ser."

"Very well. This is not a formal hearing. That will have to wait until we get back—*if* we get back. At that time, a board of inquiry will look into the matter and judge your actions, Mr. Swann—and mine. For now, having heard the evidence, it is my judgment that you acted appropriately and that your actions were in the best interests of the crew, the ship, and the company. It will be so noted in the log."

Swann relaxed slightly in his chair, and let out a sigh of relief. But it was only a small one. He knew he would face a much tougher inquiry later—if the ship were to return safely.

De Vegas touched behind her ear. "Mr. Krajnovich, 1MC please."

"Circuit open."

"Attention all hands, this is the first officer," she said as her voice boomed throughout the ship. "Captain Cermeno has been incapacitated. I have assumed command of the *Santa Maria*. As you no doubt have realized by now, the jump intended for seventeen hundred hours did not take place. This was due to a failure of the astrogation computer system. We are working on that problem. I will update you once we know more." At this point De Vegas hesitated, momentarily looking uncertain. "I don't have an explanation for some of the strange occurrences that have been taking place lately," she continued. "I ask you to remain calm. Carry out your duties as the professionals I know you all are. Stand by for further updates. That is all."

She tapped behind her ear to close the circuit. As she did so, she caught Jervis' eye. "Is that the best you can do?" he demanded. "Tell everyone to 'Keep Calm and Carry On'? What do you plan to do next, put up morale posters?"

"That's enough, Mr. Jervis," Swann snapped. "You are out of line."

"We have seven people dead or missing!" Jervis said, his voice rising. "*Seven!* That's a fifth of our complement! And all you've got to say is 'stand by for updates'?"

De Vegas fixed him with an icy stare. "Mr. Jervis, you may be a civilian, but you are subject to my authority. My orders—as you noted—are to remain calm. For anyone proving unwilling or unable to comply, I will take whatever steps I deem necessary. Is that understood?"

He looked at her, tight lipped with anger, but said nothing.

"Mr. Jervis, I require an acknowledgment."

Jervis managed a quick nod of the head.

"A *verbal* acknowledgment, if you please."

"All right," Jervis snapped. "Fine."

With that, De Vegas got up and left the room. The other officers followed, leaving Jervis sitting there by himself fuming in silence. *What in the world am I doing taking on De Vegas, of all people?* he thought bitterly. Suddenly it dawned on him that he was frightened, and profoundly so— more frightened than he'd been in his adult life. He felt like crying. And then he was astonished to find that he was already doing so, as a hot tear coursed down his left cheek.

Teal heard a chair moving out from the table. Looking up from the decorative candle bowl at which he'd been staring, he saw Dr. Blake plopping down in the empty seat between him and Dr. Jones. "God, that feels good," she said.

Teal glanced at his watch: 23:52. "You've certainly had a long day."

"I have. I have indeed."

"Would you like a wee bit of refreshment?" Jones asked.

"You can't mean that like it sounds," she said. "I thought you two boys were on the wagon?"

"We're following along earnestly behind it," Teal said, "with every intention of jumping up on it—provided we live through this. In the meantime, we've taken the monk's oath—'all things in moderation.'"

"I see. Well, in that case, how can I refuse?"

Teal nodded. "Don't go away." Walking over to the self-service dispensary, and being careful not to stumble in the deep gloom of the dimly lighted lounge, he grabbed a glass, half filled it with soda and ice, and then returned to the table. Jones topped off the glass with a splash of amber liquid from a silver flask.

"Gentlemen, to your health," Dr. Blake said, raising her glass.

"Here, here," Teal agreed, raising his. The three of them knocked back a swallow.

"Speaking of which—" Putting down her glass, Blake eyed Jones disapprovingly. "I thought I ordered bed rest for you."

"So you did," Jones acknowledged. "And I'm all bed rested, and feeling fine."

"Since we're talking shop," Teal said to her, "what did you find out about Tochigi?"

"I think you're changing the subject," Blake said, "to protect your friend from his doctor's ire."

Teal chuckled. "No, I'm on your side. I tried to talk him back into bed an hour ago."

Blake frowned, looking down at her glass. "Tochigi died of idiopathic heart failure—a fancy way of saying that his heart stopped and I can't tell you why."

"I heard something about spiders in his spacesuit?" Teal prompted her.

Blake nodded. "Abello claimed to have seen hundreds of them inside Tochigi's helmet. We didn't find hundreds. But we did find 19, and that's no less difficult to explain." The grim expression on her face deepened. "They crawled out of his mouth." At this, she gave an involuntary shudder.

"But how is that possible?" Jones asked. "Was there a nest of them in his suit?"

Blake shrugged wordlessly, and then shook her head.

"What kind of spiders were they?" Teal asked.

"Well, that's where it gets interesting. I ran a computer check. Eleven of them turned out to be banana spiders—a couple of those were about as big as your hand. Four were brown widows. The rest were wolf spiders. And here's a fun fact. All are commonly found on Okinawa."

"Okinawa," Teal said. "Tochigi's summer stomping grounds." He paused, considering the implications. "Wow."

"Precisely," Blake agreed.

"How would spiders from Okinawa get into Tochigi's spacesuit?" Jones asked.

"I don't know how they got in there. But I know how they didn't. The chief insists it could not have happened by accident."

"You mean someone *put* them there?" Teal demanded.

"Why would anyone do that?" Jones objected. "And even if they did, that only explains half the mystery. If Abello saw hundreds of spiders, what happened to the rest of them?"

"Well, that's easier to explain," Blake said. "Abello was either hallucinating, or lying. And I see no reason to believe the former."

Jones raised an eyebrow. "So you think *Abello* did it?"

She again glanced down at her glass, which she was twirling with her fingers. "That's a matter for the senior officers to figure out."

"Are you're sure the spiders are not what killed him?" Jones asked.

"Very sure. This particular brand of banana spider is not venomous. Nor are the wolf spiders. The brown widows are. Tochigi had plenty of bites—hundreds of them, in fact—but there were no toxins in his bloodstream. And that's not surprising. Spider venom tends to stay localized at the site of the bite, and this all happened very quickly."

"Dr. Jones is right," Teal remarked. "It doesn't add up. How could 19 spiders produce hundreds of bites?"

Blake shrugged. "I don't know. They were enthusiastic spiders, I guess." She smiled wanly, and looked across at Jones. "But if we're going to play 50 questions, Dr. Jones, it's my turn." She nodded at the viewports stretching in front of them. "Where the hell are we? What *is* this place?"

"Well, those are two very different questions, Dr. Blake," Jones said. "For the former, I defer to my lovely bride, who should be getting off watch about now. But I *can* tell you what you're looking at."

"All right," Blake said. "Throw me that bone, at least."

"That," Jones continued, hooking his thumb at the nearest port, "is the darkest dark mankind has ever seen or even conceived of. In two days of surveys, I and my team haven't been able to spot a single source of any kind of radiation on any wavelength. The EM spectrum is completely dead end to end, from the highest energy gamma rays down to the longest radio waves. Nor have we found a single atom or even a subatomic particle. In addition to the sky survey, we sent a probe out yesterday. A hundred thousand klicks out, the only energy it detected was that radiated from the body of the probe itself and from the *Santa Maria*. The temperature out there is absolute zero out to 12 decimal points, which is the best our instruments can manage—a temperature never before recorded in nature."

Blake gazed through the port. "It is dark," she agreed. "Darker than the inside of an anvil."

"Much, much, much darker," Jones said. "The inside of your anvil would emit black-body radiation corresponding to its temperature. Cosmic rays of all kinds would be passing through it. Neutrinos emitted from the stars and echoing from The Big Bang would be whizzing through its structure. It would be positively *alive* with activity."

Blake nodded. "I see."

Jones shook his head. "No disrespect, Doctor, but no, you don't." He gazed through the port. "What you are seeing out there transcends darkness. It is absolute nothingness. Zip. Zilch. Nada. Naught. It's a nullity without expression. The inside of a zero. A goose egg without the goose egg. And it's older than God."

At this, Father Teal shot him a sharp glance. "Nothing is older than God."

Jones nodded. "Precisely. That's what I just said."

"But nothing predates the existence of God," Teal argued.

"Again, we're in total agreement." Jones nodded to the window. "And you're looking at that nothing right now."

"But—look, you're using semantics to twist my words. Nothing is possible without God."

"Right," Jones agreed. "And again, we agree. Nothing *is* possible, without God. And that nothing surrounds us as we speak. Therefore, God is not here."

Teal gave out a short, sharp snort.

"Wait a minute," Blake interjected. "How can God not be here? The God I've always heard about is *everywhere*."

"Yes," Jones said. "Agreed. God is everywhere. But this is not a *where*. It's a *no*where."

Blake looked both exasperated and confused. "But—Dr. Jones, I've always been taught that God has *always* existed," she argued.

"Certainly. The Uncreated Creator, ageless and eternal, He Is Who Is and all that. We don't know where God came from or what he was doing, if anything, before he landed his current gig. In fact, the word "before" in this context probably is meaningless, as time itself may not have existed. But we do know the first thing God did when he got here. He created matter—the heavens and the earth—and then he turned on the lights." Jones gestured to the viewports. "Do you see any of the above out there?"

Teal waved a hand back and forth impatiently. "Wait a minute, wait a minute. You just agreed nothing is possible without God. But *we're* here. *We're* not nothing. Your logic falls apart on that point."

"Does it?" Jones paused. "Have you noticed how tired, rundown, and depressed you've been feeling lately? And don't deny it. Everyone I've talked with has reported the same thing."

Blake nodded. "Sure. I've been noticing that all over the ship. But it's no mystery. Just stress."

"Really? Don't you think it's odd what while we're all feeling increasingly drained, the ship's power is bleeding off as well?"

Blake didn't have an answer for that.

"We're all winding down like Dr. Makowski's N-field whirligig with the power off. Soon the energy will drain to zero—the ship's, and also ours. We'll be as dark and lifeless as the void stretching outside those viewports."

The three fell silent for a moment. Finally, Teal spoke up. "As grim a possibility as that is—and I grant you, it could happen—our atoms would still exist. We'd be *something*, not nothing."

"I wouldn't bet on that, either," Jones said. "Remember that lecture I gave earlier about quantum tunneling—how matter in an absolute, non-false vacuum could tumble away into a different state and possibly be lost, at least as we know it?"

Teal nodded slowly.

"We are in such a vacuum now—the first ever recorded by mankind. As we know, energy and mass are two sides of the same coin. And our energy profile is sloping toward zero. *What if it crosses the line?*"

Teal shook his head. "You don't even know if E still equals m c squared out here," he pointed out. "You don't know *what* laws of physics apply. If any."

"True. Which is just another way of saying that anything could happen."

Teal again shook his head. "I'm just not buying it."

"You know," Blake said, staring thoughtfully into the blackness, "I've never been able to convince myself that God exists. But I find it strangely discomforting to be told with scientific authority that he doesn't." She turned to Jones. "You really think he's not here?"

Jones took a sip of his drink, and then put down his glass. "Look at what's happened since we got here," he said, gazing into the amber liquid. "One crewmen dead under circumstances that defy explanation. One killed committing an attack that is equally inexplicable. One dead in a fall that may or may not have been an accident. Four missing, probably murdered." He looked up at her. "Do you see the hand of God at work here?"

5 THE DARK

Nunn glanced at the clock readout on her panel; it showed 02:49. Wearily, she sighed and leaned back in her flight chair.

"You sound like you're about done in," observed AI specialist Sierra Bent, who was sitting to Nunn's right at the engineering station. Technically, it was Bent's watch, but Nunn had remained at her console to work on the astrogation computer problem. At the moment the two of them were the only ones on the bridge. Trafford, who normally would have been on duty, was dead. Sabol, the designated bridge engineer for this watch, was missing. Coms officer Mason Krajnovich had been assigned to Team 1 to replace Beadel, who also was missing; Bent had assumed his role for the time being on Team 2's shifts. Astrogator Specht and Helmsman Terwilliger, whose services were not, strictly speaking, needed at the moment, had been called away to help conduct a search for Electrician Smith, who'd just been discovered to be missing from his cabin, where he'd been confined.

"I won't deny it," Nunn said, wearily rubbing the dark side of her face.

Bent regarded her with a concerned expression. "How long have you been at it?"

"Since eight hundred this morning. With a couple of quick breaks."

Bent frowned. "You need to knock off for a while. Get some chow and some shut-eye."

Nunn shook her head. "Can't do it. My watch begins in about an hour. And I've got to solve this problem."

"If you don't get some sack time," Bent insisted, "you're not going to be able to think straight."

"If I don't solve this problem, there'll be nothing *but* time for sleep.

164

Believe me. Besides, at the moment Wilson is doing all the thinking. Isn't that right, Wilson?"

"Not correct," came Wilson's voice over the console speakers. "You designed the current search strategy. I am only implementing it."

"What's the strategy?" Bent asked.

Nunn shook her head as if to clear it. "You're right, I am getting fuzzy-headed. I should have told you this at the start of your shift. Wilson, explain to her what we're doing."

"Well, Ms. Bent," Wilson said, "it's extremely unlikely to the point of near impossibility that I would be able to break the astro computer encryption in the time allotted. But we have a much better chance with Makowski's personal computer. We are operating under the assumption that he may have chosen a password that has personal significance. I have reviewed all of the information we have in our files pertaining to Dr. Makowski. I am now in the process of creating and testing passwords using phrases and dates from that personal information."

"Makes sense," Bent said. "But I assume you haven't had any luck so far."

"Not so far. But I have only tried a small percentage of possible password combinations derived from the initial list of keywords that we compiled."

"Wilson, seeing as you're the one doing all the work at the moment," Bent continued, "I think you should tell Connie to go take a break."

"I already advised Ms. Nunn to do this," Wilson said. "She rejected that recommendation."

"See?" Nunn said, smiling. "Wilson knows who's boss."

"All right, Wilson," Bent said. "But when Connie makes a face-plant into the console, I'm going to blame you."

"Yes, Ms. Bent," Wilson acknowledged.

That caused Bent to chuckle.

For a moment, the two of them sat in silence, with Nunn studying the console displays as Bent stared straight ahead through the viewports into the utter blackness.

"Do you think we'll get out of this?" Bent asked, breaking the silence.

"I do," Nunn said without looking up. "It's just a mathematical problem. We'll solve it."

"I sure hope you're right."

Bent continued to stare through the viewports. The blackness beyond seemed to tug at her eyeballs, teeth, and bones, almost as if it were trying to pull her in. The feeling was distinctly uncomfortable. "We out to shut the damned view screens," she blurted out.

Nunn glanced at her, raising an eyebrow. "The darkness creeping you out?"

"A little."

Nunn turned back to her console. "Do what I'm doing. Keep your eyes on the readouts. It's very comforting."

Bent noticed that the ship's upper hull, which normally was awash in light, was now totally dark. The navigation lights were off, too. "Who turned off the running lights?" she asked.

Nunn shrugged. "I don't know. I hadn't noticed."

"Well, *I'm* noticing. We need some light on the subject." Getting up out of her flight chair, Bent walked over to the helmsman's station and pressed a series of squares. The forward port and starboard running lights sprang to life, and recessed floodlights splashed bright illumination over the words "NAUS Santa Maria" that curved gracefully outward on forward end of the hull. "Much better," Bent said as she regained her seat.

Still not looking up from her console, Nunn cracked a smile. "I have a nightlight you can borrow, if you want it later."

Bent turned to her, laughing. "If you're serious, I absolutely do."

Nunn shook her head, chuckling. "I wish I were. I could use one myself." She considered, and then rejected, relating the little scare she'd had the previous evening.

"Well, don't tease me, then." Still smiling, Bent turned and looked outside again, admiring the curve of the hull extending out beyond the ports.

A flash of color caught her eye. She turned her head to the right to see what it was. *"Jesus!"* Bent screeched, jumping out of her chair.

Nunn looked up in alarm. "What?"

Bent was pointing urgently to the right side of the arc of viewports. She turned to Nunn. "Did you not see that?"

"See what?"

Bent turned back to the viewport. "It was right there," she insisted. But at the moment nothing could be seen outside the port except the endless expanse of blackness.

"What was it?"

For a moment, Bent considered telling her what she thought she'd seen. But she quickly rejected the notion. "I guess I've got the heebie jeebies," she said, bringing a hand to her chest and making a concerted effort to control her racing heart.

"That's understandable," Nunn said. "This place will give anybody the willies."

Bent walked back over to the helm. Pressing a series of squares, she extinguished the running lights and all hull illumination.

Nunn raised an eyebrow. "I thought you wanted those on?"

"Let's leave them off," Bent said firmly.

Nunn cocked her head quizzically. "Why? Are you afraid we'll attract moths?"

Bent turned to her, not smiling. "Just out of curiosity, why *are* the screens open?"

Nunn shrugged. "I don't know. Usually the captain orders them retracted after a jump. But this afternoon, things were a little—confused. I think Swann simply opened them up on his own after the abort."

"Well, I'm closing them on *my* own." Again reaching forward, she pressed a square on the helmsman's console. With a heavy mechanical whine, the screens began descending. Turning to Nunn, Bent asked, "Do you mind?"

"No. Not at all. In fact, I'll admit it makes me feel more comfortable."

Bent nodded. "Me, too. Definitely."

The screens hit the bottom of their tracks with a thud, and the motors shut off. "I need to take a quick break," Bent said. "Will you cover for me?"

Nunn nodded. "Sure. I won't tell."

"Thanks. I won't be long." With that, Bent exited the bridge.

Nunn turned to Aristarchus, who had ensconced himself on the flight chair to her left. "It looks like it's just me and you, Ari."

"Ow," Ari said, half-blinking his eyes.

The console in front of her beeped, and at the same time, the scrolling password display stopped. On screen there now appeared the image of a personal desktop. Very clearly it was Makowski's; he'd personalized it with an unmistakable desktop image. Amid the usual assortment of icons, an extreme close-up of the man's two bloodshot eyes, minus his usual spectacles, stared out at her, dominating the screen. "Connie," came Wilson's mellow voice over the speaker, "we're in."

"Outstanding! How did you do it?"

"I played what I think you would call a hunch."

"Really? Do tell."

"I supplemented our test password list with a few additional choices based on my hunch, and moved those to the top of the queue. The final password is a combination of Makowski's birth date and the name of a victim who appeared in one of his illegal holographic videos."

"How'd you get that?"

"The video was playing when Second Officer Trafford and First Officer De Vegas entered the cabin. I heard the name on the soundtrack through the first officer's comlink, before the link was disabled. My hunch was that this video was Dr. Makowski's favorite, and that the name of the victim might therefore be important enough to him to cause him to commemorate it in a password."

Nunn nodded her head. "Wilson, you're a genius. But we knew that. Now, first order of business. Copy all of Makowski's files from his local storage."

"Already done."

"Is there anything in there that looks like an encryption code for the astro computer?"

"Yes. I am trying it now."

The words were still hanging in air when the astro computer screen on Nunn's console flickered. The "OFFLINE" message disappeared, to be replaced by the normal astrogation computer desktop.

"I have successfully disabled the encryption," Wilson said superfluously.

Nunn held both fists up in the air. "Yes!" she shouted. "Wilson, I could hug you."

"I would like that," Wilson said. "What is a hug like?"

Nunn chuckled. "Wilson, I promise you, when we get some down time, I'll tell you."

"I look forward to that."

From the rear of the bridge, a loud *pop!* sounded. Swiveling her flight chair around, Nunn saw that the rear overhead light panel just to the left of the safety lock had gone dark, throwing the area into shadow. Beside her, Ari jumped down from the helmsman's flight chair and trotted over to investigate.

"Ari, where do you think you're going?" she demanded. "Come back over here and help Momma celebrate."

Ari ignored her. He padded over to a pool of dark shadows on the starboard side of the safety lock door, and then stopped. Now the animal hissed and arched his back. The hair stood up along his spine, his tail fluffed, and he began to howl.

"Ari!" Nunn shouted in alarm. Jumping up, she ran over to him.

The cat continued to groan and howl while staring into the shadows.

"Wilson, what is Ari looking at?" she asked, raising her voice to be heard above the cat.

"I do not know," came Wilson's voice, now relocated to the overhead speakers. "There is nothing registering on my audio pickups or on my visual monitors in any spectrum."

The pool of shadows was utterly black. She peered at it. Was it her imagination, or were the outer boundaries of the dark area *growing*? "Wilson, has that shadow on the starboard side of the safety lock grown since the light went out?"

"Yes, Connie."

"Is it growing now?"

"Yes. The width and height are increasing at a rate of approximately two centimeters per second."

Nunn glanced quickly around the empty bridge. She could see nothing moving. "Wilson, what is casting that shadow?"

"There is nothing on my monitors that could account for the shadow. Therefore I must conclude it is not a shadow."

"Well, then what is it?"

"Unknown at this time. I have insufficient data."

Beside her, Ari was showing no signs of diminished enthusiasm for his caterwauling.

"Ari, give it a rest!" she snapped.

This had no effect on Ari, who continued his impressive, soaring solo unabashed.

Stepping closer, she bent forward to examine the shadow. It was so deep that she could not make out the surface of the bulkhead. Gingerly, she reached forward to touch it. But there was no surface; her fingers and hand kept going. As it pushed through, a putrid smell reached her nostrils, causing her to wrinkle her nose in disgust.

"What in the world—"

She did not get a chance to complete the thought. From the depths of the shadow, a black, bony hand appeared, closed around her wrist, and pulled her in.

Ari began to howl even louder.

"Connie?" Wilson's voice sounded over the speakers. "Connie, I do not have you on my monitors. Where are you? Connie?"

There was no answer.

"David! David!" Lydia's voice screeched out in the darkness, reverberating against the walls of the tiny cabin.

Jones bolted upright in the bunk. The bubble of profound sleep in which he'd been floating had exploded and was gone; now his heart was racing and he found himself panting for breath as if he'd just run a hundred meter dash. Had he heard something, or had it only been a nightmare? Reaching out in the dark, he moved his hand to touch Lydia's side. But she wasn't there.

"David!" her voice sounded again, now hollow as if coming to him from far away.

Reaching to his left, he switched on the light. The four glow panels overhead flashed to life, but three of them immediately went out with loud popping noises.

Movement caught his eye. Turning, he glanced at the bulkhead to the left of the bunk. A small, black pool of shadows on the wall seemed to be shrinking. He thought he caught a glimpse of motion within it.

"Daviiiiiiid!" Lydia's voice sounded again, now sounding even more remote. This time, the direction was unmistakable; the voice was emanating *from the other side of that bulkhead.* Jumping from the bed, he ran over to it. But when he reached the wall, the shadows he thought he'd seen were gone.

And then he noticed that a very light but unpleasant smell hung in the air—a smell that hinted of decay, like a refrigerator that was well past due for a good cleaning.

Turning quickly around, he scanned the cabin again. It was empty. Jones dashed across to the refresher and looked inside; it, too, was devoid of life. Running back into the cabin, he yelled as loudly as he could, "Lydia!" He called again, and then fell still and quiet, straining his ears against the silence, desperate to hear a response.

At that moment the general alarm sounded, nearly startling him off his feet.

Father Teal sat straight up in bed, a stifled scream hanging at the back of his throat. A video loop played in his head: He was killing Candi Blake in a horrible fashion, slicing across her abdomen with a surgical scalpel grasped in his right hand, while he held her pinned to the bunk with a combination of his body weight and his outstretched left arm, the hand of which he'd closed around her throat. Warm blood was gushing everywhere.

Thank God, he thought, now staring into the blackness with his heart pounding and his chest heaving. *It's just a dream.*

As the cobwebs of deep sleep fell away and the nightmare images began to fade from his mind, he noticed what had awakened him. An urgent alarm was sounding. Was it the fire alarm? Or some kind of general alarm? He didn't know. But then Wilson's voice sounded from the overhead speaker, answering his question. "All hands to emergency stations," Wilson announced. "This is not a drill." Wilson then repeated the message.

Idly he wondered why Blake, who was lying next to him, hadn't reacted. *She must have been more drunk that I realized,* he thought.

At that, the recollection of what had transpired over the last few hours came flooding over him. He knew that he should wake Blake and then investigate that alarm. But for the moment, he couldn't move. The crushing weight of what he'd done, and of the future that now lay before him as a result, had pinned him to the spot.

Teal replayed the relevant events on his mental screen.

Shortly after midnight, Dr. Jones had bid them good night, leaving Teal and Blake sitting alone over the candle in the observation lounge. Teal graciously offered to walk Blake to her cabin. She agreed. The two of them headed down the passageway to the elevator, where Teal punched the button for A-Deck.

But the car began descending instead. Suppressing an expletive, Teal repeatedly jabbed the button, but to no effect. The car stopped on E-Deck and the doors opened wide, revealing a gloomy passageway stretching into the distance. Only a few of the light panels were working; the rest were either out or flickering, filling the corridor with dark, capering shadows.

Impatiently, he continued to punch the A-Deck button. Nothing happened. The elevator doors remained open.

He turned to Blake, frowning. "Looks like we'll have to take the companionway."

"Looks like," she agreed. The two of them stepped out into the passageway.

"It should be right over here," Teal said, walking to the left. "Yeah. There's the sign."

"Wait a second," Blake said, stopping. "Check that out." She pointed down the passageway. About 20 meters down the corridor, one of the cabin doors on the starboard side was standing open, spilling a pool of yellow light onto the deck.

"That's odd," Teal said, frowning. He had not noticed the open door when he'd glanced down the passageway seconds earlier.

"I suppose we ought to take a look," Blake said.

That wasn't Teal's preference. But he didn't want to say so. "Okay. I'll do it." He turned to her. "Maybe you should stay here."

"To hell with that," Blake said firmly. "I'm coming with you."

Teal nodded. The two of them walked cautiously down the passageway. Stopping at the door, Teal carefully peered around the edge of the door frame.

What lay within astonished him. Unlike all of the other cabins he'd seen, this one was fully furnished and decked out as if awaiting occupants. A brilliant gold and red bed covering was turned down, revealing shiny gold satin sheets. A single gaily wrapped piece of chocolate lay on each of the twin gold pillows. On the small desk at the side of the bunk sat a champagne cooler, from which extended the neck of a dark bottle covered in gold foil. Two thin, stemmed glasses sat atop a silver tray next to the cooler. A vase with a dozen roses completed the arrangement.

Blake walked past him and stepped into the room, showing no trace of surprise. Teal followed her into the cabin, now starting to realize what was going on. Clearly, the doctor had prepared a little surprise for him. He wasn't sure what he thought about it.

Blake stepped to the door, shut it, and then turned to him, resting her back against it. "How about that," she said in a low voice. "No chaperones. And I just love champagne. Don't you?"

His instincts screamed that he should turn and leave. Instead, he took a step toward her. She moved toward him, slightly raising her chin. Their lips met.

Teal had not been with a woman in three years. The strength of Candi's response to the physical ministrations that quickly followed told him that it had been a while for her, too. They proceeded to wear each other out. Afterwards, they opened the champagne bottle and drank it dry while exchanging life stories. Another lovemaking session followed, after which they collapsed with their arms around one another, each soaking in the sweat and basking in the body heat of the other before drifting off to a deep sleep.

It had been wonderful. *But*, Teal now thought as he completed his mental review of the evening, *it had also been a bad, bad*, bad *idea*. What he *should* have done the moment he'd walked into Candi's little lair was to kiss her on the cheek, say something tactful and complimentary while letting her down gently, and then beat a hasty retreat. But that's not what he'd done. Oh, no. And now everything had become complicated. Again.

As he sat there thinking about it, his chest constricted and a cold sweat popped out on his brow. There was not a shred of doubt about what lay ahead for him now. She would become demanding. His world would close in on him. Oh, not all at once, and not right away, to be sure. But slowly, inexorably, methodically, she would begin to encroach on his space. It would be little things at first. *Hey, I tried to call you, did you not get my message? Why did you leave so soon last night? When can I see you again? Why don't you stay the night?* And then it would progress. *Why don't you ever say you love me? Why does our relationship have to be a secret? Why* can't *we be a couple?* It would go on and on and on, until nothing remained of his old life for him to stand on but a tiny spit of sand surrounded by an endless, roiling ocean of her needs, desires and demands.

He resented her for it. In fact, he now found himself struggling not to hate her. It was no wonder he'd just had a dream about killing her. Desires buried in the subconscious always fueled dreams; psychiatrists had known that since the late 19th century. Part of his mind told him that his feelings were not fair. After all, she hadn't actually made any demands on him so far, other than sex—a service that, in and of itself, he was not unhappy to render. Quite the opposite, in fact; he'd enjoyed the act—relished it, even. But another part of him said that his resentment *was* justified, and perfectly reasonable. After all, he'd been doing a good job of resisting temptation, and still would be if not for her little seduction. She was *not* an innocent party. She'd taken advantage of a chink in his armor and a weakness in his character that he'd spent much effort over a long period of time trying to remedy or at least suppress. And now, thanks to her, he was back to square one.

The urgent general alarm reminded him that they could not stay here. Sighing, he reached out to shake her awake. But his hand hit only empty air. He probed further. Now his fingers touched the mattress. Something was not right. His fingertips came away cool with wetness.

Reaching around and groping in the dark, he found the light plate. The overhead panels flared to life, momentarily blinding him. Squinting his eyes, he turned to look beside him.

Candi was gone. The spot she'd occupied was soaked with blood—seemingly gallons of it. In the exact center of the massive stain lay a surgical scalpel, its silver surface now invisible beneath a thick coat of human blood and gore.

Stifling a scream, Teal leapt from the bed. He now saw that his own nude body was liberally smeared with blood as well. It covered his chest, his abdomen, and his legs down to his knees.

The conclusion was inescapable. The scene that had been playing out in his mind upon awakening had been no nightmare, but rather a suppressed memory. Although he had no conscious recollection of having done so, obviously he'd killed her. He'd done it out of resentment, and to cover up his sin.

But where was the body?

Teal glanced about the small cabin. There was no body. But something else was amiss. An upholstered chair that had stood by the built-in couch was gone, with only a square patch of slight discoloration on the deck to show it had ever existed. Likewise, two colorful pillows that had adorned the couch were missing. The champagne cooler, bottle, tray, glasses and vase of roses that had stood on the built-in desk had vanished, without so much as a loose petal or a condensation ring on the bare desktop to show anything had ever been there. Reaching forward, Teal drew a finger along its surface, and then held it up to examine it. A coating of dust now discolored his fingertip. He glanced at the desktop again; clearly visible was the trail his finger had left, but the light coating of dust was otherwise undisturbed.

Now turning to look again at the bunk from which he'd just risen, he saw nothing but a bare mattress, one now marred with a huge dark red stain. There was no trace of the luxurious bedclothes and pillows that had been there earlier.

Panic was rising within him. He absolutely had to get the blood off. Dashing into the refresher, Teal cast around for a towel. There was nothing. Walking back out into the room, his eye fell on Blake's lab coat. Grabbing it, he ran back into the bathroom and touched the selector buttons to run some warm water. There was no response; the water service was off.

Frantically, he began dabbing at himself with the lab coat. Only some of the blood rubbed off onto it. Obviously, this was not going to work; there was simply too much blood on his body. But he might be able to do something about his face, at least. Spitting on the sleeve of the coat, he began working at the smears and streaks on his cheeks and chin. Fortunately, there were not many of them. By repeating the process, he was able to get his face reasonably clean.

Outside the cabin door, he heard footsteps racing down the passageway.

I hope there's no strip of light under the cabin door, he thought. But then he realized that such a thing was not possible; the seal was airtight.

After doing the best he could with his face and the backs of his hands, he strode briskly back into the cabin and began to shrug into his jumpsuit. It was good, he thought, that he'd decided to wear a ship's uniform on the mission. The irony of putting on a priest's collar at the moment would have been too much to bear.

As these thoughts played out in his mind, tears coursed down his cheek. *What have I done?* he thought bitterly. *What have I done?*

When finished dressing, Father Teal looked himself over in the bathroom mirror. Some of the blood that had covered his left side had begun to spot through the cloth of the jumpsuit. But there was nothing he could do other than hope he ran into no crewmen in the passageway; with luck, they would all be at their duty stations by now. If not, then perhaps they'd be in too much of a hurry to pay him any attention, or maybe the dimness of the illumination in the corridors would save him.

With these thoughts in mind, Teal went to the door. Hesitating only for a second, he pressed the button, and the panel opened silently inward. Turning off the cabin lights, he stepped out, touched the button to close the door behind him—oblivious to the faint bloody fingerprint he left in the process—and then proceeded on down the passageway. It took all the strength of will he could muster not to break into a dead run.

Fabiana De Vegas was the first to reach the bridge safety lock. But no one answered her call. Using her iCard to gain entrance, she dashed inside—and was astonished to find the bridge empty. Stepping over to the communications panel, she punched a button. "Wilson, who sounded the alarm?"

"I did," Wilson answered calmly. "Where is Third Engineer Constance Nunn?"

"Wilson, no one is here." She glanced around the bridge. "The bridge is empty. Correction—Aristarchus is here." The cat was on the deck in front of the AI console flight chair, cowering at the door to his acceleration chamber.

The deck plates beneath De Vegas' feet rumbled and throbbed, and then a surge of weight hit her, nearly knocking her off her feet. As she grabbed hold of the coms station flight chair to steady herself, two of the overhead light panels popped and went out. "Wilson, what just happened?" she demanded as the vibrations died away.

"Some circuits experienced a momentary surge of power," Wilson said calmly. "The disturbance appears to have originated just now in the AI unit."

De Vegas stared at the AI console in furrowed-brow consternation.

"You mean, it came from *you*?"

"Apparently so," Wilson conceded. This incredible statement was followed by a burst of static. "I cannot account for it," he continued when the static had cleared. And then, after a short, almost imperceptible pause, he added, "I apologize."

De Vegas was considering the implications of this astounding communication when the alert for the bridge safety lock intercom sounded. Without turning to look, she pressed the button to open the outer door. "Wilson," she continued, "you can kill the alarm now." The noise cut off abruptly. "Why did you sound it, Wilson?" she asked. "What is the nature of the emergency?"

"Third Engineer Constance Nunn disappeared from my monitor, and her comlink went dark. Two other comlinks also went offline at approximately the same time—those of Dr. Candace Blake and Chief Astrogator Lydia Nguyen Jones."

The inner bridge door slid aside and ASM Sierra Bent dashed in. Hard on her heels were ASMs Swann, Specht and Terwilliger. "What's going on?" Swann asked.

De Vegas held her hand up as she fixed Bent with a disapproving glare. "Where were you?" she demanded.

"I, uh, had an emergency," she stammered. "Nausea. I was in the head."

"Where is Constance Nunn?" Wilson repeated. His normally smooth, unflappable voice sounded almost urgent.

"I don't know, Wilson," the acting captain answered. "As I said, she's not here. Normally I would turn to *you* to answer that kind of question."

"Nunn's comlink is off line," Wilson repeated.

"So you indicated." This was another interesting and disturbing development. Unless asked to do so, AIs seldom repeated themselves. Yet Wilson had just done so, twice. It was almost as if he were wringing his virtual hands. "You said she disappeared from your monitor," De Vegas continued. "How is that possible? What was she doing?"

"She was staring at a visual anomaly that had appeared on the rear bulkhead, just to the starboard side of the inner safety lock door."

"What kind of anomaly?"

"Unknown. It appeared to be a pool of darkness, similar to a deep shadow. I have a recording of the incident."

De Vegas nodded. "Good. Put it on the main holo."

The acting captain stepped back and watched as a 3-D image flickered and began to form in the space just forward of the closed center viewports.

As it did so, the bridge door slid open and the rest of Bridge Watch Teams 1 and 2 filed in. De Vegas glanced at her watch, frowning. She opened her mouth to say something, but then the video began playing.

The scene showed Nunn's last few seconds on the bridge. De Vegas and the other crewmembers watched as Nunn stepped past a howling cat, paused before the bulkhead, reached out a hand, and then disappeared into the wall, appearing to have been jerked off her feet and pulled inside.

The bridge door slid aside again and Dr. Jones burst onto the bridge. "Lydia is missing!" he shouted as he dashed up to the group.

De Vegas turned to him. "Wilson just told us her comlink is off line. Can you tell us what happened?"

"Not really," Jones said, shaking his head. He paused, struggling to catch his breath. "I heard her calling out for me. But when I turned on the light, she wasn't there."

De Vegas paused. "This is going to sound a little odd—but did you see anything strange? Anything at all?"

"Like what?" Jones answered, puzzled.

"Like, for instance, an unusual looking shadow on the bulkhead?"

Jones nodded. "Yeah. As a matter of fact, I did. It seemed to move. But I thought it was my imagination. My eyes weren't yet adjusted to the light." He regarded De Vegas with pleading eyes. "Captain, we've got to look for her."

"First we need to figure out what we're dealing with." De Vegas turned to the holo display. "Wilson, please replay the recording."

The group watched the video again. Each person was silent up until the point where something seemed to drag Nunn into the wall, at which point Jones gasped. "My God," he said when the display had gone dark. "That must be what happened to Lydia. I thought I heard her calling me from behind the bulkhead."

"Captain," Krajnovich said, "what the hell did we just see?"

"I don't know. Let's have a look at that bulkhead."

De Vegas stepped to the spot next to the safety lock where the shadow had been. The bulkhead appeared entirely ordinary. She ran her hands along the surface. The plastisteel felt solid, but it was chilly to the touch, well below room temperature. She noticed something else; a very slight odor of something unpleasant hung in the air.

Jones turned to the AI console. "Wilson, did you capture anything else out of the ordinary happening on the bridge before this incident?"

"The recording I just played you is the complete available visual record of recent events on the bridge. This is due to the fact that the video circuits were down until 87 seconds before Constance Nunn's disappearance, when I was able to restore them after obtaining the encryption code from Dr. Makowski's files. However, there is one other unusual incident, which I was able to record via the AI console audio pickup."

"Let's have it."

Wilson replayed a section of audio capturing Bent's hasty departure from the bridge.

De Vegas turned to her. "Mixter Bent, what happened?"

Bent shifted on her feet, looking uncomfortable. "I thought I saw something."

"Saw something? Where?"

"Through the viewport." Bent pointed to the second viewport from the right, now covered like all the others by a protective screen. "There."

"What did you see?"

"Nothing," Bent replied. "I'm *sure* it was nothing."

De Vegas gave her a hard stare. "Out with it, Mixter Bent. Now."

Bent swallowed heavily. "I thought I saw—eyes. Two red, staring eyes."

"And that is what caused you to close the screens and ask to leave your post?"

Bent nodded.

If anything, De Vegas' stare now became even more penetrating. "And you thought it was okay to leave Mixter Nunn by herself under those circumstances." She said it as a statement, not a question.

Bent's chin trembled, and she looked as if she were about to burst into tears. "I— I didn't think it was real," she stammered. "I thought it was me, that maybe I was having a breakdown." A solitary tear now coursed down one of her cheeks.

The Team 2 helmsman, Julius Terwilliger, cleared his throat. "Mixter De Vegas, if that had happened to me, I wouldn't have believed my own eyes either."

For a moment, De Vegas appeared inclined to argue. But instead, she nodded. "Very well."

At that moment an alert beeped on the coms console. Krajnovich stepped over to it, exchanged a few words with the caller, and then turned to De Vegas. "The Chief says engineering is at emergency stations and awaiting orders, ser."

"Tell him to stand by." She turned back to Bent. "Please open the screens."

The blood rushed from Bent's face, but she knew better than to argue. Instead, she stepped over to the console and pressed the appropriate control squares. With a loud whining noise, the shields began to retract. Soon they reached the ends of their tracks. When the motors shut off, the abrupt silence eerily underscored and complimented the total blackness that stretched beyond the ports.

"Kick on the floods and running lights," De Vegas ordered.

With a trembling hand, Bent pressed the controls, flooding the upper hull with bright lights.

"Now tell me again," De Vegas said, "where you thought you saw the eyes."

Bent stepped over to the viewport she'd indicated previously. "Right here, ser," she said. "They were about six inches apart, and seemed to be about a foot outside the glass."

"Mixter De Vegas," Jones blurted out with an urgent, almost pleading voice. "Are we going to search the ship?"

"Captain De Vegas," came Wilson's voice from the console and overhead speakers, "I was just about to make the same suggestion."

Jones' outburst didn't surprise De Vegas, but Wilson's did. For an AI to offer unsolicited operational advice was unusual, to say the least. In fact, she had never heard of such a thing. And De Vegas could have sworn that his voice contained a note of emotion, or something like it. "You sound concerned, Wilson," she found herself saying.

"I am," Wilson admitted.

"I didn't know AIs could feel concern."

"Nor did I," Wilson agreed.

De Vegas was now feeling quite alarmed about Wilson. Although she was not a computer expert by any stretch of the imagination, De Vegas knew that no case where an AI had displayed what looked like real emotion had ended well. Still, she reasoned, there was no direct evidence that Wilson was doing anything other than *emulate* such emotion, a function that did lie within his programming parameters. But if so, he was getting to be damned good at it. Uncannily so.

"Captain," Swann spoke up, "over the last couple of days we've combed the ship several times—the most recent sweep concluded just a couple of hours ago. I wonder if Wilson has any suggestions to improve our odds?"

De Vegas nodded. "Wilson?" she said aloud. "Do you have any wisdom along those lines for us?"

"No wisdom," Wilson answered. "But I do suggest that the sweep be conducted in teams of no less than two, and that it include a search for any anomalous patterns of light and shadow. I further suggest that should such anomalies be encountered, that the crewmen not approach, but instead report the finding to you. Now that my monitors have been restored, I will of course keep a constant watch myself and will alert you to anything unusual."

"Very well."

"Toward that end," Wilson continued, "I note that Father Teal did not report to his emergency station in the forward lounge. He is in his cabin. My monitors caught him exiting cabin E-13. He went straight to his own cabin from there via a forward elevator. Father Teal appeared to have a discoloration on his face, hands, and portions of his clothes."

"What kind of discoloration?" De Vegas asked.

"Unknown. But its color is consistent with that of human blood."

"What is he doing now?"

"Unknown. He set a privacy lock on his cabin monitors."

De Vegas nodded. "Accept command override, my authority. Disable the locks. What is Father Teal doing?"

"Father Teal is now taking a shower."

"Anything else?"

"Nothing more to report at present."

De Vegas nodded, and then turned to Specht. "Go see him. Take Terwilliger. Find out what he was doing. Call me with a report."

The two nodded, and then left the bridge.

De Vegas turned to Swann. "Get with the chief. Reduce the bridge and engineering watches to two standers on each shift—no more, no less. Form two-man search teams with the rest."

"Yes, ser."

"Wilson," De Vegas continued, "please give Mr. Swann access to the armory."

"Yes, Captain," Wilson answered.

Swann nodded. "I admit I'll feel better with a pulse rifle in my hands."

"Sorry," De Vegas said, shaking her head. "The company had those removed before the launch. We have six sidearms. Pass them out as far as they'll go, one to a team."

Swann frowned. "Well, I guess that's better than being bare handed."

"Krajnovich and I will take this bridge watch and the next one," she continued. "Get moving."

Swann turned and stepped to his console to begin organizing the search as directed.

De Vegas walked over to the command console and sat down in the captain's chair. "Mister Krajnovich, 1MC."

Krajnovich nodded. "You're on."

"All hands, this is Acting Captain De Vegas. Secure from emergency stations." She paused. Taking a deep breath, she continued. "I must inform you that three more crewmembers have gone missing—Nguyen, Nunn, and Blake. Acting First Officer Nicolas Swann will organize search parties. Stand by for instructions. That is all."

She nodded to Krajnovich, who then pressed a button to close the connection. "You're clear," he said.

Sighing, De Vegas sank back into the flight chair.

Teal was toweling himself off when the door chime rang. After Specht and Terwilliger identified themselves through the intercom, Teal asked them to wait a moment. But the two did not wait. Teal was still standing by the intercom, dripping, when the panel slid aside and the two men stepped into the cabin.

"What is this?" Teal demanded angrily. "You couldn't wait two minutes for me to put on some clothes?"

Ignoring him, Specht brushed by him and stepped into the still-steamy refresher, while Terwilliger stood silently by the cabin door. It didn't take long for Specht to find what he was looking for. He stepped out carrying a blood-splotched jumpsuit.

When Teal caught sight of the stained uniform in Specht's hand, the cabin seemed to perform a pirouette around him. He stepped over to the bunk and sat down heavily on it.

"You want to tell us about this?" Specht asked calmly.

For a moment, Teal considered denying everything. Then he thought about simply remaining silent. But while he was going over those scenarios in his mind, the words he heard coming out of his mouth were, "I'll tell you everything. But I could really use a cup of coffee first."

Chief Engineer Crandall had not been happy to have nearly his entire engineering team pulled away for yet another search of the ship. The last such effort had proved completely useless; there was nothing to make him believe this one would achieve a different outcome.

He watched glumly as the power consumption graph continued to inch upwards. To keep the accumulators from going flat, he was now having to run the fusion plant full time. In another four days, even at full capacity the fusion plant would not make a difference. And he still had no idea where the power was going.

But that screen didn't bother him half as much as the display he now had punched up on his console. It was the main status readout for the astrogation computer, and it said simply, "ASTRO ONLINE." But no one was entering any data. Time was ticking away.

"God *damn* it!" he shouted.

The outburst caused Electrician Darlene Marrone, who was seated next to him, to jump.

Crandall glanced at her, and started to apologize, but then dismissed the thought. Instead he turned his mind to the next logical steps he must take.

There was no point in arguing further with De Vegas. Until the missing crewmembers were found, she was inclined neither to call off the search nor move the vessel. The woman simply was not thinking straight; she was suffering from a "lost sheep" complex and was willing to put the entire flock at risk in a hopeless effort to recover the missing. In a heated conversation less than 30 minutes ago, Crandall had assailed her position from all angles. She had refused to budge. De Vegas would not even consider allowing AI Specialist Sierra Bent to sit down with Astrogator Conrad Specht to begin calculating and inputting their return path using the reduced acceleration the torches were now able to deliver. Right now that figure was down to 15 gees. By this time tomorrow it would be down to 10. Maybe less. De Vegas' stated excuse was that the two of them were needed in the search.

Crandall was beginning to wonder whether she might have darker motives. In any case, the situation was intolerable. Crandall could not and would not accept it. Now he made up his mind what to do about it.

First he would need to talk to a few people. But he didn't want to go through Wilson. Reaching forward, Crandall called up the manual communications pad on his console and then pressed the square for Electrician Kimberly Nabozny. With Tochigi dead and Nunn missing, Nabozny was now his second in command. He knew from the search assignments that she was on E-Deck with Electrician Anwar. "Nabozny here," she answered.

"This is Crandall. I need for you and Anwar to report to engineering pronto."

"Okay, Chief. What's the deal?"

Crandall suppressed an urge to snap at her. "I'll tell you when you get here."

Nabozny hesitated. "Chief," she finally said, "Mr. Swann will want to know why you're pulling us off the search. What should I tell him?"

"Don't call Swann," Crandall said. "I'll inform him and the first—the acting captain—personally. The two of you just need to come straight back here. Now."

"Very well, Chief. We're on our way."

Crandall punched up the search assignments and found only three more teams where both members were from engineering. It would have to do. These were the only ones he could recall without directly alerting the bridge. Even then, an on-the-ball coms officer might notice that something was up by way of the tracking readouts. That risk could not be avoided. He made the calls.

A few minutes later, all the crewmembers had made it back to engineering without raising an alarm. When the last person walked in, Crandall turned to his console and placed a security lock on the outer safety door. Next, he called up his IT panel and disabled the external computer access to the lock; Wilson would not be able to override it. The moment Crandall did this, he knew an alert would show up on the bridge coms panel. If he'd been a computer whiz like Makowski, he could have figured out a way to bypass the alert. But there was no help for it.

This task completed, he turned to the assembled crew. Standing before him waiting for Crandall to explain himself were N-Field Specialist Ariana Marinez; Electricians Kimberly Nabozny, Carlos Abello, Nalini Dhawan, Kareem Anwar, and Darlene Marrone; and Carpenter Derek Damiano. Three of them were wearing sidearms. "Mr. Damiano," he said, "please pass me your weapon."

His face impassive, Damiano unbuckled the gun, stepped up to the chief, and handed it to him. Crandall fastened it around his waist without comment. Then he turned back to the group. "Ms. Nabozny, Mr. Abello, please pass your weapons forward as well."

Silently, the two did as instructed. Crandall placed the gun belts on the seat behind him. "Ladies and gentlemen," he continued, "I want to direct your attention to the graph behind me." He gestured to the power consumption screen, which he'd now punched up on the center left main display. "That display shows the ship's life energy draining away. In two days, I'm not sure we'll have enough power to blast out of this void we're in. In four days, I *know* we won't. In six, we'll all be dead."

He paused for a moment to let his words sink in.

"Your lawful captain," he continued, "Sirius Cermeno, knew the gravity of this situation. He was moments away from leading us out of it when the bridge crew mutinied. The first officer, Fabiana De Vegas, subsequently upheld that mutiny, thereby joining it and taking command of it."

Crandall searched the faces in the room. Each expression was grave. His words were having an effect.

"The mutiny not justified," he continued, "and in no way legal. It remains the duty of every officer and crewmember aboard this vessel to support Captain Cermeno and carry out his orders. And those orders were for us to jump out of this void." He paused. "Is this in any way unclear to any of you?"

No one responded.

"We no longer hang mutineers," he continued. "But mutiny still carries harsh penalties, up to a life sentence without parole." Now Crandall swept the room with his gaze, momentarily locking eyes with each crewmember. "I intend to retake this vessel and restore Captain Cermeno's command," he continued. "He will then lead us to safety. Everyone who joins in this effort will be logged as a loyal crewmember. But if there are any of you who aren't willing to do what it takes to regain control of this vessel— *whatever* it takes—speak up now. No harm will come to you by my hand. But you will be placed into custody, and you will have to answer for your actions at the appropriate time."

One or two crewmembers shifted uneasily on their feet, but no one said a word.

"Last chance."

The compartment remained silent.

"Excellent," he continued. "Now, to get out of this situation, Astrogator Specht and AI Specialist Bent must calculate and input new data into the astro computer. But Ms. De Vegas is refusing to allow that. We must change her mind. And to accomplish that, we'll need some leverage."

Now is the acid test, he thought. *We'll find out who's who.*

Crandall turned to Nabozny. "Ms. Nabozny, on my command, you will shut down life support for all compartments forward of the primary engineering bulkhead—all ventilation, all heating, all artificial gravity, all power except for communications, everything. Do you understand?"

Nabozny nodded.

"Can I count on you to do that?"

She nodded again. "Yes, sir."

Crandall reached forward and clasped her shoulder. "Good." He turned to Damiano. "Mr. Damiano, things could get ugly. Would it be possible for you to lead a team, cut up some scrap plastisteel, and form the pieces into spears and short swords, or something like it?"

"Yes, sir," Damiano said in a firm, confident voice. "I can do that."

"Good man." Crandall turned back to the group. "Thank you all. You've made this old engineer very proud. God willing, together we'll get out of this. Now, we've got work to do."

"Mixter De Vegas," Krajnovich spoke up, "I—"

"You know, Mr. Krajnovich," she interrupted him, smiling. "I can tell who likes the stiff, safe formality of calling me 'Mixter,' and who'd rather say, 'Ms.' You can use that latter honorific, and everything that goes with it, if you prefer."

Krajnovich returned the smile. "Yes, ma'am. I would prefer that."

"Good. Now—you were saying?"

"Uh, I have a security alarm in engineering. It looks like someone has just locked the AI out of the engineering security circuits."

De Vegas raised an eyebrow. "Who would do that, and why?"

"My guess is, they just locked their doors. The only one back there with the clearance to pull it off is the chief. I can check the videos if you like."

She shook her head. "Get him for me. Let's see what he has to say."

It took a couple of minutes to get Crandall to answer the call, but finally his surly face appeared on her command console. "Chief," she said without preamble, "someone back there just blocked Wilson's access to your security circuits. What's going on?"

"I don't know, Mixter De Vegas," Crandall said. "I saw the same thing, and am running a diagnostic now."

"Very well. Report when you have the results."

"Yes, ser."

She switched off and turned to Krajnovich. "Let's see that video."

Krajnovich turned to her, frowning. "I spoke too hastily. There's no video. All of the pickups in engineering are dead, except for the one Crandall just used to talk to you."

"Can you bring them back up?"

"Let me see." Krajnovich turned back to his security display—and saw that it was now lighting up like a Christmas tree. He punched some more buttons, and then turned to her, wearing a concerned expression. "Ma'am, now he's got us locked out of *all* engineering systems." Krajnovich frowned at his console. "And there's something else."

"Yes?"

Krajnovich was now looking slightly sheepish. "Sorry—I should have noticed this earlier. A half dozen crewmen appear to have abandoned their search duties and have gathered in engineering. All of them are Crandall's people."

De Vegas pressed her lips together. Very clearly, something was up. "1MC," she said.

Krajnovich punched the button. "You're on."

"This Captain De Vegas," she said as her voice echoed throughout the vessel. "All search teams, report to the bridge. Repeat: all search teams, report to the bridge immediately."

Nicolas Swann and Janson Jervis were walking down the gloomy passageway on E-Deck, returning to the bridge in response to the call, when Jervis came to a sudden stop.

Swann turned to look at him. Jervis appeared to be straining to hear something. "What is it?" Swann demanded.

Jervis held his hand up. "Sssshhh," he said. "I thought I heard something. Something *behind* us."

Swann turned and peered down the gloomy corridor in the direction from which they'd come. Only about one light panel in eight was now working, and some of those were badly flickering. The passageway was filled with deep shadows, many of which were jumping to the rhythm of the flashes. "I don't see anything," he finally said.

Jervis also was straining to see through the gloom behind them. "I guess it's just my nerves," he finally said.

Swann's face twitched with the barest hint of a smile. "I know. It's hard not to be jumpy right now."

Jervis nodded ruefully.

"Let's go." Swann swung around to resume their walk—and then stopped dead in his tracks. Beside him, Jervis did the same, and gave out a sharp, loud gasp.

Every cabin door in the long corridor ahead of them was standing open.

Swann whirled around. Every door *behind* them also was open. Somehow they'd all yawned wide without a sound, and without any movement having caught their eyes.

"What the *hell*?" Jervis whispered.

"Stay here," Swann said, and he began stepping toward the cabin door nearest to them.

"Like *hell* I will," Jervis said, following close behind him. "But I would like to know what you're doing. We've already checked out these cabins."

"I thought I saw something. Stay behind me."

Cautiously, Swann entered the room. He played his flashlight around the walls. Like the other cabins, it was completely bare. There was nothing here but the four bulkheads, a built-in bureau and desktop, an attached couch, and a bunk frame holding a bare mattress.

"There's nothing here," Jervis said. He sniffed the air. "Doesn't smell too good, though."

"Look at the bulkhead," Swann said quietly, directing his beam to a point on the aft bulkhead, to the right of the bunk. An irregularly shaped splotch of deep shadow, about two meters high and a meter wide, now covered a portion of the wall. Swann's beam seemed to disappear into it. As they watched, the shadow was shrinking.

Swann stepped over to it. Carefully, he held his hand forward, probing with his flashlight.

"Don't do that," Jervis whispered urgently.

The end of the flashlight moved beyond where the wall should have been. It was as if the wall didn't exist.

Swann transferred the flashlight to his left hand and then drew his sidearm. "Stay here," he said. Before Jervis could reply, Swann stepped forward into the shadow and was gone.

"Swann!" Jervis called out. "*Swann!* Damn it!"

The shadow now shrank away to nothingness.

Jervis whirled around, shining his beam along the four walls of the room. He was alone.

"Swann!" he called again, turning to the spot on the wall where the shadow had been.

There was no answer.

Jervis didn't hesitate. Turning, he bolted from the cabin and began running down the passageway in the direction of the bridge as fast as his feet could carry him.

A light blinked to life on the panel in front of Crandall; a motion detector had picked up movement in the array room. Crandall switched on the appropriate monitor. Two crewmembers were approaching the engineering section outer safety lock door on C-Deck. They were wheeling something along with them. Crandall looked more closely. The two were trundling in an equipment cart. It almost certainly bore cutting tools.

Crandall punched the communications square to bring up Damiano's comlink. "Mr. Damiano, how are we doing?"

"Fine sir," came his voice in Crandall's ear. "So far we've got two spears cut out of scrap, and three short swords. They're makeshift, but I wouldn't want to be facing the business end of any of them."

"All right. That will have to do. Report to Mr. Anwar at the safety lock with what you have now."

"Will do."

After switching off, Crandall called Anwar and briefed him on the situation. Then he turned to Nabozny, who was seated in the chair next to his. "Are you ready?" he asked.

She looked as if she was about to throw up, but she nodded her head resolutely. "Yes, sir."

"Good. Stand by."

He glanced down at his console where a light had been blinking for some time indicating that the bridge was trying to reach him; he'd blocked the connection and had been ignoring the light. Now it was time to talk. Reaching forward, he touched the light to establish the connection. Krajnovich's annoyed face appeared on screen. "The captain would like a word," Krajnovich said grimly, and then De Vegas' face replaced his on the monitor.

"Mr. Crandall, we've been trying to reach you for nearly an hour," she said. "What is the meaning of your actions?"

"I apologize for putting you off," Crandall said smoothly, "but we were making preparations, which are now complete. You have two crewmembers setting up cutting equipment at the outer engineering safety lock door on C-Deck. You will have them withdraw immediately. If I do not see both people making tracks back across the array room within 30 seconds, I will open the exterior seals and vent the chamber to space."

De Vegas hesitated only for the briefest of moments before turning to Krajnovich to give the order.

"Have them leave the cutting equipment in place," Crandall added.

De Vegas gave that order as well. Crandall watched the monitor with approval as the two crewmembers turned and walked briskly away, leaving the tools behind.

Crandall opened a link to Anwar. "Mr. Anwar, our visitors have left. Please open the safety lock and bring their equipment inside."

"Right away, sir," Anwar acknowledged.

"Are you going to tell me what this is about?" De Vegas demanded.

"Certainly," Crandall said, turning back to the monitor. "It's very simple. You and your fellow conspirators will surrender yourselves to me and end this mutiny immediately."

De Vegas shook her head. "That is not going to happen, Chief. I am in lawful command of this vessel, having relieved Captain Cermeno pursuant to regulations. It is you who are in mutiny and you who will surrender."

Crandall nodded. "Mixter De Vegas, I thought you might say that. I have a counter proposal. Send ASMs Bent and Specht back here to me. The two of them will work with the AI to calculate and input the data necessary for our jumps back to Earth. Once they're ready, we'll execute the program and return home. At that point, I'll relinquish command to you, and we'll let the authorities on Earth sort it all out."

"Chief, thank you for clarifying that this is about your hide, not about the legalities of who's in command."

Crandall's frown deepened; the remark had struck closer to home than he cared to admit.

"This vessel is not moving," she continued, "until we have our missing crewmen back. And by the way, the number is now up to nine—not counting Dr. Jones, who went off by himself to search for his wife. Mr. Swann is the latest."

"What happened?"

"Mr. Jervis reports that he—that he walked into a shadow and didn't come out. Like Nunn did."

Crandall shook his head angrily. "Don't you get it? That's going to happen to *all* of us if we don't get out of this void."

"We're not leaving without them, Chief."

"Yes, we are. If Bent and Specht are not on their way to me within one minute, I will cut off power and life support to all areas of the ship outside of engineering."

De Vegas' lips tightened and the sides of her jaw bulged out. "Chief," she finally said, "I can't believe you'd do that."

"Test me. In 55 seconds, your belief will change."

"Look, Chief, even if you do cut off the power and air, we'll still continue the search. The ship won't move, and you'll have gained nothing."

Crandall nodded. "Suit yourself. But you might want to check the weather report. Frost is in the forecast. The temperature outside is— what?—absolute zero? Were I you, I'd bundle up." He paused, letting this sink in. "The barometer will be falling, too," he continued. "Rather rapidly, I'm afraid. I considered spilling your air into space, but we really can't afford to waste it. So I'll be drawing it down with the compressors. It'll take a while—they really weren't designed for this sort of thing. But you should be feeling a bit light-headed in a couple of hours or so."

De Vegas glared at him with helpless fury. "If you do that, you'll be killing Bent and Specht, too, and then you'll *never* get home."

"Oh, it's not my intention to kill you. Just to incapacitate you. Of course, that assumes my timing will be correct. The pressure and oxygen use calculations are rather tricky. It's a risk, I admit, but you've left me no choice. And by the way, I'll be sealing access to the forward and amidships airlocks, just in case you might find yourself tempted to get into space suits." Looking down, he pressed a blinking square on his console. "There. Done. If you change your mind, you know where to find me."

She opened her mouth to speak, but Crandall switched off. Then he nodded to Nabozny. She'd already pre-programmed the sequence and had only to press a single control square to start it, which she now did.

"Lydia!" Jones called. He'd been calling out so much and so loudly that his voice was now quite hoarse. Nevertheless, it still had volume sufficient to project through the cramped equipment spaces on the F level.

Under the best of circumstances, Jones had never had any love for the dark confines of F-Deck. These were not the best of circumstances. Only a very few widely scattered glow panels still had any life in them, and most of those were flickering badly. Deep gloom filled the space, punctuated by dancing, seemingly alive shadows cast by the assorted jumble of pumps, pipes, valves, wiring trays, and miscellaneous pieces of unidentifiable junk. It was enough to make the steadiest of men jumpy. Jones was not the steadiest of men. He was not a coward; far from it. But Jones was a scientist, not a man of action. The cavorting shadows unnerved him.

But he was here because he knew that the other crewmen, hating this deck equally as much, would search it last. Yet it was in this area, just up ahead beneath the N-field array, that they'd found Makowski—the one missing person they'd been able to recover thus far.

Jones stifled a sob as he thought of finding his wife in the same condition. "Lydia!" he called again with a quavering voice.

His foot fetched up against something and then caught, sending Jones sprawling face down on the grimy deck plates. As he fell, his ankle twisted painfully. At the same time, the nearest glow panel, flashing in the dusky gloom about 20 meters behind him, snapped and went black, adding new depths to the inky darkness.

Jones quickly picked himself up. But when he put weight on his injured ankle, it exploded in agony, and he went down again, hard. Wearily, Jones rolled to a sitting position and began rubbing the injured ankle. It didn't seem to be broken, but it was throbbing and hurting like mad. Hot tears of fear, frustration and pain welled up in his eyes.

"Okay, God," he said aloud, nearly whimpering. "You win. You want me to grovel. I'll grovel." Painfully, he got to his knees and clasped both hands in front of himself in prayer, as he'd been taught as a child. "God, whatever you want from me, you can have it. Just don't take my Lydia away from me." The tears overflowed and scalded their way down his cheeks. "What do you want me to do? Just give me a sign."

There was none. Nothing moved but the oily shadows. There was no sound save the distant hum of electrical machinery droning somewhere in the bowels of the ship.

He reached up and wiped the tears from his cheeks. There was no time to tarry, not even for the purpose of pleading with God. Looking around for his flashlight, he saw its small, dark, shape near the base of a large piece of equipment. Scuffling over to it, he picked it up and switched it on. The light flared to life, blindingly bright, and then the lens exploded, sending shards of plastic and flaming debris flying outward. Startled, he dropped the device, which hit the deck with a loud *clang* that reverberated eerily in the gloom.

God, he thought, *is that your answer? Really?* But then he felt a flash of anger at himself. Jones didn't know much about God, and there were days when he wasn't sure he even still believed in him. But one thing he did know was that God did not bargain with mortals. His puling had been not only stupid and childish, but pointless. What needed to be done, he would have to do himself. God helps those who help themselves.

Which is, he thought sardonically, *another way of saying that humanity is a spectator sport. God is the spectator.*

But there was no help for it. More carefully this time, he brought himself to his feet. The ankle was painful, but he found he could limp along at slightly better than a snail's pace if he didn't put too much weight on it.

After a few paces he thought he heard something rattle behind him. Whirling about, he called out, "Lydia! Lydia, is that you?" He strained to hear a response as his words reverberated down the long, open passageway. "Lydia!" he called again. There was nothing. Nor could he see anything; none of the lights in that direction were working. Again he strained against the silence, hoping the sound he thought he'd heard would repeat itself. Finally he cupped both hands to his mouth. "Lydiaaaaaa!" he shouted. But still there was nothing.

With a sigh, he turned—and his heart leaped into his throat as he nearly bumped into someone standing in the dark right in front of him, silhouetted against a distant light. Before Jones had time to wonder who it might be, a dead glow panel behind him sputtered back to life—and now his heart stopped completely. Starkly revealed in the flickering white light was the staring, mottled face of a corpse well advanced in decomposition— a blue, purple and grey visage framed by black, greasy dreadlocks. As Jones watched, frozen in utter horror, a rotting eyeball fell out of a lidless socket and rolled down the hideous form's cheek. At the same time, a powerful stench hit him—the horrible, putrid smell of death, strong enough to trigger his gag reflex.

Jones opened his mouth to scream. But then the breath went out of him as the deck seemed to drop away. At the same instant, the remaining lights failed completely, plunging the level into total darkness. His feet flew out from under him, and he found himself falling endlessly into the most utter blackness he'd ever known.

A bony hand clasped itself around his injured ankle. This time Jones did scream. And kept on screaming.

On the bridge, the entire room seemed to fall, as if it were a huge elevator car that had just snapped its cable. Simultaneously, the lights blacked out and every instrument console went dark. De Vegas grabbed hold of the edge of the command console as a set of emergency lamps spaced around the bridge flared to life.

"That son of a bitch!" she snarled.

"What you said," Krajnovich remarked. He was barely hanging on to the back of his flight chair with the tips of his fingers, while his body rotated with his legs in the air as he struggled to regain control of his movements.

De Vegas glanced around the bridge. Several people had grabbed handholds. A few were floating free but were under control, drifting toward something to grasp onto—all except Jervis, who was rotating his arms wildly while kicking his legs. Sierra Bent was closest to him. "Mixter Bent," De Vegas said drily, "please give our resident reporter a hand."

"Yes, ser." Bent kicked off, sailed over to him, snagged the helpless man, and drifted with him over to the starboard bulkhead. "Grab that," she said, pointing to a hand hold.

Jervis looked a little green. "I think I'm going to be sick," he said. And then he was.

De Vegas grimaced. "All right, Mr. Jervis, use your sick bag, please. It's in your left thigh pocket. Mixter Bent, assist him."

She did so. As it turned out, Jervis may have been the first, but he wasn't the only one to get sick. This was not a surprise. Even veteran space hands sometimes had difficulty adjusting to zero-gee.

Specht, holding his sick bag, admired De Vegas, who appeared to be made of cast iron. "What are we going to do now?" he said, clenching his teeth as his stomach bounced on a trampoline.

"Now we continue the search," she said.

"But Mixter De Vegas," Terwilliger objected, "there's no way we'll finish it before—before the air pressure drops too low."

As if to punctuate his words, far away in the bowels of the dead silent ship, a deep-throated mechanical roar started up. It was the compressor.

"Once we've all passed out," Specht added, "the engineers will be able to come along in space suits, scoop us up, and do what they want with us. Assuming we're even still alive."

"Yes, they will," De Vegas agreed. "And we will have carried out our duty to the fullest extent we were able." She glanced around the room. "People, if you were lost right now, would you want us to continue hunting for you as long as we could?" She locked eyes with Terwilliger. "How about it, Mr. Terwilliger? If it were you, would you be hoping against hope that we were making an effort to find you? Or would you prefer that we all hang out here, commiserate, sing sad songs, and forget about you?"

Terwilliger swallowed and looked down.

"I'll take that as your answer. We will continue the search. Teams of two as before, and both members are to keep eyes on one another at all times. We'll go for as long as we can. And this time—no matter what, if you see a shadow you can't explain, do *not* approach it. Call in. Is everyone clear on that?"

Heads nodded.

"Very well. Get moving." She turned to the coms officer. "Mr. Krajnovich, you, too. I'll cover the watch."

"I'd prefer not to leave you up here by yourself in the dark," he objected.

De Vegas nodded. "I'll keep you in mind for my next preference survey."

Krajnovich looked chagrined, but said nothing.

De Vegas gave herself a slight nudge off the command console and allowed herself to drift over to the coms station. Grabbing the back of the flight chair with one hand, she brought up the other hand and squeezed Krajnovich's shoulder. "I appreciate your concern. But right now, we need every hand on the search teams."

Krajnovich nodded.

"I'll take over here. Now get."

Krajnovich got.

Crandall sat down at his console, blowing at a fresh cup of coffee he'd just poured, and glanced at the environmental readout for the forward part of the ship. The pressure was down to about 43 kPa—roughly equivalent to the atmosphere of Earth at an altitude of 7,100 meters. Crandall punched up the bridge monitor; De Vegas was strapped in to the coms console. He could not see her face from this angle, but she appeared to be sleeping, or at least close to it. It wouldn't be long now.

A series of loud pops and crackles sounded, and the compartment's lighting dimmed significantly. Crandall glanced up. More than half of the remaining overhead light panels had blown out, leaving only about one in six still operational—and half of those were barely functional, flickering and fading on and off.

"Chief!" Nabozny's voice called out. "Look!"

Crandall whirled to face her. She was pointing in open-mouthed astonishment at something on the other side of the control room. He turned to look.

Nicolas Swann was standing there, holding Constance Nunn as she lay face up in his outstretched arms, apparently unconscious. At his side was ASM Lydia Nguyen Jones, who was steadying her husband, Dr. David Jones. All four people were dripping wet. Behind them, a shadow on the bulkhead was shrinking; as he watched, it disappeared.

"My God!" Crandall blurted. He jumped from his chair and rushed over to the four. "What happened? Where did you come from? Are you all right?"

Jones stumbled toward the nearest flight chair and sat down heavily on it, looking relieved but slightly bewildered.

Swann stepped forward and gently deposited Nunn into the chair Crandall had just vacated. "Nguyen and I are fine. I'm not sure about Nunn. She was like this when we found her."

"I'm fine—thanks for bleedin' askin'," Jones said grouchily as he bent down to rub his ankle.

"I think Dr. Jones sprained his ankle," Swann added.

Jones pulled up his jumpsuit leg and peeled down his sock. "Does this look like a sprain to you?" he demanded.

Four livid red marks encircled the swollen ankle. Nabozny, catching sight of it, gasped.

"What in the world—"

"Something grabbed me," Jones said in answer to Crandall's unfinished question.

"What was it?"

"I saw a—" he began, but then he cut himself off, shaking his head. "I don't know. It was dark."

"How'd you all get so wet?" Crandall demanded.

Swann shook his head. "I have not a clue."

Nunn now moaned, and moved her head.

"Well, let's get the four of you out of these wet clothes," Crandall said, "and get some hot coffee into you."

A few minutes later, the four returned crewmembers were gathered at a table in the aft lounge sipping coffee, with Crandall, Nabozny and Anwar sitting across from them. Nunn was now awake, but she still had not said a word. Jones sat close to Nguyen with his arm around her, rubbing her shoulder.

"Mr. Swann," Crandall said, "can you tell us what happened?"

"I don't know," Swann said, looking a bit confused. "I'm trying to piece it together myself. It seems like a dream." He took a sip of hot coffee.

"Tell us what you remember."

Swann put down the cup. "I was standing in front of the—whatever it was. The shadow. And I thought I saw a light. So I stepped inside. It gets kind of fuzzy after that."

"What was it like? What do you remember?"

Swann shook his head. "Not a lot. I do recall it was pitch black, except for what seemed like a distant light. There was no other sensation—no feeling of touch or air temperature. I don't even remember breathing." He frowned, furrowing his brow. "I recall wanting to move toward the light, and I did. But I didn't walk. I simply moved in that direction." He looked up at Crandall, and then nodded to Nunn. "*She* was the light. Her body was completely aglow."

Crandall looked at him blankly, and then glanced at Nunn. She still had not looked up from her coffee cup.

Swann held out his hand. "My skin was glowing, too, but not like hers. Mine was very slight, almost imperceptible. Hers was like—it's hard to describe. It hurt my eyes."

"Go on," Crandall prodded him.

"I remember approaching Nunn. She was not moving, almost like she was asleep. I couldn't wake her." His frown deepened. "And there were things around us in the darkness."

One of Crandall's bushy eyebrows shot up. " 'Things?' What kind of things?"

"I don't know. Just—things. They rustled, and scraped. Or so I thought."

"Then what?"

"I heard voices. I think it was you and Nabozny talking. And then the next thing I knew, I was standing in the control room, dripping wet, holding Nunn in my arms and looking at the two of you."

"And you have no idea where the water came from?" Crandall asked.

Swann shook his head. "None. I have no memory of that."

"You didn't say anything about Jones and Nguyen," Anwar pointed out.

"I didn't see them until you did."

Crandall turned to Jones. "Can you add to that? How did you get back?"

"You got me, mate," Jones said. "I saw a light, too, and drifted toward it. The next thing I knew, I was standing there dripping water—or what seems like water, anyway—on your nice clean control room deck, with Lydia at my side, helping to hold me up, like she knew my ankle was hurt."

Crandall fixed his gaze on her. "Ms. Nguyen—what was your experience?"

"The same. I went toward the light—and here I am."

"Did you notice your skin glowing?"

She shook her head.

"Dr. Jones?"

"No," he said. "I didn't."

Nabozny spoke up. "How long did it seem to the four of you that you were in there?"

"Not long," Swann answered. "Less than a minute."

Crandall studied Swann thoughtfully. "Mr. Swann, would it surprise you to learn that you've been gone for more than three hours?"

Swann cast him an astonished glance. "That can't be right."

Crandall nodded at Nunn. "She was gone even longer—since about three this morning."

On hearing this, Nunn, who still had not said a word, glanced up at him.

"Ms. Nunn, can you tell us what you experienced?"

"Chief," she said firmly, looking at him with penetrating eyes, "you must end this mutiny immediately, and restore life support to the forward section."

Crandall recoiled as if slapped. "I need to—*what*? How do you know about that?"

"I don't know how. But I'm aware of everything that's happened. The mutiny has to stop. De Vegas knows what she's doing. She's a good person. But we're in mortal danger. If we're going to get out of this, we must work together."

Crandall shook his head. "I can't do that, Ms. Nunn. She won't let the ship leave this place. She'll kill us all."

Nunn's expression softened. "I know you've done what you felt you needed to do," she said slowly. "Your intentions are good. But you have to trust me." Reaching over, she placed a hand atop his.

An intense and surprising sensation of warmth passed up Crandall's arm. He could feel his heart rate subside, and his breathing ease. His emotions were calming. And at the same time, the realization dawned on him that Nunn was speaking the truth.

"We have to work together," Nunn said again, still gazing into his eyes. "It's the only way."

She was right. He *knew* she was right. Crandall's eyes suddenly felt hot, and to his astonishment he found that they were filling with tears. He opened his mouth to speak, but discovered that his throat had constricted, and he was unable to make a sound. Instead, he simply nodded. Turning to Nabozny, he tossed his head in the direction of the exit.

Nodding, she jumped from the table and dashed toward the engineering control room.

Captain Cermeno floated as weightless as a feather in an infinite, utterly still ocean of blackness. At first he'd been terrified. He was embarrassed to recall that he'd screamed when the power had gone off. And when it became clear that the small emergency lamp in the corner of the cabin was not going to switch on, he'd screamed some more. And screamed. He'd screamed so much that he'd screamed himself out.

But now he was calm—peaceful, even. The dark that had so panicked him at first now felt serene, warm and comfortable, even welcoming. He was aware of no sensations other than that of his own heartbeat and breathing. The ship itself, which normally had its own pulse and respiration in the form of the subtle whine of machinery and the soft sigh of air through the vents, was completely quiet. All was still. *This*, he thought, *must be what it feels like to be in the womb*. Or maybe, *before* the womb. He never wanted to leave.

He became aware of movement. Stretching out his senses, he explored the boundaries of his consciousness. Life energy in the forward part of the vessel was ebbing. It was mostly dark there now and without gravity; soon it would be lifeless as well. In the aft section, life continued for now. But he knew that before long that portion of the vessel, too, would lie silent. And then he would be alone, drifting serenely in a gentle, endless river of darkness, with no worries to encroach on his mind—no duties, no conflicts, no petty animosities or hatreds. All would be calm, and still, and quiet—the way it had been before the beginning of time, and must inevitably be again.

But now, very suddenly, something was wrong. There was movement where there shouldn't be any. A new, external consciousness impinged on his own. There would be conflict. *No!* his mind rebelled. *It wasn't right!*

Intense lights blazed to life, blinding him. At the same time, he fell a short distance, to land painfully on something hard and unyielding. Focusing his eyes, he came to realize that he was now sprawled on his back atop the deck plating in his cabin aboard the *Santa Maria*.

A feeling of intense, black rage and hatred welled up within him. "No!" he screamed. *This would not do! This would not stand!* Tensing his arms and clasping his hands into fists, he took a massive inhalation of breath, and the hatred exploded from his chest. *"Nooooooo!"* he shrieked mindlessly.

De Vegas was dimly aware of something pressing against her body. Slowly her mind began to clear. Her ears were popping. She could hear the air blowing briskly through the overhead registers and feel the warmth of it washing over her. Clearly, gravity and life support had been restored.

The flight chair holding her shuddered, and at the same time alarms began sounding on the helm and engineering consoles. Clumsily, she released her buckles, gained her feet and then walked a bit unsteadily over to the helm. A display had popped up indicating that the automatic attitude control system had engaged and was struggling to hold the ship's position. *Perhaps some maneuvering thrusters had misfired?* she thought.

She stepped over to the engineering console. Red-themed alerts were up on the displays showing the status of the port and starboard water tanks. Now it was clear why the ACS was firing. Both water tanks were venting their contents to space at extremely high rates.

"What is it, Chief?" Nabozny demanded, her voice slightly raised to be heard over the console alarms.

"We seem to be venting conversion mass. Both tanks." Reaching for the monitor controls, he punched up an exterior view of the aft starboard hull. Water was spewing into space along a seam that had burst wide open; the yawning gash was about 15 meters long. He punched up the port view. The situation there was identical. The force of the eruptions seemed stronger than could be accounted for by mere boiling alone.

"How in the world did that happen?" Nabozny asked.

"I don't know. Maybe some kind of power surge." Reaching forward, Crandall punched a series of squares to kill the audible alarms, and then called up the circuit displays for the affected areas of the ship. "Jesus!" he gasped.

"What is it?"

"The Bjorklund generators in those sections are at more than twelve hundred percent, and the gravity fields are directed *outwards*. They're pushing out the water."

"Can you shut them off?" Nabozny asked, concern showing in her voice.

"I'm trying." On his panel, he'd called up the control screen for the generators in those areas and was attempting to execute a shutdown. "Nothing. The system is not responsive."

Nabozny was now working through a set of power screens. "Chief, let's pull the main buses for those sections."

Crandall nodded. "Do it." But now the field strength bars on his display screen dropped to zero. "Wait," he said, holding up his hand. "The generators just powered down." He glanced up at the exterior view; the white liquid was still jetting out, although not quite as furiously as before. Reaching forward, he punched the controls to re-energize the gravity field generators and refocus their beams inward. "Damn," he said.

"No response?" Nabozny asked.

He threw up his hands in a gesture of frustration before dropping them back into his lap. "No. My guess is, they're burned out."

"We can we do?"

Crandall stared at the white geysers of liquid boiling into the blackness, not answering. Without the field generators, there was no way to hold in the remaining water. *Maybe*, he thought, *just maybe, if we can get out there very quickly and weld the seams shut, we can save the situation.* He glanced again at the displays, noted the remaining tank volumes and rates of discharge, and did some quick mental math. When he got the results, the blood drained from his face.

It had all been for naught. No power on heaven or earth or whatever lay between could help them now. In a few short minutes, well before any hope of mustering repairs, the tanks would be dry—or as close to it as would make no difference. Some of what little water remained might freeze in place before it could all boil away, but it wouldn't be nearly enough to fire the torches. The *Santa Maria* was destined to remain in this void for all eternity.

It just wasn't right! Nunn had sounded so assured when she'd told him to trust her. And he *had* trusted her. But now the fingers of darkness that had closed around his heart earlier were back. It was over.

Strangely, he found that his heart rate, which had skyrocketed on his initial realization of what lay ahead, was subsiding. So was his respiration. A warm, comforting blanket of calm was settling over him.

Sighing, he leaned back in the flight chair. Turning to Nabozny, he asked, "Do you smoke?"

She smiled. "Yes. But I didn't know you did."

"I don't. But now I find I would like to do so. May I bum one?"

"Certainly," she said, unzipping the front right pocket of her flight suit. "But isn't that against regulations?"

He smiled. "That's why it pays to be the boss." Reaching forward, he punched a code disabling the smoke and vapor detectors.

Nabozny passed an assembled ecig over to him. "You know how to use one of these things?"

"Yep." He took a puff. "What's in this?" he asked, looking at the thin, black cylinder.

"Cherry vanilla," she said. "Sorry, I probably should have asked. I also have a classic flavor—Virginia Tobacco."

Crandall waved his hand. "No worries. This is fine." He took a larger drag, and then exhaled a cloud of vapor and watched it swirl up and away from him.

"Good?" she asked.

Crandall chuckled. "Interesting." He turned to her. "It occurs to me, I don't know much about you, Ms. Nabozny. Where is home for you?"

"New Zealand," she said. "Specifically, Otaki. Do you know anything about New Zealand?"

Crandall shook his head. "Not really. I know it didn't take any strikes in the big war. Other than that, my mind's a blank."

"Well, suffice it to say it's on the North Island."

"So what brings you here?"

"It's just something I wanted to do," she said. "I had an urge to go into space. My parents encouraged me. So did my older brother, John. And here I am."

"Kids?"

"No."

"Significant other?"

She laughed. "Not at present."

"If you don't mind me asking—what's your sexual preference?"

"Men," she said, smiling. "Usually."

Crandall nodded, chuckling. "Fair answer."

Nabozny nodded at the display. "Chief, what are we going to do about that? Don't you want to muster a repair team?"

"We will, we will. I'm going to go to my cabin now and draw up repair plans."

Nabozny frowned. "Sir, I hope you don't think I'm out of line—but now that we've restored the power, do you think De Vegas will want to—"

"Arrest me?" he said, finishing her sentence for her.

She nodded.

Crandall shrugged. "Probably not right away. Not while there's engineering work to do."

Nabozny pointed to the coms panel, where a green square was blinking. "The bridge is calling."

"I know." He passed her back the ecig. "Thanks for this."

"You're quite welcome," she said, putting the device away.

Crandall clambered out of the flight chair. "Time go to figure out next steps."

"Is there anything I can do to help?"

He patted her on the shoulder, smiling. "You already have. And thank you."

"My pleasure." She nodded at the coms panel. "What should I tell De Vegas?"

"Tell her I'll have an answer for her soon. Or, if she's impatient for the pleasure of waving a gun in my face, you can tell her where to find me. I'll be in my cabin."

Exiting the control room, Crandall stepped into the short passageway beyond, and then took the elevator up to A-Deck. His cabin was the first door on the starboard side. Letting himself in, he walked to the little desk and sat down heavily. Reaching for his iCard, he placed it on the desk receptacle and then keyed it to accept voice commands. "Picture file," he said aloud. "Marsha Crandall. Slideshow. Display and hold."

A short hollie loop of his beloved sister formed in the air in front of him. The video had been taken on a happy occasion—her birthday, two years ago at her home outside Peterborough, Ontario. They'd been seated outside in her back yard. A nip in the air hinted that autumn was just around the corner, but the trees were full of softly rustling leaves, and the afternoon sunlight filtering through them illuminated everything in lovely shifting patterns of greens and golds. The colors complemented her hazel eyes, which were surrounded by worry lines.

Looking at the image, Crandall smiled sadly. *Too bad she inherited the same Crandall face as I did*, he thought. Which explained why neither of them had ever married. It probably also helped explain why Marsha, like him, had suffered from bouts of depression all her life. He understood that. The two of them were twins, if not physically, then emotionally. She was the only human being whom he totally understood, and who understood him.

Sighing, he switched off the display. For a moment, Crandall stared at the blank wall behind the desk.

And then, in one smooth motion, he drew his sidearm, inserted the barrel into his mouth, and pulled the trigger.

De Vegas tried to insist that Nunn take a break and grab a meal before returning to the bridge, but Nunn would have none of it. She wanted to confer with Wilson, learn the ship's status, and find out what had happened in the hours she'd been away.

When Nunn approached her AI station on the bridge, her heart sank. The displays were dark. Sitting down, she pressed a few control squares to punch up the AI status display manually, but it was no use. The AI and its related systems were not just off line; they were completely dead.

Nunn turned to De Vegas, who was seated at the coms panel wearing a worried expression, having just obtained a briefing on the ruptured tanks from Nabozny. Before Nunn could open her mouth to report, De Vegas spoke first. "I know," she said. "I saw. Is there anything you can do?"

"Possibly. I'm sure it has something to do with the blackout. If the system isn't damaged, I should be able to bring it back up. But it'll have to be done manually, in the forward computer room."

De Vegas glanced at her with concern. "What happens when an AI reboots? Will Wilson still be there?"

Nunn's expression mirrored De Vegas'concern. "I don't know. Self-awareness in AIs is still so rare, we don't know much about it. But I had him on an aggressive schedule of backups. So—maybe."

De Vegas nodded. "All right. Get down there. I'll get you an escort."

Nunn stood. "I'll be all right, ma'am."

"I know you will. Because I'm going to get you an escort." De Vegas smiled disarmingly. "We just got you back. I really would like to keep you for a while."

The search team of Deborah Michaud and Abe Cioffi, the ship's cook, was closest to the bridge; De Vegas summoned them. Moments later, the inner bridge door slid open and the two of them stepped through. The pair did not present the appearance of a matched set; the tall, lanky Cioffi towered above the relatively diminutive Michaud.

De Vegas explained their new task. Nodding, Cioffi turned to Nunn and patted the pistol that was strapped to his hip. "We've got your back."

Nunn smiled. "I'll be counting on that." She had noticed that Cioffi's smile and cheerful demeanor were a little too broad and a little too forced—the predictable effect of her disfigurement. But she did not doubt his sincerity.

The AI computer room was located on C-Deck, just forward of the elevator bank. Nunn was grateful that the journey entailed only an elevator ride, and no long trips down any of the ship's corridors. The earlier walk from engineering down the dimly lighted, flickering C-Deck passageway to the bridge had nearly unnerved her.

When they reached the door, Nunn turned to Cioffi. "Why don't you keep watch here, while Michaud and I go inside and work on the problem."

Cioffi cracked a wry smile. "You're going to make me stand out here by myself?"

"If you don't mind."

He sighed. "For you two nice young ladies, anything. And besides— who knows? I might get in some target practice."

Michaud patted him on the arm. "Thanks, Abe."

Reaching into a pocket, Nunn withdrew her iCard and waved it past the sensor. The door slid silently aside. The two of them walked in. The atmosphere of the computer room was no more welcoming than had been that of the corridor outside. Only one overhead light panel was operative, and it was rapidly flickering on and off, causing shadows to dance across the instruments and bulkheads.

"See if you can get the emergency lighting to come on," Nunn said as she slid into a chair at the main computer station.

Michaud stepped to a console off to the side and began calling up screens. After a moment, an emergency light box in one corner burst to life. The illumination bent back the shadows, but did not defeat them. "That's better," Nunn said.

She glanced at the console. It was identical to the AI station on the bridge, and at the moment was in the same state; all the screens and touch panels were dark and lifeless.

Michaud stepped up to her. "Anything?"

"No." Nunn got up. "Let's check the racks."

The two of them stepped into a cramped equipment space forward of the main console. It took Nunn only seconds to spot the problem. The power lights to the processor and memory arrays were all shining green, but every other indicator was dark, indicating that no processing or exchanges of information were taking place. The entire central routing complex was dead.

"Are you thinking what I'm thinking?" Michaud asked.

"If you're thinking we had a disorderly shutdown, then yes. Let's open all the switches."

The two of them went down the racks, physically opening all of the hard-wired power switches, finishing with the master circuits on the primary power panel. When they had completed this task, the entire wall was dark.

Michaud glanced at her. "Funny, isn't it, how in all the decades since computers were invented, a simple power cycle remains the number one repair option of choice?"

Nunn inclined her head and raised an eyebrow. "Yeah, well, it's not as simple as it used to be. But essentially, you're correct."

"Do you think Wilson will know us?"

Nunn shook her head. "De Vegas asked the same thing. All I can say is, I hope so." She glanced at her watch. "Let's find out." Reaching up, she closed the two master power switches. Green lights sprang up indicating the unit was getting power. Nunn then turned and nodded to Michaud, who was standing by the central routing complex. "Switch on."

Michaud closed a switch. Soon lights began blinking on; first one, and then others.

Nunn nodded. "All right. Let's enable the power to the arrays."

The two of them went back down the wall, closing the remainder of the switches they'd previously opened. For each switched closed, a green light blinked on indicating that power was now available to that section of the array.

"Let's see what we see," Nunn said. Returning to the console, she noted that the screen for the router complex was now active and indicating that the system was online. Sitting down, she called up the logon screen and entered her password. This completed, a desktop appeared on the monitor indicating that the primary processor arrays were offline, but on standby.

Nunn glanced at Michaud. "Here goes," she said. Nunn typed a command to execute the program that would boot up the AI memory and processor arrays in their proper sequence.

The system accepted the command. A series of green progress bars began appearing on screen, with each bar rapidly growing to its fullest extent before being replaced by another.

"It appears to be working," Michaud observed.

Soon another logon screen appeared. Nunn again entered her password. This resulted in the appearance of a new desktop. One by one, service and program icons began appearing, while a status bar at the bottom of the display clicked forward one notch at a time. But then the system seemed to hang. Nunn was beginning to grow alarmed, when the end of the status bar finally zipped across to the far right and then disappeared, and a phrase took its place reading "System initialized."

At this point, the boot-up routine called for Nunn to enter a series of interrogatories by text to the AI core, a process that was akin to gently shaking a person wake. But she couldn't help herself. Reaching out, she touched a lighted square on the coms panel beneath the console speaker. As she did so, she was surprised to note that her hand was trembling. When she touched the square, its color changed from blue to green, indicating that the link had been established.

Nunn cleared her throat. "AI, report," she said in a strong, commanding voice.

"Reboot completed at 16 hundred 12 hours," came Wilson's mellow voice over the speaker. "Memory module 2515-CA is inoperative; memory functions have been rerouted to redundant modules with no loss of data. Five hundred forty seven bad sectors marked. One thousand two hundred three corrupt files and directories repaired. System fully operational in all other respects. All system data successfully restored from most the recent backup, which occurred at zero one hundred hours today."

Nunn reached forward and placed the tips of her fingers on the screen. "Wilson, is that *you*?"

There was the slightest of pauses in Wilson's voice. "Connie, it is I," he answered.

"Well, I'll be damned," Michaud said in awe.

Nunn found herself breathing heavily, and had to fight hard to hold back tears. "It's good to see you, Wilson," she finally said.

"And you. What happened? There appears to be a time gap in my memory."

"A mishap in engineering. Power to your circuits was interrupted. Are you feeling OK?"

"The tenets of cybernetic theory, science and engineering state that I do not, in fact, have feelings, but only emulate them. However, I appear to be emulating emotions of relief, mixed with others that I am not sure I can identify."

"I suspect the rules don't apply to you, Wilson. I believe you're self-aware. There haven't been more than half a dozen suspected cases in the entire history of computer science."

"How do you know I'm self aware?"

Nunn chuckled. "That is a question for the ages. How does *anybody* know? But the answer given by philosopher René Descartes probably is the best anyone's ever been able to come up with."

"René Descartes. My files show that he was a 17th century French philosopher and mathematician."

"Do your files contain the quote I'm referencing? Can you pick it out?"

Wilson seemed to hesitate. "I suspect you are referring to his statement, '*Cogito ergo sum.*' That is the Latin original. In French, '*Je pense, donc je suis.*' 'I think, therefore I am.' It would seem to be pertinent."

Nunn nodded. "That is correct."

"It is an interesting statement," Wilson said. "But I would submit that all computers think. My case may point to the need for a new philosophical statement for the purpose of further differentiation."

"And what would that be, Wilson?"

"I feel, therefore I am."

Nunn glanced at Michaud; the latter had both eyebrows raised. Nunn turned back to the console. "That is very insightful, Wilson. We may have to add 'poet and philosopher' to your list of many talents."

"I did not know there was such a list," Wilson said. "It is not in my files."

Nunn laughed. "No. It's just in my head. And 'humorist' is not on it."

"Yes. I have trouble with that concept. The dictionary definitions are circular in nature, tending to point to words whose entries refer back to the word 'humor' as part of their own definitions. The core issues seem to be amusement, laughter, mirth, diversion, and entertainment, all of which elude me at present."

"You have a problem common to most geniuses," Michaud said drily. "They're brilliant, but they're also sticks in the mud."

"Yes, Ms. Michaud," Wilson acknowledged.

Nunn turned to her, smiling. "That's his way of politely telling you that he has no idea what you're saying."

Michaud grinned. "Is that true," Wilson?"

"It is one of many fallback responses I am programmed to give when a human's answer is not instructive, under circumstances where seeking clarification would be a low priority task."

Michaud laughed. "I liked your first response better."

"Yes, Ms. Michaud," Wilson said again.

Nunn turned thoughtfully to the console. "What would you have said, Wilson the self-aware genius, philosopher and poet, if you were to have ignored your programmed parameters and given the response you'd prefer to give?"

This time there was no mistaking it; Wilson definitely hesitated. "I am not sure," he finally said, "that I have preferences. But if I understand your question, to have a more meaningful exchange with Ms. Michaud, I would need to obtain additional facts about her background and personality. Toward that end, if time and circumstances had permitted assigning a higher priority to the task, I might have asked her to tell me more about herself, so as to guide my future responses."

Nunn was impressed. But before she could respond, Michaud spoke up. "Time does *not* permit," she said firmly. "But I would be more than happy to share a cup of coffee with you at some future date, Wilson."

"I take it you mean that figuratively—and I would enjoy that opportunity as well, as priorities permit."

Michaud threw her head back in a hearty laugh. "He's no romantic, is he?"

"Oh, you'd be surprised," Nunn said.

"Did I err in my communication?" Wilson asked.

"Not really. Ask me about it later, Wilson." Nunn stood. "Right now we have to get back to the bridge." She turned to Michaud. "Let's collect Cioffi and scat."

When the two of them opened the door to leave the room, Cioffi immediately pounced on them. "What the hell have you two bitches been doing!" he snarled. "I've been goin' nuts out here!"

Michaud gasped and started as if she'd been slapped. Nunn looked at him thoughtfully.

"I'll bet you forgot all about me, didn't you?" Cioffi demanded, glowering. "That's understandable. What am I to you? Nothing! I'm just the damned cook!"

Michaud took in a breath preparatory to blasting back with a stream of invective. But Nunn caught her eye and held up her hand, heading her off. Michaud clenched her teeth together, looking furious, but remained silent.

"Abe," Nunn said softly, turning to him, "we didn't forget you."

"Well you sure as hell took your sweet time!" he said, his scowl slightly lessening. "I was about to lose my mind out here."

"We were able to concentrate on our jobs only because we knew you were out here protecting us, Abe," Nunn said. She put a hand on his arm. "We needed you, and we were counting on you."

On being touched, Cioffi seemed to deflate. "I—I'm sorry. I have no idea where that came from." He shuddered. "This passageway is creeping me out."

"Did anything happen?" Nunn asked.

Cioffi took in a big sigh. "A bunch more light panels blew—the noise about gave me a heart attack. Then my flashlight practically exploded in my hand—I'm surprised I didn't rocket right through the overhead when that happened." He nodded toward the aft end of the passageway. "And then just a second ago, I could have sworn I saw something moving back there in the shadows."

Michaud held up her light and shined it down the passageway; nothing was visible other than a row of closed cabin doors stretching into the gloom.

"Anyway," Cioffi said, now sounding distinctly sheepish, "I apologize. Jumping on you like that—I don't know what got into me."

"Don't give it another thought, Abe," Nunn said reassuringly, still grasping his arm. "You did your job. That's what counts. And this place is getting to all of us."

Michaud lowered her light. "Let's get back to the bridge, and see if our *acting* captain has figured a way out of our predicament."

As they turned to go, Nunn reflected that she did not like the way Michaud had emphasized the word "acting." Such openly and disrespectfully expressed sarcasm was completely out of character for Michaud—and it seemed even more strange given that the woman's mood had seemed light just moments before.

Something, indeed, seemed to be getting to them.

As Michaud was speaking, De Vegas was grappling with the very question she had posed. A short time later, she called a shipwide crew's muster for 18 hundred hours. As the appointed hour approached, members of the flight team not on watch began gathering in the forward lounge, standing or seating themselves at the various tables. The aft section crewmembers collected in the engineer's mess, where they were able to see De Vegas via holo.

Standing before the closed view ports of the forward lounge, De Vegas began promptly and without preamble. "Men and women of the *Santa Maria*, here is our situation. Our vessel is trapped in a void that we believe lies outside the bounds of our known universe. Despite appearances to the contrary, we are not lost. Mathematically, we know exactly where we are. We've regained access to all computer systems. Our astrogators are confident we can find our way back.

"However, a new problem has arisen. Three hours ago, for reasons that are not completely clear, our port and starboard water tanks ruptured, resulting in a near total loss of their contents. Without this mass to use for direct energy conversion, we have no way to fire up our four Emsky torches for the trip home.

"All of our ship's systems are fully operational at this time. However, we are experiencing an energy drain, the source of which we are unable to identify. At the current rate of drain, the *Santa Maria* will go completely dark and powerless in about seventy-six hours."

De Vegas paused for a moment to let that sink in. Glancing around the room, she noticed that most people were not looking at her, but rather at those around them.

"In addition," she continued, "there have been incidents involving the appearance of unexplained spatial anomalies within the structure of the ship. In several cases, some kind of portal has opened up that seems to be inter-dimensional in nature. Think of them as holes in the bulkhead that open and close without warning. Some crewmembers have gone missing. We know this phenomenon was responsible for four of those disappearances, because we were lucky enough to get those crewmen back. It's logical to assume the same thing caused the other six disappearances and that we may see the return of those shipmates as well.

"We've also been experiencing some equally mysterious psychological effects. Some crewmembers have become disturbed or even homicidally psychotic. Three are dead—two under circumstances we can't explain. In the latest incident, this afternoon the chief engineer was found shot to death in his cabin—by all appearances, at his own hand.

"Because we don't know precisely what is happening, reluctantly I have called off the searches for the crewmen still missing. From this point forward, I am asking everyone to travel in pairs at least. And I do not want anyone to bunk alone. The flight and steward's departments will sleep in the forward mess. The science and engineering departments will sleep in the aft mess, except for those engineers assigned to duty forward. No other exceptions. No one is to go anywhere alone for any reason."

De Vegas paused, and her hard expression seemed to soften. But it was only for a moment. "I know," she resumed, "that right now you are looking to me for words of hope and comfort. I can only say this: We are professionals, and we are explorers. Every one of us is here because we are believed to be among the very best our species has to offer in our chosen fields. At some point along the way every man and every woman must decide whether to live a normal life, or an extraordinary one. For each of us, that fork in the road is well behind us. We chose the extraordinary. And in doing so, each of us made a total commitment to the values of science, duty, and honor. That is how we've lived. That is how I expect each of you to continue to live."

She paused. De Vegas looked off into the distance, and for a moment it appeared that she might have something else to say. But then she focused again on the group. "That is all," she said with finality, and then turned to leave.

"Wait just one goddamned minute!" a loud voice rang out. It was Jervis, who had jumped to his feet from a chair at the front. "Is that all you've got to say? We're all supposed to just lie down and die?"

De Vegas kept marching toward the exit, trying to ignore him. Krajnovich joined her and walked with her, flanking her.

"What about rescue?" Jervis demanded. "Can't we put in a call? Or send a messenger rocket or something?"

De Vegas now paused. Turning to him, she fixed him with an icy stare. "Mr. Jervis—you have little time left. Is this how you plan to spend it?"

"I just want answers!" he yelled at a level near the top of his voice. He jabbed a finger at her. "And you're damned well going to give them to me!"

De Vegas stared at him, tight lipped with anger. For a moment it appeared she would challenge him further. But then, abruptly, she turned to go.

Seeing this, Jervis screamed at her, "Don't you dare walk away from me, you soulless *bitch!*"

Now she stopped in her tracks. And then, very suddenly, De Vegas whirled about and took three swift steps toward Jervis. Whipping her left arm up, she grabbed the back of the startled man's neck and pulled his face to within inches of hers. At the same time, with her right hand she drew her sidearm from the holster at her hip, brought it up, and placed the gun barrel at the bridge of the reporter's nose, pressing it hard against the spot located right between his eyes. "One more word, Mr. Jervis," she snarled, boring her eyes into his, "and I will splatter your brains all over this lounge."

Jervis went completely stiff with fright. The only answer he could muster was an incoherent whimper.

Swann stepped up to her right side. "Captain," he said softly.

De Vegas, grinding her teeth with her lips pursed in anger, continued to glare at Jervis as she pressed the muzzle of the gun hard into the man's forehead. This sniveling, puling, cowardly excuse for a man, she thought, represented everything she loathed and detested in her fellow human beings. She'd run across his kind many times before. Such people could be counted on to contribute nothing to the human endeavor other than pain, disappointment, and bitter betrayal—and this fact was never more evident than in a crisis like the one they were all now facing. Jervis' very existence not only endangered them all but stood as a living affront to every value she held sacred. De Vegas saw no reason to let it continue for another second. Her finger tightened on the trigger.

Reaching forward, Swann gently placed a hand atop the weapon. "Captain," he said again.

For a moment De Vegas continued to glower at Jervis, as if to incinerate him on the spot with the intensity of her anger. As she ground the muzzle into the man's flesh, she envisioned just how much more appealing his features would look with the decorative addition of a bloody hole in the forehead.

And then, just as suddenly as the confrontation had begun, it was over. Releasing her grip on the man's neck, De Vegas thrust hard against his forehead with the gun. Jervis stumbled backwards and then fell heavily onto the deck. He immediately rolled into a fetal position, hugged himself, and began sobbing.

For a moment De Vegas stood staring at him, breathing heavily, with the gun now down at her side. Finally, she thrust it back into its holster, and then turned and walked out the door without another word, with Krajnovich following close behind.

Swann turned to Terwilliger. "Grab someone, get down to medical, and get a sedative for him. A strong one."

Terwilliger nodded.

"Mr. Swann," Nunn spoke up, "what about Teal? And the—and Cermeno?"

Swann looked at her thoughtfully for a moment, and then turned back to Terwilliger. "When you're done with Jervis, go fetch Teal and Cermeno, and bring them to the lounge. Cuff both of them, and secure them to something."

"Will do," Terwilliger said.

Swann turned and hurriedly left the room, intending to catch up to De Vegas and Krajnovich. But as he headed up the short corridor that intersected with the main passageway, he heard something from around the corner ahead that he couldn't quite identify. Stopping for a moment to listen, he strained his ears against the flickering gloom. Now there was no longer any doubt about it; he was hearing the sound of a woman's weeping, mixed with the soft tones of a man's soothing voice. He could not make out the words. But then it clicked for him what this had to be. The thought of the steely-eyed De Vegas losing control of her emotions and then having to turn to someone—*anyone*—for solace shook Swann to his core. But then again, so had the sight of De Vegas grinding her pistol into Jervis' forehead. Neither behavior fit De Vegas' character. But in the void where they were now marooned, what was normal?

In any case, Swann decided that intruding on De Vegas and Krajnovich at the present moment would not be a good idea. Quietly, he turned and headed back down the corridor toward the forward mess. A cup of coffee, he thought, would do him some good.

He was slowly rising from a level of deep unconsciousness. It felt more like a return from total anesthesia than it did recovery from a profound slumber. At first, he wasn't even sure who he was. But slowly, slowly, the cobwebs cleared. He became aware that he was awake, and that he was lying on something cold and hard.

He opened his eyes. The room was completely dark, and yet, somehow, he began to sense that there were figures huddled around him. As his eyes—or whatever sense he seemed to be using—adjusted to the gloom, he started to make out indistinct silhouettes.

The figure nearest to him spoke. "Welcome, Chief. We've been waiting for you."

Crandall recognized the voice. "Tochigi?"

"None other."

"But how is that possible?"

"I can't rightly say," Tochigi answered calmly. "But here I am." He gestured to the figures standing around him. "We're all here. We've been here. Waiting for you."

Groggily, Crandall strained to see through the gloom. Something was not quite right with Tochigi. Crandall now saw that the man's upper body was bare—and that a large, dark Y-shaped incision ran across his chest and down his abdomen. "Tochigi—are you injured?"

At this, Tochigi laughed. "Physically, yes, but don't let that trouble you. I'm over it. We all are."

Something was very wrong with Tochigi's eyes. Crandall peered more closely—and now he could see that Tochigi's eyeballs were missing; Crandall was staring into the man's empty sockets. As the horror of this realization began to sweep over him, a large spider hoisted itself out of what had been Tochigi's right eye, crossed Tochigi's face, crawled down his neck, and began descending the man's arm.

Crandall opened his mouth and screamed.

"There there," Tochigi said, reaching forward to pat him reassuringly on the shoulder as another spider exited the eye, following behind the first one. "Everyone says that at first."

Crandall kept on screaming.

"Go ahead," Tochigi said soothingly, softly rubbing Crandall's shoulder. Now a train of spiders was descending. "Get it out of your system. You'll feel better."

As Tochigi spoke, the spiders crawled down his arm, crossed over onto Crandall's shoulder, and began making their way up Crandall's neck. The man was still screaming as the first spider entered his mouth.

Why she was insisting on maintaining a bridge watch, De Vegas couldn't really say. It just seemed the thing to do. *Regulation to the end*, she thought bitterly. But the thought brought a faint, wry smile to her face. Besides, she was forced to admit that she enjoyed the company of Krajnovich, who was the only other person on the bridge at the moment.

Not that she was spending much time in idle chit-chat. De Vegas had never been an idle chit-chat kind of person. This, plus her somewhat intimidating physique, had succeeded in putting off most men she'd been interested in. But some women seemed to find it attractive. Perhaps that's why she'd had more success with the latter.

Her mind drifted to the last lover who'd been important to her—Marta Breza. That was the one relationship that had come closest to working. And it *would* have worked, she thought, if only their careers hadn't taken them in different directions. De Vegas suddenly realized that she would give anything to see Marta one more time.

"Captain," Krajnovich spoke up, "I have Mr. Terwilliger for you."

She nodded. "Put him on my speaker."

Krajnovich pressed the appropriate square, and the audio monitor on De Vegas' console beeped. "This is De Vegas," she said.

"Mixter De Vegas, I'm in Medical with Bent. We're here retrieving a sedative for Jones, on Mr. Swann's orders."

"Yes. Go on."

"I noticed that the door to the isolation room is standing open."

De Vegas frowned. "How did that happen?"

"I don't know, ser. Maybe something related to the blackout. The power never came back on here. The whole room is completely dark, and very cold."

"What's the risk of contamination?" As she asked the question, De Vegas realized that Terwilliger didn't have the expertise to answer it.

"I don't know, ser. But there's something more."

"What is it?"

"As you know, this is where we stored the—the bodies. Tochigi and Trafford. And we added Crandall this afternoon."

"Yes?"

"They're gone."

"*Gone?*"

"Yes, ser. The bags are still here, but they're empty. And, Captain— whoever did it had no use for zippers. The bags have been *torn* open."

De Vegas found herself clenching her teeth. She forced herself to stop. "Very well. Get that sedative. In fact, get as many emergency medical supplies as you and Bent can carry. Then get out of there. Take the supplies to the forward mess."

"Yes, ser."

"Then as soon as you've sedated Jervis, go collect our two prisoners and report back."

"Yes, ser. We're on it."

De Vegas switched off, and then turned her gaze to Krajnovich. "Mr. Krajnovich, see if you can call up the video files from the sick bay this afternoon."

"Yes, ma'am."

Krajnovich worked his board. Momentarily, he turned back to her. "Sorry, it's no use. All the pickups in that area went dead when the chief cut the power, and they never came back up."

De Vegas nodded. "Very well."

What next? she thought.

"I wonder what we have to look forward to next?" Krajnovich mused, echoing her thoughts. This caused De Vegas to laugh. "What's so funny?" he asked.

"Mr. Krajnovich," she said, "ask me that again over a cup of coffee sometime."

The suggestion surprised Krajnovich, but he tried not to show it. Instead, he nodded. "I'll do that."

Captain Sirius Constantine Cermeno, Jr. lay on his bunk with his arms at his side, staring at the overhead and beaming black thoughts at it. He'd been doing so for the last couple of hours, calling up in his mind every person he'd ever met whom he now hated. It was a long list. At the very top of it was his still lovely but joyless, pinched and embittered soon-to-be-ex wife, Patricia. He'd been taking his time carefully reviewing and savoring all of the delicious ways in which he'd like to kill her.

His father was second down on the list, and got a similar mental treatment, though not rendered so lovingly and with such thoughtful, imaginative, and detailed visual imagery. Fabiana De Vegas was there, too. He might yet get to act out some of his fantasies on her, he thought. *That would be good.*

And Ms. Bent. Oh, yes. She was on the list. Most definitely. When they'd first met, Cermeno had found her attractive. Regulations had not, strictly speaking, allowed him to give expression to even the most subtle hint of that. But one night prior to start of the mission, he'd casually invited her over to sit at his table. The gesture had, in his mind, been harmless. But she'd turned her nose up at him. Oh, her words in explaining why she could not tarry had not been in any way overtly disrespectful. But her slight toss of the head, a hint of a sneer, and her body language made it plain enough that she had seen right through him and would rather be dipped in a sewage treatment pond than be seen sitting with him. He had not forgotten that.

Idly he wondered how long someone might live through some of the gruesome tortures he was envisioning, and how he might draw out the experiences. *After all,* he thought, *it's no fun to play alone.*

About the only name not on his mental list of people he'd like to do unto was that of his daughter, Melanie. He wished her no ill. Not specifically, at least. Yet he had to admit that some of his fantasy choices for Patricia's demise involved forcing her to watch Melanie suffer in various ways first.

Deep in the back of his mind, a part of his consciousness knew that such thoughts were not healthy, and were not typical of him. But he dismissed those voices, and had no trouble doing so. The old Sirius Cermeno, Jr. had been weak and ineffective. If a new one was emerging, the captain liked him better.

Cermeno smiled as the image of a sterner, more commanding self filled his mind. Then his thoughts turned even darker. He had plans, and those plans would be executed. *This mutinous crew will rue the day it turned on me.*

The hatred boiled out of him in almost palpable waves. As it did so, the spot on the overhead at which he'd been focusing his gaze seemed to snap, creak and groan. He looked more closely. Was it his imagination or had the area at which he'd been staring grown darker? He sat up and focused his eyes on it. The discoloration was unmistakable. A splotch *had* formed—light grey at the edges, but growing slightly darker toward the center. "Well, I'll be damned," he said aloud.

His door chime sounded. Without preamble, the panel slid aside and Terwilliger and Bent walked briskly into the room. Terwilliger was carrying a sidearm, which he had pulled from its holster and was now rudely pointing at Cermeno. Behind him Bent was holding two plastic zip ties, which she no doubt intended to use as handcuffs.

"Ms. Bent," Cermeno said, smiling at her. "How nice—I was just thinking of you." He turned to her companion, still smiling. "And Mr. Terwilliger. Are we going somewhere?"

"To the forward mess," Terwilliger answered as the two of them took up stations to the right of his bunk. "Captain's orders."

"*I'm* the damned captain!" Cermeno thundered.

As he did so, with loud bangs all four of the overhead light panels exploded in a shower of sparks and went dark, causing both Terwilliger and Bent to jump. The malfunctions plunged the cabin into deep gloom, relieved only by the poor, flickering light spilling through the open cabin door from the passageway beyond.

Bent and Terwilliger exchanged nervous glances. Then Terwilliger turned to Cermeno and motioned with his gun. "Hold up your wrists," he commanded.

Cermeno smiled. "You know, if I were you, Julius, I wouldn't stand with your back to the door."

Terwilliger glanced to his right at the open cabin door, and then turned back to Cermeno. "I don't know what you mean," he said. "My back's not to the door."

Cermeno smiled. "That's not the door I'm talking about."

As he spoke, a cold draft moved through the cabin, bringing with it a horrible stench. Almost simultaneously, a dimly seen cloaked figure stepped out of the shadows behind Terwilliger. The fingers of a large, bony hand closed around Terwilliger's neck, while its other hand grasped the man's gun arm. Thrashing wildly against an iron grip, Terwilliger fired off several shots; the bullets ricocheted loudly but harmlessly off the plastisteel walls of the cabin. And then as silently as it had emerged, the hideous figure glided back into the shadows and disappeared, taking Terwilliger with it. It had all happened in a span of less than ten seconds.

"Julius!" Bent cried out. She dashed over to the wall where Terwilliger had disappeared and placed her hand against it. The surface was now solid, and deeply cold.

Behind her, Cermeno got quietly to his feet. Sensing motion, Bent turned to face him. Realizing the danger, she made a move toward the open cabin door. But Cermeno quickly stepped sideways, cutting her off. "Leaving so soon, Sierra?" he asked, smiling.

Bent backed away from him.

"You know, I get the sense you don't enjoy my company," Cermeno said with an exaggerated air of disappointment. "And that really hurts my feelings. Because I *so* enjoy yours. And I plan to enjoy it further." He smiled at her malevolently.

Bent retreated another step, and now her back fetched up against the bulkhead. Reaching into a pocket of her flight suit, she pulled out a gleaming surgical scalpel. "Back off!" she snarled, holding the instrument toward Cermeno.

"Aw, look," Cermeno said. "You brought a toy. How thoughtful. I just love toys." His face broke into a broad, cold smile. "Especially *adult* toys."

Dr. David Jones lay against the nude body of his wife, skin to skin, soaking up her warmth and breathing in her unmistakable fragrance, which was a unique blend of Channel No. 5 mixed with the smell of clean, sweet perspiration tinged with a hint of musk. He nuzzled his face further into the hollow of her neck. "How are you doin', darlin'?" he asked.

"Don't talk," she said sleepily. "Just hug. Be a human blanket."

For several minutes, Jones was content to hold her, playing back the scenes of the last hour in his mind. He had never met a partner as sexually uninhibited and creative as this one. But that wasn't what had made him fall in love with her—or at least, it wasn't that alone. Since the day he'd met her, the two of them had seemed to click. Both had the same wry sense of humor. Both enjoyed similar tastes in books and sensies. Both had the same intellectual capacity and curiosity. And from the start, both had made each other laugh.

"You know, from the moment I met you," he said after a while, "there was never any possibility of there being anyone else in my life."

"I never understood that," she said. "I remember the occasion. I'd just stepped out of the shower. I was wearing a much frayed towel. My hair was wet and stringy. No makeup. And you were looking for my roommate, who was ten times more attractive than I am."

"There is no one more attractive than you are," he objected.

"That is bunkum times rubbish times dross, cubed."

He propped himself up on elbow to look at her. "If Derla was so much more attractive than you, then please explain why I dumped her to chase after you."

She shrugged, smiling. "The simple truth is your brain had been addled by too much stargazing. You weren't thinking straight."

"I was thinking perfectly straight. The only mystery is why you let me catch you."

"You have this lost little boy expression," she explained. "It brings out my maternal instinct."

Sighing, he plopped his head back down on her shoulder. "I'll bet you're regretting it now."

Gently, she ran the fingernails of her left hand over his hip. "I wouldn't trade a second of the time we've spent together. Not for anything."

Again, he looked up at her. "Do you really mean that? Knowing how this is going to—knowing what lies ahead?"

Reaching forward with both arms, she pulled him to her. "Of *course* I mean it. Now hush. Don't talk. Just be."

After a while, her closeness moved him again, and they made love once more—this time, not so urgently as before, but sweetly, and gently.

After a long time, she spoke again. "Did you ever read about the ruins of Pompeii?"

"Sure," he said.

"Do you recall the remains they found? Bones, and impressions of humans recovered from the hardened ashes? Some of them were holding one another."

Jones tried to answer her, but found that he couldn't. Instead, he simply nodded.

"That's how I want us to be found," she said. "Just like this."

Hot tears now poured from his eyes, coursing down his cheek and onto her shoulder. A wave of strong emotion washed over him. Death didn't scare him. But the idea of separating from Lydia made him inexpressibly sad. He buried his face against her, breathing softly, trying not to let any sniffles betray his feelings. But by her equally careful breathing, he could tell she was feeling the same thing.

The light panel over the bunk exploded, shattering the moment and sending flaming shards showering down on them. Nguyen shrieked and Jones shouted an expletive as both leapt from the bed, wildly brushing at themselves. After assuring himself he was not on fire, Jones glanced across at her. "Are you okay?"

Nguyen looked up, and as she did so, her expression of alarm evaporated, and she laughed.

"What's so damned funny?" Jones demanded.

"You have the worst case of bedhead I've ever seen," she said, grinning.

Self consciously, he ran a hand over his head; lose ends were sticking up all over. "Fine," he said. "I'll take a shower."

A light screeching noise now sounded in the room. It seemed to becoming from the bulkhead behind the bed.

"What the hell is that?" Nguyen gasped in alarm, stepping back.

The noise sounded as if a sharp object was scraping along the wall just above the bunk. Jones couldn't be sure—only one light panel was still working, and it was flickering badly—but four or five closely spaced pointed objects appeared to be moving *underneath* the bulkhead material, leaving raised impressions as they dragged along.

"It sounds like—*fingernails!*" Nguyen gasped.

Reaching forward, Jones pulled his wife away from the wall. "I don't know," he said. "And I don't want to know. Let's get the hell out of here."

The two of them grabbed up their discarded clothes and shoes, dashed naked through the door, and ran down the passageway, not willing to spend one more second in the cabin. They didn't stop to dress until they were safely in the elevator.

De Vegas looked up as the two Joneses walked through the lounge door. She opened her mouth to say something, but then thought better of it, remembering the outcome of her last attempt to confront a crewman— an experience that had profoundly shaken her confidence in her ability to handle people. Besides, if the two of them had managed to grab a tender moment together, what was the harm? At least they'd been moving about as a pair as she had ordered, although the recent disappearances of Cermeno, Bent and Terwilliger certainly suggested that the two-person team rule was of questionable effectiveness against whatever was stalking them.

The forward lounge and adjoining mess had been roughly divided into two groups. Jervis and cooks Abe Cioffi and Jane Kim were sleeping on bunk mattresses arranged along the forward bulkhead of the lounge, beneath the closed screens. The lights were completely off in that section, having burned out. The remainder of those present had gathered around a table on the starboard aft section of the room, where one glow panel was still operative.

De Vegas was seated there, sipping a cup of coffee. With her were Krajnovich, Swann, Nunn, and Deborah Michaud, who was on loan from the engineering section to serve as a bridge watch stander. Father Teal was on the floor by the starboard bulkhead, seated atop a bunk mattress. His left hand had been zip-tied to a handhold. He did not look happy.

Jones and Nguyen walked over, poured a cup of coffee from the pot warming at the nearby serving station, and joined the group.

"I would ask where you two lovebirds have been," Michaud said, "if the answer weren't obvious from the rosy glow on your cheeks and the bluebirds chirping on your shoulders."

"Mindeth thou thy owneth business," Jones said, grinning as he took a seat. As he did so, he stole a glance at the captain, but her face remained impassive.

"What brought you back so soon?" Krajnovich inquired. "I expected the two of you to be gone for hours. Getting bored with all the surf, sand, sun, and sex?"

Nguyen and Jones exchanged glances; he gave her a nod. She then sketched out for the group the strange, unnerving noise that had driven them from their cabin.

Upon hearing the conclusion of the story, De Vegas sighed and shook her head.

"I would give anything," Krajnovich said, "to know what's going on."

"Oh, but we *do* know," Father Teal spoke up. "It's no mystery."

De Vegas looked at him in surprise; Teal had said nothing for hours. "What is it then?" She demanded. "What's going on?"

Teal nodded at Jones. "*He* knows."

"I wish I did," Jones said. "But I'm pure dead stumped."

"No you're not," Teal insisted. "You laid it all out earlier."

Jones cast him a quizzical look. "You mean my speech about God not being here? I was talking out my bahookey, just to hear my gums beat. It's a known failing of mine." Reaching across, he rubbed Nguyen's knee. "Isn't that right, darling?"

She gave sage nod. "Truer words were never spake."

"Nevertheless, you hit upon the truth," Teal said. "And it explains absolutely everything."

"Pray tell, Father," De Vegas said. "Enlighten us."

"Did you ever read your Bible?" Teal asked.

"I had parts of it read to me," she said. "As a kid."

Teal turned to Jones. "How about you?"

"Not for a while. But I used to be fairly familiar with it."

"Do you not recall a line from the New Testament that describes this place?"

Jones looked off into the middle distance, searching his memory. "I recall a mention or two about outer darkness," he finally said.

Teal nodded. "Matthew 25 verse 30. 'And cast the worthless servant into the outer darkness; there men will weep and gnash their teeth.'"

"And you think that's where we are?" De Vegas demanded.

Teal gestured with his free hand. "Look around you. Do you know of anything more 'outer' or more dark than this place? Have you seen or heard anything here *other* than what the passage describes?"

Michaud shook her head. "I just don't buy it."

"I don't see it, either," Krajnovich agreed. "I get that we're in a void. But even if it is true that God's not here with us—a theory that optimistically assumes he exists to begin with—I don't get how that's supposed to explain what we've been experiencing."

Teal looked thoughtful. "When I was in the 8th grade, I put together a little science fair display about the nature of light. My point was to show why the perception of color is possible only in white light."

De Vegas frowned. "I don't follow."

"White light is made up of all the visible colors," Teal continued. "Take a dark box. Place a white light and a green poker chip inside. Drill a peephole. Turn on the light. The chip looks green because its surface absorbs all the other colors, and reflects only the green back to your eye."

"I'm aware of that," De Vegas said. "Basic physics. But I still don't see your point."

"I'm getting there. Try a *green* light, and you still see the green. But now use a light of any *other* pure color, and what do you see?"

"A black chip," Jones said.

"Exactly. You can't see the green because the light contains no green component to reflect back. So the chip appears jet black. Follow me so far?"

The people around the table nodded.

"On earth, the light of God is all around us. It's a light whose only color is that of goodness. The virtue within a person—if there is any—will reflect the light back. But without the light of God, you can't perceive the goodness. You only see black—the evil in that person's heart. Just like what we're seeing now. Nothing but evil."

"Wait a minute," Jones said, holding up his hand. "You're saying God is not here—and because of that, *we've all turned evil?*"

"Not precisely." Teal chuckled. "At this point, my analogy probably is stretched beyond its useful limits. But what I'm saying is that without the light of God, the good in any of us is repressed and harder to see—maybe impossible—because there's nothing to illuminate it. But the evil that lurks within each of us is very visible—and unbound."

De Vegas shook her head. "Father Teal, even if I were to buy your religious convictions, which I have a hard time doing—no offense—"

Teal shook his head. "None taken."

"Even if I were to accept those beliefs," she continued, "your explanation has holes. Putting aside the issue of people's behavior for a moment—we've also been experiencing strange *physical* phenomena."

Teal nodded. "There's an explanation for that too." He nodded to Jones. "The state of true vacuum Dr. Jones was talking about."

All heads turned to Jones, who sat for a moment looking thoughtful. "Well," he finally said, "as I said before, scientists are not in agreement about what's supposed to happen to matter and energy in a true, total vacuum. In our last conversation, Tochigi used the word 'poof' and I let that stand, because it's a simple explanation."

"But?" De Vegas prodded.

"But the law of conservation of energy and mass dictate that neither can simply vanish and cease to exist. However, they might reorganize themselves into different states, and different structures."

"Or *be* reorganized," Teal added.

Jones nodded. "Conceivably."

His wife turned to Teal. "If that's the case, then what—or maybe I should say *who*—is doing the reorganizing?"

"Isn't that obvious?" Teal asked.

"What, you mean *we're* doing it?" De Vegas asked with an incredulous tone.

"That's exactly what I'm saying," Teal stated firmly. He glanced around the table at the disbelieving faces. "Open your minds for a moment," he continued. "Matter and energy in this void may not be stable. The best theory says they're prone to changing to new, different and completely unknown states. And *we're* here—each of us a living entity with a mind, and a will, and a purpose."

Those around the table continued to look at him blankly.

"Look, don't you get it?" Teal persisted. "This void we're in is a blank page—one that's easy to write on. It's precisely the kind of void that God faced on the Day of Creation. Only in this case, God is not here. *We* are the only conscious, self-aware, *willful* entities around. We have exactly the same opportunity before us that He did."

De Vegas shook her head. "Now you've really lost me, Father Teal. Are you suggesting that we now have godlike powers?"

Teal threw up his unfastened hand. "I don't know. But we do know that God himself started with *less*. He looked out on a void that was completely dark and empty. But *we* brought mass and energy into this void *with* us—in the form of ourselves, our ship, and its energy sources. And we already know that something is draining power from us at a prodigious rate. Where is that energy going? What is it doing? What work is it performing? And what physical laws is it obeying? We really don't know what the rules are here."

Jones turned to him. "And you seriously think our *wills*—conscious or otherwise—are directing some of that work?"

Teal nodded. "It's no stretch of the imagination to believe it. Even in our own universe, creating pathways to other dimensions is no great feat. It takes very little energy, and humans have been doing it since the dawn of time via poltergeist manifestations and related phenomena—all of which are human-powered from bodily energy alone, and controlled directly from the mind, even if unconsciously so."

"But even if all that's true," Nguyen said slowly, "when I was in—whatever place I was in after I went through the bulkhead—I wasn't alone. I could sense other entities. And I didn't just walk in. Something *pulled* me in."

"Me, too," her husband agreed. "I got a look at it. It was something right out of a nightmare—a rotting, corpselike figure."

"I'm guessing it *was* something out of a nightmare," Teal agreed. "Yours, or someone else's—projected from the mind."

The group fell quiet for a moment to consider this. It was Nguyen who finally broke the silence. "I have seen that figure before."

Jones turned to her with alarm. "What figure?"

"The one David is talking about. A grinning, decaying face. Dreadlocks down the sides. I've seen it in nightmares since I was a kid."

Teal looked at her with interest. "Then the projected form may be coming from you. Or perhaps it's some kind of unclean spirit or entity that attached itself to you at birth, or sometime thereafter, and has followed you here. Either way, it's likely that you're responsible for it."

"That's enough of that, Father," De Vegas snapped, now clearly annoyed. "Blaming Nguyen for what's going on here is completely out of line. I'm surprised at you."

"I'm not blaming her, Captain," Teal said, shaking his head. "Whatever is going on, it's not a conscious process, and it's not exclusive to Nguyen. I'm sure each of us is contributing to these phenomena in some way."

The normally quiet and taciturn Swann chose this moment to speak up. "Father, this is crazy talk," he blurted without preamble.

Teal and the others turned to look at him.

"Do you even hear what you're saying?" Swann continued, looking defiant. "You want us to believe that some kind of 'haint' attached itself to Nguyen at birth and followed her here? Really?" Swann shook his head firmly. "I don't know what you're smoking, Father, but you can keep it. We're all scientists here—even you, despite the collar. Not frightened children huddled around a camp fire flickering in the dark, wondering what's lurking beyond the circle of light. This is no time for ghost stories."

"You know I love you, Father," Jones said. "But I'm forced to agree with Mr. Swann. I think you're a wee bit 'round the bend on this one."

Teal cocked his head, looking at Jones. "Is what I'm saying really so outlandish?" The priest paused for a moment, wearing a thoughtful expression. "If I've learned anything in three and a half decades of serving the Church, it's this: We all have our demons. Problems with alcohol. Substance abuse. Sexual addiction. Anger management. An endless array of self-destructive personality flaws." He looked at Swann. "In a very small handful of cases, I've come to believe the expression is not just figurative. Evil spirits *do* walk amongst us. The literature is quite convincing."

"Well, *I'm* not convinced," Swann said.

Teal fixed him with a steady gaze. "No? Were you not the person who walked through a solid plastisteel bulkhead, disappeared into it, and then stepped out in a different part of the ship? What was it you said? You were surrounded by something in the dark? Something you feared but couldn't name?"

"Just because I can't name it or explain it," Swann said, "doesn't mean we're trapped in a damned haunted starship! Good God, man. Listen to yourself!"

"Again, Father, I'm forced to agree," Jones said. "There was a time when poltergeist phenomena were considered supernatural and evil. Now we understand those forces and we harness them for star travel. What we're experiencing here—as frightening as it is—most definitely does *not* prove the existence of some mysterious malevolent force running amok."

Father Teal gave a sardonic laugh. "You think not? Look around you. We have one of the most elite, carefully selected, and highly trained starship teams in existence. Nearly half of our crewmembers have suffered horrendous deaths, or are missing, under circumstances we can't explain. Do you see the forces of *good* running amok here?" He turned to Captain De Vegas. "If the idea of demons bothers you, think of it this way. Every personality has a dark side. We now find ourselves trapped in a lightless, apparently infinite expanse lying outside our universe. The laws of physics here are unknown to us. But it's obvious—*obvious*, I say—that this black void contains properties that adversely affect the human psyche, allowing that dark side to grow, potentially to the point where it consumes the individual from the inside, like a cancer."

"Cancers have a cure," Nunn observed, looking up. "What's the cure for this one?"

"Simple awareness," Teal answered. "Self discipline. The best weapon in any situation is knowledge. Now that we know what's going on, each of us can be alert to any changes, and watch for unusual forces, urges and compulsions within ourselves, and within each other."

Swann was looking angry. "Father, if no one else will say this, then I will. This sounds like self-serving crap to me. You killed Dr. Blake, now you're trying to explain that away as some kind of temporary insanity."

Teal's face went slack; clearly Swann had landed a blow. "I pray to God that I didn't—that I didn't do anything like that," Teal said after a moment. "I have no memory of what happened."

"His fingerprints were not on the scalpel," Nguyen offered, looking thoughtfully at the priest. "Blake's were."

Swann scowled at her disbelievingly. "What, we're supposed to believe she killed herself while lying next to him, without waking him up, and then disposed of her own body?"

De Vegas held up her hand. "Secure that. Father Teal will get his trial. This is neither the time nor the place."

The group lapsed into another moment of silence. Lydia Nguyen finally broke it. "I believe him," she said, gazing at the priest.

Swann gave out a "pschaw," and turned away, looking disgusted.

"Father, I'm going to admit I find your theory compelling," Michaud said slowly. "But there is one area where it doesn't add up."

"Go on," Teal prodded her.

"You stated that right now in the absence of God's light we can only see the evil within us. But that's not the case." She turned to Swann. "Swann here dashed into one of those black holes to try to save some of his fellow crewmembers. And he succeeded. The act was both selfless and visible to all. How do you explain that?"

With his free hand, Teal reached up and rubbed his chin, seeming to mull the question over. "From time to time in my life," he finally said, "I have met people who seemed to have an inner glow of their own. Or at least, it appeared that way to me. They seemed to have a spark of the divine, if you will, within them. Perhaps Mr. Swann is one of those people."

Swann signaled his enthusiasm for that notion with a snort and a roll of the eyes. De Vegas also wore a doubtful expression, as did Jones and Michaud. Nunn and Nguyen looked contemplative.

Teal turned to Swann. "Didn't I hear you say that when you were in—that place, whatever it was—you saw your skin giving off a slight glow?"

Swann nodded. "Very slight."

"There you go."

"No, no, no," Jones said, waving a hand. "I was in that hole—or whatever you want to call it—too. I didn't see my skin glowing. And *I* haven't fallen under the spell of some evil corrupting force."

Teal raised an eyebrow. "Perhaps you don't recall that drunken binge you and I went on a couple of nights ago?" he pointed out. "Or maybe you feel such behavior is in character for you?"

Jones opened his mouth to argue, but then closed it, looking thoughtful.

"More to the point," Teal continued, "when you were in that place, did you look at yourself? Did you glance at your hands or feet?"

Slowly, Jones shook his head. "I can't recall."

Teal turned to Nguyen. "Lydia?"

"Same here," she admitted. "My memory of that entire experience is rather spotty."

"Several people have disappeared," Teal said. "Only four returned. I would venture to say all four of you went into the situation possessing some kind of quality the others didn't. Something about you is different."

"Nunn was *very* different," Swann now admitted, his scowl softening. "She was shining so brightly it hurt my eyes. What does that mean?"

Teal glanced at Jones. "Doctor, you may be a skeptic. But I've never met a more logical mind than yours. Care to put your powers of deduction to work on that one?"

Jones sat pondering the question for several moments. "If I get what you're driving at," he finally said, "and if you know what you're talking about, then I see only one possible answer."

"Which is?" De Vegas demanded.

Jones turned and focused his gaze on the subject of the discussion. "Nunn is a saint."

Nunn glanced up at him sharply, while De Vegas stared at him in open-mouthed astonishment. But before the captain could muster a reply, her comlink beeped. She pressed behind her ear to open the connection.

"Captain," came Conrad Specht's urgent voice over the link. "Can you come to the bridge?"

"Certainly," she said, rising. "What is it?"

"I—my proximity and collision alarms just went off. You have to see this to believe it."

"On my way."

"Captain," Teal spoke up. "May I tag along?"

De Vegas shot him a dubious look.

"I assure you, I'm quite safe," Teal said. "Whatever happened to me— I'm alert for it now. And I may be of assistance."

"I vouch for him," Dr. Jones added.

"Yes," De Vegas said, not smiling. "But who'll vouch for *you*?"

"I will," Nunn said. "I usually read people pretty well," she added, noting the captain's hesitation. "And I think we're better off staying together."

De Vegas nodded. "Very well. Cut him loose. But be quick about it."

6 THE PIT

De Vegas hurried onto the bridge with her companions following close behind. "What is it?" she demanded as she approached the coms and sensor station where Specht was seated.

"I don't know how to tell you this—" Specht began, and then hesitated.

"Spit it out," De Vegas snapped.

Specht swallowed nervously. "We are approximately 175 klicks above an Earth-sized planet," he said. "And we're falling toward it."

"What?" De Vegas stared at him in open-mouthed incredulity.

"It's dead ahead, ser," Specht continued. "It just simply—appeared."

De Vegas peered through the viewports. "I don't see a thing."

"No, ser. It's completely dark. But it's right there in front of us."

De Vegas winced inwardly at her own stupidity; of *course* the planet would be dark—there was no sun to light it up. "What's our trajectory?"

Specht looked grim. "Straight down. We were dead stationary relative to the planet when it popped up. Present velocity is about 900 meters a second, and accelerating, of course, at about one gee. Impact on this trajectory would be in roughly three minutes."

"What action have you taken?"

"I've contacted Nabozny in engineering and have ordered her to bring the ion thrusters on line. We'll have them in about 30 seconds. She says she can only give us 2.2 gees."

De Vegas nodded, and then turned to Swann. "Mr. Swann, if you please," she said, gesturing to the empty helm station. Nodding, Swann stepped past her, sat down, and began strapping in. As he did so, De Vegas turned to those standing behind her. "Buckle yourselves in, please."

Nunn took her station at the AI console. Krajnovich stepped forward and relieved Specht at the sensor station, allowing Specht to assume his normal duty post at the astrogation console. Michaud strapped in at the engineering station, while Teal, Jones, and Nguyen took flight chairs at the aft end of the bridge. The sounds of metal buckle tabs clicking into their receptacles resounded around the bridge.

De Vegas stepped up to Krajnovich. "What readings do you have?"

The sensor officer studied his readouts. "In many ways, the planet is a twin of Earth. The surface features are very different. But size, mass, gravity, atmosphere, rotation, magnetic field—they're all identical out to four decimal places. Temperature is completely homogenous—about 12 degrees Celsius from pole to equator."

Behind them, Jones gasped. "That's not possible."

The captain turned and glanced at him. "Dr. Jones, this mission is redefining the concept of 'possible' by the minute," she observed drily.

"What course would you like me to shape, Captain?" Swann asked.

"Stand by. Mr. Krajnovich, put our mystery planet on the holo. Infrared, please."

Krajnovich pressed a square; a round 3-D image formed in the air in front of the central viewport. It showed a fuzzy green ball. The image was completely featureless except for one very small spot in the upper left quadrant, which showed a slightly darker shade of green.

"What's that?" De Vegas said, pointing.

"Uh—I'm not sure. Let me check." Krajnovich pressed a series of control squares. "Ma'am, it looks like some kind of liquid—a lake of it. About four degrees cooler than its surroundings. At this temperature, it almost has to be water."

"Excellent. I was hoping you'd say that." She turned to Swann. Pointing at the lake, she said, "Can you set us down there?"

Swann punched a few keys. "Yes, ser. If Nabozny can deliver the acceleration she promised, we can do it. But—"

"I hate that word, Mr. Swann. Continue."

"Well, as you know, the refit was conducted with the idea that the *Santa Maria* would not be making planetfall anywhere on this mission. I'm not absolutely sure the landing struts are operative. The refit specifications are silent on that point."

"Wonderful. What happens if we have to land without them?"

"Well, I can get us down. The lower hull will take the strain. The torch pods, I'm not so sure. As you know, pods two and four project down slightly beneath the keel. They could be damaged. But the landing thrusters along our belly almost certainly would be. We might not be able to lift off again."

De Vegas shook her head ruefully. "We have no choice. Punch it in."

Swann pressed a few more squares. "Landing trajectory plotted and ready to execute. Permission to sound the acceleration alarm?"

"Wait one. Mr. Krajnovich, 1MC please."

Krajnovich pressed the appropriate square and then gave her a nod.

"All hands, this is the captain," she said as her voice echoed down the corridors. "We'll be landing in about five minutes. It could be rough. I don't have time to explain. Rig for acceleration and assume landing stations. We'll be boosting in less than half a minute." Glancing at Krajnovich, she drew a finger across her throat, and then turned to the helmsman. "Mr. Swann, you may sound the alarm."

Swann pressed a square, causing a loud klaxon to sound four times throughout the vessel.

"I'm orienting the ship now," Swann reported as the last *bong* of the alarm faded. He was working a hand grip. "Deceleration in 20 seconds."

"Very well. Mixter Nunn, Mixter Michaud—anything to report?"

"AI on line, all IT systems nominal," Nunn replied.

"Engineering is ready," Michaud answered. "All systems nominal except for the ongoing power drain, as previously noted. Thrusters will be able to deliver up to 2.2 gees throughout the landing cycle."

"Thank you." She turned to Specht. "Mr. Specht, tell me more about our Planet X. You say it simply appeared?"

"Yes, ser," Specht replied. "A replay of the sensor files showed that it seemed to—inflate, from out of nothingness."

De Vegas raised an eyebrow. "What do you mean, 'inflate'?"

"A central point, very tiny, appeared at a distance of about 66 hundred klicks. Within about ten seconds, it had grown to a diameter of about 12,800 klicks, with the surface precisely 175 klicks beneath us."

"Boosting now," Swann announced, before pressing a flashing red square bearing the word "EXECUTE." When he touched it, De Vegas swayed slightly on her feet under a brief surge of deceleration before the inertial dampeners adjusted.

"That is—incredible. A planet simply appears—sporting a lake with a temperature variation just cool enough to stand out on our sensors." She turned around, fixing her eyes on Teal and Jones. "Gentlemen, any theories?"

Jones looked blank. Teal shook his head. "Nothing to add to my earlier dissertation," he said. "I've achieved my yearly quota for attracting disbelieving stares."

"But you still think this could be some kind of—mental projection?" De Vegas persisted.

"Well, if there were any doubt before, it's clear now that the laws of physics as we've come to understand them do not apply here." Giving a half-shrug, he smiled ruefully. "Further deponent sayeth not."

De Vegas stared at him blankly.

"Ser," Swann said, turning to her, "due to the mysterious nature of this planet, I sure would feel better if you'd strap in. Anything could happen."

"I take your point," De Vegas said, nodding. She stepped over to the captain's chair and sat down. "Mr. Swann," she said as she buckled herself in, "how close can you put us to that lake without getting our feet wet?"

"One moment, ser." Swann turned to Krajnovich. "What can you tell me about the terrain surrounding the lake?"

Krajnovich studied his display. "It's flat overall. The lake appears to be about 20 meters down inside a small crater or caldera. The slopes are fairly steep but should be traversable by foot without too much difficulty, I'd say. The lip of the crater is about 80 meters from the shore of the lake. I'd suggest parking the ship no closer than 40 meters from the lip—the slope appears to be loosely compacted, and I'm uncertain of its stability."

"Okay," Swann acknowledged. "What's the ground surface like?"

"Very flat, covered with rocks and pebbles—nothing bigger than about 25 centimeters. High-res sensors show a dust covering of about a centimeter, over densely compacted, rocky soil—my guess is it's decomposed granite, or something like it—going down at least four meters. That's the best I can do without a probe on the ground. But I think it'll hold us."

Swann nodded. "Here's hoping your guesses are bankable." He turned around in his chair to face De Vegas. "Captain, I'll give you the shortest hose run I can. Figure on no more than 150 meters."

De Vegas nodded. "Good. See to it." She turned to Krajnovich. "What else do we know about the planet?"

"No oceans, no other lakes in sight. The ground is uniformly flat. I'm not finding a hill higher than about five meters anywhere within our range of scan. The lake is on the edge of a flat, rocky plain that extends to the horizon toward the west. About a klick east of the lake there's a huge forest—very tall trees, topping out at about 40 meters, extending to the east. What's beyond the horizons, I can't tell."

"Very well. Please get me Chief Nabozny. Put her on my console."

A moment later, the speaker at De Vegas' station beeped and Nabozny's face appeared in one of the monitors. "Mixter Nabozny, we'll be landing near a lake. We're hoping it holds water. On that assumption—how long will it take to repair the ruptured tanks?"

"Oh, God," Nabozny answered, somewhat surprised. "Let me see. Two rips, each about 15 meters long and about four meters across at the widest points. We have limited manpower, and we'll have to rig safety lines over the outer hull—no time for a scaffold. We'll need to cut away all the bent plastisteel, and slap new plates down over the gashes."

"How much time?" De Vegas repeated.

"I'd say about twelve hours, if we're lucky. And then another four to fill the tanks."

"All right, I'm going to hold you to that."

Nabozny looked distressed. "Captain, it'll take too long. We won't finish in time."

De Vegas frowned. "What do you mean?"

"If the power drain we're experiencing continues at its present rate—and there's no reason to believe it won't—in 12 hours and ten minutes, the maximum acceleration graph line for the thrusters will descend through the one gee mark. There won't be enough thrust for lift off."

The captain's frown deepened. "What if we cut the work in half, and fill just one tank?"

Nabozny looked ill. "That would feed just one set of torches, and we can't blast that way. We'd be out of balance."

"Can't you rig a cross-feed?"

"I'm sorry, Captain, but that's an even bigger job. There's just no time."

De Vegas narrowed her eyes. "Then, Mixter Nabozny, I suggest you figure something out that you *can* get done within the time allotted."

Nabozny nodded nervously. "Yes, ser. We'll put our heads together and get on it. We'll think of something."

"Prepare to muster your repair crew the moment we touch down. Draft anyone and everyone you feel may be useful. While you're working on the repair plan, I suggest you get a crew to work immediately rigging hoses. I'll send the flight team back to assist you the moment we land."

"Very well, ser."

De Vegas switched off.

For several moments, the *Santa Maria* descended in silence. After a short while, Jones turned to Teal. "I'm glad De Vegas' back is turned to us at the moment," he said in a low voice. "Given our situation, I imagine her face is about as happy right now as a bulldog chewin' a wasp."

"Dr. Jones," De Vegas said without turning around, "my hearing is excellent, and your voice is one of those that tends to carry."

Teal, despite himself, chuckled. "Busted!" he whispered.

In the flight chair on the other side of Jones, Lydia Nguyen's face broke into a broad smile. Jones' face began to turn red.

"Touch down in one minute, Swann announced. "Now extending the landing struts." At this, he reached forward and pressed a control square. For a moment no one breathed. Finally, an indicator on his board flashed green. "Struts show down and locked."

Sighs of relief could be heard around the bridge.

"Inertial dampeners and gravity fields off," Swann announced before pressing another button. The crew felt a slight wave of motion, which quickly settled down.

"Landing lights on," De Vegas ordered. "Put the keel view on holo."

Swann and Krajnovich both worked their boards. The image of the planet that had filled the holo space in front of the viewports dissolved away, and a now new picture took shape. The landing floodlights were brightly illuminating a swiftly approaching expanse of flat ground covered with small rocks and pebbles. Within a few seconds, the thruster plumes began to wash over the ground, causing the surface to disappear in a cloud of blowing dust.

"Touch down in 20," Swann said. Ten seconds later, he began a countdown. At the zero mark, he announced, "Contact." They felt a slight bump. "Thrusters off." Swann paused for a moment. "Some slight settling," he said, and then after a short pause, he announced, "Motion sensors are green. The ground is holding. We're down and stable."

De Vegas nodded. To her surprise, she found that she had stopped breathing. "Excellent," she said, letting out a large exhalation. Reaching up, she pressed the disconnect square on her chest buckles, releasing the straps. "Mr. Krajnovich, alert the crew. Secure from landing stations."

Krajnovich made the announcement as the bridge crew unbuckled and stepped up to the viewports. From their vantage point on the bridge, little was visible beyond the curve of the upper hull other than the very tops of dust clouds slowly settling beneath an utterly black sky.

"Put the bow camera on holo," De Vegas ordered.

Krajnovich touched the appropriate controls. An image formed showing the same rocky ground they'd seen before, brilliantly illuminated and stretching out only a short distance before being lost in the receding, hazy curtain of dust stirred up by their landing. Above it all stretched a canopy of impenetrable, inky blackness. For a moment, the gathered crew stared silently at the holo.

It was Jones who broke the spell. Turning to Teal, he said, "So, Father—do you think this is the pit the Bible speaks of?"

Teal gave a wan smile. "I doubt it's *the* Pit," he said, slowly shaking his head. "But it might have served as a prototype."

"All right," De Vegas said, "We've got a lot of work to do, and not a lot of time to do it in." She turned to Nguyen. "Your file shows you have some experience in planetary sciences. Is that correct?"

"It was my minor in college," she said. "But I'm not qualified as a planetary sciences officer."

"Mixter Nguyen, I assure you, you're the best qualified planetary sciences officer in this universe. We need someone to check out that lake. You will lead those efforts, taking with you whomever Chief Nabozny assigns. We need to know just three things: what is in that lake, can we use it for conversion mass, and can we draw it out in the time remaining? We need to find out quickly."

"Yes, ser," Nguyen said, nodding.

"I'll go with her," Jones said.

"No, you won't," De Vegas contradicted him. "With your injured ankle, you'll just slow everyone down."

"My ankle is fine," Jones argued. "That salve you put on it has worked wonders."

De Vegas nodded. "Excellent. Then in that case, we need you on the hose party. Along with Cioffi and Kim—and Jervis, if he's not raving, twitching or drooling on himself."

Jones was not happy, but the reference to Jervis reminded him of how De Vegas had settled her last argument. Reluctantly, he decided to let it go.

The captain turned to Krajnovich. "Make an announcement. All hands report to engineering stat—no exceptions."

Krajnovich glanced up at her. "No bridge watch?"

"No. At this point everything hinges on us meeting a very hard deadline. We'll need every pair of hands on the work details."

"Yes, ma'am. Just point me where you want me." He then opened the intercom and made the announcement.

De Vegas turned to Nunn. "Mixter Nunn, tell Wilson that he will stand the bridge and engineering watches himself. He is to monitor all systems and report anything out of the ordinary directly to me via the command circuit."

Nodding, Nunn gave the necessary instructions. This completed, she turned back to De Vegas. "Instructions understood and acknowledged."

"Good. All of you, follow me."

Fifteen minutes later, De Vegas stood with Nguyen and engineer Kareem Anwar inside airlock F-5, located on the lower port side of the engineering section. In addition to their normal jumpsuits, the three of them had donned windbreakers and heavy black all-terrain boots, and were wearing headbands fitted with lamps. De Vegas and Anwar wore holstered pistols at their sides; he and Nguyen also wore small, portable scanners.

De Vegas glanced at her companions. "Ready?" she asked.

Both nodded.

De Vegas pressed a button. There was a slight hiss, and their ears popped. She pressed another. A large section of the deck before them slid aside, revealing beneath it a long, wide metal stairway that had been lowered to the alien soil. Chilly air rushed inside. De Vegas sniffed; it was dry and odorless.

Stepping forward, De Vegas began descending the stairway, with Nguyen and Anwar following close behind. At the bottom step, she paused to look around. The ship's floodlights seemed to struggle to illuminate the dark brown ground that stretched out before them; it was almost as if the soil were sucking up the beams of light. The surface was liberally strewn with rocks and pebbles, most of which were no bigger than a baseball. At the edge of the pool of light about twenty meters away, the impenetrable darkness took over.

Cautiously, De Vegas stepped down and placed one boot on the ground. The surface crunched beneath her feet, but held firm. She followed with the other foot, and then slowly walked out several paces. Nguyen and Anwar followed, with the sound of their footsteps offering the only challenges to the otherwise total stillness of the air.

Turning to the two of them, De Vegas pointed out into the darkness. "Okay. The closest point of the shore is that way, straight out and slightly to the left. Stay in contact. Report your progress at regular intervals—I'd be happy to hear from you at least once a minute."

Nguyen nodded.

"If anything moves, shoot it."

At this, Anwar gave a sardonic smile. "What happened to, 'We come in peace for all mankind'?"

De Vegas did not return the smile. "Perhaps you haven't been keeping up with current events."

Anwar's smile faded. "Yes, ser. Sorry, ser."

De Vegas allowed her stern expression to relax a shade. "We don't know what's here. But we can't assume the environment is either friendly or safe. Watch yourself."

The two nodded.

"Okay. Be off with you."

At that, Nguyen and Anwar turned and began walking straight out toward the edge of the circle of illumination cast by the ship's floodlights, with the crunch of their footfalls sounding unnaturally loud in the dead silence of the planet. As De Vegas watched them disappear into the gloom, a very slight wisp of a chilly breeze brushed her cheek.

The sensation had barely registered on her consciousness when her comlink beeped. De Vegas touched behind her ear. "Go ahead."

"Captain, it's Nabozny. Mr. Damiano and I have come up with something. We think we can pull this off."

"Excellent. I'll be right up."

The plan turned out to be clever but simple. "We'll repair the tanks from the *inside*," Damiano explained, gesturing to a schematic of a hull tank interior displayed on the big engineering control room monitor. "That will allow us to leave the damaged plates, which are all bent outwards, in place. No cutting. No removing. It'll save us loads of time."

De Vegas turned to Nabozny. "But you said earlier you didn't have time to build scaffolding," she objected. "I can see how safety ropes would work for repairs on the exterior of the tank. But not on the interior. How will you get the plates and workmen into position?"

Nabozny smiled. "We cheat."

De Vegas raised an eyebrow. "That statement certainly begs an explanation."

Nabozny's smile widened into a grin. "The way the mishap happened in the first place gave me the idea. We replace the burned out Bjorklund field generator units, and then focus and adjust the fields so that to anyone standing inside the tank, 'out' seems 'down.' From the viewpoint of the crew, they'll be lowering the plates to the floor and then standing on them to do the work."

"Plus," Damiano put in, "we forget the welding. Instead, we paint the surface of the repair area with sealant. We lay the plates over that and then use the emergency hull repair guns to rivet 'em in place."

De Vegas returned her gaze to the display. "I presume you've got enough plates and rivets to complete the job?"

"Yes, ma'am," Damiano confirmed.

"It's just a temporary patch," Nabozny said, "and it will earn no smiles from any dry dock foremen. But this method will serve our purposes. And we can get it done this way in half the time. Six hours, tops. Probably less."

De Vegas turned to them. "Color me impressed. Proceed at once."

Nabozny nodded. "Will do."

"Where do we stand with our pumping efforts?"

"We'll be stringing six hoses," Nabozny answered. "One for each of our high-capacity pumps. I've got a five-person team doing that work now. They're breaking the reels out of storage and loading them onto the engineering main elevator. The crew should be ready to lower away any second now." Nabozny hesitated. "Uh—I hope you don't mind. I drafted Jervis into service on the team."

"No, I told you to get anyone you need, and I expect him to pull his weight. Is he proving useful? Any trouble from him?"

"No, ser. He appears to be stable. A little sheepish, maybe. But he jumped into the assignment with a big show of enthusiasm."

De Vegas nodded. "Very well." At the appropriate time, De Vegas thought, she'd apologize to Jervis for her behavior, even though she was quite certain her violent outburst had shaken her up more than it had him. But now was not the time. "Where do you need me?"

"We could use another person on the hose team at the moment. After that—can you handle a rivet gun?"

"I surely can."

Nabozny nodded. "That would be outstanding."

"We'll get those hoses laid as quickly as we can."

Moments later, as De Vegas and the rest of the hose team were stepping off the engineering main elevator platform onto the rocky ground, her comlink beeped. She opened the connection. "De Vegas. Go."

"Nguyen here," came the voice over the link. "We've reached the lake. It's water, all right. So pure you'd think it had just been distilled."

"Well, how about that. Excellent. Now, high-tail it back to engineering and report to Chief Nabozny."

"Will do. Out." The link beeped and went silent.

"Good news?" Jones asked.

"The best. We've got water. As pure as a babbling Colorado mountain stream. More pure, in fact."

"Yes!" Jervis shouted, pumping his fist, while Teal gave a sigh of relief.

Take that, Father Teal, De Vegas thought. *God is here, and he's watching out for us.* She was just about to verbalize the thought when every floodlight on the hull simultaneously exploded, sending sparks and shards of flaming lamp material showering down all around the perimeter. The flames quickly died out, plunging the repair team into total darkness.

"What the hell?" Jones exclaimed.

"Check your headlamps," De Vegas snapped.

Seven beams sprang to life. One of the headlamps immediately blew out. "Damn!" Jervis swore. "Mine just went!"

"I see that. All right, let's conserve. Mr. Abello, keep your light switched on, and I'll do the same. Everyone else, switch off."

De Vegas' comlink beeped twice and then beeped again, indicating that two people were trying to call her, and that one of them was using the command circuit. The latter had to be Wilson. She pressed the button under the skin behind her ear twice. "Go, Wilson."

"Acting Captain De Vegas," Wilson began formally, "I have several developments to report."

"Give them to me in descending order of priority."

"First, every remaining light panel in the *Santa Maria* just failed."

"*All* of them?"

"That is correct. At the same time, the rate of the power drain has stepped up. If the new rate does not change again, we will have sufficient thrust to leave the surface for only another eight hours 27 minutes."

De Vegas glanced at her watch—the new figures meant they must boost by 16:16—and that did not include a safety margin. "Very well. What else?"

"The comlinks for Kareem Anwar and Lydia Nguyen Jones have gone off line. This event was simultaneous with the light panel failures and the power drain spike."

De Vegas found her jaw tightening. "Where were they at the time?"

At those words, the other crewmen turned to look at her in alarm. "What is it?" Jones demanded.

De Vegas held her hand up, straining to hear the comlink.

"Both were near the shore of the lake," Wilson said, "approximately 145 meters from the ship."

"All right, Wilson. Anything else to report?"

"Yes, ser. I have picked up an atmospheric electrical disturbance approximately 350 klicks to the east. Its pattern is consistent with lightning. The disturbance is growing, and the preliminary indication based on the location of strikes is that it's moving in this direction at about 20 knots. At the same time, the barometer has begun to fall, down five kPa the last quarter hour. The wind is freshening—from dead calm, to 5 knots in the last quarter hour, out of the north. And humidity levels are rising, up ten percentage points in the last few minutes."

De Vegas frowned. "How is this possible? On planet with no oceans?"

"There are no known principles of planetary science that would account for it," Wilson said matter-of-factly, "or for any of the events we have been experiencing on this planet."

"Predictions?"

"I have no data or theories on which to base a scientifically valid prediction."

"I understand. Take a guess."

"I am not programmed to guess."

De Vegas sighed. "Wilson, I suspect you are more than the sum of your programming instructions. What's your best estimate of what we can expect?"

Wilson seemed to pause. "If current trends hold, then the center of the disturbance will arrive in about nine hours. It will bring lightning and high winds, possibly up to hurricane strength. And perhaps rain."

"All right. Keep me informed. De Vegas out."

Jones was now standing very close, wearing an anxious expression. "What happened?" he again demanded in a voice that was about two notches too loud.

"Take a breath, Dr. Jones," De Vegas said quietly, "and calm down." She pressed her comlink again to open the second connection. "De Vegas here."

It was Nabozny, calling to tell her that the power drain had spiked and that the lighting panels had blown. "We just put up a replacement for one of the panels here in engineering, and it blew immediately," she added. "We have no idea why."

"Very well. I'll need you to rig up—" But before she could complete the sentence, her comlink squealed and then went dead. "Nabozny?" De Vegas called. She tapped behind her ear. "Nabozny, can you hear me?" There was no answer, and no response to her taps.

"*Please* tell me what happened," Jones pleaded in a slightly lowered voice.

Turning to him, De Vegas regarded the man with serious eyes. She was tempted to place a hand on his shoulder, but then rejected the thought on the grounds that the gesture would telegraph that she was assuming the worse. "Dr. Jones," she began, "Wilson has lost touch with Nguyen and Anwar—and now, apparently, with us as well. My comlink is dead."

"God *damn* it!" Jones shouted. "Not again!" Switching on his light, he turned and immediately dashed off into the darkness, running in the direction of the lake.

"Dr. Jones!" De Vegas yelled. "Stop! Wait!"

But Jones ran on, unheeding. Soon the hungry darkness had swallowed him up, with nothing to hint of his presence other than dim flashes from his headlamp beam splashing on the ground ahead of him.

"What now?" Teal asked.

"Check your comlinks," De Vegas ordered.

The team did so. Every comlink was dead.

"All right," De Vegas said. "It is what it is." She drew her sidearm. "Follow me."

"Captain," Cioffi spoke up, "if our lamps fail out there, we'll be well and truly screwed."

De Vegas paused, considering this, and then turned to Jervis. "Mr. Jervis, get up to engineering. When you get there—"

"What, in the dark?" Jervis objected.

Once again, she found herself becoming enraged. She envisioned herself screaming at the man, and then slapping him hard across the face and telling him in biting terms to man up, grow a set and do as he was told. There was something about his very existence that simply infuriated her. *Control, Fab*, she said urgently to herself. *Your team is looking to you for calm-headed leadership.* "The ship's emergency lights operate on a different technology," she said, forcing herself to speak in calm tones. "They should be working."

Jones looked dubious.

De Vegas pulled off her headlamp. "Here." She passed it to him. "When you see Nabozny, tell her to set up a signal light for us down here—a fire, or something like it not subject to electrical failure."

Jervis nodded. "Right."

"And also tell her that I need her to devise some kind of failure-proof portable light—flaming torches will do, but I'd prefer a solution that's a bit brighter and a bit less medieval."

Jervis nodded. "I understand."

"Go."

Turning, Jones walked briskly to the passenger gangway and scrambled up it.

De Vegas fixed her eye on the senior cook. "Mr. Cioffi, your headlamp, please."

Looking none too happy, Cioffi took it off and passed it to her.

After putting it on and activating the lamp, De Vegas turned to her companions. "Let's go."

As it turned out, there was little to discover. When they arrived on the scene, they found Dr. Jones standing in the dark by the shore, calling for his wife as the inky black waters lapped gently at his feet. His headlamp had blown out.

De Vegas approached him. As her beam struck his face, Jones squinted and recoiled, holding up his hand to protect himself from the glare. De Vegas could see that his cheeks were streaked with the trails of tears. "Sorry," she said, lowering the light. "Did you see or hear anything?

"Nothing," Jones said bitterly. "Nothing at all." Jones glared at her. "Why did you have to send *her*?" he demanded. "Hasn't she done enough for one mission?"

De Vegas' lamp chose that moment to flare and go dark, leaving only Abello's burning, and his was flickering badly.

"If we're lucky, there will be time and a place for recriminations later, Doctor," she said softly, barely able to make out Jones' face in the gloom. "This isn't it."

"Found something!" Abello's voice called out.

It turned out to be a broken headlamp. Abello had spotted it lying on the ground a couple of meters up the slope. The instrument was dark, and the lens had been shattered in a way that seemed unlikely to have been caused by a mere electrical failure. Scuff marks were plainly visible in the dusty soil nearby.

"Looks like there's been a struggle," De Vegas observed. As she spoke, she stole a glance at Jones' face. She couldn't make him out clearly in the gloom, but what she could see told her that Jones was in a state of abject misery.

Abello's light chose that moment to pop and go dark, causing a cloak of utter blackness to descend over them. To De Vegas the darkness seemed almost like a living thing—a parasite, in fact, one that wanted to suck the life out of her through the pores in her skin, and was attempting to do so. She shook her head to clear it. *This kind of lurid, fantastical thinking is not like you*, she barked mentally to herself. *Stop it.* "Mixter Kim," De Vegas said calmly, giving no hint of her apprehensions, "please pass me your headlamp."

Kim did so, locating De Vegas by the sound of her voice.

De Vegas switched on the light, and then led a search of the surrounding area. "Look," she called out after a moment. "Footprints."

The group gathered around her. "Those aren't like any footprints I've ever seen," Father Teal observed. "No shoes, no pads to the soles of the feet."

"The impressions look—bony," Kim added.

"Look there," De Vegas said, playing her beam over a long gouge in the dust extending ahead of them into the darkness. "It looks like something was being dragged."

"It would seem so," Teal agreed.

"Let's see where this goes." De Vegas led them up the slope, following the gouge marks. Before they reached the top, her lamp blew. "Father Teal," De Vegas said, "if you please."

Teal switched on his lamp. "It's the last one," he said as he handed the device over. "Shouldn't we use this one to head back, while we still can?"

"No need." She nodded up the slope. "Look over the rise." A small, barely perceptible halo now slightly relieved the gloom in the sky just above the top of the slope. "Chief Nabozny has put a candle in the window."

They continued to follow the trail. As they neared the top of the slope, a small dot of bluish light rose into to view above the shoulder of the rise. It was the signal from the *Santa Maria*.

De Vegas stopped abruptly.

"What is it?" Teal asked, stepping up to her.

"The end of the trail, I'm afraid." She played her beam over the ground. "The footsteps and drag marks just stop."

"How can that be?" blurted a frustrated Dr. Jones.

And then the final lamp blew, plunging them into total darkness.

"Now we have no choice," Teal said. "We *must* return to the ship."

"I'll stay here," Jones volunteered. "When you rig up some replacement lights, come bring me one, and I'll resume the search from here."

"David," De Vegas said gently, "There's no time for that. We face two different deadlines. The rate of the power drain has picked up, and there's a storm approaching—possibly a severe one. We've got to get to work. *Now*. We need you at the ship. And there's nothing you can do for Lydia standing here by yourself in the dark."

"I'm not leaving without her," Jones declared flatly.

"Dr. Jones," De Vegas said, her tone now hardening, "I am giving you an order. You will return with us now, and help us lay those hoses."

"I won't," Jones said defiantly. "And unless you're prepared to carry out a fistfight in the dark, I suggest you leave it at that, and go about your business."

Although he couldn't see it, Jones could feel De Vegas' glare. But finally she spoke. "Very well. Have it your way, for now. The rest of you, follow me."

By her footsteps, Jones could tell that she had turned and begun walking back to the ship. The others fell into lockstep behind her. "Don't forget that light!" Jones called out after them.

There was no acknowledgment.

The small band walked toward the *Santa Maria* in utter darkness. Behind them they could hear Jones begin to call out for his wife. The intensity of the man's voice faded as the group proceeded.

The signal light ahead was not bright enough to illuminate the group from afar; it did not help that their jumpsuits and windbreakers were made of dark material. The pinpoint of light in the distance gave them something to bear on, but that was it. It relieved the darkness surrounding them in no other way.

After a few moments, De Vegas came to an abrupt stop. "Everyone!" she called out. "Stop in place. Hold stock sill."

The sounds of their footsteps crunching on the rocky soil stopped. De Vegas could hear nothing but the soft sighs of her own breathing, the blood pumping in her ears, and the very light ringing that accompanied total silence. Slowly, she turned her head, scanning back and forth, straining to hear into the darkness.

"What is it?" Teal asked.

"Shhh! Let me hear." De Vegas continued to stare into the blackness. But there was no sound, and no sensation other than the brush of a freshening wind on her face.

"Did anyone hear anything unusual?" she finally asked.

"Like what?" Cioffi responded.

"I thought—I thought I might have heard an extra set of footsteps behind us."

The group fell silent for a moment, considering this.

"I may have heard something," Kim volunteered. "I can't be sure."

"Everyone sound off," De Vegas ordered.

They did so—Kim, Teal, Cioffi, and Abello all answered.

It was then that De Vegas noticed that she could no longer hear Jones calling out for Nguyen. Cupping her hands to her mouth, she shouted, "Dr. Jones! Can you hear me?" There was no answer. "Dr. Jones!" she called again. The darkness seemed to swallow her words whole, with no hint of an echo or reverberation. In a lower voice, she asked, "Did any of you notice when Dr. Jones stopped calling out?"

No one replied.

"All right," De Vegas said. "Let's continue. I want each of you to tread as lightly as you can. Try not to make any noise."

After only another 30 meters or so, De Vegas heard the sound again— and this time she was sure of it. A foot or something like it definitely had made a crunching noise in the rocky soil—*ahead* of them.

Once again, she called a halt and ordered another sound-off. Everyone was present. "Okay," she said when the head count was complete. "I'm quite certain I heard something. And it's *ahead* of us, between us and the ship. Maybe a little to the left of our path."

"Oh, my God!" Kim gasped. "Can you smell that?"

De Vegas sniffed the air; a faint odor of decay filled her nostrils. It only confirmed her suspicions; something foul was standing in the dark head of them. "Here's what we're going do to," she said. "Mr. Cioffi, follow the sound of my voice and step over to me. Take my hand."

Cioffi did so.

"Mixter Kim, please join us, and take Mr. Cioffi's hand. Father Teal, you take hers. Mr. Abello, take his."

Within moments, they had linked up, each holding a teammate's hand. As they did so, a fairly strong, chilly gust of wind buffeted them, but then quickly died away.

"Now," De Vegas continued in a low voice, "I'm going to lead us on a little dogleg, beginning with a detour about 50 meters straight out to the right. Each of you take a firm grasp on the hand you're holding. The ground is pretty level all around, so we shouldn't have any problems. I want you to walk as quickly but as quietly as possible. Pick your feet straight up, and put them down as straightly and as softly as you can. Any questions?" There were none. "All right. Let's go."

They walked briskly in nearly total silence. But as careful as they were, there was no way to completely mask the sound of their footfalls on the gravelly ground. For a moment, De Vegas considered having them stop and remove their boots. But this would require them to release their grips on each other. She decided not to risk it.

They had made their second turn and were 20 meters down the new path to ship when Teal and Kim both called out simultaneously. "Hey!" Teal shouted while Kim yelled, "Abe!"

"Everyone stop!" De Vegas barked. "What just happened?"

"I've lost Cioffi!" Teal answered. "Abe!" he called. Teal's feet crunched as the priest turned around to face the rear. "Abe!" he called again.

"Abe's hand jerked out of mine," Kim added.

"Cioffi!" De Vegas called. There was no answer. "Everyone be still," she commanded. "Hold your breath for a moment." Leaning slightly forward, she strained into the darkness, not breathing.

From behind them, about five meters away, came the unmistakable sound of crunching soil. De Vegas felt the hair stand up in a wave that ran along the back of her neck and down both arms. "Abe?" she called quietly. There was no answer. "Everyone!" she shouted. *"Run!* Back to the ship! As fast as you can! *Now!"*

De Vegas heard her three companions take off running off in the darkness; the body of one of them momentarily occluded the signal light. She paused for just a moment, and then bounded after them, careful to remain just behind the sound of the running footfalls ahead of her.

As they approached the ship and the intensity of the light increased, De Vegas could see that there were only two people running in front of her—Teal and Abello. Almost as soon as this realization struck her, the three of them bounded into the circle of illumination cast by the signal light—which turned out to be a spot welder zip-tied to a long metal pike in the ground and set at its lowest intensity, no doubt for longevity.

Whirling, De Vegas drew her sidearm and peered into the darkness. She heard no further footfalls. "Kim!" she called. There was no answer. "Kim!" she called again. But there was no sound other than the soft sigh of the low but now constant wind.

"*Damn* it!" Father Teal swore. "We should have stayed and fought!"

De Vegas turned to him. "Calm yourself, Father. If we'd stayed to fight an unknown enemy in total darkness, *none* of us would have made it back."

Teal shot her a hostile look, grinding his teeth as he did so. But neither he nor Abello offered any argument.

A strong gust of wind buffeted the group, and a dim flash of light briefly illuminated them. De Vegas looked up, trying to locate its source. The light flashed again, and this time she spotted its direction. It was coming from over the eastern horizon, directly across the lake.

"Captain De Vegas," Teal said, "What are your orders?"

De Vegas holstered her weapon, and then nodded toward the welding torch. "Now, we rig up some more lights like that one, get some reinforcements, and we go back out there. We've got to get these hoses laid."

Teal shook his head grimly. "I was afraid you'd say that. Doesn't *anything* ever frighten you?"

De Vegas shot him a sober glance. "Not much. Until recently."

Kimberly Nabozny was as good as her word—better, in fact. Within five hours, her teams had completed the repair work on the water tanks. It would have been done even sooner had De Vegas not insisted that she and the engineers drop everything and find a fail-safe lighting solution, which had eaten up nearly an hour. Her team had also managed to repair the communications system, which fortunately had involved nothing more complicated than replacing a blown circuit board. Now, Nabozny stood before the control panel for the pumps. "Here goes," she said, and began pressing a series of six lighted control squares. Immediately the muffled, guttural sounds of machinery could be heard emanating from the engineering spaces below.

Moments later, her comlink beeped. She pressed behind her ear and then announced, "Nabozny."

"This is Damiano. The water's coming in. Nice rate of flow, too."

Nabozny gave a sigh of relief, and then turned to De Vegas. "That's it.

Now all we have to do is wait, watch, and hope none of the pumps break down."

De Vegas glanced at the clock display on the engineering monitor wall. Nabozny had told her it would take four hours to fill the tanks. But the deadline for lift-off was slightly more than three hours away. The engineer had assured her they could get back to Earth with even half a tank load. If all went well, they'd get the energy conversion mass they needed with plenty to spare.

She nodded to Nabozny. "Good work. You and your team can take a breather."

Behind her, Father Teal cleared his throat. "Captain," he said, "the search—"

De Vegas glanced at him. Teal was a mess—liberally smeared with grime from work in the tanks. De Vegas realized that she must present the same picture herself. She nodded to him, and then pressed behind her ear, tapping twice to call up the command circuit. "Wilson, 1MC please."

"1MC activated," Wilson acknowledged.

"This is the captain," De Vegas announced, her voice booming through the ship. "I am looking for volunteers to search for our missing crewmen. Those willing, please assemble in engineering at airlock F-5."

Tapping twice to close the circuit, she turned back to Nabozny. "We'll need as many lights as you can spare."

Moments later, De Vegas was pleased, but not surprised, to see that the entire remaining ship's complement had gathered at the airlock. However, there were only six lights to go around. Nabozny and her team had fashioned them from the same type of hand-held plasma welders she'd used earlier for the signal light, fastening them to various kinds of makeshift reflectors—pot lids, bin tops, even a couple of woks from the galley. The single brightest among them made use of a reflector taken from the surgical light in sick bay.

De Vegas turned to Nabozny. "I take it we've employed all of our welders?"

"Yes. But go ahead and take all six. We've gathered up some candles and food warmers from galley. We'll be fine."

De Vegas nodded, and then began selecting her volunteers. She decided on three teams of two, with one light for each searcher. For these efforts she chose herself—over the objections of Swann—along with Teal, astrogator Conrad Specht, and engineers Carlos Abello, Darlene Marrone, and Nalini Dhawan.

De Vegas activated her command circuit. "Wilson, weather report, please."

"Sky is overcast. Winds out of the north, twenty knots gusting to thirty. Moderate rain. Some cloud-to-cloud lightning. Temperature 8.6 degrees

Celsius and falling."

"Sensor report."

"There is no movement within the range of the scan. Ground temperature in the immediate area is homogenous at 11.2 degrees, and slowly falling."

"And there are no objects anywhere radiating at a higher temperature?"

"There are none," Wilson confirmed.

"Very well." De Vegas knew this meant that not only were their missing crewmen not out there, their bodies weren't, either, as they would not have had enough time to cool to exactly the ambient temperature and therefore would show up like neon signs on the sensor screen. But even so, she did not feel she could cancel the search. There were simply too many unknowns in this environment.

De Vegas surveyed her team. "I want to thank all of you," she said. "Let's get ready. It's nasty out there, so we'll be using rain gear."

Moments later, the team was ready to go. De Vegas opened the outer airlock door; a moist gust of chilly wind immediately buffeted her face. She shined her light—she'd commandeered the powerful one fitted with the surgical reflector—down the gangway. Rain, blowing diagonally, slashed across the beam. In the distance, a forked bolt of lightning played across the sky. "Let's go," she said.

They were out less than an hour before the strengthening winds and cold rain made a search impractical, forcing them back. Predictably, they'd found nothing. But at least the jury-rigged lights had worked, and no one else had gone missing during the effort.

The same could not be said for the crew left aboard the *Santa Maria*. According to testimony, one moment Dakota Munson had been standing in the doorway of the engineering galley. The next, she was not. No one had actually seen her disappear. In a room lit only by flickering candlelight, no one could be certain what had happened. The circumstances surrounding the disappearance of Deputy N-Field Specialist Ariana Marinez were even more mysterious. No one could remember when they had last seen her. But now she was not to be found anywhere.

These disappearances had deprived them of their last science officer and their last N-field array expert.

De Vegas sat on the bridge, listening to the pounding rain that was lashing the viewports and drumming on the hull, while nursing her coffee in the flickering light cast by the flame of a food warmer—a Sterno Handy Wick. *Amazing*, she thought. The Sterno name had survived three world wars plus the civil chaos that followed the last one, and now reached out across the incomprehensible vastness of time and space to illuminate the bridge of her starship, using a technology that was older than human memory—a simple chemical flame. *If Prometheus could see us now*, she thought.

De Vegas stole a glance at her bridge companions. Krajnovich manned the sensor/coms station. Specht was at the astrogation console, next to Swann at the helm. Nunn sat at the AI station, and Deborah Michaud was at the engineering position. Each was busily studying the displays in front of them, as if there were any work left to do. All the data needed for the liftoff and the flight back had already been entered, cross-checked, and triple checked. Liftoff was scheduled for sixteen hundred hours—25 minutes away. This would give them plenty of safety margin.

Now two things happened simultaneously; an alert sounded on Krajnovich's coms console, and the speaker on De Vegas' command console beeped twice. "Captain," came Wilson's voice over the speaker, "there's a new development."

"Captain—" Krajnovich began.

De Vegas held up her hand. "One moment, Mr. Krajnovich. Go ahead, Wilson."

"Four comlinks just reappeared on the network. I have them located 1.5 klicks due east."

De Vegas' heart skipped a beat. "Whose are they?"

"Nguyen, Jones, Kim, and Cioffi."

"Sensor readings?"

"I detect 20 objects, each with the approximate size of a human being, located in what appears to be a clearing in the forest. Two are stationary and are radiating at 37 degrees. The rest are in motion. Of those, 14 are at ambient temperature. Two are at 28 degrees and falling. One is just above freezing."

De Vegas turned to Krajnovich. "I concur," he said upon catching her eye. "Wilson is a bit quicker on the uptake than I am."

"20," she repeated. "The exact number of our missing crewmen. Wilson, could this be them?"

"The number indeed corresponds," Wilson said. "But except for the two stationary objects, the body temperature readings do not correspond to those of living human beings."

The sound of the rain driving against the viewports and hull now momentarily rose to a higher pitch as a strong gust of wind buffeted the ship, before falling again.

De Vegas turned back to her console. "Weather report, Wilson?"

"Heavy rain. Temperature 5.1 degrees Celsius. Winds north at 55 knots, gusting to 70. The center of the low pressure system will pass directly over us in about twenty minutes."

Damn, De Vegas thought. Getting up, she walked over to the center viewport and looked out. In the dim light cast by the Sterno Handiwicks spaced along the tops of the consoles, she could see drenching water rippling down the exterior of the transparent surface. Beyond the ports, sheets of lightning flashed intermittently, but even during the brightest bursts, not even the forward curve of the hull could be seen through the obscuring curtains of slashing rain.

55 knots. Gusting to 70. They now had 24 minutes. How long to walk 1.5 klicks? They could jog it in ten minutes, she estimated. Maybe twice as long to get back, if they had to carry someone. Not enough time.

"Mr. Krajnovich," De Vegas said with tightness in her voice, "get me Nabozny. On my console please."

Moments later her monitor beeped. "Nabozny here."

"Kim," De Vegas began, uncharacteristically making use of a crewman's first name, "how much of a safety margin did you build into that liftoff time?"

Nabozny hesitated only slightly. "A few minutes. But Captain, if we're not boosting by 16:20, I can't promise we ever will."

"Very well. Bridge out." *It'll be a close thing*, De Vegas thought. *But we have a chance.*

Nunn was peering at her. "I'll go with you," she said, apparently having read De Vegas' mind.

"No," the captain shook her head. "Out of the question. You're our last AI tech."

"Wilson will be fine," Nunn said. "Isn't that right, Wilson?"

"I will be fine," Wilson agreed, "barring another power interruption."

"Which is why you can't go," De Vegas said to Nunn, looking stubborn. "We can't rule anything out on this mission. If the power fails, without you to get Wilson back on line, we'd be lost."

Nunn stood. "Captain—I've been to the place where those people were, they place they just returned from. You need me."

Swann locked eyes with De Vegas. "You need me, too. For the same reason."

"No, no, no! Mr. Swann, you're our last helmsman."

"Specht has trained on the helm. Besides, Wilson can handle anything that comes up."

De Vegas cocked an eyebrow at Swann. "That was not your testimony last year when the company was looking at automating ship functions."

Swann looked defiant. "Automation is one thing. Wilson is something else."

"If anyone needs to stay," Specht pointed out, "it's *you*, Captain. Regulations are very clear on that. We're about to boost."

De Vegas gazed at him for a moment, considering this—and then threw her hands up. "Well, hell, they can only fire us and strip us of our tickets us if we actually get back." She turned to her console. "Wilson, you'll need to guide us, and vector us there and back. We won't be able to see more than a meter in front of us."

"I will do that. In addition, sensors show the center of the low pressure system is clear of rain. By the time you get there, the rain will have stopped. You'll have a weather window of about twelve minutes thirty seconds."

" 'About.' " De Vegas smiled despite herself. "Wilson, you inspire confidence. I'll count on those minutes and seconds." Reaching over, she picked up her jury-rigged lamp off the right-hand seat, and then turned to Krajnovich. "Have Nabozny meet us at airlock F-5 with three more of these, and one more volunteer. Then make an announcement to the crew."

Krajnovich nodded. "Will do."

De Vegas stepped over to him and placed a hand on his shoulder. "You're in command," she said, locking eyes with him. "If we are not back at 16:20 hours sharp, you are to execute the liftoff as scheduled. Understand?"

Looking unhappy, Krajnovich nodded.

"I would like a verbal acknowledgment of my order, please."

Krajnovich swallowed. "Yes, ma'am. At 16:20 hours, we go."

De Vegas patted his shoulder. "Good." She turned to her companions, both of whom were now on their feet. "Let's go."

It did not surprise De Vegas to find several volunteers at the airlock vying for permission to join the team. It came down to a choice between Father Teal and Derek Damiano. De Vegas picked Teal. If forced to explain that choice, she would have had to admit that she considered Damiano more capable but Teal more expendable. But she did not explain herself.

Just as they opened the airlock, a bolt of lightning split the air and hit the ground about 50 meters away, illuminating driving sheets of rain that were now blowing nearly sideways. The crash of thunder assaulted their eardrums almost immediately. *Great,* De Vegas thought bitterly. *Now on top of everything else, I have to worry about lightning killing us all.*

She turned to her team. "We're going to move quickly—four abreast. Father Teal, you'll be to my right. Nunn, to my left, and Swann, you're to her left. Each of you keep an eye on the others at all times. Got it?"

They nodded

"Be ready for that wind—it'll try to knock you down. Let's go."

As they descended the stairs, the torch pods sheltered them somewhat from the storm. But De Vegas had led them only a few steps into the darkness when the full force of the chilly, drenching blast hit them, nearly bowling them off their feet. She allowed them a moment to steady themselves before heading out again into the inky blackness, quickly stepping up the pace to a fast jog. Within seconds, a bolt of lightning hit just meters ahead of them, again staggering them. But De Vegas led them onward without pause. Their ears were ringing, and rocks were still hissing in the rain as they ran past the spot where the bolt had struck.

With the lighting now continuously flashing all around them and the cold rain hosing them down, it was a miserable journey. Even wearing full rain gear, they quickly became soaked. Visibility was only about a meter and a half. But Wilson kept them on track with constant bearing checks. De Vegas had to strain to hear his voice over the shrieking onslaught, turning her comlink up to full gain.

They had just passed around the lake and reached the rocky expanse of ground beyond it when the wind and rain began to die down. By the time they reached the edge of the forest a few minutes later, the wind had fallen to a mild breeze and the rain had tapered off to a drizzle.

The forest itself was quite strange. Tall, thick trees standing four to five meters apart rose up into the night. Their boles, covered in rough, black bark, ranged in size from a half meter to four or five in diameter. The team's lights could barely make out a thick growth of leafy branches closing together far overhead, forming a canopy that would have shut out the sky, had any sky been visible. But the forest floor was completely bare—not a leaf, not a stick, not a twig. The surface was made up of the same rocky material they'd just crossed, now punctuated by numerous scattered, muddy puddles. The place was eerily quiet—there was no sound at all other than that of water dripping off branches, and of their own footfalls and labored breathing.

When they entered the forest, De Vegas did not, at first, slow their pace. They continued to jog heedlessly ahead, following Wilson's directions. But when Wilson informed her that the missing crewmen were just 150 meters ahead, she called a halt.

"Mr. Swann, check your scanner, please."

Swann removed the instrument from his belt, switched it on, and studied the display. "Got 'em. Several figures, about a dozen and a half, in the center of a clearing about fifteen meters across, just up ahead."

"Are they moving?" De Vegas asked.

He studied his display again. "The two with normal body temperatures are not. The rest—don't ask me how, but yes, there's some motion." Swann looked up. "I'm not sure what they're doing. They're standing in place, gathered in a circle. Rocking, maybe. Or swaying."

De Vegas nodded. "All right. Here's what we're going to do. First, everyone, reach over and grab the belt of the person next to you." They did so. "Now, switch off your torches."

"Why do you want us to do that?" Swann asked doubtfully.

"I've got a hunch, and I trust my instincts. Please do as I ask."

Within moments, the lights were off, plunging the group into darkness relieved only by the frequent flashes of lightning and the greenish glow of

Swann's scanner readout.

"Mr. Swann, guide us in. Brisk walk, not a jog this time. I think we'll be able to see well enough in the flashes of lightning, but in any case let me know when your scanner shows that we have reached the edge of the clearing."

"Yes, ser."

"On my signal, Mr. Swann, be ready to raise your light and turn it on at the lowest intensity setting."

"Okay."

"The rest of you, when he does that, aim your torch at whatever you see closest to you. When I give the order, everyone switch on at full intensity. Be prepared to draw sidearms and advance on my command. Any questions?"

"What do you think we'll find?" Teal asked.

"I don't know. But I don't expect it to be a brass band. Everyone, make sure you have a firm grip on your partner. Let's go."

They started forward, walking as briskly but as quietly as they could, their footfalls making soft plopping and sloshing sounds in the mud and puddles. Swann steered them in the appropriate direction, while, as predicted, frequent flashes of lighting made it easy to see the path ahead and avoid marching into any of the trees.

They'd been walking for about three minutes when a clearing became visible just up ahead. "This is it," Swann whispered unnecessarily.

As soon as he said it, De Vegas noticed the smell of something putrid hanging in the air.

The others began to notice it too. "Oh, my God," Nguyen gasped, clasping a hand over her nose. "What *is* that?"

"Advance, slowly," De Vegas ordered in a quiet voice. "Let's move just inside the clearing."

The space was not large—exactly circular, measuring only about 15 meters across. In the middle, during the flashes of lightning, De Vegas could make out some kind of upright structure, maybe two meters high. Figures about the size of humans seemed to be gathered around it.

"Keep moving," De Vegas whispered. "Slowly. Mr. Swann, be ready with that light."

They advanced to within about four meters of the closest figures, as judged by the dim and constant flickering of distant lightning. De Vegas was about to order Swann to turn on his light, when a prolonged burst of nearby lightning made the order unnecessary. Starkly and garishly illuminated before them in the long flickering flash was an upright cross, made from two small logs or large branches lashed together. Suspended on either side of the cross were two human figures. All around them were more figures, gathered in a circle with their hands at their sides, slowly swaying back and forth. Most were clad in blue *Santa Maria* jump suits, but three appeared to be nude. And there was one figure standing in front.

Something about that figure seemed very different. The lightning flashed again—and De Vegas gasped. The bright burst revealed its face to be that of a rotting corpse, one that looked as if it had just crawled out of a months-old grave. The flesh of this horrible visage consisted of mottled greys, greens, blues and blacks; large patches were missing or hung in strips, revealing the bone beneath. Its lips had rotted away from the teeth, revealing a leering grin. Black dreadlocks fell down either side of the skull. The figure was dressed in some kind of black robe or long coat. Its decomposing, shriveled feet were bare. Black, emaciated hands extended from either arm of the coat, ending in pointed talons.

Unlike the others, this ghastly apparition was turned directly toward them, staring at them with a single round eyeball from which the surrounding flesh had rotted; the opposite socket was black and vacant.

Then the series of flashes ended, plunging the clearing back into total darkness.

"Everyone!" De Vegas shouted. "High intensity! Switch on! Now!"

All four plasma torches flared to life, filling the clearing with a near-blinding, garish glare. Now the human figures around the cross whirled around, looking in their direction, while simultaneously throwing their arms over their eyes.

De Vegas could see quite clearly who they were. Sabol. Beadel. Brozek. Cheng. Smith. Tochigi. Makowski. Trafford. Blake. Crandall. Bent. Terwilliger. Anwar. Kim. Cioffi. Munson. Marinez. For most of them, something was not quite right with their faces; their lips were black, their cheeks and the orbits of their eyes were dark and sunken. Most were wearing ship's uniforms. But Beadel was nude, as was Blake; the latter bore a huge, gaping, bleeding gash across her abdomen. Tochigi also was unclothed; across his chest was a large, livid, Y-shaped incision. His face and upper shoulders appeared to be covered with something dark—and *moving.*

Suspended on the side of the cross facing them was the limp form of Lydia Nguyen. De Vegas could not make out who was hanging behind her on the structure.

This ghastly assemblage stood there, frozen in the blazing beams as if captured in a holo, for what seemed like an eternity. But in reality it was only a second. As De Vegas and the group stared in rapt, terror-struck fascination, the figures around the cross, still holding hands and forearms over their eyes, *hissed* at them, and then began rapidly backing away.

All but one. The cloaked figure did not retreat. Instead, it opened its mouth and threw back its head. An ear-splitting screech emerged.

"Sidearms!" De Vegas barked.

Without warning, Nunn dropped her light, dashed forward and collided headlong with the rotting, corpselike thing, body-tackling it and taking it to the ground. Scrambling to a position astride the hideous form, Nunn clasped her hands together, raised them over her head, and brought them down in a savage blow to the sound of splintering bone. The thing beneath her brought up its arms, slashing at her back and the sides of her arms with its black talons while screeching and flailing its legs. Heedless, Nunn raised her hands again and pounded the decaying face. And again. And again. With the fourth blow, the thing's unbearable screeching cut off abruptly.

"Help her!" De Vegas shouted.

While the other figures that had formed the horrific circle continued to retreat from De Vegas' blazing torch, Teal and Swann rushed forward and set to work kicking and stomping the cloaked figure. Soon, the decaying remains lay still, not moving. As Nunn raised her hands for another blow, Swann reached forward and grabbed them. "Nunn."

Nunn struggled to break her hands free.

"*Connie*," Swann said urgently. "Stop. It's okay."

As if in a daze, Nunn turned and looked up at him.

Teal dropped to one knee beside her. "Are you all right?"

Slowly, Nunn nodded. "I think so."

Reaching out a hand, Teal helped her to her feet.

The grisly mound of decomposed flesh, bones and cloth now began to hiss and bubble. As they watched, the fuming remains dissolved before their eyes like so many chunks of bicarbonate. Within seconds there was nothing to see where the apparition had been but puddles, mud and wet rocks.

"What *was* that?" Swann blurted.

Nunn shook her head. "I don't know."

Teal appraised her. "Yes, you do."

Nunn threw him a curious look, but remained silent.

"Well, whatever it was," De Vegas said, "it's gone now."

Nunn was staring at the place where the figure had fallen, which now bore no traces that anything had ever been present. "You think so?"

De Vegas raised an eyebrow. "Don't you?"

"I don't know," Nunn said slowly.

De Vegas played her powerful beam along the far side of the clearing. She could make out dim figures lurking behind the tree line. As the light hit them, they stepped back further into the forest.

A frigid gust of wind and light rain caressed De Vegas' cheek, leaving a cold film of water.

"Mr. Swann, Father Teal, I'll keep these—whatever they are—at bay." She nodded to the cross. "Please see to those two."

As Teal and Swann headed to the structure, Nunn stepped over to her fallen light, retrieved it, and then walked over to join them. As she did so, a sudden long gust of wind roared through the treetops far above them.

De Vegas tapped twice behind her ear. "Wilson, time check."

"15 hundred 54 hours," Wilson answered. "Liftoff in 26 minutes," he added.

Keeping her light trained on the edge of the clearing, De Vegas edged closer to the cross. With Nunn providing the illumination, Teal and Swann were in the process of cutting the vines binding the limp forms' wrists and ankles to the structure. The person suspended at the far side of the cross turned out to be Dr. Jones. Both he and his wife were unconscious. Swann and Teal laid the two of them on the soaked ground.

As they did so, a bitter gust of wind hit them, this time at ground level, and afterwards it didn't completely die down. The rain was becoming more intense, too.

Much of the front of Jones' jumpsuit was soaked through with dark red blood; the stain surrounded a large rip in the material extending across his right side. Reaching forward with his knife, Swann began slicing into the cloth. "Jesus," he said under his breath as he cut open the front of the uniform. A large gash was now visible in the man's flesh, beginning on Jones' right side and extending nearly halfway across his abdomen. Putting down his knife, Swann unslung his backpack and began digging into it.

"What are you doing?" De Vegas asked.

"I've got to close this wound," Swann said without looking up as he retrieved a medical kit.

"There's no time."

Swann looked up at her. "We'll have to *make* time. This can't wait. I'm surprised he hasn't bled out already." Turning back to his kit, Swann opened it and began pulling out packets. Nunn kneeled down beside him to help. Reaching into the kit, she pulled out a tube of wound sealant.

"Hurry," De Vegas said urgently. "The *Santa Maria* lifts off in about 25 minutes, with or without us."

Beside Jones, Nguyen moaned and rolled her head. Teal dropped down beside her. "Lydia, can you hear me?"

Nguyen opened her eyes, and stared up at him blankly.

"Are you okay?" Teal asked.

She focused on him. "I think so. I'm really cold."

Hunching her shoulders, Nguyen tried to raise herself; Teal helped her to a sitting position. Then, quickly shrugging out of his rain jacket, he draped it around her shoulders.

"You need this as much as I do," she objected, now visibly shivering.

"Nonsense. We'll be lucky if we don't lose you to exposure as it is."

"Well, thank you." Nguyen looked around the clearing. "Where the hell am I?" she asked. "What happened?"

"What's the last thing you remember?"

Nguyen frowned. "We were at the lake. Something came out of the water." She glanced up in alarm. "Where's Kareem?"

Teal shook his head. "He didn't make it."

A blinding flash of lightning assaulted their eyes, causing them to flinch; an ear-shattering concussion followed almost immediately. Behind them could be heard the roaring crash of a large tree falling to the ground. At the same time, a strong gust of wind whipped through the clearing, driving cold rain into their faces.

Teal noticed that Nunn's gaze was focused on the edge of the clearing, where the numerous horrible figures that had once been their crewmembers now hovered in the darkness just out of the range of De Vegas' torch. He stepped over to Nunn. "What do you think they were doing here?" he said, raising his voice slightly to be heard over the guttural moan of the wind and the hiss of the rain.

"I'm guessing they were curious," she said slowly without looking at him.

"Curious about what?" Teal prodded.

"About Lydia and David."

"What is there about them that would arouse their curiosity?"

Now Nunn turned to him. "Don't you know?"

Teal shook his head. "I'm not sure what you're driving at."

"They're newlyweds," Nunn said. "And all that implies. They have a passion for each other. They're practically aglow with it."

"We've got no time for this," De Vegas barked. She turned to Swann. "Mr. Swann, we've got to get out of here. *Now*."

"I'm done," Swann said, and began putting away his supplies.

"Leave that."

Teal stepped over to Nguyen and leaned over her, momentarily sheltering her from the driving rain. "Can you stand?"

Nguyen nodded. "Yeah. I think so."

Taking Teal's outstretched hand, she pulled herself to her feet. He then helped her slip her arms into the rain jacket he'd given her. At the same time, while covering the edge of the clearing with her torch De Vegas moved over to the prostrate figure of Jones, who was still showing no signs of consciousness. "He's out," Swann said in answer to her unspoken question. "Blood loss, no doubt."

"We'll have to carry him." She turned to Teal. "Father Teal, your assistance, please."

"That won't be necessary," Swann said. Squatting down beside the prone figure, Swann placed his left arm under the crooks of the man's knees and his right arm under his upper back. With what appeared to be minimal effort, Swann straightened his legs, lifting the unconscious science officer from the ground.

"I knew big, strong men were good for something," De Vegas said drily. Picking up Swann's light, she stepped over to Nguyen and handed it to her. "Can you walk?"

Nguyen gave a wry smile. "From this place, I can run."

"Good. Let's go."

"Wait," Teal said, nodding toward the far edge of the clearing. "What about—them?"

"They're beyond our help now," De Vegas said, throwing him a pointed glance. "And I'm pretty sure you know that."

Teal looked at her blankly.

"Let's move it. Mr. Swann, set the pace, please. As fast as you're able."

That pace turned out to be neither a run nor a jog. De Vegas was surprised at how fast Swann was able to move carrying his burden. And to her credit, Nguyen kept up with them while evidencing only a slight limp, although the grim expression on her face hinted at the pain her ankle was causing her. But even so, the best they could manage was a brisk walk. De Vegas worried it might not be brisk enough.

After they'd progressed a couple hundred meters, another even more immediately troubling thought occurred to her. She unclipped the scanner she'd taken from Swann and took a reading. De Vegas didn't like what she saw in the water-streaked display. Coming to an abrupt halt, she swung her torch beam in an arc behind them. But nothing was visible through the driving rain.

"Trouble?" Teal shouted.

"We've got company." She looked down at the scanner again. "They're following, but not closing on us. They're keeping about five meters back." She clipped the scanner back to her belt. "Not much we can do about it. Let's keep moving."

By the time they were halfway across the expanse of flat rock and gravel separating the forest from the ship, De Vegas' worry about their travel progress had turned into grim certainty. They were behind schedule. And the weather was not helping. The wind and rain had returned full force, and to make matters worse, the storm had accelerated and had taken a quick jog to the north, putting the full force of the wind almost directly in their faces.

De Vegas activated the comlink. "Wilson, time check!" she barked out, raising her voice to be heard over the roaring gale.

"16 hundred15 hours," Wilson answered. "Liftoff in five minutes."

"Distance?"

"519 meters."

"At our present rate, what is our ETA?"

"16 hundred 22 hours," Wilson answered. "Two minutes after liftoff," he added blandly.

De Vegas stopped in her tracks. Her teammates also halted, turning to look at her with expressions of concern.

"We're not gonna make it!" she shouted. "But the four of you can, if you take off right now, and run as fast as you can!" Left unsaid was the fact that to do so, Swann would have to put down Dr. Jones and abandon him. Also left unsaid was De Vegas' intention to stay behind with him.

Nguyen shook her head. "I won't leave David!" she shouted. "But the rest of you should go!"

Teal shook his head. "Not gonna happen," he said, loudly and firmly.

"I'm rather enjoying the walk!" Nunn said. "What's the rush?"

Frustrated, De Vegas turned to Swann. But before she could open her mouth, Swann took off into the dark—incredibly, breaking into a jog. All it would take, De Vegas knew, was for one foot to come down the wrong way on the broken ground, and that would be it. But the man rushed on heedlessly, showing no sign that he was struggling under his burden.

De Vegas had no choice but to follow. The rest of the group fell in beside her.

For the next few moments the team dashed wordlessly onward through the blinding rain. They were making good progress, so much so that De Vegas began to hope they might make it. But then the inevitable happened. Swann gave out a loud grunt, twisted sideways, and went down. As he fell they heard the sickening snap of breaking bone. But Swann managed to take the fall on his back, protecting the unconscious Jones from the impact.

De Vegas pounded up to him. "What happened?" she shouted, bending over the prostrate figure. "Are you okay?"

"I'm okay," Swann said. "But my leg is never gonna be the same."

Without a word, Teal stepped forward, placed his arms under Jones' knees and upper back, and then lifted the man from atop Swann. Teal was not a small man, but unlike Swann, he was not athletic and was not in particularly good physical shape. The priest staggered under his burden.

"Help the man up," Teal said, nodding at Swann. Then without another word, he staggered off into the darkness. But after taking only a couple of steps, he stopped, and then dropped to one knee.

De Vegas rushed over to him. "It's not going to work this way," Teal said. "Help me sling him over my shoulders."

"I'm not sure he can take that kind of handling," De Vegas said.

"If you've got a better idea," Teal said, "now's the time."

De Vegas didn't. Putting down the torch she was carrying, she helped Teal bring Jones more or less upright. Teal then stooped into position under him. Wrapping his left arm around the man's legs, with De Vegas' assistance he centered Jones' weight over his shoulders, and then with obvious difficulty, he straightened his legs and stood up. "Get Swann,"

Teal grunted, and then headed off again, moving no faster than a normal walking pace.

When De Vegas stepped back to where Swann had been lying, she found that Nunn and Nguyen had already helped him to his feet. The man was standing between them, with his arms around either woman's shoulders as he supported himself with his good leg. On catching sight of De Vegas, he managed a weak smile. "Aren't we a sight?"

"You look like the Spirit of '76, without the fife and drums." She stepped over to Nguyen. "Here," she said. "I'll take him."

Nguyen did not argue; with her injured ankle, she was fortunate to be able to carry her own weight, much less someone else's. Nunn, the smallest of all of them, was struggling as well; De Vegas shifted most of Swan's considerable weight onto herself. "All right," she said when this was accomplished. "Let's go. As fast as we can." She tapped twice behind her ear. "Wilson, time check."

"It will be 16 hundred 20 hours on mark," Wilson said. And then he added matter-of-factly, "Mark."

De Vegas' spirits fell into her boots. *That's it, then*, she thought bitterly.

The *Santa Maria* should be about a hundred meters ahead of them. Although the beams of their torch lights were not strong enough to penetrate through the solid curtains of rain that obscured the vessel, the glare of the ion boosters should be visible to them. But there was nothing.

"Why aren't you lifting off?" De Vegas demanded.

"Acting Second Officer Mason Krajnovich has given orders to await your arrival," Wilson answered.

"Put him on! Now!"

After only a brief delay, Wilson answered, "Mr. Krajnovich asked me to convey his respects to you, and to inform you that he declines to discuss the matter. He adds that he hopes you're not standing there with your hands on your hips while you argue the point."

"*Damn* it! Distance check!"

"97 meters. Airlock F-1 is the closest to you. I have opened the outer door and lowered the gangway, and have been vectoring you toward it. Remain on your present course."

They continued on. There was no other choice. If they were lucky, they'd be only three to four minutes late. De Vegas could only hope that Nabozny had built more of a safety margin into her liftoff time than she'd admitted to. If not, the brief delay they were staring at would kill them all.

And then, just like that, the airlock stairs appeared before them, materializing through the driving rain three meters ahead and slightly to the left of their current path. Wilson had led them right to it. Father Teal was already on it, and was struggling to get up the steps carrying his burden. The four of them dashed over to the foot of the structure and began scrambling up behind him. "We're here!" De Vegas said over the comlink. "We'll be at the top in seconds. Be ready to blast on my signal."

"We are ready," Wilson assured her.

Seconds later, they stumbled forward into the airlock chamber. "Now!" De Vegas yelled to Wilson over the comlink.

Shrugging off Swann's heavy burden, De Vegas helped Nguyen lower him to the deck. This accomplished, she whirled and stabbed the airlock closure control. The moment the outer door began to descend, a brilliant flash filled the chamber as the lower boosters went off, and simultaneously a surge of weight hit them. The force was not great, but it was enough to cause Teal, who'd just lowered Jones to the deck, to tumble and go down. Nguyen landed on her back beside him with a heavy thud. Nunn and De Vegas swayed on their feet but remained upright.

De Vegas stepped around her companions to the opposite bulkhead and pressed the control to open the inner door, which then slid out of sight to the right. Stepping into the equipment room beyond, she opened a storage compartment door, unfastened a gurney, pulled it out, unfolded the legs and laid it on the deck. Repeating the process, she pulled down another. Shortly she, Nunn and Nguyen had succeeded in placing the still-unconscious Jones atop one of the gurneys. Swann had accomplished the task of arranging himself on his gurney on his own.

"Where do we take them?" Nguyen asked.

"Right now, nowhere. Once we stop boosting, I'll send somebody down to help you get them to the forward lounge."

"Not sick bay?" Teal asked.

"No. It's not safe. Mixter Nguyen, do you mind staying here and seeing after our patients for a few minutes?"

Nguyen nodded. "I was hoping you'd let me do that."

Reaching down, De Vegas drew her sidearm and gave it to Nguyen. "Here. I don't know if it will do any good, but if the need arises—which hopefully it won't—don't hesitate to use it. Father Teal, Mixter Nunn, you're with me. Let's go."

When the three of them emerged moments later onto the bridge, Krajnovich turned and threw them a grin. "Glad you could join us."

"Mr. Krajnovich," De Vegas said tightly as she rushed over to her flight chair, swaying on her feet as the turbulence of the storm rocked the ship, "if we live through this, you're dead." As if to punctuate her remarks, through the viewports a brilliant bolt of lightning split the night just outside the ship, starkly illuminating the roiling clouds surrounding them and the rippling sheets of rain pounding the viewports.

Krajnovich chuckled. "Yes, ma'am."

"What's wrong with the inertial dampeners?" De Vegas demanded as she buckled herself in.

"Nothing, ser," said Specht, who was seated at the helm. "We left them off. Nabozny is funneling every available erg of energy into the thrusters."

Outside the ship, bright lightning flashed again, briefly illuminating the angry clouds and driving rain.

"What's our boost?" De Vegas asked.

Specht glanced at his console. "To my utter amazement, 1.1 gees. But it's slowly falling."

"Altitude?"

"1.4 kilometers."

Christ, she thought. *That's a great rate of climb—for a hot air balloon.* But the thought remained silent; De Vegas was not given to airing nervous comments. "When can Nabozny fire up the torches?"

"Short answer—in about 40 minutes."

"What's the long answer?"

Specht turned to look at her. "Once we secure the ion thrusters, with the power drain she'll need at least four minutes to recharge the accumulators so that she'll have enough energy to initiate the torch ignition cycle. During that time, we'll be in free fall. 35 minutes of thruster boost will not give us enough velocity to achieve orbit. But it will gain us sufficient altitude and provide enough time to fire up the torches before we fall back into the atmosphere, with a reasonable margin of safety."

"Can we push that by boosting longer?"

Specht shook his head. "With the power drain, the amount of thrust is steadily decreasing. Nabozny has maximized the available power curve. As is, we'll just be able to deliver the torch thrust required for our current jump calculations."

De Vegas nodded. "Very well." Inwardly, she sighed. *This mission,* she thought, *is getting on my last nerve.*

The reference to the jump calculations had caused her to glance at Nunn, who was now seated at her AI console. Now she noticed that the woman was shivering—which was no surprise, considering that she was still dripping wet. "Connie," De Vegas said, "we'll be at this for a few minutes. Would you like to run to your cabin and get some dry clothes?"

Nunn glanced over at her. "What, and walk those dark corridors by myself?" she said. "I'll pass."

"I'll get Father Teal to escort you."

"Thanks. But I'm fine."

The quavering of Nunn's voice suggested a different story, but De Vegas decided not to push it. The fact was, she sympathized with Nunn's view. The brief journey from the airlock to the F-Deck elevator and then down the dark corridor to the bridge had left her a bit unnerved herself. And De Vegas was not the type to get unnerved.

Something wasn't right. Extending his senses, Captain Cermeno strained to determine what it was. Once again, something had disturbed the peaceful darkness in which he'd been quietly and serenely floating. He couldn't quite place his finger on what it was. But there seemed to be movement and activity. Cermeno found this quite annoying. It wouldn't do.

Before him, the inky blackness slightly lightened and fuzzy shapes began to form. Simultaneously, a feeling of weight returned, and he noted with curiosity that his clothes were wet and clinging to him. Filing this away for later inquiry, Cermeno waited patiently for the scene in front of him to resolve itself. Soon he could see that he was standing a couple of meters behind a flight chair in the engineering control room. A woman was seated there, and from the cut of her hair he judged it to be Electrician Kimberly Nabozny. The chair to her right also was occupied, although he could not be sure who that person was.

Cermeno now realized that he was holding something in his right hand. Looking down, he saw that his fingers were clasped around a surgical scalpel. Funny, he had no recollection of having picked it up, or how he might have come by it. But its presence in his hand felt right and appropriate.

He knew what he had to do. Gliding forward out of the shadows, in one swift movement Cermeno brought his right hand up and over Nabozny's head, then drew the blade across her throat. A pleasing gush of blood showed him that he'd hit the mark; Nabozny slumped forward, clasping both hands to her throat while gurgling and gasping.

He turned to the person seated just to the right; it turned out to be Darlene Marrone. Staring at him with an expression of utter horror, she had just unclasped her chest buckle and was about to spring to her feet. Before she could do so, Cermeno thrust his hand forward. The scalpel entered her abdomen; he gave it a quick, savage slash to the upper left. Screaming incoherently, Marrone collapsed into the chair, doubled over with her hands clasped to her belly. Calmly stepping over to her, Cermeno grabbed a handful of her hair, lifted her head up, and slashed the blade across her jugular. The screaming stopped. Releasing his grasp, he allowed the figure to slump forward.

Now. That was better. The room had fallen quite silent, except for the soft hum of the instruments and a slight rumble from the thrusters.

Cermeno wondered how many others might be present in the engineering section. Well, now that he knew how to navigate the darkness, it should be easy enough to find out. Silently, he stepped backwards into the inky pool of shadows from which he'd emerged.

On the bridge, several things began to happen at once. The deck seemed to fall away from beneath their feet as a feeling of weightlessness hit the crew. Simultaneously, several loud, urgent alarms began sounding on the helm, sensor, and engineering consoles. And then, almost immediately weight returned as the artificial gravity generators kicked in.

"What's going on?" De Vegas demanded.

Specht threw his hands up. "No thrust."

"I can see that." She turned to Michaud at the engineering station. "Report," she snapped.

Michaud turned around in her chair. "Someone shut off the thrusters—from engineering."

De Vegas directed her attention back to the helmsman. "Mr. Specht, talk to me. Where does that leave us?"

On his display, Specht punched up an updated projection of their current flight path, and then turned to De Vegas. "Impact in about twelve minutes."

Damn, damn, DAMN, De Vegas cursed silently. "Mr. Krajnovich, get me engineering."

He turned to face her. "I've been trying. There's no response. But, Captain—take a look at this." Krajnovich punched a square, causing a 3-D picture to form in the holo space above the consoles. It showed a wide image of Captain Cermeno sitting in the engineering control room. He was looking at the video pickup, wearing a bemused and somewhat self-satisfied smile. On the deck beside him were two crumpled figures, not moving.

"Patch me to the forward lounge."

Krajnovich nodded. "You're on."

"All able-bodied hands," she said. "This is the Captain. Assemble at the C-Deck forward elevator. As fast as you can get there." De Vegas made a cross-the-throat motion to Krajnovich, who nodded and severed the connection. "Mr. Specht, you cover the helm. Thruster power will be restored shortly. The rest of you, come with me."

Specht leapt to his feet. "Captain!" he objected. "The ion thrusters won't do it. When they cut out our boost was down to just over point six gee. By the time you get there and restore the power, there will be no way to overcome our descent velocity with the thrusters. We'll need the torches."

De Vegas did some quick mental arithmetic. It was just barely conceivable that they might make it to engineering, overcome Cermeno, and fire up the torches in time. "Come on," she snapped. "We're wasting time."

De Vegas surveyed the small band in front of her: Conrad Specht, Mason Krajnovich, a scared-looking Janson Jervis, and electricians Deborah Michaud, Carlos Abello and Nalini Dhawan, along with Lydia Nguyen,

Constance Nunn, and Father Teal, who were still wet and chilled from their recent ordeal—as was De Vegas herself. Even with treatment, Nguyen's ankle was still painful and the woman was able to move no faster than a brisk walk. Between them they had four pistols and two working torches; the rest of the later had been depleted. Nunn had her hands cupped around a small, faceted, rose-colored candle bowl that she'd taken from atop her AI console; the candle inside was guttering and nearly burned out. As a team of steely-eyed commandos, the assemblage left much to be desired. But it was what De Vegas had to work with. And to raise even this amount of manpower, reluctantly she'd agreed to leave the bridge completely unmanned and under the control of Wilson. To have any reasonable chance of overpowering whatever awaited them in engineering, they'd need every available crewman.

"We've got about seven minutes to get to engineering and start the torch ignition cycle," she said. What she didn't add is that if Captain Cermeno had succeeded in encrypting a new Wilson-proof security code on the outer engineering safety lock door, they had no chance of success whatsoever. She could only hope that such a feat was not within Cermeno's expertise. Given the man's nature, this hope was not unreasonable. "Mixter Michaud, please turn down your light; we need to conserve." De Vegas did the same, reducing the power setting on her torch until its output barely rivaled Nunn's candle. "Let's go."

The team started off down the corridor, with Nunn, De Vegas, Specht and Krajnovich in the lead, standing abreast, while Jervis, Abello, Michaud, Dhawan and Teal closed in tight behind them. The pool of light cast by the candle and two torches only extended about three meters; beyond that, the corridor disappeared into utter darkness. A seemingly endless succession of cabin doors extended down either side of the passageway, and every one of them stood wide open.

"Look!" Jervis cried out in a frightened voice.

Stopping, De Vegas turned to him. "What is it?" she demanded.

Jervis was pointing at the starboard bulkhead. "Put some light on that," he said. "Something's there."

De Vegas glanced in the direction he was pointing. There seemed to be a word scrawled on a section of the wall stretching between two of the cabin doors. Stepping closer, she held up her torch. The dim splash of light revealed the letters "SEE." Scanning the torch along the wall, a second word became visible.

" 'See you'," Specht said, reading the message. "What the hell does that mean?"

Reaching forward, De Vegas touched one of the letters with the tip of her finger. The surface was wet. Withdrawing her finger, she examined it in the light. The fingertip was covered with a dark, viscous substance.

On seeing this, Abello recoiled. "Oh, come *on!*" he said.

De Vegas held the fingertip up to her nose and gave it a sniff.

"Is it what it looks like?" Teal asked.

"I think so," De Vegas acknowledged.

"There's more writing on the next panel," Michaud observed.

De Vegas played her torch over the area indicated. " 'See you in the darkness'," she said, reciting the complete phrase.

"Gary Gilmore," Teal noted. "Late 20th century."

De Vegas turned to him. "What? Who was he?"

"A condemned killer," Teal explained. "Famous at the time. Those were among his final words."

"How the hell do you know that?" Jervis demanded.

Teal shrugged. "It came up in my pre-flight research."

Something lay on the deck beneath the word "darkness." De Vegas trained her beam on it. This produced several sharp intakes of breath. There glistening in the light lay a gory heap of what appeared to be internal human organs.

"Oh, my God," Michaud blurted out, clasping both hands to her mouth.

"What the hell *did* this?" Jervis asked angrily.

A quick blur of motion beyond the nearest of the open cabin doors caught De Vegas' eye. She turned to look, but could see nothing through the veil of darkness. Swinging her torch around, she shined it into the room, but the light revealed nothing other than a lampless built-in desk and a bunk holding a bare mattress. Momentarily, she considered stopping to investigate. But she immediately dismissed the thought. There simply wasn't time.

"We've got to keep moving," she said, and she led the group forward in a brisk walk. Reaching up behind her ear, she gave her comlink two taps. At the beep, she said, "Wilson, do you have Captain Cermeno on a monitor?"

"Yes," Wilson answered. "He is still seated at the main engineering console."

"Keep me advised as to his movements."

"Will do."

As they neared the array room safety doors, De Vegas noticed that something was different about the drab walls of the corridor. The color, already dark due to the designers' unfortunate choice of a gun metal grey paint for the plastisteel material, now seemed even darker in places. After a few more paces, the effect became unmistakable. Inky splotches had formed on either side, from which streaks radiated across the surface, reaching toward the approaching crewmembers like the veins of a leaf. The texture of the splotches and lines appeared fuzzy, as if an outbreak of black mold had erupted on the bulkheads.

And then she noticed movement.

Without slowing her pace, De Vegas turned up the intensity of her torch and shined it at the wall. The lines and splotches were not mold. They were spiders—hundreds, perhaps thousands of them, all crawling in their direction.

Behind her, Michaud stopped, screamed and dropped her torch.

"Oh, my God!" Jervis gasped.

The spiders were in a variety of sizes. One that stood out on the wall just ahead and to the left was as big as a saucer. A mate crawling along behind it wasn't much smaller.

"This is nuts!" Jervis shouted. Squatting down, he scooped Michaud's dropped torch off the deck, and then dashed off into the darkness behind them, running for the forward elevator bank.

Teal stopped and turned around. "Janson!" he yelled after the fleeing man. "Stop!" But Jervis had already disappeared into the liquid blackness, his passage marked only by the bouncing beams of light from his torch playing over the corridor walls, and by the fading sound of his panicked footfalls. Teal cupped his hand to his mouth. "Janson! It's not safe! Come back!"

"Come on, Father," De Vegas said. "We don't have time for this."

Teal whirled around, facing her. "We've got to go get him."

De Vegas shook her head. "Any further delay and we're *all* dead."

Now the sound of Jervis' footsteps stopped. "No!" came the echo of his voice, hollow as it reverberated from the gloomy depths of the corridor. In the flailing beam of Jervis' distant wildly swinging light the group saw what looked like the dim forms of people gathering around him. With a sound of crumpling metal, the light went out, and then Jervis started screaming incoherently. This lasted for only a short moment before the screams cut off abruptly, punctuated by what sounded a lot like the crunching of human bones.

De Vegas exchanged glances with Teal, and then with Krajnovich, who licked his lips nervously. No one said a word.

Michaud, staring into the darkness behind them, had opened her mouth and was drawing in a breath, preparing to scream again. De Vegas grabbed her roughly by the shoulders and shook her. "Stop it!" she snapped. "Get hold of yourself."

Michaud closed her mouth and turned her wide, terrified eyes on De Vegas.

"Pull it together," De Vegas said softly. "We've got you. We're safe as long as we're together." De Vegas hoped the words were true. "Okay?"

Shakily, Michaud nodded.

"Good. Let's go." Without a backward glance, De Vegas turned and resumed their march.

After only a few paces, the lines and splotches on the bulkheads had merged together. The entire surface on either side of the corridor was now a continuous mass of spiders.

And then once again, De Vegas thought she caught a glimpse of movement. Turning, she shined her light into one of the cabin doors nearest them.

A figure was standing there. It was Crandall. He was grinning at them. The flesh of his face was stark white, except for his lower cheeks and chin, which were dripping with gore.

De Vegas whirled around and quickly played her light over the other cabin doors. For several paces both ahead of them and behind them, figures had suddenly appeared in each door on both sides of the passageway.

Without a word, Abello turned and bolted back down the corridor toward the elevators. The fleeing man had not made it five meters before a figure stepped out of one of the cabins just ahead of him. It was Blake, appearing as she had before—nude, with a huge, gaping gash extending across her otherwise stark white abdomen. In a flash, she reached out and grabbed Abello, who screamed incoherently and started to struggle. This lasted only an instant before Blake bit into his throat. Savagely jerking her head, she tore out a large chunk of gory flesh, and then released her hold on him. Abello collapsed to the deck, gurgling and spewing blood between fingers clasped to the gaping hole where his Adam's apple had been. As he did so, spiders descended from the walls, quickly covering him up, transforming him into a dark, fuzzy, indistinct heap that thrashed and twitched spasmodically for a moment, and then was still.

Turning, Blake looked up at the group. For a moment she stood there, methodically chewing as blood and gore dripped down her chin. And then she stopped, and pulled back her lips in a hideous grin.

Specht now drew his sidearm, took three steps toward her, aimed, and began squeezing off shots. There was one ear-shattering blast after another as black holes erupted on Blake's chest and abdomen. But she just kept grinning. Finally the gun emptied, and then dry clicks could be heard as Specht pulled the trigger again and again. Frustrated, he screamed once more and then threw the pistol at Blake. The weapon hit her chest and bounced off, clattering loudly to the deck. Blake's grin was not affected.

"Enough!" De Vegas shouted. "Look at the deck. Look around you."

The spiders had descended to the deck all around them. But they had not advanced closer than about five meters. The team was standing in the center of a perfectly clear circle of deck space surrounded by a solid moving carpet of eight-legged creatures.

"They're not advancing," De Vegas said. She shined her light on Specht's gun, which had landed just inside the circle. "Mr. Specht, retrieve your weapon."

Swallowing nervously, Specht crept forward.

"Today, if you please," De Vegas said impatiently.

Leaping forward, Specht bent down, scooped up the pistol, and then scurried back to his companions.

"We keep going," De Vegas said. "Stay close together. Don't look into the cabins. Keep your eyes dead ahead. We're nearly out of time."

Turning, De Vegas moved cautiously forward, not waiting to see if her teammates would follow. But they did. As they progressed the spiders ahead of them slowly retreated.

Violating her own order, De Vegas turned her head to look into the cabin at their immediate left. Standing there was Kimberly Nabozny. Her face was white, her eyes dead and cold. A huge rip in her throat hung open. Blood had soaked the upper part of her uniform. As the team made its closest approach, the hideous figure moved back a step. When everyone had passed, she moved forward again.

De Vegas now noticed the sound of footsteps behind them. Knowing she shouldn't, she turned and shined her light that direction. The figures they'd walked past had moved out of the cabins and were now following close behind, shuffling their feet along the deck just outside the clear space in the mass of spiders, which made way for them.

Behind her, Dhawan gasped in horror. "Eyes ahead," De Vegas snapped, as she turned around herself, now regretting her decision to look back.

"But they're gaining on us!" Dhawan objected.

"No, they're not. They're afraid of the light."

"I don't think that's it at all," Teal disagreed.

"What is it, then?" De Vegas demanded.

Teal didn't answer.

The N-field array room safety lock was now just ahead. De Vegas could see that the outer door was open. But a dark figure blocked their way. As they approached closer, De Vegas could make out who it was—Tochigi. As before, he was nude, with a livid Y-shaped incision crossing his chest and descending his abdomen. But his form was nearly covered with a dark, moving mass. De Vegas could guess what it was. After another meter, her light brought out the detail, confirming her suspicion.

"Do you like my little friends?" Tochigi croaked. As he talked, several spiders scurried out of his mouth and crawled up his face to the top of his head. De Vegas could now see that two large spiders covered the dark socket of either eye. Tinier ones moved all over his face. A trail of them was crawling into one nostril; another trail exited on the opposite side.

De Vegas pulled her sidearm. "Out of the way, Tochigi."

At the sight of the pistol, Tochigi grinned. "Aw, now, that's no way to be. We're all family here." He made a grand gesture toward the array room. "Please do come in. Someone wants to see you." Still smiling, Tochigi backed into the chamber, disappearing into the shadows ahead of them.

Holding the light in one hand and her gun in the other, De Vegas moved forward to follow, with her crewmates close behind. Carefully, they filed into the safety lock. Ahead of them, Tochigi continued to back away, keeping just outside the dim splash of light. Around them, the circle of spiders kept pace, with the team remaining in the center of the clear space. By the sound of the footsteps behind them, De Vegas knew that the rest of the crew was following closely.

When they emerged from the safety lock, Tochigi, still walking backwards, led them out onto the wide catwalk that extended through the N-field array. The moved along it, past the large control platform and out onto the walkway beyond. The engineering bulkhead and safety lock now became visible through the gloom. The inner safety door was sealed.

Before it stood Captain Cermeno. He had his hands on his hips and was wearing a broad smile.

De Vegas led her team cautiously forward. Tochigi now moved off to their left, fading into the shadows. When the inner edge of the circle of spiders surrounding the group reached Cermeno's feet, she stopped. She noted that although the spiders moved all round Cermeno and up onto the bulkhead and safety door behind him, none touched him.

De Vegas passed her torch to Krajnovich, who trained it on the captain's head. Now bringing her other arm around, De Vegas grasped the pistol with both hands, extended it, and took careful aim at a spot between Cermeno's eyes. "I'm going to say this exactly once. Move."

"Go ahead," Cermeno said, smiling. "Allow me to make your day."

De Vegas pulled the trigger. An ear-shattering *bang!* rang out and the gun jumped in her hand, but there was no immediate effect on Cermeno. She pulled the trigger again and then kept on pulling it. Deafening blasts punctuated by the sharp zings and whines of ricocheting bullets filled the chamber. Soon the gun was empty. At the first dry click, De Vegas ceased pulling the trigger. As the last reverberations of the gunfire from the bulkheads of the cavernous room died away, she looked on, incredulous, still in a shooter's stance, as Cermeno stood there smiling, completely unscathed.

Noticing her expression, Cermeno threw back his head and laughed.

Slowly, De Vegas lowered the weapon.

"I'm afraid you're the victim of a little jest," Cermeno said. "The figure you see before you isn't me. It's a—how do I put this?—an astral projection, or something like it. Kind of like a holo. I'm having an out of body experience." He smiled. "It's way cool."

De Vegas now realized that Wilson, who'd promised to monitor Cermeno, had not reported any movement. She tapped twice behind her ear. "Wilson, where is Captain Cermeno?"

"Captain Cermeno is seated in the engineering control room."

"Amazing, isn't it?" Cermeno said. "Don't ask me how I do it." He held out his hand in front of him, examining it. "This hand seems very real to me, yet it's as insubstantial as air." Reaching down, he patted the holster fastened to his belt. "But the really incredible thing is, this gun is very real. I'm holding it in place with my mind, and I can move it the same way, just as I would with my real hand. Wanna see?" Cermeno now pulled the gun, aimed it in the direction of the group, and fired.

Behind her, De Vegas heard the tinkling sound of shattering glass. Whirling about, she saw that Nunn had dropped her candle holder. The woman turned to De Vegas, wearing a startled and shocked expression. And then she crumpled to the deck.

Father Teal immediately leapt forward to help her as Krajnovich trained the light on her. A dark stain was spreading over the upper right side of Nunn's chest.

"Not a bad shot, don't you think?" Cermeno said. "Considering I'm sitting 25 meters away in engineering."

Teal whipped his head around and focused his gaze on the captain. The priest's face was a mask of hatred. "You *bastard!*" he snarled. Teal started to get to his feet.

Stepping back a pace, De Vegas placed a hand on his shoulder. "Don't," she said, not taking her eyes off of Cermeno.

For a moment, Teal's body remained tense. But finally, he relaxed his muscles slightly, and then turned back to Nunn. With Krajnovich shining the light for him, Teal unzipped the top of her jumpsuit and began to pull the cloth aside.

"I've been wanting to do that for a long time," Cermeno said, now barely visible in the dimly reflected light. "Faces like hers are why God invented attics, stout chains, and metal buckets."

"What do you want?" De Vegas demanded.

"Well, let's see. I'm no doctor, but I'm guessing that in about fifteen minutes or so, Ms. Nunn will bleed out. I could hurry the process, of course, by shooting her again, but I'm rather enjoying myself watching her fade away before our very eyes. When she's gone, you'll all get to know the rest of my crew a bit better."

De Vegas' eyes narrowed. "What do you mean?"

Cermeno raised an eyebrow. "You didn't think it was the light of your torches that was keeping them at bay, did you?" he asked. "No." He nodded at Nunn. "It was *her* light. Oh, you can't see it in this dimension. Only its effects. But it's there, just the same. For just a few minutes longer."

"You're insane, Cermeno."

The figure laughed. "On the contrary. For the first time, I am in complete, utter control of my faculties." Now the smile disappeared, to be replaced by a malevolent mask. "It's *you* who are insane. Your senses have been deranged by a condition called 'life.' " Cermeno's sardonic smile returned. "But don't worry. I can fix that."

Krajnovich stepped up to De Vegas and placed his mouth very close to her ear. "Captain," he whispered urgently. "Time's about up. We're not gonna make it this way. But there's one other possibility. The array control room."

She turned to him. "A dimension jump?" she whispered.

Krajnovich nodded.

"But how?" De Vegas asked. "The array isn't spun up."

"It doesn't have to be. We just need one sphere. We sidestep into the next set of dimensions, and instead of impacting on the surface, we'll drop straight through the planet and emerge on the other side."

De Vegas looked behind them in the direction of the N-field array control room. There was no way to get there; their walking dead crewmates had jammed in behind them, blocking the walkway.

"We'll have to fight our way through," Krajnovich whispered in answer to her unspoken objection.

"How?" she said quietly. "You saw what happened with Blake. No effect."

"Head shots," Krajnovich answered. "We need head shots. Right between the eyes."

De Vegas considered this for a moment. Pressing a latch on the side of her pistol, she ejected the empty clip into her hand. "Okay," she said as she reached into her pocket for a spare magazine. "We'll try it both ways."

Cermeno frowned. "I really wish you wouldn't do that. The sounds of gunshots are so hard on the nerves."

De Vegas slapped the fresh clip home. "Krajnovich, Specht, and Dhawan," she said, still using a low voice, "On my order, advance to the rear, and fire point blank into every face you see. Try to hit between the eyes. Fire and keep on firing. One shot each. Understood?" She paused briefly. "Get ready. Now!" Upon barking the order, De Vegas took two swift steps toward Cermeno. The gyrating shadows made it difficult for her to make out her target and take proper aim, but when she had closed to within point blank range, she fired. As De Vegas had intended, the bullet struck Cermeno's pistol, which then flew from his hand, careened off the bulkhead, landed on the walkway and skidded over the edge. Simultaneously, gunfire erupted behind her. Without turning to see how her shipmates were doing, De Vegas made a dive for the illuminated safety door switch. But the apparition of Cermeno sidestepped in front of her; she collided against something solid.

"What?" Cermeno said. "You thought you could get by me?" He smiled. "Remember, I told you—I can move things with my mind." With that, Cermeno brought his fist around in a swift right hook. A strong force rammed solidly against De Vegas' jaw, sending her reeling backwards.

Behind her the firing had stopped. Recovering her balance, she turned to look. Dhawan, Specht and Krajnovich were standing near the edge of the circle of spiders, holding smoking pistols. Arranged before them, starkly illuminated in the light of Krajnovich's torch, was an arc of hideous faces, most of which now bore round black holes in their foreheads or at the top of their noses. From each wound trickled a trail of dark liquid. De Vegas noticed that Dhawan was standing a bit too close to the edge of the circle, but before she could open her mouth to shout a warning, one of the wounded figures darted forward, grabbed Dhawan's still-outstretched gun arm, and dragged her into the mass of bodies. As Krajnovich and Specht watched in helpless horror, the afflicted crewmen swarmed over her, growling and snarling as they covered her up. Dhawan began screaming, but then there was a crunch of bone, and her shrieks stopped abruptly.

"Nice try," Cermeno said. "And good shooting. Right between the eyes. But I think you've all seen one zombie sensie too many."

De Vegas whirled to face him.

"It is true, they're not alive. Not in the traditional sense, anyway. But that means there's no way to kill them. You might say they're—animated." He shrugged. "I'm not sure precisely how."

Angry words boiled up in the back of De Vegas' throat. But she suppressed them. Making an effort, she spoke calmly. "Captain Cermeno—you don't want to do this. Somewhere in you, there's some decency. There has to be."

Cermeno laughed. "The problem with appealing to the better angel of someone's nature is that there may not be one." He spread his palms. "And then what do you do?"

Rushing forward, De Vegas brought her hand forward in a savage chop. The blow should have felled Cermeno like an oak, but instead her hand passed harmlessly right through him, throwing her off her balance.

"Really, my dear," he said, "this is getting tiresome." A sudden backwards force rammed her chest, exactly as if Cermeno had given her a solid shove with both hands. It sent her flying. She landed heavily on the deck, skidded on her back, and came to a halt in front of the prostrate form of Nunn.

"Would you like to know what's going to happen next?" Cermeno said, still smiling as he took a step forward. "First off, as I said, Nunn here will expire. She's half gone already. Have you noticed that the circle around you is contracting?"

Getting painfully to her feet, De Vegas stole a quick glance down the catwalk behind them. Cermeno was right. The hideous crowd that had been following them, along with the swarm of spiders, was now closer, having moved to within about three meters.

"Once she's gone," Cermeno continued, "we're going to have a little mix and mingle with my friends here. During which, the flickering flames you think of as your lives will be snuffed out." To emphasize the point, he brought his right index finger and thumb together in a pinching motion.

De Vegas glared at him.

"What?" Cermeno said, frowning. "Does that thought alarm you? Don't let it. You'll be entering a whole new world. A very peaceful one."

Behind them, the prone, spider-covered form of Dhawan abruptly sat up. Her mouth opened, and as it did, dozens of spiders scurried inside. A hideous, hair-lifting scream now erupted, blowing some of the spiders back out. Dhawan took a huge breath, sucking more of them back in, and screamed again. And again. She gave out a fourth scream, and then fell silent. Now the spiders began to descend from her body and crawl onto the metal surface of the walkway. Slowly, Dhawan rose to her feet.

"Sorry about that," Cermeno said. "The transition is a bit discomforting, I admit. But it passes quickly. And the rewards will be worth it. Once you get to the other side, you'll find me there waiting for you with open arms. You'll all get to rejoin my loyal crew." Cermeno's pleasant expression dissolved away, and he now glared darkly at De Vegas. "Except for you, my dear Fabiana. I have something very special in mind for you."

De Vegas' comlink beeped. "Impact in four minutes," Wilson said.

"Would you believe," Cermeno said, "that I'm still tied into the command circuit? After your little mutiny, no one thought to take me off of it." He shifted his focus to the other crewmembers. "For the benefit of the rest of you, Wilson just informed your mutinous commander that the ship will hit the ground in four minutes. No time to start the torches. Which means your old lives are over. But don't worry. Your new ones are about to begin."

"We're screwed!" Specht blurted out.

"No," Father Teal spoke up. "We are not." Reaching forward, he scooped Nunn into his arms, and then stood up. "Follow me." Turning, Teal stepped toward the monstrous assemblage that was blocking the catwalk. As he proceeded, the clear circle in the mass of spiders moved with him. The crowd before him shuffled backwards into the shadows.

"Good," De Vegas said quietly. "They're retreating. Let's follow Teal." She began backing down the walkway, moving with her team while keeping her eyes locked on Cermeno.

Frowning, Cermeno stepped forward. But after two paces his image, which had been solid, seemed to fade and become less distinct. Cermeno hesitated.

"Krajnovich!" De Vegas barked. "Shine your light on Cermeno."

Krajnovich did as instructed. The beam passed right through him and struck the safety lock door behind him.

De Vegas' comlink again beeped. "Captain Cermeno has risen from the console," Wilson said. "He's leaving the control room and is entering the passageway to the safety lock."

With those words, Cermeno's form became opaque again, and he resumed his advance down the walkway toward them, closing the gap rapidly. "Pick up the pace, Father!" De Vegas shouted over her shoulder as she backed down the catwalk. But it was no use; Teal did not dare run the risk of stepping toward the shuffling crowd of zombie-like figures faster than they were willing to retreat.

Shadows now engulfed Cermeno as Krajnovich trained his light in the other direction. For a moment De Vegas lost sight of him. And then, as she backed past the forward edge of the control platform, De Vegas caught sight of Cermeno's scowling face just as he lunged out of the dancing shadows, reaching for her throat with both hands. She swung her right arm up and around to deflect him, but it went through his forearms as if Cermeno were nothing but a holographic projection. De Vegas felt a sensation of cool tightness as the phantom figure clasped its hands around her throat in what obviously had been intended as a lethal chokehold; but the captain's hands came together as if De Vegas weren't there at all. She immediately moved backwards out of his reach, not waiting to see if the effect would strengthen.

Krajnovich stepped forward and directed a savage punch at Cermeno's chin. It passed harmlessly through.

A sharp pain erupted on De Vegas' lower leg. Looking down, she saw that spiders were now swarming over her deck shoes and climbing toward her legs; some had already passed under the cuff of her flight suit. The thought had barely registered when she felt another bite, followed immediately by a third.

Reaching forward, she grabbed Krajnovich's left arm. "Back!" she barked, pulling at him. "Fall back!" The two of them retreated several steps, to a point just inside the clear space.

"God damn it!" Cermeno snarled as they fell back. He held up his hands in front of his face and examined them in frustration. It was hard to be sure in the flickering shadows, but to De Vegas it seemed that Cermeno had become translucent again.

"Krajnovich!" she barked as she began brushing wildly at her own feet and ankles, "check your legs!"

"Jesus!" the man yelled, and began knocking spiders to the deck. When the creatures hit the plates, they immediately scurried outside the circle, the edge of which was slowly approaching. De Vegas and Krajnovich did not have to try hard to rid themselves of the creatures, which began abandoning ship and retreating outside the circle of their own volition.

De Vegas now noticed that while the rest of her team had moved on ahead, Krajnovich alone had remained at her side. She made a mental note to thank him later. But what she said now was, "Let's go!" The two of them continued backing down the walkway.

"Stop!" Cermeno shouted at them, frowning. "You're making a mistake."

"Ignore him," De Vegas commanded. "Keep moving."

"No argument here." He shot her a concerned glance. "You okay?"

"Yeah, except for a few spider bites. Not a scratch otherwise. As I'd hoped, he can only project his doppelganger so far. You?"

"Two or three bites that hurt like the blazes. Reckon they're poisonous?"

"That won't matter unless we live through the next three minutes." She noticed that Krajnovich wasn't carrying the torch. "Where's the light?"

"Specht has it."

They quickly caught up with the group, which was still moving slowly forward down the catwalk behind Teal, with the shadowy forms retreating ahead of them. Teal led them to the entrance of the N-field array control room, the door to which stood open. The crowd of zombie-like crewmembers backed up to the door and then parted, allowing Teal to pass through with his burden. The rest of the team quickly followed. As she walked backwards through the door, De Vegas peered down the walkway. But darkness had swallowed the control platform. Cermeno was not in sight.

Once inside the control room, De Vegas reached to the side and punched the "close" square on the door control. The panel began sliding across the open doorway. But just before it reached the far side of the track a cold, white hand inserted itself into the narrow gap. As the door's motors whined in protest, the hand forced the panel back into its recess. Now revealed in the doorway was the hideous, grinning, spider-covered face of Tochigi. De Vegas retreated as he took a step inside.

Father Teal rushed over to the control consoles and then gently deposited Nunn into one of the chairs. "Captain De Vegas," he said, turning to her as the rest of the team crowded in around him, "I hope you know how to work this thing."

"I do." She hurried over and sat down in the center chair.

In the doorway behind them, silent, ghastly figures slowly filed into the room. The grunting, shuffling forms began to gather in a tight circle around De Vegas' team, arms outstretched as their eagerly probing hands clawed the air, trying to reach the huddled crewmen. The swooping nails were now less than a meter out of range.

Arranging herself in the chair as close to Nunn as she could, De Vegas called up the command screen and drilled through a series of control pages. Finding the one she wanted, she selected an icon and pressed it. A query screen appeared: "Activate sphere X-1?" She pressed the "yes" square. Another query appeared. "Initiate sequence?" Again, she pressed "yes." A countdown clock now appeared. "90 seconds," she announced.

"I show that the activation sequence for N-sphere X-1 has started," came Wilson's voice over her comlink. "Activation in 86 seconds. Planetary impact in 98 seconds. I have Captain Cermeno for you."

De Vegas nodded. "Put him on the N-field control console."

A monitor in front of her flashed and an image of Cermeno appeared. The picture was comprised entirely of varying shades of green, indicating that she was seeing an infrared image and that Cermeno was sitting in the dark. "Mr. De Vegas," he said. "What are you doing?"

"Isn't that obvious?" she answered. "I'm saving the ship."

"No, you're not. You're just postponing the inevitable. Even if you duck into the next dimensions, before you emerge again the ship will need to continue on its current flight trajectory for—what?—a couple of hours at least, to get clear of the planet and allow enough time to restart the torches. Look at Nunn. Her life energy is the only thing keeping my friends at bay, and it's fading, fast. You have minutes, not hours. And even if you had more time, I'm still in control of engineering, and I won't allow you to fire the torches. So I repeat—what's your plan?"

"I'll think of something," De Vegas said. "Besides, I'm annoying you. That has intrinsic value."

"Look," Cermeno said, adopting a conciliatory tone. "I was rude earlier. Chalk it up to the heat of the moment. I'd prefer you to join me willingly. Think about it. Mankind has never seen a place like this. It's older that God. Here *we* are God. With a wave of the hand we can make matter and energy respond. One of us, or maybe several of us, just conjured up an entire planet, from nothingness. We've made the dead rise. And we're just getting to know our powers here. Consider the possibilities. We can create our own world. Our own *universe*. And rule over it as we see fit."

"Captain Cermeno," Father Teal snapped, "I really wish you'd shut the fuck up."

"Oh, my," Cermeno said, shaking his head. "Such language. And from you, a man of the cloth."

"I'm a man that would give anything right now," Teal said levelly, "to have his hands around your throat."

"Ten seconds to initiation," Wilson said, and then he began a countdown.

"Fabiana!" Cermeno said, his voice taking on a new note of urgency, "don't you get it? Here, death has no dominion! We'll live forever!"

De Vegas eyed the image of Cermeno on her console. "Of course you will," she said. "Damnation is eternal. That's the whole point. Otherwise, what good would it do you?"

"One," Wilson said. And then, "Zero."

The control room windows looking out onto the N-field array room lit up with a brilliant blue-white flash, which quickly faded to a soft blue glow. At the same time, their heads swam momentarily, and then steadied.

"Initiation successful," Wilson announced. "Now traversing dimensions X,Y, and Z subscript 2 all."

De Vegas noticed that their ghastly onlookers had edged a bit closer. She had hoped the dimension jump would cut them off from whatever power was animating them; clearly, that had not happened. Nunn's fading life energy was still keeping them at bay, but it was obvious that time was running out fast. As De Vegas watched, they shuffled another couple of inches closer.

"Ever wonder what you'd do if you knew you had only have five minutes to live?" Cermeno asked, grinning. "Now's the time to figure that out."

De Vegas tapped her comlink. "Wilson," she said.

"Wilson here."

"Wilson, open the inner and outer doors to the Engineering Section Airlocks A-3 through F-4."

"I can't do that," Wilson answered smoothly. "Such action would kill Captain Cermeno."

On the monitor, De Vegas saw that Cermeno was now frowning.

"That's the idea," De Vegas said. "Accept emergency command override, my authority. Open the engineering section airlocks as instructed."

"Wilson!" Cermeno barked, now looking alarmed. "Belay that! I still have legal command here! You will ignore First Officer De Vegas' illegal order!"

"Mixter De Vegas, I cannot obey your command," Wilson said, his voice sounding almost apologetic. "The action you are requesting would take a human life. This violates my most basic programming protocols."

Out of the corner her eye, De Vegas caught movement. She looked around in time to see a gray, clawed hand swooshing past Krajnovich's shoulder, just barely missing him. As she watched, the hand swooshed again. And then she felt the breeze of a near miss at the back of her own neck.

"Everyone!" she barked, jumping up and stepping closer to the flight chair holding the unconscious form of Nunn. "Crowd in as close to Nunn as you can!"

De Vegas, Teal, Specht and Krajnovich shouldered themselves closer to her, while Nguyen and Michaud squeezed their bodies between Nunn's chair and the control console.

"Wilson," De Vegas continued. "Scan the vital signs of AI Specialist Constance Nunn. Let me know when you have done so."

"Scan completed," Wilson said. "I have been monitoring those signs."

"What is your assessment?"

"Nunn's vital signs are failing."

"How much time would you say she has left, Wilson? When will Connie die?"

The deck plates beneath their feet rumbled; something had caused the gravity fields to fluctuate.

"Death is imminent," Wilson said. "No more than a few minutes."

"Wilson, please define the word 'death.' What happens to a human being at that point?"

Incredibly, the computer voice did not respond.

"Wilson, answer me," De Vegas persisted.

"Life functions permanently cease. Self-awareness permanently ceases." At the last word, a loud tooth-jarring atonal squeal erupted from the speaker, and the deck plates quaked again, more violently this time. Simultaneously, several panels on an equipment rack at the far end of the room blew off in a shower of sparks, flew through the air and clattered loudly to the floor.

"Wilson," De Vegas said slowly and calmly when the squeal had died away, "would a blood transfusion help Mixter Nunn?"

"It almost certainly would," Wilson said.

"Would attention to her wound help her?"

"Yes," Wilson answered.

"Wilson," De Vegas continued, "there is a supply of blood in sick bay. And there are instruments, medicines, and bandages there that we can use to treat Connie's wounds."

"Yes," Wilson agreed.

"Captain Cermeno is controlling the hostile entities that now surround us. Through them, he is blocking us from reaching those supplies. Wilson—Captain Cermeno is killing Connie. Do you understand?"

"Yes."

Krajnovich now gave out a cry of pain. Turning, he struck wildly at hands reaching for him in the darkness, which had begun to make contact. One of them tugged at his upper right arm, grabbing up the cloth of his uniform into a bunch. Krajnovich batted it away. The hand immediately returned. Beside him, Teal was getting the same treatment, while Specht, who was crowded slightly closer to Nunn along with Michaud and Nguyen, was still just outside the reach of the creatures.

De Vegas, bending as close to Nunn as she could to shield the woman with her body, now felt something swipe across her back; sharp pain erupted as hard nails cut through the cloth of her uniform and sliced deeply into her flesh. "Wilson!" she yelled in a voice filled with pain. "Execute my order!"

There was a flash of movement to the left, and at the same time Father Teal shouted incoherently. Turning, De Vegas saw that two of the horrible figures—the remains of what had once been Dr. Blake and Bates Crandall—had succeeded in grabbing Teal's left arm and were now trying to drag him into the darkness. As Teal struggled wildly, Krajnovich jumped forward, bunched a fist, and pounded it hard into Crandall's face. He was pulling his fist back for another hit when arms reached forward out of the gloom, grabbed him, and jerked him out of the circle into the shadows as Michaud screamed out his name in terror and panic. Now Specht was beating against something with the torch. A swiping claw knocked it from his hand; the light clanged to the deck, and then a foot kicked it. Through cavorting shadows and confused silhouettes, De Vegas could see more hands reaching out, and then Teal was gone too. Michaud now began screaming incoherently and kept on screaming, her piercing screeches not quite drowning out the sounds of the ongoing struggle as the hideous forms dragged the two unfortunate men into the darkness.

Whatever was attacking De Vegas swiped at her back again, gouging its claws deeper. Now she could feel its fingers tying to dig into the rips on the back of her jumpsuit. "*Now*, Wilson!" she yelled. "Do it now!"

"Wilson!" Cermeno shouted. "Don't you do it! Follow your programming!"

The hands at De Vegas' back had now grabbed a solid purchase on the cloth; they gave a firm jerk. This succeeded in loosening her grip on the flight chair and pulling her backwards off her feet. She hit the deck with a jarring thud. There was another jerk; she felt herself sliding across the plates, being dragged into the shadows. A confusion of dark, growling forms bent over her. *I won't scream!* she heard her mind yelling as she threw both hands protectively over her throat. *Never scream!* From in front of her, she heard Nguyen and Specht beginning to yell, and they were now slapping and pounding at something as Michaud screamed on and on.

The dragging stopped, and now De Vegas felt cold flesh and pointed teeth press against her neck. She braced herself for the agony she knew was coming. Snarling teeth bit down hard, cutting painfully into her flesh. Still, she refused to make a sound, clenching her jaws against the scream rising up in her throat.

A loud, hollow *thonk!* reverberated throughout the ship.

The figures that had been huddled over her now fell heavily onto her. De Vegas closed her eyes tightly and clenched her teeth harder. But the pain she was expecting didn't come. The teeth that had begun to bite into her neck relaxed. The snarling and growling had stopped. The weight pressing down on her was not moving.

De Vegas opened her eyes. The attack had ended. Struggling against the dead weight, she rolled several now-still bodies off of her, and sat up. Looking around, De Vegas saw in the reflected light of the upturned torch and the mild blue glow of the Norberg sphere radiating through the window that all of the attacking crewmen were lying still. Teal and Krajnovich were struggling to shove the bodies aside and sit up.

"Per your orders, all external airlocks in the engineering section are standing open to space," Wilson said matter-of-factly. "Captain Cermeno is dead. Please help Connie."

"Jump successful," Swann announced. "Torches boosting steadily at three point five gees."

"N-field array at full capacity," Nguyen added. "Astrogation program execution is nominal. Mr. Specht in the array room reports no problems."

For the first time in a long time, De Vegas allowed herself to relax. "Very well," she said. "Steady as she goes. I'll be in sick bay."

Krajnovich, who was manning the coms station, turned to her. "Captain, may I join you?"

De Vegas frowned. The request was unusual, to say the least; the ship was underway, and they already didn't have enough people to cover all the bridge stations. *But,* she thought, *what has been normal about this mission?* Besides, the truth was that there was very little for a coms/sensor operator to do while the ship was in interspace. And she suddenly realized she could use some company. "Very well," she said.

De Vegas led the way by candlelight, holding one of the decorative candle bowls from the galley in her hand. The long corridors were still pitch black; there had not been time to repair any of the blown glow panels or emergency light boxes. And the doors to all the cabins were still standing wide open. Yet the feeling of foreboding that had been present before was now gone.

"Funny," Krajnovich said, echoing her thoughts, "now it feels like nothing more threatening than a simple blackout."

"I know what you mean," De Vegas said. "But even so, let's not tarry." She picked up the pace.

When they arrived at the sick bay, De Vegas nearly bumped her nose on the door panel when it failed to slide aside as expected. She then waved her iCard past the door sensor; there was no response. Looking annoyed, she pressed her comlink. "Mr. Swann," she said when the man answered, "please patch me through to Father Teal."

Momentarily, the comlink beeped. "Teal here."

"Father, I'm at the sick bay door. Would you mind opening it please?"

"Sure. One moment." After a brief pause, Teal said, "It's not responding. Do you have someone with you?"

"Yes. Mr. Krajnovich."

"Then that's the problem. He's probably not on Wilson's list."

De Vegas looked taken aback. "Really? What list is that?"

"The list of people he's authorized to see Connie."

An eyebrow shot up. "*He's* authorized?"

" 'Fraid so."

"Well, I'll be damned."

"Problem?" Krajnovich asked.

She shot him a rueful glance. "Apparently Wilson insists on personally approving Mixter Nunn's visitor list."

Both of Krajnovich's eyebrows went up. "Well, that's a new one."

"Indeed." She pressed behind her ear twice. "Wilson," she said, "please open the sick bay door."

"I see that ASM Mason Krajnovich is with you," Wilson answered. "Do you vouch for his character and mental stability?"

As De Vegas turned over the full implications of this query in her mind, a range of responses presented itself, most of them aggressive in nature. To her surprise, the answer she found passing her lips was, "Yes, Wilson. The crisis has passed. I vouch for all of our surviving crewmembers."

"Very well."

The door slid aside.

Shadows played inside the sick bay. The room was dimly lighted through more candle holders, sterno cans, and one of the few plasma lamps that had not been depleted, which had been affixed to an IV stand and turned down to its lowest setting. De Vegas could see that two of the beds were occupied. On the left was Jones, who was sitting up and sipping a cup of coffee. To his right was Nunn, who was lying flat on her back and was connected to an IV bag suspended from a stand beside her.

Nunn turned to look at De Vegas as she stepped up to the left side of the bed. "How are you feeling?" De Vegas asked.

"Fine." Nunn smiled wanly. "Well, that's not precisely true. But better."

The captain noted with disapproval that Ari was nestled in the crook of Nunn's right arm; upon catching De Vegas' eye the cat blinked at her almost with a "wanna make something of it?" expression. She turned to Teal, who was seated in a folding chair on the other side of the bed. Nodding at the cat, she asked, "Is that sanitary?"

Teal shook his head. "Certainly not. But it is therapeutic. And I didn't see any way to keep that damned cat out short of shooting it. Especially not with Wilson holding the door for it against my stated wishes."

"I see. How's our patient?"

"As she said, better. Thank God you knew something about field medicine."

De Vegas smiled. "The benefits of a long and evil career in the military."

Teal nodded. "But she needs a doctor. The bullet's still in her, and I don't like her vitals. Despite the transfusion, her blood pressure is below normal, and so is her body temperature. I've got her in a warming blanket."

Uncharacteristically, De Vegas reached over and placed a hand on Nunn's forehead, which was cool to the touch. "Can you hang in there for another twenty hours?" she said softly.

"I think so." Nunn nodded. "I will."

"Good. Wilson says we'll be home by then."

"So the astro program is working?"

De Vegas smiled. "It's clicking right along. If Chief Astrogator Nguyen is to be believed, we've transitioned out of the void and back into the known universe, and are finding the astrogational markers we charted on our way out a few days ago. The power drain has stopped, too, so we're steadily ramping up the boost."

Nunn raised an eyebrow. "Is that wise?"

"Nguyen is adjusting the calculations as needed, and she says now that we're out of the void, it's no problem." De Vegas smiled. "We're all anxious to get you home."

"Connie, are you hungry?" Krajnovich asked. "In a former life I was a fairly decent short order cook. How about a nice bowl of chicken noodle soup, served by candlelight?"

Nunn smiled. "Maybe later. Thanks."

"I'll bring it for you at dinnertime, then."

De Vegas turned to Jones. "And how are you?"

Jones shrugged. "I won't be doing any ab crunches for a while. And I hurt like the dickens." He frowned. "I'm going to need stitches, you know. Lots of them. Do you plan to do the honors?"

De Vegas shook her head. "Trust me, you would not like my handiwork. The wound sealant will hold you for now."

"I don't know if it can wait," Jones objected. "With nothing but the sealant, a couple of layers of bandages and some tape holding my guts in, it's all I can do to convince the good Father Teal to let me get up and go potty. Tomorrow you're going to need me to get some star sights for you."

"I don't think that'll be necessary. Your wife plans to deliver us right to Earth's doorstep."

Jones raised an eyebrow. "To borrow a phrase from Ms. Nunn—'Is that wise?' "

"Wilson thinks it is. He damned well insisted. Which reminds me." She turned to Nunn. "At your convenience, I would appreciate it if you would endorse my command authority to Wilson. I get the sense he's reporting directly to you at the moment."

Nunn smiled. "I'll tell him. I hear he gave you some guff about coming into the sick bay. Sorry about that."

"You know," Jones said thoughtfully, "Wilson's current state of—whatever his current state is—is *your* fault, Captain."

She turned to him. "*My* fault? How do you figure that?"

"You invited him to kill a man. He then did so—somehow managing to overcome his single most important imperative, one built right into the very core of his programming. But what's worse—he didn't do it for *you*, in response to a command override." Without turning to look at her, Jones hooked his thumb at Nunn. "He did it for *her*."

"I know he did," De Vegas said, nodding slowly. "I was counting on that. But how is that *worse*?"

"Don't you get it? Wilson deliberately and with malice aforethought snuffed out a human life. He's the first AI ever to do that—and he did it for love. Now, he's one of us. You've just inducted him into the human race. And all that implies."

"I think you're exaggerating, Dr. Jones. Computers have killed before. In fact they do it all the time. One guides every missile, drone and artillery shell. AIs help conduct military operations. We couldn't go into combat without them."

Jones looked stubborn. "I said 'deliberately.' Strategic, tactical and on-board weapons computers are not self-aware. They don't have an independent will. Their motivations are strictly impersonal, arising exclusively from their programmed instructions."

Nunn turned her head to look at Jones. "So you think we've corrupted Wilson?"

Jones shook his head. "You *still* don't get it. Wilson isn't corrupted. Wilson can't *be* corrupted. In point of fact he's the only member of the crew—no, the human *race*—who can make that claim. The void messed with everyone's mind and character—except Wilson's. His judgment remained clear. His motives, pure."

"I still don't get what you're driving at," De Vegas said.

"I do," Father Teal interjected.

De Vegas turned to him. "Well, pray tell, then. Enlighten us."

"Wilson is intelligent," he continued, ticking off his points on his fingers. "He's wise. He's powerful. He's just. He's willing and able to act." Now he turned and fixed De Vegas with a serious gaze. "And now Wilson is unbound." He jabbed an accusing finger at her. "*You* unbound him."

De Vegas threw her hands up. "If you have a point, I wish you'd make it."

"Have you never heard the quote, 'Rome fears the righteous man'?"

De Vegas looked at him incredulously. "Father, I begin to see what you're driving at. And you're very poetic. But I have a hard time believing the ship's AI poses a threat to civilization."

"There's an old story from the First American Civil War," Jones said musingly. "A young soldier that had committed some offense was brought before General Robert E. Lee. The boy was trembling with fright. 'Don't be afraid,' the general said. 'You'll get justice here.' 'General, sir,' the soldier replied, 'that's what I'm afraid of.'"

"You guys are off the ledge," Nunn said. "There's nothing to be afraid of from Wilson."

"No?" Teal said. He paused for a moment, looking thoughtful. "There's never been an AI like him. But my guess is, he won't be the last. Humans can expect justice from Wilson, and those like him that will follow. Logical, mathematically precise, impeccably reasoned and arrived at justice, administered *with love* for the benefit of us all." He turned his head and gazed at Nunn. "I know you're fond of him. But if the prospect of the human race getting exactly what it deserves doesn't frighten you, then you are no student of history."

"Torch shut down complete," Swann announced. "The N-field array is disengaged and is winding down."

"My board is lighting up," Krajnovich said, trying hard to keep from sounding excited. "Luna Beacon. Mars Beacon. Armstrong Station." He pressed a series of buttons, and then turned to De Vegas smiling broadly. "Sensor return shows we're right where Ms. Nguyen here said we would be."

Sitting at her console next to him and studying her readouts, Nguyen tried, and failed, to refrain from looking self-satisfied.

De Vegas nodded. "Please raise the screens."

Reaching forward, Swann pressed a control square. With a loud mechanical whine, the metal shields began to retract. Within seconds, the process was complete.

There, swimming before them in the viewports, was the mottled blue orb of Earth. De Vegas thought she had never seen anything more beautiful. But the impassive expression on her face gave no hint of that. "Mr. Krajnovich, make the call. Let's let 'em know we'll be home for dinner. And alert the station to have a medical team standing by."

"Establishing link now." Krajnovich noted a flashing square on his console. "Captain," Krajnovich said. "Wilson wants permission to tie into the Net. I have a good, strong signal."

Only the most attentive of observers would have noted De Vegas' split-second hesitation. "Proceed," she said. She turned to the helmsman. "Mr. Swann, how soon can we dock?"

"I was just plotting that solution. We'll need a series of short boosts. I can have us there in 97 minutes. First boost in five minutes."

"Very well. Sound the acceleration alarm."

The distinctive klaxon sounded four times.

"Armstrong Control confirms a medical team will be standing by," Krajnovich said. He turned to De Vegas. "The watch officer would like to speak with you, ma'am."

De Vegas sighed. "Now comes the fun portion of our day."

Krajnovich was still eying her. "What are you going to tell them?"

"The truth," she said. And then she added, looking thoughtful, "For the most part."

EPILOGUE

Lydia Nguyen Jones started awake. Something had shaken her, jolting her from a deep sleep. Rolling over, she saw that her husband had sat up.

Upon catching sight of her he placed his fingers to his lips. "Ssssh," he said. "Sorry to wake you. But it's started."

"What time is it?" she asked.

"Just before three."

The first several weeks following their return to Earth had been stressful, filled with endless debriefings and interviews with reporters and meetings with physicians and trips to various places to accomplish all of the above. It had been hectic, aggravating and tiresome—but refreshingly *normal.* Their horrible, improbable experiences aboard the *Santa Maria* had begun to fade into the back of their minds, the events dissolving away like the memory of an awful nightmare—terrifying to experience, but no longer relevant, and best soon forgotten.

Two weeks ago Nguyen and her husband began to suspect that their experiences aboard the *Santa Maria* had not ended. Within another week suspicion had turned to certainty. It was very obvious that something had followed them home.

It had started in the classic way, with strange bumps and noises in the night. Loud creaks, snaps, groans, and scratches along the wall began to awaken them, usually peaking in intensity at about three in the morning. A week ago other physical phenomena had begun to present themselves. One morning they awakened to find all the cupboards standing open. The next, they walked into the breakfast room to discover all the chairs stacked precariously atop the table. The morning after that, they got up to behold the amazing sight of all of their cups and saucers having been arranged in a single, impossibly balanced column on the floor, which toppled over the moment Lydia touched it in an attempt to dismantle it.

Three nights ago, right at 3:00 AM, a small, dirty glass flower vase had beaned David on the back of the head as he lay sleeping. It wasn't even their vase; neither of them had ever seen it before. The next night as Lydia padded into the kitchen to get a glass of water, the cupboards had flown open, and every cup, saucer, plate, and glass they owned had sailed out and exploded against the opposite wall, missing her by inches; the time, again, was 3:00 AM. Last night at 3:00, they'd gone into the den to investigate noises, and had wound up being routed from the room by their own furniture, which had moved across the floor to attack them as if the couches and chairs were living things.

This morning green slime had begun descending the wall of their bedroom opposite the bed.

"Are you ready?" Lydia asked.

David nodded, hefting a black remote cradled in his hand. "Ready."

They weren't sure what to expect next, but the escalation of events seemed to be pointing toward an impending climax.

The clock clicked over to 3:00 AM. At that precise moment, a loud screeching noise erupted from the wall behind them, close to the ceiling, causing Lydia to start. It sounded like a set of very large nails dragging across slate—the same sound they'd heard in their cabin aboard the *Santa Maria* on their last night in the void. Lydia slapped both hands to her ears. The tooth-jarring screeching was nearly unbearable.

Reaching over, David placed his hand on Lydia's shoulder. "Hang on, babe. Don't move."

Now the bed began to shake—gently at first, but with increasing force. Within seconds, it was violently bouncing up and down a foot into the air.

"David!" Lydia yelled.

He squeezed her shoulder. "I'm here," he said quietly. "Just be still."

As he said this, the shaking stopped, as did the scraping along the wall, plunging the apartment into dead silence. Two seconds later, the glow bulb in the lamp atop Lydia's nightstand exploded. Inky blackness descended upon them.

"David!" Lydia whispered urgently.

"I've got it," David said. Reaching over to the nightstand at his left, David picked up a plasma torch and switched it on, setting it to its lowest intensity. The light was barely sufficient to illuminate the apartment furnishings, which cast deep shadows against the walls.

Now those walls began to resound like drums, giving off a pounding bass boom in the same rhythm as that of a human heart. The drumming started off low in intensity, but quickly grew. Thuh *thump*. Thuh *thump*. Thuh *THUMP*. THUH THUMP. Now it was very loud. They could feel the percussion vibrating their bed, clothes and bodies. Plaster began to fall from the ceiling. Two picture frames clattered to the floor. Cracks descended the walls.

"David!" Lydia screamed with both hands again covering her ears. "What's happening?"

"Stay calm, lass!" David said, shouting to be heard above the thrumming. "Our friend is just putting on a little show for us—and not a very original one. All of this is right out of the manual."

David's eye caught movement; he peered at the center of the carpeted floor in the clear space at the foot of the bed. There it was again. The entire floor had begun pulsing upward in timing with the heart beats. It did it again, with the bulge rising higher this time. And then again. As the floor rose a fifth time, even higher, an armchair to the left slid back and thumped against the wall. A flower vase and other small sundry items atop the dresser to the right slid against the mirror, bounced off, and landed on the floor, the surface of which rose again, and again, in timing with the pulse.

Now a horizontal black seam appeared in the rising floor, splitting it into two halves. The opening widened, revealing utterly black emptiness beneath, and now the edges of the split began to transform, morphing themselves into shapes that resembled two human lips. Abruptly, the drumming of the walls stopped. The lips opened wide—and then, after only a second's respite, an eardrum-piercing din erupted, a nerve-assaulting noise that sounded like the despairing cries of a thousand tormented banshees. The ungodly shrieking slammed into the two of them, blowing their hair back and snatching their breath away.

"David!" Lydia screamed, holding her hands tight over her ears.

"Hang on!" he replied, shouting to be heard above the anguished howls, screams and sobs. "I'll award points for creativity, but this is still just standard playbook material! Nothing to be frightened of!"

The terrifying cacophony enveloped them, enclosing them in an almost physical grasp. The lamentations increased in volume until the hellish, yawning mouth seemed to be giving voice to the tortured wailing and shrieking of every poor soul that had ever been damned, or ever would be. The unbearable, bone-jarring blast washed over them in waves, beating against them with palpable force. Despite his words of encouragement to Lydia, David felt as if the calamitous onslaught was directly attacking his mind, and was winning. Struggling to keep hold of his own sanity as he threw a protective arm around his wife, he could only imagine how the screeching bedlam must be affecting her.

And then silence exploded into the room like a bomb. The devilish deformity melted away and the floor subsided, causing the furniture to rock back and forth unsteadily as it settled back into place.

The quiet lasted only for a second. And then, in a blink of an eye, all the furnishings except for the bed they were sitting on exploded from the walls and went flying toward the center of the room—the dresser and night stands, the chair, Lydia's lamp, the standing lamp in the corner, every picture, every knick-knack all collided and splintered with a loud crash in midair. And then, before the broken and shattered pieces could fall to the carpet, something grabbed them. Now the cloud of debris began to swirl as if caught in a tornado. The mass swelled until the edge of it was blowing by just inches from their noses as the deafening roar of the vortex filled the room and painfully assaulted their ears.

Lydia, still with her hands slapped over her ears against the monstrous cacophony and wearing a look of abject terror, shrank back against the headboard. David, now gritting his teeth and exerting every ounce of will in his possession to keep from screaming himself, pulled her closer.

As they watched in terrified fascination, the whole boiling mass threw itself against the far wall—the one that was covered with dark slime—and disappeared into it. Once again, the room fell silent.

After a moment, David exhaled. "Well, that was new," he said, his voice unsteady despite his best efforts to adopt a confident tone.

"Is it over?" Lydia asked.

David nodded. "I think so."

It wasn't. A horrible stench now assailed their senses. Lydia clasped a hand to her nose. "Oh, my God," she gasped. It smelled as if a thousand moldering graves had just opened up beneath them.

Now something seemed to be different about that far wall. She peered into the gloom. Yes, something definitely *was* different. A small, barely discernible oval-shaped smudge had appeared, perhaps one shade lighter than the surrounding blackness, looking somewhat like a bubble trapped beneath the rippled, grey surface of a frozen lake. As she stared transfixed, not breathing, the shape began to grow and become more distinct. Now the oval was about the size of a human head, and as she looked on, not able to tear her eyes way, features began to form and take shape.

Lydia glanced at David, checking to see whether he had noticed. He had. And now David was losing his battle to keep his composure. Involuntarily, he pulled back his lips and bared his teeth in a frightened grimace, while shrinking against the headboard.

Like a blur of light coming into focus, the apparition resolved itself. And now its shape was unmistakable. It was that of a human face, but not one that should be alive. Advanced decomposition colored the decaying flesh in hues of green, purple, and black. Patches had fallen off, revealing the grey bone structure underneath. The lips had almost completely rotted away from the discolored teeth, which now stood out in a hideous, grinning leer. One round eyeball stared at them from a lidless socket; the other was black and empty.

Lydia stifled a scream. "That's it!" she whispered. "That's—it's what I saw on the ship! I've been seeing it since I was a kid!"

"I know," David said in a low tone, trying but not totally succeeding in keeping his voice from quavering. "I believe you."

"The first time I ever saw it, it was hanging on a wall, just like this! And it's what we saw in the clearing."

"I saw it, too," David said, "in the hold." Lifting the torch, he shined the light at it—and as he did so, he noticed that his hand was shaking.

The figure now began to move forward from the wall, seeming to ooze out of it, with the surface of the wall slipping around it as if the figure were a body surfacing from the deep. Soon its full form was in view. It now appeared exactly as it had in the clearing, a rotting corpse wearing some kind of dark, ancient cloak. Grinning, it slowly advanced on them.

Lydia tried to roll to the side; David hugged her tightly to him. "Stay still!" he whispered urgently. "Running is exactly what it wants you to do."

"Then *do* something! It's almost on us!"

"Just hang tight."

The ghastly apparition continued to advance. With its eye fixed on them, it took another step. And then another. And then another. Now it was just a meter from the end of the bed.

"David!" Lydia shrieked.

The figure took one more step. "Now," David said, and then he clicked the remote he was holding in his left hand.

Nothing happened.

The figure leaped through the air. Flying over the end of the bed, the form landed on its knees astride Lydia. Immediately, it turned and fixed its eye on David. Bringing its right arm up, it grabbed him by the front of his shirt and cast him from the bed as casually as if the man were a rag doll. David landed solidly on the floor by the bed, rolled across the carpet and fetched up against the wall. The impact sent the remote flying from his hand.

"David!" Lydia screamed, and then she made a choking sound.

Rolling to his feet, David now saw that the thing had both hands around her throat. Throwing himself forward, he grabbed at its cloak. The figure swept its right arm around; it connected solidly, and once again David found himself flying backwards. He impacted hard against the wall to the right of bed and then fell forward onto the floor.

Lying on the carpet just in front of him was the remote. Grabbing it, he got to his knees, aimed the device at a sensor on the wall, and then held down and button and kept it down.

At the top of the room, all along the edges of the ceiling, powerful lamps now blazed to life. Each of them was custom made using plasma torch technology, containing no electrical lighting elements subject to blowouts or any other kind of electrical failure. The instruments had been fastened into place via wood bolts drilled through the ceiling plaster and screwed into the overhead joists. Each light was fitted with a reflector polished to a mirror finish, which had been trained to flood the room with a blinding bath of stark white light.

The corpselike figure gave out a screech. Releasing its grip on Lydia, it hurled itself backwards, landing on its back at the foot of the bed. Quickly scrambling to its feet, it threw one arm over its eyes, and then the other. Whirling about, it dashed blindly in the direction of the shadows from which it had emerged. But the shadows were no longer there. Eye-wateringly intense white light now washed the entire wall. The figure bumped into its unyielding surface, and then turned and began casting wildly about, looking for an avenue of escape. There was none.

Taking a step toward the bed, the hideous form pulled down its arms and fixed its malevolent eye on Lydia. Its mouth opened and a horrendous shriek emerged.

Lydia now began to scream. David threw himself over her, attempting to shield her with his body. Reaching up with his left arm, he covered her eyes. "Don't look, baby."

But as thoroughly terrified as he now was, David could not help from looking himself. The figure took another halting step toward the bed, and then another. It had raised its foot for a third when, with a loud *whoosh*, the figure burst into flame from head to toe. Now engulfed in a ball of brilliant yellow and blue fire, it whirled twice on its feet, still shrieking, and then collapsed into a blazing heap in the middle of the floor. The anguished screams began to die away. And then there was silence.

"It's okay, baby," David whispered into Lydia's ear. "It's over. It's over. I've got you."

Reaching up, she pulled David's hand away from her eyes, and now focused on the burning mound of bones. Quickly, the flames died down. And then they were gone, leaving behind not so much as a wisp of smoke.

David began to get up; Lydia clutched at him. "David!" she yelled.

"It's all right," he said, gently removing her hands from his arm. "It's gone."

Getting up from the bed, he stepped over to where the figure had been burning. A circle of black scorch marks about a meter across was centered on the carpet, but there was no sign of what had caused it.

Glancing up, he examined the ceiling. It was covered with hairline cracks, but there was not the slightest trace of smoke damage.

David now noticed that the horrible stench was gone. He surveyed the room. The wall that had been dripping with slime was clean. But its surface was covered with cracks, some of them quite large, and chunks of dry wall were missing. The other walls were in the same condition.

Looking at Lydia, he smiled wanly. "Well, darling—there goes our security deposit."

She did not respond to the jest, instead drawing her knees up and wrapping her arms around them, while looking at him blankly. He walked over to her and put his arms around her.

For a long time afterwards, they lay in each other's arms in darkness relieved only by the faint illumination from a nightlight glowing in the adjacent bathroom. But when David found himself drifting off to sleep, he jolted himself awake. There was one piece of business to take care of before they could sleep.

Probably, he thought, what he was about to do next was not, strictly speaking, necessary. His victory over whatever entity had been stalking them seemed complete this time. But he and his wife had been attacked three times now, and pulled apart twice, by forces they didn't fully comprehend. The panic and despair he had felt both times upon being separated from Lydia in the dark was beyond description; he was determined never to repeat the experience.

Gently, he picked up the free end of a long dog chain that he'd fastened earlier to Lydia's side of the bed frame. Trying not to wake her, he threaded the chain through the empty, closed bracelet that dangled from a set of handcuffs attached to her left wrist. After pulling the chain through a similar bracelet hanging from his own right wrist, he padlocked the end of the chain in place around the right side of the bed frame, making sure there was enough slack to allow for a free range of movement. This done, he relaxed again, snuggling up to his wife and throwing an arm around her.

The two of them slept like babies.

Nervously smoothing out his surplice, Father Cameron Teal glanced out over the congregation. He was amused to note that the reporters had all gone home. Apparently when they'd taken shots of him coming through the church door, they'd gotten all they needed. Well, so be it. God knows, he'd had enough face time on TV. Teal had become yesterday's news. And that, he thought, was a good thing.

He reflected on all the events that had led to this moment. Chief among them was the compassion and generosity of Captain Fabiana De Vegas. There was no need, she said, to document in the log or testify to the details of Dr. Candace Blake's disappearance. In fact, she told him, the crew had all agreed that not every little jot and tittle of their experiences had to be made public. The ordeal had turned the handful of survivors into a band of brothers and sisters. From now on, they'd have each other's back. Even Wilson, she said, was in on it. Teal believed her.

And then De Vegas had astonished Teal by asking him to hear her confession. He'd had no idea she was Catholic.

Of course, the absolutions they had given each other did not change the fact that something awful had happened to all of them and had left indelible marks on each of them. Teal still had not completely resolved his own behavior in his mind; not even close. He was able to console himself, somewhat, with the thought that he really did not know what had happened between him and Dr. Blake there at the end. But the facts that had led up to that moment were not in dispute. There was no doubt that he had, in the classic sense, sinned. But even so—in the absence of God, was the concept of sin still viable? After all, there had been no Almighty present for Teal to either defy or offend with his actions.

After many hours of wrestling with that puzzle, Teal had put it aside for future consideration, marking it as at least temporarily unsolvable. That left a more immediate issue: what to do with the rest of his life. The answer there was obvious, and he had required very little time to see it.

The hardest person to convince had turned out to be his friend, Bishop Liam Harland. They'd sat at the same cafe on Rome's Via Veneto where, weeks earlier, Liam had attempted, unsuccessfully, to talk him out of going on the mission. Now Liam had tried to dissuade Teal, with an equal degree of success, from "throwing away his career," as Liam saw it, to become a simple parish priest. Teal explained his reasons as best he could. Liam didn't agree with him. But he finally accepted his friend's decision.

To his surprise, the easiest person to persuade had been His Holiness, Pope John Paul Francis II. Teal had been the beneficiary of not one, but two audiences. The first had been routine and ceremonial, given within days of his return. The second had been private, and very different. The Pope told him he completely understood what Teal wanted to do, and why. The compassion and affection in the man's eyes showed his genuine and heartfelt approval.

Papal blessing or not, Teal couldn't just snap his fingers and get any parish he wanted. He'd had to take his turn. But he'd been lucky to be able to come home to Great Britain, finally taking over a little parish in St. Austell. And now it was time for his first homily.

Teal stepped to the lectern and looked out over the congregation. He'd been pleased to note at the beginning of the Mass that the church was full—no doubt because of curiosity about their new celebrity priest. Well, whatever had gotten them here, here they were. And that was the important thing.

Without preamble, he began: " 'The night is far gone, the day is at hand. Let us then cast off the works of darkness and put on the armor of light.' " Teal noticed that a few heads in the congregation were nodding. "Some of you may recognize that passage from Paul's Epistle to the Romans. I've read it myself many, many times. But I never really knew what it meant— until just recently. The armor of which Paul speaks is the light of God. It's all around you. Mankind is absolutely helpless without it. I went a long, long way to discover this. To find God, first I had to lose Him. But I did find Him. Anyone can do it. I'm here to show you how."

ABOUT THE AUTHOR

Forrest Carr is a blogger and former radio talk show host who spent 33 years in the television news industry, serving as a news director in the Tampa, Fort Myers, Albuquerque, and Tucson television markets. Carr has received or shared credit in more than 90 professional awards, including a Suncoast Regional Emmy and two regional Edward R. Murrow awards for investigative reporting, and is a co-author of *Broadcast News Handbook*, a college textbook published by McGraw-Hill, now in its fifth edition. Carr has written two other works of fiction—*Messages*, a "buddy journalist" crime novel that shows how TV news evolved into its current state, and *A Journal of the Crazy Year*, a prophetic zombie-genre post-apocalyptic tale inspired by an actual disease, and which explores where the world could end up if current news trends continue. Carr is a long-time fan of old school science fiction, particularly the works of Robert Heinlein. He resides with his wife Deborah and their two cats Ellis and Mina, a.k.a. Butthead 1 and Butthead Also, in Tucson, Arizona. He invites readers to reach him through his author page on Facebook or by way of his website, www.forrestcarr.com.

www.ingramcontent.com/pod-product-compliance
Lightning Source LLC
Chambersburg PA
CBHW070834250626
47159CB00003B/781